WANT
IT
ALL

A BANKSIA HOUSE OMEGAVERSE

WANT IT ALL

HOLLIE HARTWRIGHT

PINDIKA PRESS

CANBERRA

Want It All (A Banksia House Omegaverse)
Published by Pindika Press
Canberra, Australia
Copyright © 2025 Hollie Hartwright
Cover design copyright © 2025 Rachel McEwan

All characters in this novel are over the age of 18.

Paperback ISBN: 978-0-6456731-4-2
Ebook ISBN: 978-0-6456731-5-9

For my husband, who told me he liked this one best.

AUTHOR'S NOTE

This is an omegaverse novel.

It might seem like a strange thing to say, but I actually don't recommend this story as an introduction to the genre. Trust me, I want you to read this – but if you haven't read omegaverse before, it can be a lot to take in, and there are other stories that might be better for a first-timer. My personal recommendations for starter omegaverse are *Baby + the Late Night Howlers* and *Lola & the Millionaires* by Kathryn Moon. These novels give a fantastic overview of the elements that make up the genre, along with being beautiful, emotional stories (with plenty of spice). However, if you're a new omegaverse reader and determined that this novel will be your first, I've included an overview below.

Omegaverse (sometimes known as A/B/O or OV) is a shared playground, with authors putting their own spin on some basic constants, the main one being the premise of designations.

In this work, the designations are alphas, betas, and omegas, and all people will 'reveal' as one, usually between the ages of eighteen to twenty.

Alphas carry an innate sense of dominance, which they can turn on others, and are often (but not always) physically larger and/or stronger than betas and omegas. They are made to protect, and this is often their main function in a pack. Male alphas have a 'knot' at the base of the penis, which swells just before climax, and can lodge them inside their partner. Female alphas have a 'latch', a collection of extra muscles lining the vagina, which they can tighten during penetrative sex.

Betas have scents, but otherwise are pretty much everyday people. This omegaverse has a slightly dystopian vibe, and in this future world, betas are often not valued the way they should be.

Omegas have three-monthly, hyper-fertile periods called 'heats', during which they crave constant sex. Both male and female omegas have extra nerve endings within their bodies which allow them to take pleasure from an alpha's knot, and thick, copious arousal called 'slick', which has self-healing properties and keeps them lubricated during their heat. In this universe, some male omegas have extra reproductive organs which allow them to become pregnant and birth children.

This is a non-shifter omegaverse, meaning that the characters are human – with some added wolf-like traits. They have distinct scents, and sometimes (but not always) live in polyamorous 'packs' based on complementary scents. They have an enhanced sense of smell, and can growl, snarl, whine, and purr; alphas may also channel their dominance through a 'bark'. They can create bonds with partners through a bite, and their canines will push down to facilitate breaking the skin for this purpose.

If you need more information than this, an internet search for 'what is omegaverse?' should set you right up. My favourites include Kathryn Moon's *Sweetverse* novels, Eliana Lee's *Bond Dissolution* novels, Lola Rock's *Pack Darling*, Roxy Collins' *House of Omega*, Elizabeth Stephens' *Dark City Omega*, and Devyn Sinclair's *Slate City Omegaverse* books, but there are many, many more to choose from.

This omegaverse is an explicit, high-heat, multiple point-of-view MMMF why-choose romance, and contains M/F, M/M, menage, and group scenes. While the female main character was written to be the heart of this pack, all points of view and all connections between characters are explored. If any of this isn't for you, please choose a different book. The main characters in this novel are all between the ages of twenty-six and twenty-seven.

<u>**Content warnings include**</u>:

○ A character dealing with trauma and PTSD-like symptoms

○ Hospitalisation (in the past), medical monitoring, and medication, including the non-consensual use of tranquilisers

○ Kidnapping and being held against one's will

- ○ The traumatic death of a close family member (in the past) and associated ongoing grief
- ○ Main characters putting other main characters in dangerous situations for their own gain
- ○ The implied threat of sexual assault (not by a main character, and not carried out)
- ○ Delving into someone's past without permission, including the reading of confidential journals
- ○ Violence (in the past) and an associated court hearing (in the past)
- ○ A lot of swearing.

The main characters in this novel aren't always good people, and some make choices they come to regret; this may not sit easily with some readers. Please also be aware that this omegaverse includes widespread medical scent suppression and government intervention and tracking.

If you think I have missed something from this list of content warnings, please contact me; I am committed to keeping my readers safe.

The setting for this book (Banksia House, its grounds, and its nearby cliffs and beaches) is fictional, an amalgam of various places along the Australian NSW South Coast (which is *not* fictional). SECU is also fictional, though, as a long-term employee of an elite university, I apologise in advance for the various soapbox critiques scattered throughout the story inspired by my own experiences.

This book uses Australian English – except when it comes to the word *arse*, which just feels less … *sexy* … than *ass*. One day I will try to make it work, but it is not this day.

ROSE

'ARE YOU SURE THIS IS IT?'

The boundary wall was made of aged sandstone and stood at least three metres high. The rideshare driver put his car in park and stared at the wrought-iron gates, which were wide and topped with spikes. To our right, bronze letters fixed to the sandstone bricks spelled out two words.

Banksia House.

My fingers tightened around my phone. 'This is it.'

'That is some gothic novel bullshit right there,' the driver muttered. 'Will they open the gates?'

'The instructions said to wait here. Someone will come and get me.'

The driver turned and shot me a doubtful look. He was fair-haired and hazel-eyed, and his relaxed citrus scent – light, sweet, and faint – told me he was a beta. Though citrus was a scent I didn't love, I inhaled deeply, raking it in. I wouldn't be scenting anyone for months; scent-blocking medication and scent-cancelling sprays were non-negotiable requirements for attendance at Banksia.

'It looks like an institution,' he said.

'It's part of the South-East Coast University,' I returned absently, checking my bags and gathering up what I could comfortably carry. 'So you're not wrong, I suppose.'

'Mate, I've been to the SECU campus, and it doesn't look like this.' He turned around to study the iron gates once more. 'Are you rich or something?'

My stomach lurched with sudden nerves. *I* wasn't rich, but I assumed everyone else here would be. Banksia House gave out two scholarship positions per year, and I had one of them. All the other students would have paid their eye-watering tuition fees up front – and they would have done it happily.

Banksia House was the only school of its kind in the country, catering exclusively to postgraduate Humanities students. Its entrance requirements were beyond insane, its fees high enough to bankrupt small countries, its standards punishing to the point of cruelty. And yet, Banksia received thousands of applications per year, because it was also the best, by any measure. Every year, its graduates emerged as the bright new stars of their fields, because they'd already studied under the biggest names in their discipline. Though Banksia retained a core group of tenured staff, part of its allure for students was its practice of employing professionals to teach on a yearly basis, offering salaries large enough to routinely attract Nobel Laureates, bestselling authors, Cannes-winning producers, and Archibald-Prize artists. If you were a student at Banksia House, you knew you were walking out with the skills, knowledge, and contacts to make an impact on the world.

And I was here.

'Or something,' I said at last.

The driver turned to eye me again. 'Look, you're not being trafficked or anything, are you? I'd prefer not to have that on my conscience.'

'You can sleep soundly. No trafficking, I promise.' I opened the car door and pushed my bags out, wrestling with my larger tote. 'Thanks for checking, though. I appreciate it.'

'Well,' he said, tapping an address into his GPS, 'make sure you carry some scissors around, yeah? Just in case there's a wife in the attic.'

'I'd stab Rochester first,' I muttered, and closed the car door behind me.

The air was heavy with eucalyptus and salt; the coast wasn't far away. The driver waited until I'd hauled my bags away from the car, then reversed and swung around, offering me a wave and a last, doubtful look. I waved back, trying to pretend I wasn't trembling with apprehension.

A noise came from behind the gates. A moment later, they swung open, revealing a car idling behind them. The car was some kind of vintage classic, the sort that was a huge inconvenience to own in Australia and must have cost a fortune to maintain. I knew nothing about cars, but even *I* knew that whoever owned it had more money than they strictly should.

The driver's door opened, and a man stepped out, older, with dark eyes and a kind expression. I inhaled, but caught no hint of his scent on the slight breeze. 'Rosemary Morris?'

I gave an awkward wave. 'That's me.'

'I'm Harry. I'll drive you up to the house. Would you like some help with your bags?'

I nodded gratefully, and he gathered them up, packing them into the boot. My messenger bag was a comforting weight across my chest, so I left it on, even after sliding into the passenger seat. There were no seatbelts – a mark of just how old the car must have been; even before the Unveiling, cars had seatbelts – and I failed to push away the feeling of vulnerability as Harry settled into the driver's seat and the engine rumbled to life.

'The drive isn't too long,' Harry called over the noise, his tone apologetic. 'But it's a bit hard to manage with luggage. We organised a bus for the students who arrived yesterday, but thought that might have been a bit overwhelming for you, being the only one to come today.'

'Sorry to put you out. My flight was delayed.'

'It's no trouble at all. We were watching the storms over Melbourne and thought your plane might not be able to take off. You're our only first-year student from Victoria this time.'

I stared out the window, hoping to catch a glimpse of the Banksia House manor, but the drive was bounded by high hedges, still covered in the blossoms of late summer. 'How long have you worked here?'

'Five years,' Harry answered. 'I trained in horticulture at the main SECU campus, then was invited to apply for a groundskeeper role here.'

'Are the grounds large?'

'Two hundred acres in total. The manor block is only a couple of acres, though, and that's where most of the work is.'

Two hundred acres with sea views in the heart of the New South Wales south coast. I didn't want to think about how much the land would be worth.

'Are you from Melbourne, Rosemary?'

'Just Rose is fine,' I said. 'My family lives just outside Melbourne, but I was actually born not too far from here, in Wollongong.'

We chatted about Melbourne for a few minutes – Harry had a sister who lived there – but as the car crested a rise, I fell silent.

There were pictures of the Banksia House manor on its website, of course, but they were oddly elusive – a corner here, the front doors there, a snap of one side of the gardens. The pictures gestured at what the manor was, but never captured it in its entirety, leaving it a mystery – even for those applying to call it home for years to come.

The rideshare driver had been right. It *was* some gothic novel bullshit, and it took my breath away.

Four storeys of stained sandstone rose before us, with hundreds of high windows glittering like eyes, and a motherfucking *turret* nestling to one side. The manor's wide entrance doors were accessed by a stone staircase that spilled before them like a ridged tongue, and I was fairly sure I could see a *clock tower* rising from the back of the building.

The grounds, however, were purely Australian, almost in defiance of the European style building at their centre. Grey and white-barked eucalypts swayed in the breeze, native grasses spilled silvered shades of green over the earth, and wattle flowered in yellow flames around the drive.

The contrast was enough to make my head ache.

'Beautiful, isn't it?' Harry said proudly.

'It's … incredible,' I managed. *And my home for the next three years, at least.*

Fuck, I hope there's plumbing.

Harry pulled the car up at the foot of the staircase. 'I'll take you to your room.'

I forced myself to leave the car, clutching the strap of my bag. From here, I could see the cliffs a few kilometres away, and the glittering sea stretching all the way to the horizon.

If there's no plumbing, the view will make up for it.

Harry grabbed my bags and led me up the staircase. I hesitated before the yawning double doors, but I shook myself and squared my shoulders. I'd maintained a high-distinction average across all subjects *and* had won a national award for my outreach program for high-school history students to get here. I wasn't about to be cowed by a *doorway*.

I still swallowed when I stepped through it, though, and Banksia House manor closed over my head.

The inside was only slightly more modern-looking, with patterned wallpaper and a grandfather clock looming disapprovingly in the entranceway. Corridors stretched to both sides, and a staircase opened ahead of us, made of polished wood with sweeping bannisters. The wall to my right proclaimed the Banksia motto: *audeamus – let us dare.*

I inhaled. It was a reflex, an attempt to identify the scents around me, to categorise them so I knew who smelled safe, and who to avoid.

There was wood polish, and, somewhere, the muted smell of fresh paint. There were traces of wattle blossom and eucalypt from the trees outside, with an undertone of turned, wet soil. From further away, I caught the smell of cooking food – roasted vegetables and chicken.

But there was no human scent with its warm, musky base. Not even a *hint* of it wound through the air.

I chewed on my bottom lip, feeling a mix of relief and consternation.

'Your room is on the first level, in the south wing,' Harry said. *Of course* this place had *wings*. I was going to need a map on my phone, because I had zero clue where *south* was. 'They group students based on their projected study paths, so you'll be close to people with similar interests.'

I perked up at that. I'd completed my undergraduate degree online because it had taken me a long time to adjust to my designation, and it wasn't entirely safe for me on campus. It meant I'd graduated without any real friends, and my high school best friend, Chloe, had moved back to Singapore with her family two years ago. I missed her awfully, and I was hoping I could make some new friends a little closer to home.

I followed Harry up the staircase, trailing my fingertips over the silk-smooth wood.

'Every room has its own bathroom and kitchenette,' he told me over his shoulder. 'But meals are served in the dining hall, so most students use their kitchens for cups of tea and comfort food. Breakfast is from six to nine am, lunch is from eleven to one, and dinner from six to eight pm. The kitchens are closed to students between those times, but the dining hall itself is always open, and there are always snacks. Tuesdays and Thursdays are cookie days,' he went on, shooting me a kind smile. 'Wednesday is slice day, and Friday, pie and crumble. Mondays are by request – you can submit suggestions through the Banksia app.'

The stairwell spilled into more corridors; Harry turned down one to the left. I followed him past a row of closed doors until he stopped outside one marked *Fourteen*, spelled out in brass letters.

'This is yours.' He settled my bags down before it and unlocked it with his swipe card. He didn't step inside, a courtesy I appreciated; my instincts would have bristled at a stranger entering my room. 'Your swipe key should be on your table, along with your welcome package. You can download the app from the Banksia student intranet. It will tell you everything – your schedule, how to book study rooms, how to submit assessments, your mailing address, how to lodge a ticket with the housekeeping team, see the doctor … Everything. You can also book appointments with the administrative team or the campus support officer if you need to talk it through.' He gave me another smile. 'Good luck, Rose. I hope you have a wonderful time here.'

I thanked him, then waited until he'd disappeared back down the hallway to drag my bags inside, locking the door behind me. There was a wide window directly opposite the door, open, and the scent of lemon myrtle laced the air.

I exhaled, trying to calm my nerves.

The room was laid out like a studio apartment, with a queen-sized bed to one side and a wide TV on the wall opposite. A large study desk sat beneath the screen, with a fancy-looking ergonomic chair wrapped in plastic waiting to one side. The kitchenette held a sink, a stove top, a small convection oven, and a new kettle, still in its box. Opposite the kitchen was a closed door; I opened it to find a modern-looking bathroom, tiled in white and mint green and boasting a bath-shower combo, a long mirror, and a toilet.

Considering what I'd seen of student accommodation when researching other schools, it was amazing. Everything was spotlessly clean and new. The wallpaper was a neutral cream-and-silver, patterned with branches and birds. The window made the room light and airy, and there was even an armchair against the wall, upholstered in a light grey velvet. I spotted a built-in wardrobe next to the bed and decided to start unpacking.

I loved unpacking, no matter where I was. It felt as if I was claiming a space as my own, even if I would only be there for a short time. I hung and folded my clothes, then placed my favourite tea on the kitchen bench. The mattress was brand new, still wrapped in plastic, so I unwrapped it and covered it with my own sheets and my pastel-pink duvet, taking a moment to catch my breath once I was done. I placed my laptop on the study desk, along with my eReader, a speaker, and my tablet. I climbed up on the bed to string fairy lights along the wall, then folded my favourite throw blanket over the armchair.

By the time I was finished, I was happy with the way it looked. My bed needed more cushions and I wanted extra fairy lights to string over the desk, but I could do some online shopping later. Ideally, I would hang a canopy around the bed, too, but there were no hooks in the ceiling and I wasn't sure how I'd manage it.

My welcome pack waited on the table. I thumbed through the brochure, then downloaded the student app onto my phone. *Banksia Online*, its icon proclaimed. I checked my timetable and my academic contacts before a pop-up message let me know that my first week would be full of orientation activities – the discipline mixers sounded great, though I was less keen about kayaking in the nearby river – and that class started in the second week, bright and early on Monday morning.

When my stomach rumbled, I realised the sky was darkening and it was time for dinner. I took a quick shower, reapplying my scent-cancelling lotion afterwards, then pulled on my favourite outfit for luck. I sprayed myself with synthetic perfume, gathered my hair into a loose bun, then stuffed my key and phone into one of my dress pockets. Before I left my room, I swallowed my nightly dose of scent blockers.

According to the Banksia app, the dining hall was on the ground floor, along with the gym, the administration and student support offices, and a small indoor pool. I found the main staircase and followed the corridor east, checking the online map as I went. The ground floor seemed relatively public; it reminded me of an English historical house, open to visitors, with placards detailing which famous person once sat at *this* ornate writing desk, or that *this* print once belonged to *that* distinguished artist. I suspected I would be dreaming of wallpaper for years to come; acres of the stuff stretched above the smooth wood panelling, interrupted only by doors with shining bronze handles.

Another corridor opened to the left and I veered down it, drawn by the sounds of chatter and cutlery. I didn't walk far before I spotted the lettering on the wall, reading *Dining Hall*, with an arrow pointing to an arched walkway.

It wasn't as big as I'd expected. The hall held four long tables, each able to seat twenty or so, positioned parallel to two central food stations which seemed to hold salads and desserts, respectively. Beyond them, a few students queued before a serving station that looked very much like an airport cafe, trays in their hands as they chatted.

I headed towards them, offering a tentative smile to a woman at the back of the queue who caught my eye. She seemed a little older than me, possibly one of the later-year students, or perhaps someone who stayed on to undertake a prestigious Banksia PhD.

She smiled in return. 'First year?'

'First year, first day.' I held out my hand. 'I'm Rose.'

'Marina,' she said, shaking my fingers. 'Welcome.'

My nose itched, but it wasn't from her scent; with more students around, the metallic tang of scent cancellers was thick in the air. I inhaled, but caught only the myriad aromas of food, twitching my nose at the sensation. Even though I couldn't scent Marina's designation, she had the straight gaze and upright posture of someone used to getting their own way; in other words, she seemed like an alpha. Nevertheless, it was freeing not to know.

And even more freeing not to tell.

My instincts didn't like it – human scent was the way we made sense of the world, the way we knew which people were for us, and which weren't – but I loved it. Everybody here was on equal footing – in one way, at least; it would be the height of ignorance to pretend other power imbalances didn't exist. But not having to be ruled by designations – not living every day braced for the possibility of scents that made my skin crawl or my stomach churn, or *worse*, the rare scents that were complementary and sent my instincts into a spin – was something I'd been dreaming about for *years*. The scent-blocking tablets and cancelling sprays and lotions we used were medical grade, supplied by Banksia, and they were much better than anything you could buy over the counter. They were free, too, for me at least; no doubt the fees from paying students covered the cost many times over. If I'd had to use the same blockers and cancellers outside, I'd bankrupt myself – and my parents – in a matter of weeks.

It wasn't just scent that was controlled here. The terms of our enrolment dictated the use of hormone stabilisers which minimised the frequency of ruts for alphas, and of heat suppressants for omegas. Banksia's rules were strict, but they reflected the government's laws about mandatory scent blockers in all educational institutions. With the stabilisers, suppressants, blockers, and cancellers, it was as if the Unveiling – the time when designations first began to appear a few hundred years previously, stalling our technological development and causing massive social upheaval – never happened.

'How are you settling in so far?'

'I'm not sure I've been here long enough to know,' I admitted, then asked Marina which discipline she studied.

The Banksia House curriculum was different to other Masters programs at Australian universities. It was three years long, for a start, and all students began with a general knowledge and research skills stream before they chose their specialisation. The second year was all coursework, and the third gave students a choice between more coursework or research, the latter which was subsumable into a PhD if you were good enough to secure a place. Banksia cohorts were tiny, capped at thirty students per year, which meant that once you chose your specialisation, you were guaranteed one-on-one tutoring from experts in your field for the rest of your degree.

My suspicions about Marina turned out to be correct; she was a PhD student in the ancient history stream, the same discipline as my undergraduate degree. I tried to block out the noise around me as she talked about her research, determined to remember every word falling from her lips.

The noise increased as more students filed into the dining hall; my stomach growled at the smell of cooking meat and roasting vegetables wafting from the kitchen. I'd signed up for the vegetarian option with some trepidation, but I needn't have worried. A woman at the serving station gave me a healthy portion of delicious-looking zucchini pie with a huge pile of roast vegetables as a side, then pointed me towards the salads, most of which seemed to be meat-free.

Once we had our food, Marina smiled at me. 'Would you like to sit with me? Or have you seen someone else you know?'

I wasn't about to pass up the opportunity to make a friend, especially one who knew her way around and who was a fellow history dork. Between mouthfuls of roasted chicken, Marina told me about living at the manor – she complained about her apartment, which told me she was definitely *not* a scholarship student – and gushed about the gardens, recommending them for walks but advising me to stay away at nighttime, unless I wanted to see students fucking in the bushes.

I mean, I wasn't averse to the idea, but it wasn't what I'd come here for.

No pretty face or complementary scent is worth your future, Rosie, Chloe had said. *Get your degree and get out. No distractions.*

'You seem like a beta to me,' Marina said, studying me. I met her eyes, but didn't answer; my designation was my secret to keep. 'Be prepared. Some students come here for the degree; others come to find a pack. It's simpler here: a lot of the groundwork is already done. You know you're getting someone smart, someone driven, someone who has the potential to succeed. Some alphas here will be …' She searched for the right word. *Tenacious.* It's good we don't see too many omegas here,' she went on. 'They'd be bitten and bonded before census date.'

I pushed a potato around my plate, my appetite suddenly gone. I'd read the student statistics before I'd applied: ten in every hundred students were betas, and one in every hundred an omega.

'Oh, don't worry,' Marina said breezily, mistaking my silence for concern. 'Just be clear on your boundaries. And probably keep your door locked at night.'

Well, that's not ominous at all.

'I read a little about the Banksia Prize,' I said, trying to steer the conversation elsewhere. 'But I'm still unclear on how they award it. It's just for first years, right?'

As prizes went, it was one worth having. Two years of personal mentoring with the expert of your choice, a reserved place in the Banksia PhD program, and a hefty scholarship to go with it, all the way to graduation. Recipients were routinely head-hunted the moment they got their testamur, with residencies, exhibitions, book deals, fellowships, and jobs scattered at their feet like bouquets.

I wanted it so badly I could feel it in my *bones.*

Marina nodded. 'There are other prizes for second and third years, and another set again for research students. The prizes are generally academic, based on the top marks. But the Banksia Prize is a little different. No one is really sure of the criteria.' She shrugged. 'But the Revels fund the scholarship and organise the mentoring, so they have the final say on who wins.'

My heart skipped a beat. 'The *Revels* fund it? The secret society?'

Marina snorted. 'The Revels are more of a club these days, though it's still invitation-only, and I've heard rumours they still haze potential members. But they've left behind anything that might get them sued, and they're one of Banksia's main sources of funding – other than student fees, of course – so SECU politely pretends they don't exist. I'd join, if I could,' she said, sounding slightly wistful. 'What a thing to have on your CV. Or better still, pack up a Revels member. All the benefits, without the extra work.' She lifted her fork to her mouth, then froze. 'Oh,' she murmured, low and quiet. 'I was wondering when he'd show.'

I followed her gaze, turning in my seat – and stopped breathing.

Designations could be kept private here, but there was no way he was anything but an alpha. Six-foot-six and every limb curved with muscle, his black shirt clinging to rounded pecs, black jeans wrapping around thick thighs. Tattoos peeked up past the collar of his shirt and wound down his arms, a mix of floral motifs, illustrations, and text. A messenger bag – just like my own – was slung across his wide chest, pulling his shirt tight across his abs.

I swallowed, my eyes travelling up to fix on his face.

He had a square jaw, a straight nose, black brows, and stormy grey eyes above cheekbones so sharp I could cut a finger on them, all framed by waving hair so dark a brown it was almost black.

Alpha, my instincts purred, immediately taking notice. *Alph* –

They fell silent when they saw his wrists.

The government monitored us all. When alphas and omegas revealed their designations – usually between the ages of eighteen and twenty – they were forced to report their status and be added to a national database or face jail time. We all completed monthly online surveys, monitoring changes in mood and habits, and collecting information about how our designations affected our daily lives. Some of us occasionally sat through awkward visits from official agencies during what the government termed *wellbeing sweeps*. Omegas were monitored more than most, with heats and any offspring tracked by the Omega Support Agency, but there was one group who was watched even more closely.

With our designations came our instincts, and with alpha instincts came the chance of what the medical profession termed *instinct blackout* – periods of time when humanity took a back seat and the alpha beneath the skin ran the show. It was uncommon; when it did happen, instances were reported to the Alpha Protective Force, who intervened to monitor the *at-risk alphas*.

The popular consciousness had a different term: feral. The APF didn't help matters, in my opinion, by making at-risk alphas wear wristband monitors – just like the ones this alpha was wearing.

I shivered, my skin breaking into goosebumps from an odd mix of a hot flush and a chill. From what I understood, instinct blackouts rarely occurred in alphas so young – he couldn't have been much older than me – and I'd never imagined a feral alpha to be so handsome.

'Who is he?' I whispered to Marina, unable to tear my gaze away.

'Byron Griffiths. He's the new Dean's son.' Marina lowered her voice. 'I heard that she negotiated his enrolment here as part of her contract.'

His eyes snapped towards us, as if he'd heard. His gaze lingered on Marina for a moment, before shifting to me.

Alpha, my instincts whimpered. I had the sudden urge to tip my chin to the side and bare my throat. I fought the compulsion to drop my gaze, trembling as his grey irises darkened.

His brow creased – as if in surprise – and he murmured one word. He didn't say it loudly, but silence had fallen over the dining hall in the wake of his arrival, so his soft voice was as clear as a shout.

'*Omega.*'

BYRON

I KNEW IMMEDIATELY THAT I'D MADE a huge fucking mistake.

The colour fled her cheeks and her jaw went tight. Her knuckles were white as her fingers tightened around her fork.

Perhaps with the intention of using it – on me.

The dark-haired woman across from her started, her eyes wide, her lips parting in an astonished *o*; the news was clearly a surprise.

You fucking fool, B, Tina's voice said, disgruntled. *You just outed an omega.*

I hadn't meant to, but my intentions didn't matter. I'd been told that omega students at Banksia House rarely disclosed their designation to their peers and sometimes graduated with the other students none the wiser, but then I'd seen her, covered in scent cancellers – there was no trace of natural perfume in the air – and yet so obviously, blatantly an omega. And a fucking delicious one at that, all curves wrapped in a plaid pinny and cream silk shirt, her thick auburn hair pulled back into a loose bun. Her light brown eyes had looked me over with interest, but now shone with a mix of fury and unshed tears.

I'd just fucked up her life, after all.

Omega, my alpha growled. *Frightened. Sad. Make it better.*

I can't make it better, I told him. *I caused the fucking problem.*

'Omega?' Whispers began to circle the room, which was a surprise to literally no one. This place was overflowing with alphas, some already building packs, and I'd just announced the prize of all prizes – an omega who was *here*.

I'd made her a walking target.

I took a step forward, an apology forming on my tongue, but she looked deliberately down at her plate. With a quiet dignity I never could have mustered in her place, she gathered up her meal and glass and took them to the waiting bay, most of her food untouched.

A woman stepped towards her, her eyes dark with intent. 'Omega –'

I snarled.

The sound ripped through the room; the other alpha straightened. It wasn't just because of the sound; she'd caught sight of my monitors.

No one wanted to fuck with an alpha who was at best unpredictable, and at worst, dangerous.

At least not on the first night of orientation week.

The woman stepped back, giving the omega some space.

The omega didn't look at me; I didn't expect her to. She just walked with a straight spine through the dining hall, disappearing into the maze of corridors that made up the bowels of this pretentious hellscape.

It was then I noticed that other students had their phones out, their camera lights blinking.

Might as well give them a finale.

'If anyone touches her without her express and ongoing consent,' I ground out, my voice dangerously low, 'or makes her feel uncomfortable, or so much as *looks* at her if she doesn't want it, I'll tear their fucking arms off.' I wouldn't do any such thing, but they didn't know that. I pinned the woman who'd approached her with my best glare; she dropped her gaze to the ground. 'Just *try me.*'

I spun on my heel and stormed from the dining hall, guilt like a weighted blanket across my shoulders.

Fuck, B – you couldn't have waited until class started to make a scene?

'Helpful, Tina, thanks,' I muttered to the memory voice.

My phone vibrated against my thigh; my monitors lit up with a matching flash. I fished my phone from my pocket, knowing I had no choice but to answer. 'Hi, Dr. Ford.'

'Byron.' My APF liaison officer was always polite and well-mannered. 'Your mother just called me.'

If I'd had any doubts about how quickly the rumour mill worked at Banksia House, I wouldn't any longer. Someone in the dining hall must have live streamed the entire fucking thing for my mother to hear about it that swiftly. 'Dr. Ford –'

'To be clear, Byron, I'm calling to ask how you are.'

I inhaled slowly. Dr. Ford wasn't bad. In fact, he was great. But he got paid to keep an eye on me, and it was a job he took seriously. I couldn't help but feel like a toddler, or something squirming under a microscope. 'I feel like an utter fool. And a complete asshole. I can't believe I did that.'

'I saw your face,' he said gently. 'It wasn't intentional – it was a gut reaction. You were surprised. Being an asshole is generally a deliberate choice.' He paused. 'How did you know? That she was an omega, I mean? Aren't you all taking scent blockers?'

It was a difficult question to answer. She just *was*, as if it were something so innate she couldn't hope to hide it. She wasn't smaller than everyone else – it was a popular misconception, and one encouraged by TV, books, and film, that all omegas were tiny – and nothing about the way she looked made it obvious. Anyone could have auburn hair, brown eyes, and a cute button nose.

It was the way she *felt* – as if she should have been at the centre of the room, at the centre of *everything*. As if I should have fallen to my fucking knees and prayed for her to notice me, to let me serve her, to let me worship her like the goddess she was.

'I'm not entirely sure,' I said, because it was the only answer I could give.

There was a short silence. 'What will you do?'

I stopped in the corridor and looked out the window. The view was of Banksia's grounds, then all the way down to the cliffs and the sea, made inky by the oncoming night. It was pretty, even if I generally preferred things to be wilder, a little less tamed. 'I'll try to apologise, I guess, although I'm sure she won't want to hear it. I won't force my company on her. The least I can do is leave her alone.'

'You could try an apology from a distance – an email, perhaps. Something she could read in her own time, in her own space. It could be less intimidating.'

He meant that *I'd* be less intimidating, but he was right, either way. 'That's a good idea. Thanks, Dr. Ford.'

'I'll check in tomorrow,' he said. 'And Byron?'

'Mmm?'

'You're doing really well. I'm proud of you,' he said quietly, and ended the call.

I stuffed my phone back into my pocket. It was nice to hear, but moving forward sometimes felt like walking through mud, as if I'd trekked for days, weeks, months – but when I looked back to see how far I'd come, it seemed like no distance at all. And as much as I loved them, my parents didn't make matters any easier.

When they'd told me that mum had been offered the position here, I'd thought for a moment she and dad would come alone. But then she added that she'd negotiated a place for me, too, and any illusions about newfound autonomy flew straight out the window.

I couldn't mind, though, not really. Not with what my parents had been through. Even though most twenty-seven-year-olds didn't stay quite so close to their parents.

'Most twenty-seven-year-olds aren't *feral*,' I muttered to myself.

On the plus side, my apartment was in the student accommodation, not with my parents in the staff wing. They had said pointedly that they'd check in often, but the reins were looser than they'd been before.

My stomach interrupted that train of thought with a loud rumble, reminding me that I'd left the dining hall without eating.

I scowled out the window. The omega's plate had been almost full when she'd returned it to the service bay.

Fuck.

She might have had some food in her room, but I certainly didn't. And while I could head to my parent's apartment to steal a sandwich – or even some bacon, if my dad hadn't eaten it all – she might not have been here long enough to make friends who could provide the same.

'Well, this will be embarrassing,' I said to the window.

I headed back to the dining hall. All the chatter stopped the moment I stepped foot inside. I ignored the sudden silence and the loaded looks and joined the line for food. While I was waiting, I sent my mother a message.

I know you saw what happened. I need a favour. The omega didn't finish her food. I need to take her some, but I don't know where her room is.

Mum must have seen the message immediately, because three dots appeared on the screen, showing she was typing. They disappeared a moment later, and I knew she was weighing up what to do.

That isn't something I can tell you, B.

My father called a moment later.

'South wing, first floor, room fourteen. Her name is Rosemary. Love you, B, you silly goose,' he said, and hung up.

I sent him two emojis – a heart and a goose.

When I had a tray laden with two plates of dinner food and piled with different desserts, I walked to the south wing. My apartment was in the east, and another floor up. I didn't like where her room was: she was close to the stairwell, and my instincts hated that anyone might walk by her private space, but there was no good place to put an omega here. A corner room would be too quiet, with too few people to help if something went wrong, and too many ways she could be penned in; a room in the middle of the wing would see her surrounded by alphas.

'Not your problem,' I told myself.

Her door was, unsurprisingly, closed. I put the tray down on the plush carpet and knocked.

'Omega?' I called softly. 'My name is Byron. I know it won't mean much, but I'm sorry for what happened in the dining hall. I noticed you didn't finish eating, so I brought you some dinner.' I paused. 'Would you prefer the zucchini pie or the roast chicken?'

There was no answer.

'I know you don't want to talk to me, which is both totally understandable and shows impeccable taste on your part, but I'm leaving food here regardless, and I'd prefer to leave something you'd like to eat. I don't really want to guess, because I don't know you at all, and will absolutely get it wrong.' There was no response, but I caught a faint scuffling sound, and suspected she was looking through the door's peephole. 'Chicken or zucchini?'

'Zucchini.'

Her voice was quiet, barely a whisper. Even so, I soaked it in, memorising the sounds.

'Good choice.' I picked up the plate with the chicken and grabbed one of the cutlery packets. 'Good night, omega.'

She didn't open the door until I was out of sight, and I couldn't blame her. As I climbed the stairs to the second floor, I heard the soft hiss of a door sliding over carpet, and the clink of cutlery as she picked up the tray.

I would have been lying if I said I didn't feel a stab of satisfaction at the thought of her eating the food I'd brought to her, the food I'd chosen. It was an instinctual thing, the alpha beneath my skin preening at the notion of serving the beautiful omega. If she were mine, I'd want to make sure she always had the best of everything – preferably from my own fork.

If my alpha tried to fuck with my meal planning, I'd eat them, *instead.*

I didn't hear Tina all the time anymore. I heard her when I needed advice, or when she would have shaken her head at me – or knocked me up the back of mine. She was always right, and this time was no exception, no matter what my instincts had to say about it. Alphas had one main job: to protect. Sometimes, ensuring safety was physical; that was why my six-foot-six frame was draped in muscle, despite me spending most of my time on my ass with my nose in an eReader. Sometimes, ensuring safety was psychological.

An alpha can fuck up a mind as easily as they can fuck up a body, Tina had told me once. *Remember that, B.*

As if I could ever forget.

When I got to my apartment, I flicked on a streaming service and started a comedy I'd watched a hundred times, because I knew there was no way I'd be able to concentrate. I shoved food past my lips, chewing and swallowing until it was all gone, but I hadn't tasted a thing. When I finished, I realised something.

The omega – *Rosemary* – was on the first floor. In the single rooms.

I didn't have a pack, but I'd been given a pack room simply because my frame wouldn't fit on the smaller beds. It meant my apartment had two bedrooms instead of one, with king beds in each, and a third room nestled between them with a low ceiling and small windows that could be used as a nest. There was a second door to one side – securely locked, of course – which opened into my neighbour's apartment, so that bigger packs could have more space if needed. The nest in my room was empty, still smelling of new carpet and fresh paint, but at least it was there.

The single rooms didn't have nests, I remembered. But nests weren't just for heats. They were an omega's sacred space, a place they ruled, a place where every detail was to their liking, somewhere they felt entirely safe.

Did the administration think Rosemary wouldn't need one?

I pushed my plate away and grabbed the Banksia brochure, frowning. The rules around taking scent blockers and wearing cancellers were strict; I skimmed through them.

Omegas will remain on heat suppressants during teaching periods and mid-term breaks.

My frown grew deeper. Suppressants were fine; nine times out of ten they worked with no problems and minimal side effects. But it was a mistake to think they were infallible. It usually came down to a clash of medications – generally antibiotics – but I'd also read a study where a scent match had triggered a heat, despite the omega being on suppressants.

Not your omega, not your problem, I reminded myself.

I couldn't help but feel responsible for her, though. I'd taken away her secret and her safety. The least I could do was keep an eye on her.

Surely I owed her that much.

TRISTAN

'HAVE YOU SEEN THIS?' Sebastian hissed, showing me his phone.

I *had* seen it. Banksia House had strict rules about what could be shared on social media; no photos of the manor or its immediate grounds, and no photos of any enrolled student or staff member taken on the property could be shared. To make up for it, Banksia had its own – albeit simple – social media app, and the clip of the dark-haired alpha snarling in the dining hall after outing the pretty little omega had been posted multiple times.

'Yeah, I saw it,' I nudged his plate. 'Eat.' I opened my laptop.

'Aren't *you* going to eat?' he said pointedly.

I shoved a forkful of chicken in my mouth and clicked into the student administration system.

I'd gained access before we'd arrived; for an institution with so much cash flow, I'd have thought they'd have better system protections.

We already knew who the alpha was: Byron Griffiths, youngest child of Banksia House's new Dean, Professor Carla Griffiths. The omega in question was more of a mystery.

'Rosemary Morris,' I murmured a moment later. 'Twenty-six years old.' My eyebrows rose; I pushed my glasses up my nose. 'A graduate of our university, same year, same faculty. She majored in ancient history.' I looked across at Sebastian. 'Surely we would have had some of the same classes.'

'You can take history online,' Sebastian said.

An emerging designation was a shock to anyone, but it was especially difficult for omegas. Their hormones took longer to settle, and their heat cycles could be erratic for several years. They were more sensitive to scent than any other designation, so public places could be an uncomfortable experience. In that context, online study made a lot of sense.

I clicked into her offer documents; my eyebrows rose further. I cleared my throat. 'She's a scholarship student.'

Next to me, Sebastian went still. I met his clear blue gaze.

The pretty omega could be his biggest threat.

All the students at Banksia House were impressive. But the scholarship students were next level. There were *thousands* of applications for the two scholarship places each year, and the students who got them deserved them. They hadn't bought their place here, not with money, nor their family name. They'd *earned* it.

Sebastian was, without a doubt, the smartest person I'd ever met. His parents were all Banksia alumni, but while his mother had gone on to win a Nobel Prize, and his fathers to win awards that were equally impressive – if not as well known – none of them had ever won a prize at Banksia.

Despite Sebastian's achievements, his mother saw only his easy smile and warm manner. Nothing he did was ever good enough, and if it *was*, she'd infer he'd used his looks to get there. *Sebastian isn't serious enough*, she'd say one visit, and *he simply doesn't have the aptitude* the next. It made me livid, but it hurt Sebastian, deeply.

And so he was determined to win the Banksia Prize and prove his mother wrong.

It wasn't a healthy obsession, but I wasn't one to talk.

'You're getting that prize,' I said quietly.

He hooked his foot around my ankle. 'I know, alpha.'

He didn't know, not really. Not even *I* knew the lengths I would go to ensure his happiness.

I clicked into the pretty omega's personal information, and noted down her room number, along with a few other details – her home address, her parents' names, her birthday – before skimming through her application documents. As expected, her admissions essay was well-written, eloquent, and the perfect balance of emotive and respectful.

While I wouldn't say it was *better* than Sebastian's, it was certainly equally as good.

As I'd suspected, her education summary showed a gap of a few years after high school, probably when she'd emerged as an omega. Sebastian was right, too; she'd completed her Bachelor degree and Honours year online, after what seemed like a short-lived foray into art school on campus.

I wondered what had put an end to *that* ambition, but suspected I could guess.

When designations had started to appear, there had been a period of significant upheaval as workplaces and schools adapted to the new needs of employees and students. Tertiary academia, however, had always done things at its own pace. It had taken a few horrific – and very public – incidents caused by barely-human alphas for universities to start changing their policies around scent blocking and rut suppression, but by then, the damage had been done. Omega enrolment sank so low that the designation made up less than two percent of all higher education students across Australia. Everything was stacked against them: alpha and beta teachers who didn't understand the complex needs of an omega body, harassment from fellow students and even teaching staff, and the nature of the term structure and assessment deadlines, which demanded that omegas change to meet *them*, rather than allowing for flexibility to flow the other way.

There was a lot that needed to change.

Sebastian's foot traced up my calf. I turned to him, my lips curving into a smile, and took his fingers in mine. 'Have I ever told you that I love you?'

He rolled his eyes, grinning. 'Only a hundred times a day for the last six years.'

'Hmm. That doesn't seem like enough.' I caught a movement from the corner of my eye and looked up to see a handsome woman standing opposite us, smiling.

'Is this seat taken?'

There was a sea of seats elsewhere, many of them closer to other groups of students. I wasn't bothered so much by *that*, though.

What bothered me was the way she was looking at Sebastian, the way her eyes caressed his golden hair, traced over his lovely face, and locked onto the delicious stretch of tanned skin beneath his collarbone.

My instincts bristled. 'There are plenty of seats elsewhere.'

'I was asking the beta, not you,' she returned, her smile widening.

The alpha inside me snarled his displeasure. 'Do you mean *my* beta?'

She glanced at me for the first time. I knew what she'd be seeing: someone who was tall but slender, a messy crop of brown curls falling over his glasses.

'I don't see a bite,' she said dismissively.

I smiled, showing my teeth. 'What makes you think I'd bite his neck?'

'If you've both finished pissing on my leg,' Sebastian said tightly, laying down his fork, 'I rather think those seats *are* taken. If you're looking for a beta, might I suggest a different tack next time? Betas aren't possessions to be had.'

She scowled. 'What else are you good for?' She turned and strode away, settling near a group of students closer to the salad station.

Sebastian sighed, rubbing his eyes. 'For fuck's sake.'

'I'm sorry she was an asshole, Seb.'

He huffed. 'I'm annoyed at you, too. You might have asked first, Tris, instead of refusing her straight away. I'd like to make friends here, if that's all right with you, *alpha*.'

'She didn't want to be *friends*, baby.'

He glared at me. 'I'm not a glass vase. I am perfectly capable of finding that shit out for myself.'

I took up his hand and rubbed my cheek along his knuckles. If I'd not been on blockers, my scent would have covered his skin, marking him. 'I know you are. I'll do better next time. I'm sorry.'

He deflated. 'Urgh. I can never stay angry at you. My instincts love when you do the whole *mine* thing.'

'Maybe you could use your signal next time.' We had a long-running sign for when Sebastian wanted my help: he tapped his fingers on his thigh. 'If I don't see the signal, I'll leave you to handle it.'

'Deal.' He shot me a smile that made my stomach go tight, then peered at my laptop screen. 'Find anything interesting?'

◊◊◊

All anybody talked about for the next few days was the omega, who sensibly stayed barricaded in her apartment. Someone was delivering food; we'd seen a tray in the corridor outside her room. The administration was clearly aware of what had happened, evidenced by a worried-looking woman we'd seen knocking on her door, a woman I knew from the Banksia website to be the new Dean. Though I suspected that personal visits to students probably didn't fall within her job description, as it had been her son who'd caused the problem, she probably felt a measure of responsibility for the situation.

The son in question had also been mostly absent, emerging from his lair at mealtimes only, wearing a fierce scowl, his monitors, and clean-but-identical black shirts and black jeans each day. He was handsome as fuck, even with his face twisted into a frown. He wasn't someone who could fly under *any* radar, so as much as he tried to avoid attention, he simply didn't.

I mean, *six-foot-six*. He took up most of whichever room he happened to be in. It didn't help that he was textbook alpha: huge, muscled, and oh-so-savage looking. Whenever I saw him, I couldn't shake the feeling of a storm on the horizon, the clouds just waiting to roll in and electricity thick in the air.

I'd already stalked his socials, which consisted of erratic posts about music gigs and the occasional annotation of a quote he particularly liked; his profiles all hosted a tiny bisexual flag next to his name.

'If we were looking for a pack …' Sebastian said, his blue eyes darkening a little as he stared dreamily at Griffiths one lunchtime. 'But we're not, are we?' He'd patted me on the shoulder in a manner that was supposed to be comforting. 'We have everything we need.'

I certainly felt that way, but I was less convinced about Sebastian. He brought up the idea of a pack so regularly that he must have thought about it often. I wasn't completely opposed to it, but the problem was finding someone good enough. I'd never met *anyone* I'd considered being even close to deserving Sebastian.

I certainly didn't deserve him; I was simply selfish.

He'd already shared rumours of an upcoming scent party, where students would stop taking their blockers for twenty-four hours and shower without reapplying cancellers, then head into the gardens with alcohol and a determination to make bad decisions. Stopping blockers for a day wouldn't reveal a person's full scent profile – the blockers worked cumulatively – but it would give potential partners a taste of someone's scent, which could be enough to cement an offer to join a pack, or to pair with others who had complementary scents.

Scent parties were illegal in every Australian state and territory but the ACT, where they were thrown by the local government and strictly monitored by police. It was convention instead for students on blockers to exchange scent cards with potential partners. Scent cards were pieces of fabric, worn on the skin until they were imbued with scent, then fixed to a cardboard or thin wood backing. They were usually the catalyst which determined whether a relationship would be pursued or not; it was difficult for romantic relationships to succeed long-term if the scents involved weren't complementary.

At Banksia, I'd taken to sleeping with Sebastian's scent card beneath my pillow; it settled my alpha down when he became frantic about Sebastian's missing scent. It wasn't against the rules to have scent cards here, but university guidelines specifically mentioned that they advised against it.

Scent parties were a much wilder way to determine complementary scents, which didn't deter Sebastian, who was all but bouncing at the notion. 'Who knows,' he'd said, his lips curving into the smile I loved so much. 'Maybe you'll find your scent match.'

It was a nice thought – who *wouldn't* want to find their perfect match? – but statistically, it was more than unlikely that in a world with over nine billion people, a scent match would just *happen* to be here. In reality, if a match even existed in the first place, they were probably on the opposite side of the globe, living a life that would never weave into mine. It was why packs were usually founded on complementary scents, which were more common; research showed an individual's scent would be complementary with around ten percent of the wider population. A head alpha would bring complementary packmates together and keep them that way, taking on responsibility for the pack's physical and emotional wellbeing.

Sebastian's scent was certainly complementary to mine, but we'd been on blockers since we'd met, so I'd never felt its full force. I didn't care that we weren't a scent match – I loved him so deeply it was almost a madness anyway – and he didn't seem to mind, either. He'd been begging me to bite and bond him since our early twenties, but I'd gently resisted, wanting him to meet others with complementary scents first, to be absolutely sure it was me he wanted to bond.

I'd die if he chose not to, but at least I'd know I hadn't taken the option from him.

And if he chose me ... How could I ever want anything more?

SEBASTIAN

'OH, *FUCK*.' MY HEAD FELL BACK as my arms began to shake, my fingers curling around the edge of the desk so tightly I was surprised the wood didn't splinter. 'Oh, fuck. *Alpha*.'

Tristan swirled his tongue, then took me all the way to the base in one graceful swallow.

I almost blacked out, my vision flickering with pleasure. 'Tris, I can't –'

I wasn't sure what I couldn't do: take it, perhaps, or hold on. Tristan always sucked my cock as if he were dying of thirst and only a mouthful of cum could save him; it was dirty and desperate, and I could never get enough. He didn't have a gag reflex, and the sensation of his lips wrapped around me while my head brushed his throat made the world turn white.

It wasn't just about the physical sensations. My alpha was on his knees for me, and my fingers were tangled in his beautiful curls, giving me the illusion of control; the notion made me squirm. We were in a study room because the thought of getting caught turned us both on, but Tristan wouldn't take his pleasure here. Instead, he'd break me into pieces and put me back together again, then later, tonight, in the safety of our bed, he'd recount every detail in a series of filthy whispers until we were both writhing, panting messes.

I couldn't wait.

He moved his lips up and down my shaft, then came off me with an obscene wet sound before dipping down to mouth gently over my sac. I gave a strangled groan, needy and desperate. Tristan answered the sound with a filthy chuckle. If there was one thing in the world that Tristan Grace loved almost as much as me, it was power. He loved knowing that he could make me beg, make me squirm, make me lose my mind – and *I* loved knowing that he'd do it, and then wrap me safely in his arms until I was ready to find myself again.

'Fucking love you, alpha,' I panted; he swallowed me once more and my hips kicked up of their own accord as I came without warning straight down his throat.

I floated in the afterglow; Tristan gathered me in his arms and brushed kisses below my ears and across my scent glands. He was an alpha, after all; if alphas had one trait in common, it was their obsession with scent. It was part of the reason we did this so often: scent blockers were effective at eliminating scent from our skin – from sweat pores or scent glands – but they only minimised the taste of us in cum or slick. Tristan was obsessed with my scent – a cherry I found much too sweet – and he got his fix in whatever way he could.

I wasn't any better. His scent was a mouthwatering, elegant vanilla, and I wanted to breathe it in every moment of the day. I wanted him to scent mark me so I could smell it on my clothes, on my skin, and to have him bite and bond me so that the echoes of his scent would twine through mine, letting every other alpha know that I was taken.

But alas.

Any other alpha in his position would have bitten me without a second thought. But Tristan insisted on being *noble* about it, and so I remained unbonded. But I was open to the idea of a pack, and Banksia was as good a place as any to start looking.

I gently disentangled myself from his arms and fished in my bag for scent-cancelling spray and wipes. I was never without either, and Tristan always carried extra, too.

We knew what we'd be risking if we weren't careful.

'I want to go to the discipline mixers,' I said, coating myself with cancelling spray. The later-year and research students were hosting mixers for the first years in discipline common rooms that night. Tristan would die before studying anything but archaeology, so his specialisation was already set, but I hadn't decided yet. I'd been getting a bit bored during our undergraduate degree, even with all the time we'd taken off for Tristan to go on digs, so I wondered whether something new might be better for me.

Ancient history, perhaps, or something completely outside my wheelhouse, like literature. A different discipline, so I could do a cross-school PhD, with the added bonus of entertaining my brain for a few months while I caught up to the other students.

And I would catch up. I wasn't conceited, but I couldn't be modest about it, either. Even without my parents and their achievements, I deserved my place here.

I pushed the thought of my parents away. Banksia House had been theirs; now it was mine. I refused to spend the next few years standing in my mother's shadow, even if one of the libraries was named after her.

Not the library this study room was in, obviously. I'd never get hard again.

Tristan sprayed himself with canceller while I watched appreciatively. My alpha was so beautiful, with his even features and soulful green eyes, deep enough to drown in. He wasn't built big – not like Byron Griffiths – and people tended to underestimate him because of that, even though he was still taller than me and roped in enough slender muscle that his clothes draped and clung in all the right places. His family oozed cash – the kind that came with ancestral manor houses and invitations to coronations – and Tristan carried himself with a quiet self-assurance that I'd found irresistible since he'd smiled at me on our first day of university six years ago.

When our clothes were straight and there was no hint of scent in the air, we left the study room for the first mixer. We were early – and by *early*, we'd arrived at the first common room twenty minutes after the advertised start time – so it was just us and the later-year students. We'd started with the classics mixer, and the vibe was overwhelmingly *friendly but awkward*; a handsome PhD candidate made a joke in Latin that I responded to unthinkingly, and they paid us more attention after that. I didn't think I'd choose classics as my speciality – I didn't enjoy the rote learning aspect of languages – but I worked to charm them nonetheless, while Tristan watched with an indulgent smile.

We moved onto philosophy next, where I was greeted by a blonde man with a wide grin and eyes that dropped a nanosecond later to my crotch. I retreated and Tristan stepped forward, clearing his throat and moving his hand to rest in the small of my back.

I fucking loved it when he did that. The touch was calming, centring – but it was also a non-verbal *fuck you* to the other alpha ogling my package.

I couldn't blame him, obviously. But he could also fuck right off.

I didn't think philosophy was for me, and not just because it had been my mother's specialisation.

We left quickly, heading for more familiar ground. The ancient and modern history students had teamed up, but you wouldn't know it to look at them: it was as if a line had been drawn down the centre of their common room, with a few hapless individuals that I imagined to be Middle Ages specialists wandering between the two groups.

Tristan must have thought the same, because he gave a tiny cough, a sound that usually covered a laugh. We headed for a stern-looking woman wearing an SPQR pin on her lapel, and a few moments later, Tristan was deep in conversation about museums returning stolen artefacts.

A man smiled at me, and it was a genuine *hey-how-are-you* smile, not a *hey-I'd-like-to-be-in-your-pants* one, and I was so grateful that I proceeded to talk his ear off. Two other men watched from a distance, but I had the feeling they were keeping an eye on their packmate, not assessing a potential new one.

The man's name was Paul – I had a strong suspicion he was an alpha – and he told me about the ancient history specialisation, dropping the names of a few guest lecturers and tutors he'd had over the years. I recognised all the names, which was impressive, coming from a different discipline; Banksia House didn't fuck about when it came to their academic hires. Paul mentioned their six-monthly trips – to central Australia, Italy, Greece, England, and South America – and their links to academies overseas before he suddenly faltered.

'Gosh,' he said quietly, his eyes fixing on the door behind me. 'She's brave, I'll give her that.'

I turned. My breath caught in my throat, because standing in the doorway was a poem of a woman, pretty and curvy with thick auburn hair falling over her shoulders in shining waves. I knew immediately who she was.

Rosemary.

The omega.

The chatter in the room stopped.

She flushed the most delicious shade of pink I'd ever seen, then turned to leave. My chest gave a strange, tight squeeze of what felt like empathy for her.

'Hey, Rosemary,' I called to her, running my mouth before my brain could catch up. Tristan shot me a *what the heck, Sebastian* look, but I ignored it. 'I'm so glad you made it! Paul was just telling me about the ancient history tutors, and they're insane.' I gave her my best warm smile and held out my arm, as if I was expecting her to walk into an embrace. 'And you *have* to hear about their overseas trips.'

Her brow furrowed, but she must have been dying to hear about the specialisation – or perhaps she was simply desperate for some time out of her bedroom – because she walked slowly across the room and *stepped into my outstretched arm*, pressing herself lightly against my side. I let my hand rest on her hip, as if this was *totally what I had expected and I was completely fine with it*, and not, in fact, battling the sudden, odd urge to push my face into her hair and inhale.

Paul seemed stunned into silence, so I forced myself to chatter. Tristan was tense, but as I hadn't yet given him my *please save me* signal, he stayed where he was, though his eyes flickered between Rosemary and me. I repeated all the information Paul had already given me, and, by the time I'd finished, the man had recovered enough to keep talking about the second-year curriculum and the current third-year research projects.

Rosemary listened, her lips slightly parted. My lungs were full of a sweet floral scent, but it wasn't *hers*. It was her hair product, or fragrance, or both, and it was lovely, but my teeth were aching with the unhinged desire to rake across her scent gland to see if she would perfume. *Which would be a totally fucked up thing to do*, I told myself, trying to concentrate on keeping my fingers loose on her hip, and not tightening to pull her closer the way I wanted.

Get a grip, Sebastian.

Rosemary asked a question; her voice was rich and smooth and quiet, the kind of voice that caresses, and I could almost *see* Paul's brain break in real time. I repeated the question, drawing his attention back to me, but he gave a garbled answer as his glazed eyes fixed on my lips. Rosemary twitched uncomfortably under my hand, and I realised that our previously carefree conversation was quickly deteriorating. I tapped the fingers of my free hand against my thigh, and a moment later Tristan appeared, thanking Paul with a charming smile before murmuring *we really should go to the next mixer, baby.*

I kept hold of Rosemary's waist; there was no way I was leaving her alone in a room full of alphas, even if they were history geeks like us. She didn't resist, letting me pull her into the corridor before she broke away.

I glanced back through the doorway to see Paul shake himself. Another man stepped to his side, patting him sympathetically on the back. *Poor thing,* I thought. *He was doing so well.*

'Thank you,' Rosemary said breathlessly. 'His eyes were glazing, did you notice?' Tristan frowned, and she blinked. 'Oh. Maybe it's an omega thing.'

Tristan turned his frown to me. 'Maybe.'

Rosemary's eyes flickered between us. 'I really appreciate the save,' she said. 'I take it you know who I am, but I'm not sure of your names.'

'Sebastian Worthy,' I answered at once, as if I were saying my name for roll call. 'And this is my alpha, Tristan Grace.'

She gave a small, sweet smile. 'It's nice to meet you both. I'm *the omega*, obviously.' Her smile turned wry. 'But I prefer Rose.'

'Rose,' I repeated, but it came out as a croon, and her cheeks turned that delicious shade of pink once more.

Tristan cleared his throat. 'We're going to head to the next mixer. It's been lovely —'

'And you're welcome to join us,' I interrupted, cutting Tristan off before he could dismiss her. 'Or we can walk you back to your room.'

Her smile widened, and my heart gave an uneven thump. 'I'd love to join you.'

ROSE

Sebastian chatted easily, as if we'd been friends for years. I answered when I could; my tongue had never felt so heavy, as if I'd somehow tied a knot in the middle of it.

He was just so fucking *pretty*.

Angelic was the word I'd use. All golden hair and bright blue eyes and perfect features, with wide shoulders and a narrow waist, as if he'd walked out of a painting and hit the gym along the way. His alpha was taller, his shoulders of a similar breadth, and he was pretty, too, but in a different way; he was guarded where Sebastian was open, severe where Sebastian was welcoming. Tristan had dark, curling hair and green eyes that shone behind vintage-style glasses, a stubborn jaw, forearms to die for, and a soft English accent that was a danger to knees everywhere. I could tell he wasn't keen on his beta's sudden interest in me, but it was clear he was indulgent where Sebastian was concerned. He wasn't anything like the other alphas I'd known, but there was something about the way he carried himself that let me know I'd be foolish to underestimate him, an edge of dominance that sharpened the very air around us.

I inhaled, but couldn't catch even a hint of their scents.

Frustration spilled through me. I'd bet every dollar I had that Sebastian Worthy smelled as good as he looked.

A heartbeat later, I told myself to be grateful. I was here for a degree, not a pack. His scent didn't matter. *Their* scents didn't matter. I didn't need to know if they were nature scents, or lifestyle scents, or food scents. I didn't *need* to know if Sebastian's scent was as lovely as his eyes.

'Sociology next?' he suggested, and I shook myself, trying not to think about the weight of his arm as he settled it casually back around my waist. Sociology wasn't for me, but I hadn't seen another soul for two days, so I let myself be pulled towards another common room.

It was less crowded than the history mixer. A woman with a chain of bites around her neck welcomed us with a bright smile and answered Sebastian's questions without once losing her composure. I tried not to stare at her bites – there were four different marks, at least – and pushed down the spark of jealousy that was catching in my belly.

A degree, not a pack, I reminded myself, looking away – straight into the stare of a pair of men in the corner, who were watching Sebastian and me as if we were their next meal.

I looked away immediately, rubbing the back of my neck without thinking, uncomfortable. A moment later, Tristan stepped between us and them, blocking them from my sight.

I looked up at him, surprised, but his eyes were fixed on the woman speaking to Sebastian. His expression was polite, as if nothing had happened.

I forced myself to listen to the woman with the bites. She seemed like a beta, though without scent, it was impossible to tell for sure. Alphas were easier to pick; most of them walked around as if they owned the place and everything in it. Sebastian had drawn the possible-beta into describing the details of the sociology curriculum, and she was smiling freely, utterly charmed by him. I shifted my weight; in response, his hand tightened on my hip.

As a touch, it was almost nothing. A warm weight on a curve of flesh, the slight pressure of fingers cupping. At the same time, it felt like a claiming. *Mine*, Sebastian was saying, through the gentle touch. *His*, I said, by letting him keep his hand there. Tristan – a still presence beside us – only solidified it with his watchful gaze and easy, ready stance.

I swallowed. That was the problem – well, one of the problems – with being an omega. No matter how capable I was, no matter how intelligent, how hard-working, how independent, my instincts still wanted a pack, and they were much less picky in their search for one than they should have been. They wanted alphas who would protect me, and betas who would worship me. They didn't care about much outside that, working off the assumption that if an alpha or beta smelled good, that was all that mattered.

I didn't want that. Well, I *did*, but it wasn't *all* that I wanted. If I found a pack – a million years from now – I didn't just want complementary scents. I wanted a pack I could be myself with, a pack that would value me for my brain as much as my designation.

I wanted *love*.

I repressed a snort. I was more likely to find a scent match than love. Most alphas viewed omegas as vessels for their knots, and nothing more. Omegas were rare, and in some places overseas, we were prizes in state-run lotteries, given to packs like a holiday house or a shiny new car. It wasn't that bad in Australia – we were protected by the law, if not by popular sentiment – but I'd still heard stories about kidnaps, trades, and auctions. I only had to remember my uncomfortable attempt at art school to know that those stories could have been true.

It was why the Omega Support Agency tracked and monitored us so closely. Well, that was the reason the government gave, anyway. They wanted us registered and contactable for our protection. There were eye-watering fines and jail time for unregistered omegas; that threat was enough to have most omegas on their database within days of emergence.

'Thank you so much for your time,' Tristan said, and I realised I'd missed everything the woman had said. 'We should get going.' He gave her a wide, warm smile; Sebastian wasn't the only one who could ooze charm when he wanted.

'In a hurry?' Sebastian said, amused, as we walked from the room. His hand stayed on my hip; he didn't seem inclined to move it, and I wasn't about to ask him to.

'Neither of you are going to choose sociology,' Tristan answered. 'You're not interested, and Rose wasn't even paying attention. Plus, those alphas in the corner were getting on my nerves.'

Sebastian frowned. 'What alphas?'

I side-eyed him, realising that he hadn't noticed them. He hadn't *needed* to. Tristan had, and that was all that mattered.

I wondered what it would be like to have someone watch out for you like that.

I didn't realise what the next mixer was until we'd walked into the common room, at which point I knew *immediately* it was literature because *he* was there.

I knew more about him now: that his name was Byron; that he was the son of Banksia's new Dean; and that his Honours thesis on the modern Gothic had been published in a prestigious journal soon after he'd graduated. Along with that, I'd watched the scene in the dining hall a hundred times in different posts on Banksia's social media app, seen the horror dawn in his grey eyes after his voice wound through the dining hall.

And I also knew what he'd said after I'd left. That he'd hurt anyone who did anything I didn't want.

I hadn't quite forgiven him, but knowing it had been an accident – and knowing he'd tried to make it better by bringing me food for the last few days – went a long way.

He was trying to make himself seem smaller, keeping his hands in his pockets and his arms tight by his side as he spoke to a later-year student, but it was like asking a mountain to shrink. He dominated the room regardless, and not just because of his size. There was something about him that drew the eye; I wondered if he knew it, if the black clothes and the hunched shoulders were his way of trying to fade into the background.

He went still as he noticed me, his stormy eyes tracking from my feet to the top of my head, as if making sure I was all there. They fixed for a moment on Sebastian's hand, still hot on my hip, before he blinked and returned his attention to the conversation.

I exhaled shakily.

'Fuck, he's gorgeous,' Sebastian said under his breath, dipping his head closer to mine. I eyed him sideways; he shrugged. 'What? I'm allowed to *look*.'

'He's …' I began, then trailed off, struggling to find the right word. He – Byron – was too masculine to be beautiful, but *handsome* wasn't right, either; something about him was too hard for that. 'Yeah,' I said at last. 'He is.'

'We heard he's been bringing you food.'

I gave Sebastian a sharp look. 'You *heard*?'

He grinned. 'Okay, we saw trays outside your room and assumed it was him, because the kitchens will only deliver during term time. We were just checking you were alive, I swear.'

'It could have been anybody,' I pointed out, though he was right.

When his mother had visited me, offering apologies on behalf of herself and the university administration in a sincere, stricken kind of way, she'd suggested they set up a camera outside my door – a suggestion I'd accepted.

I may have checked it around mealtimes. For safety reasons, obviously. Absolutely not to ogle the alpha.

'He emailed me,' I blurted out. 'To apologise.'

Sebastian's gaze flew to my face. 'Was it a good one?'

It had been *really* good. *Too* good, even. 'Yep.'

'So why aren't we over there?'

I narrowed my eyes. 'Why are you invested?'

He grinned at me. 'Who wouldn't be?'

My eyes darted back to the big alpha. He straightened, and the woman he was speaking to eyed the way his chest expanded.

'Um,' I said, my mind suddenly blank.

Sebastian laughed; his fingers tightened as an excited-looking student came over to speak to us. 'Hi! We're wondering about …'

I tuned Sebastian's chatter out; I'd loved English in high school, but I wouldn't choose literature as my speciality. I was almost certain that Sebastian wouldn't choose it, either, but he kept asking questions regardless. Tristan had stepped away, although not far, and was having an intense conversation with an equally intense-looking alpha.

A movement by the door caught my eye, and I saw that the alphas who had watched us at the sociology mixer had followed us here.

'Omega,' one growled. Without thinking, I pressed myself into Sebastian's side.

The room fell silent, waiting. I waited, too, because I couldn't do anything else. They were blocking the door, my only escape.

'Walk with us,' the other said, and Sebastian trembled.

I cleared my throat and looked them in the eye. It was hard for omegas to meet an alpha's gaze; our instincts told us to lower our eyes, to stay safe, not to challenge their dominance. They both had brown eyes, short brown hair, and matching broad, tall frames; they almost looked like brothers. 'No, thank you,' I forced out, managing to keep my tone polite.

I was proud that my voice didn't shake.

The feeling only lasted for a moment because, as one, their expressions turned thunderous. 'You want to try that again?' one of them said, drawing himself to his full height, as if that would somehow change my mind.

I knew what they were trying to do. It was how omegas got trapped in unsuitable packs or were abused by alphas who kept but never bothered to bond them. Every alpha was dominant; it was what they were. And some misused that power by manoeuvring betas or omegas into situations where they couldn't say no.

'I don't,' I managed. Sebastian's fingers were digging into my hip and I concentrated on the pressure instead of ducking my head and wriggling into his arms like I wanted to. 'I don't want to walk with you. I don't want to walk with *anybody.*'

I said it as loud as I could, so that every person in the room could hear.

One of them snarled, and the hair on the back of my neck stood on end.

'I think she made herself clear,' the intense-looking woman with Tristan said; her unimpressed expression wouldn't have been out of place at the front of a classroom full of teenagers. 'Either come in and talk about the literature specialisation or move on to your next mixer.'

Sebastian huffed a tiny laugh. The dark-haired alphas exchanged a look, then melted away from the doorway.

I sagged against Sebastian, my knees suddenly shaking.

'No, you don't,' he said softly, holding me up. 'You brave little thing. Stand up straight like the badass you are, Rose.'

Tristan strode towards us, his expression tight, and I realised he'd moved since the last time I'd seen him – he'd been standing between us and the door.

Opposite Byron, who'd moved to do the same thing.

I raked in a breath, realising that I hadn't been in any danger. They'd both been there, standing between us and the other alphas.

Byron's stormy gaze fell on me, questioning.

'I think I've had enough,' I said softly.

The student speaking with Sebastian exchanged a glance with the intense-looking woman. 'We'll report them,' he said. He nodded to a corner of the room, where another woman had her phone out. 'Julianne recorded the whole thing.'

'I'd appreciate it, thank you.' I forced a smile and looked back at Sebastian. 'Would you walk me back to my room?'

'Of course,' he said immediately, and steered me gently towards the door. Tristan fell in behind us, before Sebastian paused in the doorway, looking back. 'Alpha?'

I glanced back, too, but he wasn't talking to Tristan.

He was talking to *Byron*.

Who followed us out, silently.

He didn't say a word the whole way. Sebastian chattered, not seeming to require responses, and Tristan interjected occasionally, but Byron was silent.

As was I.

I thanked them when we got to my room, uncomfortable with how much they'd done for me. Before I unlocked my door, Sebastian enveloped me in a hug.

I froze, but it was so ... *nice*. He was tall and his chest was broad and hard; his arms shut out the world. I breathed in, inhaling the scents of soap and washing detergent, underlain with the metallic tang of canceller. I could have stayed there for hours, but he let me go.

'See you tomorrow, Rose,' he said, and dragged Tristan away with a grin.

I blinked after him.

'Was there a mixer you missed, but wanted information from?'

I turned to face Byron, startled. His hands were back in his pockets, and he'd stepped back, giving me plenty of space.

'Archaeology,' I managed.

He gave a curt nod, then gestured to the door. 'Make sure you lock it behind you,' he said softly, before turning and walking away.

I slipped inside and did as he said.

Some hours later, I heard a rustling outside my door. When I checked my camera, there was a brochure on the floor outside it.

My lips curved when I opened the door to pick it up. *So you're interested in archaeology?* it read.

And on top of it rested a posy of sunny, golden wattle flowers.

BYRON

I DIDN'T ATTEND ALL THE ACTIVITIES during orientation week, but by the first day of class, I had a fairly good idea of who I wanted to avoid for the next three years.

Glynn and Dean – the two alphas who'd tried to force Rose's hand – topped the list. They were straight-up assholes, and she wasn't the only one they'd gone after. A first-year beta and a third-year alpha also lodged complaints about their behaviour. My mother asked me about it, and I answered honestly. *They shouldn't be here.*

She nodded, and I knew that she agreed, but, as usual, her hands were tied by *process*. Three complaints put them on the edge of expulsion before class had even started, but they hadn't explicitly broken any rules, and a later-year student – a cousin of Glynn's – had offered to watch over them, to *teach them the Banksia ways*. It didn't sound half ominous, but the cousin's father was a major donor, so the Banksia board opted to give Glynn and Dean one more chance.

They weren't the only ones on my list. It also included a second-year, Jacob, who tried to pick a fight with me outside the dining hall one evening, and a third-year, Melissa, who would *not* leave me alone. She was clever about it, never giving me the opportunity to refuse her outright; she just *appeared* every time I went for a meal, and my DMs were overflowing with unread messages.

I didn't want to be rude, but I wasn't interested. I was polite, but I was careful not to do anything that could be misconstrued as welcoming the attention, and I switched my social media profiles to private to make sure it couldn't happen again.

Which didn't stop me checking other people's profiles, embarrassingly thoroughly.

Tristan's feed was so casually rich it was absurd. He didn't post often; when he did, they were always photos that were taken on his phone, swift and careless, often featuring Sebastian – though never a full photo, and never of his face – with a glass of wine in hand. His captions read things like *so glad to be back in Greece* and *lucky to have the whole island to ourselves*. His New Year's Eve photos seemed to be ones he'd been tagged in by other people, people whose names even *I* knew, people who seemed to share the traits of youth, beauty, and eye-wateringly large amounts of money, partying elegantly in backdrops I'd only ever seen in films.

Sebastian's private feed was cute; he'd followed me the morning after the discipline mixers and accepted my subsequent request about five seconds after I'd sent it. His posts mostly featured his impressive balcony garden in the apartment he and Tristan had shared before coming to Banksia House. Tristan was in many of them, wearing an indulgent smile and a softness around his eyes that I was yet to see in real life. There were a couple of photos of Sebastian's family, but not many; those pictures seemed to feature Sebastian looking uncomfortable at various award nights, standing stiffly next to one of his parents as they held trophies or plaques or certificates – or, in one, an oversized fake cheque for a sum I checked a few times to make sure I hadn't misread.

I spent the longest on Rosemary's feed. Hers was a little more curated; she was obviously careful about what she posted, and her shots were so beautiful they looked almost professional. Her pictures were often about what she was reading or crafts she seemed to take up for a few months before starting something new. There were some selfies – she looked so pretty in them my mouth went dry – but I realised after a while that all of them were taken inside. Her feed didn't show her travelling, or even getting out and about in the city she'd lived in.

The world isn't made for omegas, Tina's voice reminded me. *They need a safety net. Friends, or family, or a pack. People who can help them feel comfortable as they navigate the space around them.*

It made me sadder than I could say to think that Rosemary might not have had that.

It played on my mind as I got ready for the first day of class. I always wore variations of the same outfit – black on black – so I didn't need much time to dress, though I was careful with my scent cancellers and I checked the battery on my monitors to make sure they'd last the day. After brushing my teeth, I ran my fingers through my hair, pulled half of it back into a loose bun, and packed my bag.

I was halfway down the staircase when I found myself veering to the right and knocking on Rosemary's door.

She answered a moment later, looking surprised. 'Alpha?'

Alpha.

Every muscle in my body tightened at the sound of my designation on her lips. I cleared my throat, trying to ignore it. 'I'm going to get breakfast before class. Would you like to come?'

She blinked, and then a smile spread over her face, slowly. 'Yes,' she said quietly. 'I'd like that.'

She took a few extra moments to get ready. I stayed outside her room, listening to her bustle about, a song by an Australian female indie artist playing in the background. I added the song to my own streaming library. *You're unhinged*, I told myself. *You're basically a stalker.*

'Ready.'

I swallowed as she stepped outside. She was wearing a high-waisted dark green skirt with a cream blouse, and my mind went blank. The entire outfit was tight to the skin and she had the kind of figure that belonged in a Golden Age film.

I hitched my bag on my shoulder and cleared my throat. 'Great,' I said inanely, because it was all my lust-addled alpha brain could manage.

We didn't chat as we walked down the stairs, but it wasn't an awkward silence. All I could hope was that she didn't think I'd gotten into Banksia because of my mother. The administration insisted that I sat all the entrance tests, then begrudgingly told my parents that I ranked *somewhere in the middle* of the cohort. Rosemary didn't seem to mind that I was quiet, though.

We lined up for food. She eyed the waffles with the kind of wistful look that would give me a coronary if it were ever aimed my way, but when we got to the serving station, she asked for Bircher muesli, instead.

I studied her from the corner of my eye. Omegas craved sweetness like bees needed pollen; they burned energy at a higher rate than an alpha in a rut. I knew that Bircher muesli would never have cut it for Tina. When I stepped up to the serving station and the man behind it smiled at me, I asked for an omelette *and* the waffles, which I piled with every topping I could. Rosemary blinked at me but didn't comment; I followed her through the dining hall, ignoring the stares from other students and, when we sat, I offered her a waffle.

She frowned at me. 'They're yours.'

'We can share.'

She held out for longer than I was expecting, finishing half her muesli before she tentatively slid a waffle covered in maple syrup from my plate and demolished it in small, neat bites. When I offered her another, she smiled, full and honest.

'Thank you, alpha.'

I tried to shove down the satisfaction that came with those words. My instincts were less easy to deal with, purring silently with approval as she bit into the food I'd chosen.

'Fuck, yes!' came another voice; a moment later, Sebastian plonked himself down next to Rosemary with a grin, holding a plate heaped with his own pile of waffles. Tristan followed with a plate of toast and fruit. He nodded in greeting, then sat beside me.

'Griffiths,' he said.

'Grace,' I returned.

Neither of us commented on whatever the fuck was happening, and the four of us just … sat together.

As if we were friends.

Or something.

Sebastian shot me a grin, and I forced myself not to react to it. I wondered how long it had taken Tristan to become immune to that smile, or if he ever had. Between the pretty beta and lovely omega, it was a wonder that I could concentrate enough to chew. They looked incredible together: Sebastian with his summer glow and Rosemary with her quiet autumn beauty, like two seasons come to life.

My instincts purred again.

Sebastian nudged Rosemary with his elbow. 'Are you ready for day one?'

She shoved a forkful of waffle in her mouth. 'I will be.'

'Coffee,' Tristan muttered, raking his hands through his curls. 'Need coffee.'

Clearly, I wasn't the only one struggling with my instincts.

'Griffiths?'

Tristan stared down at me, one eyebrow raised, and my stomach tightened. I shook myself, realising he was asking for my coffee order. 'Flat white. Thanks.'

He rolled his eyes in an *of course* kind of way. 'Rose?'

She gave a shy smile. 'A chai latte. Thank you.'

'Hmph,' Tristan answered, and strode away from the table.

Sebastian watched his alpha leave with a hooded smile, then met my gaze. His smile turned playful. 'Something in the air this morning, alpha? First day nerves, maybe?'

I raised an eyebrow. He knew exactly what was happening, the menace. 'Something in the air,' I agreed blandly.

Rosemary – *Rose*, they'd called her – gave us a perplexed look, so I shoved the last of my omelette into my mouth, feigning a calm I didn't feel.

Thankfully, Tristan returned quickly with the coffees. Sebastian finished his waffles, then poached a spoonful of almond butter from my plate, grinning as he licked his spoon clean in a way that made my entire body go tight.

I stood before I could embarrass myself. 'I'm out,' I said shortly. Rose moved to stand; I shook my head. 'Finish your breakfast, omega. See you in class.'

I strode away before she could respond, coffee in hand. She'd be safe with Sebastian and Tristan; they'd looked after her at the mixers, after all. I hurried up the main staircase, trying to put some distance between myself and the image of Sebastian's tongue wrapping around his spoon or the way Rose's skirt clung to her thighs.

The halls were bustling; everybody was gearing up for the first day of classes. Every person I saw had a coffee cup in hand; one harassed-looking alpha with silver hair was carrying an entire plunger, eyeing it like it was liquid gold. The morning sun streamed through the windows, and when I looked out, I could see the shifting light glinting off the sea.

I was born inland, and I'd always lived there. Seeing the ocean so often was a treat, and one I'd not yet grown used to.

Our classes were all on the third floor, in the First Year Library. Students' first year at Banksia was devoted to general studies and research skills. We would spend the year together and would be treated as a single cohort. The First Year Library was one of the few rooms in the manor big enough for all of us.

It was cavernous, its floor space filled with study desks and chairs, the walls lined with full bookshelves stretching from the floor to the roof, which was two storeys high. Stained glass windows lined one wall, wide and arched, light streaming through them in a riot of colour. Instead of the usual religious imagery, the coloured glass depicted vivid scenes of the landscape around Banksia House: the sea, the cliffs, the bush, the beach, and native animals and birds. I spotted a plaque on the wall, naming a well-known First Nations artist as their creator.

There was an area for teaching beneath the massive windows, with a lectern and a projector screen before rows of chairs with tablet arms. I assumed this was where we'd have class – all the other desks were study pods, with partitions and retro desk lamps – so I headed across the library and chose a seat in the back corner, where I could see the entire room and where the light from the windows spilled over me in a wave of warmth.

I grabbed my laptop from my bag and found the class summary. According to it, today's lesson was introductory and would cover mostly administrative stuff, so there was no required reading. I'd read the first few chapters of the textbook yesterday anyway, because we'd be starting with a unit on prehistory, which was completely outside my wheelhouse. I'd never studied anything that wasn't based on text before, and I didn't want to fall behind.

I opened a browser tab and looked through the online classroom. Banksia had its own system, independent of SECU, and it seemed pretty good – definitely better than the one at my last university. All our resources were online – you could pay extra for a bound print-out, which I'd already done; I hated annotating on a screen – and there was a certain amount of interaction expected in online forums each week. This week was a simple *introduce yourself* – preferred name and pronouns, undergraduate degree, favourite book, that kind of thing – so I typed something out as I waited, giving the bare bones that everyone else here would have already known. I'd seen the looks and heard the whispers; the students here knew

I was the Dean's son, and they knew she got me my place here. They also knew, no doubt, that I was taking up the second scholarship place. No one had said anything to me – not yet, anyway. I suspected my size and monitors were the reasons why; not many people wanted to fuck with a six-foot-six wall of muscle, especially not one who might black out at any moment.

I looked up as footsteps echoed through the library; unfortunately, it was Glynn and Dean. They scowled at me as one – as though they were mobsters or something, and not just two unpleasant rich boys with unaccountably high grades. Glynn stepped towards me before a third set of footsteps sounded. A slender man with salt-and-pepper hair walked in, an expensive-looking laptop under one arm. He strode towards the lectern and began to set up; Glynn and Dean sank into seats at the front, as far away from me as they could possibly manage.

The man looked up, catching my eye. My instincts stirred; *alpha*, they told me, and I agreed, taking in his direct stare and the confident set of his shoulders. He studied me with a blank expression before frowning and going back to his laptop. The screen to his side ascended and descended in turn, until he was satisfied with its height.

More students filtered in. By now, most of the faces were familiar. A woman named Alessia chose a seat nearby, giving me a friendly nod as she pushed her dark hair back from her face. She seemed like a beta, though I couldn't tell for sure. An alpha, Pravin, who'd done the same undergraduate degree as me, sat next to her; he shot me a smile as the seats began to fill. He'd told me that he'd known

Tristan before Banksia; their grandmothers had been at university together in Mumbai before Tristan's grandmother moved to the UK, and their families still kept in touch.

Sebastian all but bounced into the library with a sunny smile. Every alpha in the room straightened, watching as Tristan followed close behind him, Rose at his side. Her eyes were wide as she took in the library, her gaze darting to the books, then the windows, then to me sitting beneath them.

Rose's entrance divided the other students' attention. Did they ogle the breathtaking beta, or the pretty omega?

Choices, choices.

Rose must have noticed their stares, because she flushed and moved closer to Tristan, whose expression was one of bored disdain. He didn't care about the students looking at his beta, or at the omega by his side, because they weren't important enough to warrant his attention. Tristan had the air of someone who knew his worth – and no matter what, it was more than yours.

I should have hated his arrogant ass, but that unshakable self-assurance was kind of a turn on.

Rose skirted the chairs; my heart skipped a few beats as she headed straight towards me. She plonked her bag down on the floor with a muffled thump, then slid into the chair next to me. Sebastian folded to sit by her other side, and Tristan gracefully slouched next to him, kicking out his long legs and crossing them at the ankle.

Having Rose so close was as calming as it was distracting. My eyes darted sideways every time she moved, my instincts shouting at me to be of use. *Find her food, make her comfortable, keep her safe. Keep her within sight, within reach. Fuck her, bite her, bond her.*

Settle the fuck down, I told them – and myself – but my inner alpha had no intention of listening, too busy trying to push a comforting purr up my throat when Rose jiggled a foot nervously. I'd never purred for *anyone* before, and I sure as fuck wasn't about to do it for the first time during class when any asshole might hear.

That shit would be for my pack, and my pack alone.

'Good morning, first years,' the alpha at the front said. His voice wasn't loud, but everyone fell silent immediately. 'I'm Professor Brandon Heathcote, and I'll be taking you during the first semester.'

Heathcote started with an Acknowledgement of Country, then went on to tell us about his credentials, which were as long as my arm and impressive for someone so young. I glanced to the side, catching Sebastian with his mouth open and his eyes even wider, possibly a little star struck.

It was cute.

Heathcote gave us an overview of the course, then talked about the assessment. I relaxed when he spoke about the essays; I might not have known the subject matter, but I could write a solid argument in my sleep. The final exam made me a little nervous, but I figured I'd aim to do well enough in the essays and online responses that I could scrape by with a pass in the exam if I needed to.

'To begin,' Heathcote said, flicking his presentation to the next slide. He looked down, shuffling some papers. 'Alessia. What are the three key concepts which constitute the primary ways anthropologists understand human life?'

Alessia tensed. 'I … I'm not sure.'

Heathcote looked down once more. 'Sebastian,' he went on, apparently ignoring Alessia's response. 'What is the four-field approach?'

'The subfields of the anthropology discipline are cultural anthropology, linguistic anthropology, archaeology, and biological anthropology,' Sebastian answered promptly. 'Combining insights from all four fields allows a complex examination of questions or issues. This is known as the four-field approach.'

'Rosemary,' Heathcote continued, without acknowledging Sebastian; I tensed. 'What is enculturation?'

'The process through which we acquire culture,' Rose said, frowning, her voice hesitant.

My brow was similarly lowered; this wasn't what I had expected. *And was it a coincidence …?*

'James,' Heathcote said, turning to the only other possible beta in our year, who visibly shrank. *Not a coincidence, then.* I sat straighter, rolling my shoulders back as Heathcote went on. 'What –'

'Brandon?' Tristan interrupted, raising his hand in a languid half-wave. 'The class summary states there is no required reading in week one.'

Heathcote raised a black eyebrow. 'And?'

'Not all of us have a background in anthropology. These questions assume prior knowledge.'

Heathcote tilted his head to the side, watching Tristan impassively. 'You are the best of the best. These are basic questions.'

'Basic questions if you already possess an anthropology degree, certainly.' Tristan paused. 'And perhaps one of the alphas would appreciate the chance to answer.'

Heathcote's eyes narrowed. 'Do you think designations matter in academia?'

'No, I don't.' Tristan stared calmly back. 'I think it *matters* when specific students who just *happen* to belong to specific designations are asked questions in public that they may not be able to answer.'

I exhaled silently. *Fuck.*

Tristan had seemed confident, in the way that rich people always were, entirely sure that no matter where they were and what they were doing, the way *they* did it was right. He'd seemed dismissive in a similar way, as if everyone here was beneath his notice.

But the air had gone sharp with something else, something more than the staring contest between an asshole professor and his arrogant student.

Something I knew well; something I'd used to my own advantage before.

Beside me, Rose shrank back in her chair as the edge of dominance raised the hairs on the back of my neck. Sebastian's eyes were on his alpha; he hooked his foot beneath Tristan's ankle.

I tensed.

Heathcote looked away first. 'I expect all students to be able to answer all questions in my class,' he returned, then flicked the presentation to the next slide and began to read from it, effectively cutting off any further response from Tristan. The alpha two seats away from me didn't seem to care much, rolling his head from one side to the other, an eyebrow cocked ever-so-slightly in an expression of bored contempt.

Tristan had a spine of steel. I didn't know *anyone* who would willingly butt heads with a professor in the first five minutes of their new class.

Not even *Tina* would have done that.

Alessia glanced over her shoulder and shot Tristan a grateful smile.

The message icon on the online classroom flashed. I clicked on it, seeing I'd been added to a group chat.

> *Rosemary Morris says: Thank you, Tristan.*
> *Sebastian Worthy says: Way to go, alpha*
> *Tristan Grace says: It was nothing.*

I glanced across at Tristan again. His gaze was fixed to Heathcote's presentation, his expression still bored, but the hand propping up his chin was curled into a tight fist.

I had a feeling that I'd just gotten a glimpse of the real Tristan Grace, and I wondered what else was lurking beneath the surface.

TRISTAN

WHEN I'D SAID IT MEANT NOTHING, I hadn't been lying. I'd seen Alessia's grateful look, and James shot me a warm smile as we were walking out of class, but I deserved neither. I'd done it for Sebastian, and Sebastian only. If Heathcote had left him alone, I would have sat silently and let our professor target the others, just like every other alpha in the room.

I didn't deserve their gratitude.

Heathcote's obvious bias troubled me, though probably not as much as it should have. Sebastian would be fine. He was the smartest person I'd ever met, and if Heathcote continued to target him … Well, I'd be doing more than just talking back in class.

'I'm going to have to work my ass off,' Sebastian muttered. 'I bet his bias against betas and omegas comes through in his marking.'

'SECU policy states that all work is blind marked.'

Sebastian threw me a wry look. 'Yes, I'm sure he'll let that stop him.'

Disquiet churned in my stomach. Perhaps I wasn't taking it seriously enough. Sebastian already had the world working against him; he didn't need a bigoted professor with a superiority complex making things worse. 'We'll watch him,' I said, curling my arm around Sebastian's waist and pressing a kiss to his temple.

And I would.

Like a fucking hawk.

Sebastian's brow creased into a familiar frown. He stumbled on the bottom step of the main staircase, and I knew that his mind had gone elsewhere – to studying, specifically. I kept my arm around him as we descended, and it was only half for the pleasure of holding him close.

I knew from long experience what he needed: a pot of tea, some study snacks, and his classical music playlist. When we reached our apartment and he disappeared into the bedroom, I found his favourite tea and made him a pot. I'd ordered some biscuits and chocolate from a speciality shop further down the coast, so I put some on a plate, added some raspberries, then connected his phone to the Bluetooth speakers.

Sebastian reappeared as the sound of a gentle piano concerto filled the living room. His expression softened, and his perfect lips curved into a smile.

'Oh, alpha,' he breathed, and for a moment, I thought the afternoon might take a different turn. It wasn't to be, however; he bussed a kiss to my cheek and flopped down on the couch, opening his laptop and shoving a biscuit in his mouth, whole.

'I'm going for a walk.'

He glanced at me. 'In the gardens? Or further?'

'Just the gardens. I want to check out the maze.'

He nodded. It wasn't surprising; I walked as much as I could. I knew I didn't look outdoorsy, but walking was my meditation. If I didn't have anything else to do, I'd walk for miles, letting the sounds around me and the steady rhythm of my own breathing lull me into a state of quiet content. It was a trait I shared with my mother; whenever I went home, she'd plan a ramble, just for us, and they were times I treasured.

After pressing a kiss to Sebastian's hair, I headed downstairs. Later-year classes ran all day, and I overheard some workshops as I walked through the corridors and escaped into the gardens at the back of the manor.

The gardens were meticulously manicured, lying beyond a small green. They framed the maze and were bordered by flowering plants and, further away, towering trees, giving the manor a sense of seclusion. The garden was entirely planted with native species: even the green wasn't grassed, but rather a lush covering of Australian violets. I'd never seen its like and I paused to admire it, snapping a few shots on my phone to show Sebastian and to send to my mother. They both loved gardening, though Sebastian's interest was mainly in indoor and balcony plants; messy cottage gardens were more my mother's thing. It was what had changed my parents' minds about Sebastian. They'd thought I was too young to *settle down*, until he'd given them a tour of our last apartment and Sebastian and my mother had struck up an hours-long conversation about indoor gardens.

Somehow – to my parents, at least – Sebastian's care and dedication for his plants translated to care and dedication to *me*, and they came around to our relationship.

Sometimes, I wished my parents didn't know me *quite* so well.

Banksia's maze was made of lemon myrtle; it was flowering, so the sweet scent of its blossoms hung in the air, mixed with the heady citrus smell of its leaves. It was so strong that I could barely scent anything else, which unnerved me. As an alpha, my sense of smell was second only to an omega's, and we relied on scent to navigate the world around us. The heavy curtain of citrus in the air was as good as someone blindfolding me.

The maze stretched over my head, three metres or so upwards. I strode forward, my shoulders relaxing as the lush green enveloped me. I resolved to take some leaves back to Sebastian for tea. He enjoyed comfort, and that comfort often came in the form of something hot and drinkable.

The pathway forked. I chose the right-hand side; I wasn't trying to get to the centre of the maze, just wandering around it. The path led to a small clearing with four more walkways branching from it, and a small water feature in the middle like a tiny roundabout. Stone benches sat to the left and right. I snapped another picture for Sebastian, then whirled around, frowning, when I thought I heard a footstep.

There was no one there.

I inhaled, but all I could smell was lemon myrtle.

Shaking my head, I chose one of the paths and strode deeper into the maze. A kookaburra call sounded from somewhere nearby. I'd only ever seen them in zoos or at bird sanctuaries, but I knew that they were territorial and their call could mean a stranger was close. What I *didn't* know was if *I* was that stranger, or whether they were calling about someone else.

I followed the path, finding some dead ends along the way, most of them featuring some kind of statue. Banksia's art collection was worth a fortune, and I was a little surprised to see so many pieces out here in the garden, where anyone could trip over them.

A shuffling noise came from my left.

I spun, the hair on the back of my neck standing on end as my alpha rose inside me, bristling just beneath my skin. The kookaburra called once more, mocking. My hands came up, ready to strike, and my teeth ached, preparing to push down, to bite, to *tear*.

But I remained alone.

I lowered my hands, feeling like a fool, but my skin didn't stop crawling. I shoved my hands into my pockets, scoffing at myself. *It's the maze*, I told myself. It was the overpowering smell of citrus and the way the trees walled me in and cut off the sky.

Behind me, a footstep fell.

I moved, but a hand was already clamping around my jaw, and something sharp pressed into my neck.

◈◈◈

I woke in darkness, blinking slowly. I couldn't see a thing. Some kind of material scratched gently across my brow and the bridge of my nose, my eyelashes dragging against it, telling me I'd been blindfolded. My entire body ached, but my shoulders were especially sore; my arms were stretched behind my back, and the tight, shifting warmth around my wrists suggested that *someone was holding them that way.*

Rage spread through me, hot and consuming. My alpha roared, hating that someone was restricting our movement. My instincts shouted at me to struggle, to throw them off, to tear away whatever covered my eyes, and to beat my foes into submission, both with my fists and with my dominance. My alpha reared its head, ready to make someone *bleed.*

But I knew that was the worst thing I could do.

My parents had dealt with kidnap threats before. Once a year, they hired a consultant – sometimes private, sometimes from the military, sometimes a member of the Alpha Special Forces – and they'd refresh my entire family on what to do. Try not to get kidnapped in the first place, was their general advice. But if we did, we were advised to cooperate. To take in all the information we could. To study our kidnappers' faces, their voices. To talk to them. To try to forge a connection, to humanise ourselves. To always make it clear if we needed medical attention, and to only try to escape if we were absolutely sure of success.

Above all, they advised us to stay calm.

Which, it turned out, was easier said than done.

A shuffling sound came from my right; someone grunted, as if in pain. A snarl ripped through the air, raw and desperate, full of anger and fear.

I wasn't alone, then.

'Be silent.'

The voice was female, and unfamiliar; it resonated with dominance and command. The snarling stopped abruptly.

'You are in no danger,' the woman continued. 'The opposite, in fact.'

My shoulders stiffened; the ache in my body spread. From my symptoms, I suspected that I'd either been beaten to a pulp while unconscious, or I'd been given a dose of propofolyte, a tranquiliser specifically developed to floor alphas during a rut. The drug worked almost instantaneously, but its effects had a relatively short duration if the dose wasn't repeated.

And its side effects included muscle aches, cramps, weakness, and general lethargy.

Fantastic, I thought crossly, shifting as my thigh cramped; the movement earned me an unreasonably sharp hinge joint – a knee, I suspected – to the lower back.

'You're here today because we've researched you. Watched you. And we know you have something that might be valuable to us. We don't mean money,' the woman went on, as I stiffened. 'Though that can be helpful, too. We mean that there's something about you – about your drive, your connections, your skills – that could help us. Something we could use.'

I inhaled sharply, realising who'd taken me.

The Revels.

'This isn't admittance,' the woman said warningly. 'This is the first of multiple steps towards a *possible* offer. You're at a school that students would kill to attend. And we're the group that takes only the best of the best.

'Your task is in your hands.' I felt something nestle between my fingers, and I closed my hand around it, tight. 'Whether you complete it is your choice. But failure to do so will remove you from consideration. You have one month from today; after that time, if your task remains incomplete, you will be struck from our list.' She paused. 'We ask a lot of those who join us. But they get a lot in return. Your wildest dreams could be your reality.' Another pause. 'For you and your pack.'

My breath caught. I'd never cared about the Revels; I didn't need them. But *Sebastian*?

If I was accepted, I'd have a say in the Banksia Prize recipient. The PhD place he wanted would be his on a platter. Any postgraduate fellowships would be sorted – even tenure at the university of his choice.

I didn't care about my dreams; they'd already come true. But I'd do anything – including whatever was written on the slip of paper in my hands – to make sure that Sebastian got what he wanted.

'It should go without saying, but if you tell anyone about this, you'll not only be struck from our list, we'll toss you from Banksia House and SECU entirely. We'll be watching,' the woman said, and this time, I felt the needle slip beneath my skin.

◇◇◇

I woke alone, surrounded by the scent of citrus.

The kookaburra was still calling, but there was no other sound. I pushed myself off the ground, groaning. Everything hurt. I was grateful I was alone; I hated feeling weak, but I hated other people *seeing* me weakened even more. It took me more than a few moments to get to my feet and stagger across to the bench.

The sun had barely moved in the sky, which told me I hadn't been gone long, even if the air was hotter and the brightness made my eyes ache. I shielded them with one hand, then uncurled the fingers of the other.

The paper was rolled like a tiny scroll, sealed with black wax. The impression was of a plant; though the wax had smudged, I could tell it was a banksia flower. I broke it carefully, trying to keep the seal intact.

On the paper were three words, written in beautiful cursive.

Compromise the omega.

My vision tunnelled, white bleeding into the edges of my sight as rage and fear flared through me, all consuming. I could barely swallow the roar that threatened to tear from my throat.

I'll destroy them.

I was on my feet the next moment, ignoring the pain, ready to hunt down the Revels immediately. I was sprinting through the maze, crushing the paper between my fingers, before it hit me.

Rosemary. They could mean Rosemary.

I stopped, skidding to a halt. I looked down at the paper, smoothing it out.

Compromise the omega.

For a moment, I asked myself *why*. Why would they want me to do that? And what did they mean by *compromise*? I assumed it wasn't in a historical sense, where *compromising* might be as simple as being alone in a room with her. Did they mean to make her unsafe? To sabotage her work? Manipulate her emotionally?

I realised it was up to me; the Revels weren't going to give me any guidance. That was the point. They'd just watch, and wait, and evaluate whatever I chose to do.

I could do nothing.

I buried that thought before it could take root. This was for Sebastian. While Rosemary seemed nice enough, she wasn't really a friend, and now she was a target.

Compromise the omega.

I stopped at the entrance of the maze to collect a handful of lemon myrtle leaves for Sebastian, then made my way back towards the manor, my mind whirling with possibilities.

BYRON

A KOOKABURRA'S CALL WOUND THROUGH THE AIR.

It wasn't close, but I wondered what had set it off. The afternoon was hot, and it was a stupid time to be outside, especially so for me, wearing all black and heavy boots. My skin was getting burned and I was sticky with sweat; I could catch enough of my own scent to know that I needed a shower and another dose of blockers.

Scent blockers weren't perfect, no matter how much the government protested otherwise. Their mantra was *responsible scent management* and that was fine – most of the time. Low doses of blockers were added to the water supply, which covered the alphas, betas, and very few omegas in most workplaces, minimising their scent profiles. Additional scent-blocking tablets were mandatory for anyone in an educational institution, medical establishment, legal workplace, government department, or jail. But according to Dr. Ford, blockers could be affected by hormonal changes, anxiety and stress, illness, meeting a scent match, and – as evidenced by me in the current moment – just plain excessive sweating, so if you wanted them to work, you needed to be very, *very* responsible.

Banksia provided medical-grade blockers for students and staff, but it wasn't like that everywhere. Blocking tablets were subsidised by the public healthcare system, but they weren't exactly *cheap*. It was just another way that our society silently ensured that certain jobs and types of education were reserved for the rich and for alphas and betas, because omegas needed higher doses than everyone else to mask their stronger scents.

The world isn't made for omegas, Tina said in my memory again, this time sadly.

I hated hearing her sad. I wished that every memory was happy, that every word that bubbled up from my subconscious was joyful and tinged with her loud laughter. But that wouldn't be the truth. Tina was made of light and dark, just like everyone else.

My hair blew into my face; I ran my fingers through it, gathering it into a haphazard bun.

The gardens around the manor were lovely, but I craved something wilder. My dad had slipped a brochure beneath my door while I was in class, a map of walks around the Banksia property and beyond. I'd decided on a shorter one to start, mostly because it took me to the cliffs.

The view was breathtaking. The sea was a million shades of blue, and I could hear the waves crash against the rocks below, losing myself in its unceasing, sibilant roar.

Tina had loved the beach. She'd always planned to move to the coast. She loved the slower pace, the heat, the sea breeze, and the tempestuousness of the ocean.

'That's enough of that,' I told myself, standing to brush the grass from my jeans. I was having dinner with my parents later, and they didn't need me to be morose.

They were already sad enough.

The kookaburra called again, a little closer this time. The walk back to the manor took me through a patch of bush, and I followed the sandy, meandering path through the trees, enjoying the dappled light and slightly cooler air. The scent of eucalyptus was thick and cloying, and I hoped some of it would cling to me, disguising my sweeter scent until I got back to my room and could shower and take another dose of blockers. I always carried extra rut medication – essentially a mild sedative – as it was a requirement of my *recovery plan*, but I'd need to remember to carry cancellers and blockers in this heat, too, at least until I became more used to the climate.

I reached out to touch the trunk of a gum tree, tracing the mottled grey pattern on its bark. I'd been lucky enough to travel overseas with my parents a number of times, but nothing quite compared to the beauty of Australia's south-east. Parts of it were stark, and parts of it lush; parts of it were rocky, and others, verdant.

I'd never felt so much at *home* anywhere else.

A magpie carolled overhead, then gave a harsher call. A rustle came from nearby, barely audible; I froze, my heart leaping up my throat as I noticed a smooth undulation of brown and yellow through the brushy undergrowth. It was moving away from me, so I stood still until the tiger snake's scales were no longer visible, and when I started walking again, I let my feet fall heavily on the ground.

Fuck.

I'd never been so close to a snake in the wild before. It took a few minutes for my heart to stop racing, and by that time, I was back in Banksia's gardens.

The manor was as impressive from the back as it was the front. The clock tower was visible in its entirety from there, a counterpart to the turret at the front of the building. There were more windows on this side, too; *all the better to see you with*, I thought, looking up to see the shadows of students moving beyond the glass. I didn't know a thing about gardening, but I knew that Banksia's were impressive, and I caught the scent of lemon myrtle before I saw somebody stepping from the maze.

Tristan Grace.

He was flushed and sweaty-looking, and I had a few moments to study his worried expression before he caught sight of me and his face shuttered. He looked rumpled, which seemed – even though I barely knew him – to be out of character. I opened my mouth to say hello, but he gave a curt nod and strode away before I could speak, disappearing back inside the manor as if it had swallowed him up. One of his hands was full of lemon myrtle leaves;

with the other, he shoved something that looked like paper deep in his pocket.

Okay, then.

I frowned after him for a moment, feeling an uncomfortable stab of empathy for the way he'd hidden what he was feeling so swiftly, and with such ease. I made my way across the green, then stopped still as the manor doors opened, and Tristan slipped from my mind entirely.

'You look hot, alpha,' Rose said, stepping onto the edge of the green before clamping her hand over her mouth, her eyes widening in horror as she turned a delicious shade of pink. 'I mean, *it's* hot, not *you're* hot. Not that you're *not* hot, but …' She closed her eyes for a moment. 'Why is there never a sinkhole when you need one? *You look like it's hot*, is what I was trying to say.'

I snorted. 'Nice save, omega,' I said dryly, trying to pretend like every nerve ending hadn't lit up at the sight of her. I didn't move closer, because I could still catch my own scent over the eucalyptus and lemon myrtle, and I didn't want to make her uncomfortable. 'If you're thinking about a walk, I'd recommend not. I almost trod on a tiger snake.'

'Well, yes,' she returned, as if that were perfectly reasonable. 'That's what happens when you have a water source next to bushland.' She gestured towards where I'd been walking; the north border of Banksia was marked by a river. I hadn't gone that far on my walk, and I wouldn't try, not if there were more of those bitey bastards about. I wasn't afraid of them, per se, but I also wasn't foolish.

Usually.

I tilted my head. 'What are you doing out here?'

Rose flushed again. I didn't mean to be dramatic, but I would have happily dedicated my entire life to making her blush. She cleared her throat. 'I was looking for you, actually.'

I tried very hard not to lose my shit. 'How can I help?'

'Well, I was wondering if you might like to study with me.'

I blinked. *Study with her?* As in, sit next to her or across from her, while she worked? Just being generally in the same vicinity while she existed?

I would get less than zero work done, but *fuck yes*.

It was my turn to clear my throat. 'I'd like that.'

She graced me with a tentative smile. 'Are you free now?'

'I, ah ...' *How do I tell her I need to shower without seeming ... gross?* I opted for honesty. 'I think my blockers are wearing off. I need ten minutes to shower and take another dose. Where were you thinking? A study room? Or the First Year Library?'

'The library,' she answered, which was probably a good thing; my brain would melt if I spent an hour with her in the close confines of a study room.

'The library, then. I'll meet you there.'

She smiled again, wider, this time with a hint of teeth. A jolt of *something* shot through my limbs, but I waited until she was back inside before I followed her, hoping I was leaving a safe distance.

It was odd, really. A few days ago, I would have happily committed an indictable offence for a hint of Rose's scent. But now?

I still wanted it, so badly my teeth ached. But there was something … *nice* … about the tension that made the air sharp every time she was near me.

I took the staircase two at a time, realising when I got to the top that the feeling was *anticipation*. Outside Banksia, I would have asked Rose out for coffee, the subtext being *don't wear cancellers*, or asked whether she wanted to exchange scent cards. Either way, that hint of scent would have told us both straight away whether we were compatible, on a biological level, at least.

I didn't know whether Rose had a scent card here; though the rules didn't ban them explicitly, they also recommended against bringing them. Without them, we were forced to make connections the way they must have done before the Unveiling – by *talking*. It was odd and wonderful, all at once.

But if Rose scented me, that would stop. Immediately. She might like my scent – but there was a much greater chance she would *not*. The thought tied my insides in knots. What if we became friends – became *more* – and I found out her scent was jasmine? Or a sickly-sweet musk? Or some other scent that made my stomach churn?

What if she hated *my* scent?

Omegas generally disliked the scents of other omegas. It was a biological thing, ensuring that packs wouldn't get greedy and hoard precious omegas like dragon treasure. But omegas were equally discerning about alpha scents, too. I'd read stories about established packs breaking up because their new omega liked some, but not all, of their scents.

That's why our society is nonsensical, Tina's voice insisted; this was one of her favourite rants. *Omegas should be choosing packs from the beginning, not joining existing ones.*

I couldn't say that I disagreed. Tina had taught me that omegas were the heart of any pack lucky enough to have one, but that wasn't the way most alphas thought. Our world saw omegas as commodities, as trophies, as vessels for knotting and breeding. It was a rare alpha or beta who could comfortably take a knot, and an omega could bear double the number of young any other designation could manage.

And male omegas?

They were the blue diamonds, the painite, the rhodium – the rarest of the precious. There was a short history of packs resorting to crime – even as far as murder – for the chance of bonding a male omega. I had no idea whether any existed in Australia; if they did, I imagined they'd keep it quiet.

You didn't tell people you'd found a unicorn, after all; there would always be someone who wanted it more than you.

I swallowed an extra dose of blockers, shoving a spare blister pack in my bag, then showered as quickly and as thoroughly as I could. I winced as my scent filled the bathroom, sweet and strong in the shower steam. All the apartments were equipped with industrial air purifiers for that very reason. They were always running – controlled centrally – but I turned up the settings to try to flush my scent from the room. It was particularly thick; I guessed it was because of Rose. While my mind wanted to be her friend on its own terms, my body was preening like a bowerbird, preparing to entice the pretty omega with shiny things – or, in this case, my scent.

I slathered myself in cancellers and pulled on clean clothes, gathering my wet hair back from my face. As an extra measure, I sprayed myself – clothes, hair, and all – with another layer of aerosol cancellers. When I was done, my nose burned from the metallic scent, but it was better than the alternative.

I stuffed my laptop and textbook into my bag, then locked my door behind me. I surreptitiously sniffed myself again, relieved to find I couldn't catch my scent at all. Satisfied, I made my way to the library.

I didn't see Rose at first. A group of students gathered around two desks, and I could see Pravin's dark head bent over some printed journal articles. I waved to him as a head popped up over a partition and I beelined for a pair of warm brown eyes.

Rose had chosen a corner desk, which I hated because any asshole might have sat down and boxed her in. But as *I* would be the one to do that, the feeling passed quickly. I could hear the murmurs of the group's conversation – they were *not* studying – and Pravin had his ear buds in, his long fingers tapping on the desk in a rhythm which suggested he was listening to something slow and soothing.

Which was to say that when Rose shot me a shy smile and said *hey*, it felt as if we were in our own little bubble, and her smile was just for me.

You're insane, I told myself, but a better word might have been *obsessed*.

'Hey,' I said, and sat down at the desk next to her. I gave her as much room as I could, moving my chair back so she had space, but I couldn't help angling my body towards her like a flower turning its face to the sun. 'What did you want to study?'

She frowned. 'Everything, I think. I can't afford to fall behind. Not if Heathcote is going to target us like that.'

I'd already told my mum what happened in class. My mum couldn't tell me anything confidential, but my dad didn't need to be as careful, mentioning that there had been a couple of complaints about Heathcote in the last few years, and that it would help the administration if there were more. I'd submitted one already – anonymously, of course. I didn't want to help solve one problem but then cause another for my mum.

'I think he's already been warned,' I said. 'Would *you* want to piss off Tristan Grace?'

She laughed. 'No. That alpha has dominance for *days*.'

I made a noise of agreement, because she wasn't wrong. It was hard to quantify dominance. It was a feeling, more than anything else – until it was used, and then it was like an invisible wall pressing down. All alphas had it, but some had more than others; it was the force behind an alpha's bark and pack leaders, the intangible pressure to *submit* to someone stronger. Tristan might not have been the biggest alpha in the room, but I was realising he had dominance up to his eyeballs. 'Should we start at the beginning of the textbook, then?'

'That seems sensible,' Rose said, and I had the sudden notion that her little half-smile would be the death of me.

The textbook had some study questions at the end of each section, so we went through the first chapter together, taking turns to read aloud, and then talked about the questions. Rose didn't need me, not even a bit; I was getting the far better end of the bargain. She already knew all this stuff, and I was only holding my own because of my late-night cramming.

She edged closer as we talked; I tried not to notice. My nose was full of her light perfume. It wasn't her *perfume* – not that sweet, addictive omega scent that bloomed with arousal or pleasure – but rather a synthetic floral scent that clung to her clothes and skin. It was nice, but I wished that nose plugs were a thing, because it was heating me in places I shouldn't have been hot, not in a library.

I mean, I was a literature graduate with aspirations of editing at a publishing house. *Of course* I wanted to fuck in a library. But not while a bunch of random students sat a few metres away, and not outside my pack.

I wasn't *waiting* for a pack. I'd messed around plenty before ... *Before*. But there were some things that I wanted to save for them, fantasies I wanted to make true with a side of love and devotion. I knew, somewhere deep inside, *bone* deep, that I wasn't made for a pairing; I knew I'd be a pack alpha, be one of the multiple parts that made up a whole, whatever that happened to look like. There was no standard when it came to pack dynamics; the types of connection were as varied as the numbers.

But I wasn't about to scare away the first omega I'd ever been interested in by getting a little *too* riled up by her perfume amongst the bookstacks, so when her hand brushed mine, I shifted back.

Only for her to follow me, moving closer when she turned the page, and that feeling hit me again – that sense of delicious, *dangerous* anticipation.

'Everything okay?' she murmured.

I swallowed, my eyes fixed on her profile. 'All good,' I answered, lying through my teeth.

This wasn't just *good*.

This was *incredible*.

ROSE

Having Byron Griffiths stare at me was the most electrifying, heady sense of power I'd ever experienced.

He'd almost jumped out of his skin when my hand brushed his, monitors shifting as he moved away. Despite that, his body still angled towards me, his eyes fixed on the side of my face, his gaze almost tangibly hot.

I shouldn't have felt safe. I knew what those monitors meant, even if I didn't know the details. No omega would trust a feral alpha.

Except … I did. Because *this* feral alpha had brought me food. He walked me to class and protected me when I'd needed it, even when I hadn't known he was doing it. And here he was, trying so hard not to crowd me, to give me space. *I* was the one moving closer, ruining his good work.

I'd have liked to see anyone do a single thing differently. His hair was pulled back, still damp from the shower, and it brought the strong planes of his face into focus.

I wanted to map them with my fingertips.

I wondered what his lips would feel like.

'Should we ...' I turned to face him, my eyes tracking the way his throat moved as he swallowed. My mouth went dry. 'Should we look at the first assessment?'

The notion jolted me out of my pleasant daydreams.

Other than the nightmare of my failed attempt at art school, no one had known my designation during my undergraduate degree. As an online student, there'd been no need for me to reveal it. On the advice of doctors, I'd had a heat during my very first cycle to let my body adjust then taken suppressants ever since, so heats had never been an issue. None of my lecturers or tutors had known I was an omega.

But here, *everybody* knew, including my teachers. And apparently it mattered – to Brandon Heathcote, at least.

'I'm going to have to work my ass off, aren't I?'

Byron looked startled for a moment, then his expression tightened into understanding. 'We all are. That's why we're here. But you might have to work harder than most in Heathcote's class.'

◇◇◇

The rest of the week took on a rhythm. Byron waited outside my room in the morning and walked me to breakfast, where we sat with Sebastian and Tristan. We went to class together, worked together, and we had lunch together, too. In the afternoon, we went our separate ways: Byron to check in with his parents or liaison officer, Tristan for a walk, and Sebastian and I disappeared into our respective rooms. I usually watched something on a streaming service before joining Byron a few hours later in the First Year Library. Then we studied – and I tried not to flirt – until dinner.

It was comforting. *Nice.* I woke up each morning already looking forward to it. Sometimes, Alessia and Pravin would join us, either in the dining hall or the library. Marina invited me for a coffee catch up, and we spent two hours talking about her research and my ambitions over a plate of cupcakes and a plunger of coffee.

I had *friends*.

But it was Byron I spent the most time with. When he was late one morning, I started to panic before he arrived, rushed and breathless, saying he slept through his alarm.

You're there for a degree, not a pack, Chloe's voice warned.

'Who did you choose for the first assessment?' I asked him, when we were in the library one afternoon.

The first main assessment wasn't huge; it was only five hundred words, worth ten percent of the final grade. We had to write a short report on an anthropologist or archaeologist, and why we thought they deserved more recognition for their contributions to their field.

Byron flipped his laptop around to show me a journal article; he'd chosen an archaeologist who'd developed an open-source coding system where researchers from around the world could input measurements and descriptions to build an online simulation of sites they were excavating. The system was new but had immense potential, not just for archaeology but for history education too, making sites accessible for students who otherwise would have little chance of seeing them.

And the archaeologist was a beta.

I smiled at him. He blinked, then cleared his throat. I inhaled slowly, but there was no hint of scent in the air. I couldn't help but wonder what his might be. Something edible, like citrus? A woody scent like cedar? Or would it be sweeter, like lavender?

The possibilities were endless.

My gaze strayed to where his jaw met his neck, my teeth aching as I imagined raking them over his scent gland.

'Did you end up choosing Nora Cummins?'

I shook myself. Nora Cummins was the only omega working in either field as far as I knew. A few years ago, there'd been a huge controversy when she wasn't nominated for an important prize after developing surveying technology that helped identify and map archaeological sites in protected environmental areas. 'I finished a draft last night. I need to do some tidying up, and I haven't finished the bibliography yet, but I think it's okay.'

'I can look it over, if you'll read what I've done?' he offered.

I slid my laptop towards him in answer, then broke out in goosebumps when his hand brushed mine.

Keep it together, Rose, I begged myself.

It was immediately clear that he deserved his place at Banksia House. His writing was eloquent and graceful, expressive without being flowery. He addressed the topic of the report and hit every criterion on the rubric. It was the kind of paper that was academic without being impenetrable, something you might have read in a magazine or a journal.

I shifted restlessly in my chair. 'You misspelt her name in the second paragraph,' I teased, pushing his laptop back towards him. I didn't glance at the other tabs he had open; he'd trusted me with his work, and I wouldn't do anything to undermine that.

One dark eyebrow twitched; his eyes stayed fixed to my screen. 'I did not.'

'No, you didn't. It's perfect.' I fidgeted as I waited for him to finish, suddenly nervous. I felt exposed; only teachers and my parents had read my work before. It felt as if I'd been stripped naked and was waiting for him to comment.

I pushed that thought way, *way* down.

'The other students should be worried,' he said at last, sliding my laptop back to me, his grey eyes flicking up to meet mine. 'If they want to top our class, that is. You're a threat to every one of them, Rose.'

I flushed with pleasure. Compliments were nice, but there was something about being told I was an academic threat that really hit the spot for me. I sucked my bottom lip between my teeth.

His eyes narrowed in on the movement, immediately going dark. I froze in place, not knowing whether I wanted to lean in closer or flee. He shook himself, tearing his gaze away, and I exhaled, half in relief, and half in disappointment.

'Should we look at the chapter for next week?' I forced myself to say, managing to keep my voice from trembling.

He tapped my laptop. 'Finish your bibliography first. That will give me time to read through the chapter and pretend I know what you're talking about.'

Yes, alpha.

I'd always assumed I'd find an alpha through scent. That I'd catch his, and he'd catch mine, and twenty minutes later I'd be moaning around his knot while he sank his teeth into my neck. That was how it was *supposed* to be.

This – the talking, the loaded eye contact, the blushing, the anticipation – was unexpected, and it was *wonderful*. It was something I'd never imagined, something I'd never expected. And now I found that it was a kind of freedom – and a freedom I *wanted*.

After years of thinking I'd be claimed, was it possible that I could choose?

His scent still matters, my instincts reminded me.

I sighed and got to work on my bibliography.

I was woken by a flurry of buzzes.

It took me more than a few moments to realise that I'd left my phone on. My hand fumbled around my bedside table until I found it, then held it up as I blinked blurrily at the screen.

3:03am.

byron followed you.

byron sent you a message.

I tapped into my social media account, then clicked into my messages, reading the text.

I'm not sure what you like, but cats seem a safe place to start.

I watched the video he'd sent, huffing a laugh, then sent back one of my favourites.

Three dots appeared. *What are you doing up?!*

Me? I wrote back. *What are* you *doing up?!*

I'm always up, he returned, and I bit my lip against where my mind went. *I hope I didn't wake you.*

I hit the *call* button inside the app; he picked up a moment later.

'Rose? Are you okay?'

'I forgot to put my phone on airplane mode,' I said. 'But I always like cats, no matter the time.'

'Fuck, I'm so sorry.' His voice seemed deeper at night. It made my muscles go loose in the best way, made my eyes heavy and my skin warm. 'You should go back to sleep.'

'Don't want to,' I said; it came out embarrassingly sleepily.

'Uh-huh,' he said wryly. 'Sounds like it.'

'Why are you awake?'

He took a moment to answer. 'I don't sleep well,' he said at last. 'I haven't for a long time.'

My breath hitched. 'What helps?'

'Drugs,' he answered bluntly. 'I've tried everything. Meditation, CBT, yoga, more exercise, changing my diet, changing my bedroom, music, different pillows, cutting out screens, cutting out caffeine, chamomile tea, melatonin … If you have any other suggestions, I'm all ears.'

'That sounds really hard, alpha,' I said quietly.

I heard him swallow. 'It's okay, omega,' he answered roughly. 'I'm used to it now.'

I wanted to ask *why* he couldn't sleep so badly that my throat went tight, but I knew I couldn't. I didn't know much about feral alphas, but everything I'd heard – the blackouts, the loss of control – was contrary to the man who walked me to breakfast, who'd brought me food, who'd stepped between me and trouble then left a posy of blossoms outside my door. What I knew of Byron Griffiths was all gentle words and considerate actions, and I thought of the way I'd seen him standing at the literature mixer, his arms tight to his sides and his head bent as he tried to make himself smaller.

'What do you do instead of sleeping?' I found myself asking.

There was another silence, as if he was surprised. 'I read,' he answered. 'Scour the internet for cute animal videos. If it's particularly bad, I'll work out. Sometimes –' he broke off, and I heard him inhale. 'Sometimes, my dad will be awake, too. Sometimes we'll talk or go for a walk.'

'It must be nice to be so close to your parents.'

He laughed; the sound was pained. 'I love them a lot. And I'm all they have.'

It sounded like there was more to it, but again, I couldn't bring myself to pry. We'd only been on the phone for five minutes, and I already knew more about him than I had that afternoon. 'You can call me,' I blurted.

'What?'

'You can call me. When you can't sleep.'

'Rose. I'm not interrupting *your* sleep just because I'm not getting any.'

'You can,' I insisted. 'This is … This is nice.'

'It is nice,' he said, after a moment.

'See? You can message me, and if I'm awake, I'll call you.'

'Hmm,' he said, which I took to mean *I will absolutely not be doing that.*

'Try it tomorrow and see if you like it.' I couldn't stifle my yawn, and he made an exasperated noise.

'Go to sleep,' he growled; the sound sent tingles to my fingers and toes.

'Whatever you say, alpha,' I returned, letting a hint of purr into my voice, and ended the call.

Another message came a moment later.

You're an absolute menace, you know that?

I went back to sleep smiling.

◇◇◇

The next morning, we received an email saying class was cancelled; Heathcote had some kind of virus. He'd left a message on the online classroom, reminding us to submit our first assessment.

I'd already done it. I'd thought it would be a relief, but nerves were still gnawing at my stomach.

'Wonder if he'll still be marking?' Sebastian said, shoving a forkful of pancakes in his mouth.

'There are rules around when we get feedback,' Byron answered, stirring his coffee. 'Because the next assessment is due in two weeks, we need feedback for this one within seven days. Mum said Heathcote has the proper flu and will be out too long to make the deadline. They've already organised two other markers.'

'So what are we doing today?'

I frowned at Sebastian. 'Heathcote gave us work to do.'

'Rosebud.' He slung an arm around my neck; my cheeks went hot. 'Class is cancelled. It's the end of summer and beautiful outside. We're young, and theoretically carefree. We can study tonight. We're doing something today – you just have to choose what.'

'Why is this my decision?'

'Because you're the prettiest,' Sebastian purred in my ear, and my breath hitched, even though that wasn't *remotely* true.

I tried to ignore the twist of loss I felt when he moved away. 'I haven't been for a walk through the gardens yet,' I made myself say, 'Or down to the beach.'

Tristan glanced out the dining hall windows, then brought up a weather app on his phone. 'It's a perfect beach day. Overcast and warm, but not too hot.'

'Dad said there were bluebottles last week,' Byron commented, his gaze following Tristan's. 'You might not be able to swim.'

'I don't mind,' I said. 'I just want to see it. And maybe ...' I trailed off.

They waited; Tristan cocked his head to the side, watching me.

'Just get away for a bit,' I continued in a rush. 'I've never really been able to do that.'

Byron frowned, but Sebastian's expression was one of understanding. 'You know Tris has a car here, right?' he said, and I blinked at the use of *a* car over *his* car, or *the* car. *How many cars did Tristan Grace own?* 'We can take you away anytime, anywhere you want to go. Further down the coast, or north towards Sydney, or inland towards Braidwood or Canberra. We could even drive to Melbourne one weekend, though it might be a flying visit. Whatever you want, Rose.'

I inhaled, because that was a lot of possibility, far more than I'd ever considered. 'Thank you,' I said quietly. 'That's really nice.'

Tristan stood. 'But today, we're going to the beach.' Suddenly, he was all alpha; his shoulders rolled back, and his voice took on a tone that would make a high school teacher proud. 'I'll make us a picnic to take. Byron, you get drinks and sunscreen. You two –' his eyes swept over Sebastian and I '– go get ready.'

I opened my mouth to protest – I could help with the food or something, surely – but Sebastian caught my hand and tugged me to my feet. 'Nope,' he said under his breath, like he knew what I was thinking. 'Tris *lives* for this. And by this, I mean doing stuff. Usually it's for me, but today it's for *us*, so sit back and enjoy it.' He grinned. 'That's the *point* of having alphas.'

Tristan was already striding towards the kitchens, and I pitied whoever was on duty. When Tristan said *picnic*, I didn't think he meant a few packets of chips and some apples.

Sebastian pulled me from the dining hall, leaving Byron to clear the table. 'I'm so glad we're doing this,' he said happily. 'I've been studying my ass off, and Tris has been worrying about me studying. This is the perfect break.'

'You've been studying?'

'Only every spare moment. Heathcote really freaked me out.' He glanced at me sidelong as we climbed the main staircase. 'No one's ever been quite that ... *blatant* ... about their bias before. And I want the Banksia Prize. I don't want to let Heathcote fuck that up for me.'

I pondered his words as he dropped me off at my door, and what he'd said stayed at the front of my mind as I dug my swimsuit from my wardrobe and dressed, then found a change of clothes, a towel, and my sandals. Despite what Tristan had said, I slathered myself in sunscreen and packed it in my tote bag, too.

When I'd finished, Sebastian was waiting outside in a t-shirt and board shorts. He tugged my bag from my hands, ignoring my protest, then led me down the stairs. 'The alphas are getting changed. They won't be long.'

We waited for them outside the manor's mouth-like double doors. The air was warm and fresh, and I felt something inside me relax. I hadn't realised how much I'd wanted this; I'd probably needed it for *years*. For all that we liked to pretend, beneath the layer of clothing and conventions humans were just animals; we all needed to see the sky and feel the breeze on our face, at least every now and then.

Byron and Tristan arrived, and a few minutes later we'd walked to the end of the drive and were stepping outside the sandstone walls, using a small iron gate I hadn't noticed when I'd arrived. The groundskeeper, Harry, waved at us from the shade of a towering blue gum; I waved back, and we meandered along a rocky path towards the cliffs.

The cliffs lay around two kilometres from Banksia. I could just catch a hint of salt in the air and hear waves rolling, the sound carried by the strong breeze. Tristan led the way, Sebastian behind him. I followed, and Byron walked behind me, pausing when I stopped to snap some pictures of the landscape on my phone, trying to capture the glittering water stretching to the horizon, framed by bush. Being bookended by the two alphas felt a little like being chaperoned, but I wasn't about to complain; my omega was preening.

We didn't talk much; the breeze made conversation difficult, and I was unfit enough to be slightly out of breath as I navigated the rocky path with sandalled feet. My awareness flittered between the path, the view, and the *other* view – Sebastian and Tristan's broad shoulders and backs. If I was being completely honest, my gaze might have drifted down a few times, too. It was a view I shouldn't have been looking at, but surely there was no harm in just looking, especially when I was doing it respectfully.

Mostly respectfully.

There was harm, though, because I was looking at things I could never have, but after today, I'd know that I wanted them.

Sebastian looked back and shot me a grin.

Warmth spread through me, seeping through every limb, into every joint, and –

I was in trouble.

'Oh, look,' Byron said, interrupting that train of thought. 'Dolphins!'

Alpha eyesight was sharper than the other designations, but I could still make out the small pod, playing in the bay, just past where the waves were breaking. 'They're so close to the beach!'

'They get whales here, too,' Byron added, stepping beside me and shading his eyes as he looked out to sea. He was wearing a pair of aviators, but the glare from the water was fierce. 'It's later in the year, though. Humpbacks and Southern Rights, mostly, but other kinds too.'

'And sharks?'

'Ye-ep,' he said, drawing the word out. 'A few different types. But dad said there was a drone sighting of a three-metre white shark not long ago, so I think I'll be sticking close to the sand.'

Despite the warmth of the day, I shivered. I wasn't afraid of many things, but being wary of metres-long apex predators was just sensible.

'Your dad is an author, right?' Sebastian said over his shoulder. 'I read one of his novels a few years ago. *The Watch Eternal.* I really liked it. I was surprised it wasn't … bigger.'

Byron snorted. 'You and him both. He thinks it's his best work, and he gets annoyed that all anyone wants to talk about is *The Light in His Eyes*.'

'But *The Light in His Eyes* is amazing!' I exclaimed. It was the truth; I had two copies, one on my eReader and a beautiful hardcover that I refused to open; I was also unhealthily excited about the upcoming film. 'I had no idea that Carwyn Griffiths was your dad!'

'Is that why you studied literature?' Tristan glanced back, his green eyes curious. He'd jammed a straw sunhat over his curls and the lenses of his glasses had darkened in the bright light. 'Because of your dad?'

'That, and there's a certain responsibility that comes with your parents naming you *Byron*,' the alpha said dryly. 'My sister went the opposite way. They named her after Christina Rossetti, so she started an electrician apprenticeship.'

'What's it like, having a fiction author for a dad?' Sebastian asked.

'What's it like having a Nobel Laureate for a mum?' Byron returned.

Sebastian looked out to sea. 'Touché.'

'It was a serious question, if you want to answer it,' Byron said gently. 'I don't know what other dads are like. My parents are both betas, and it's just the two of them, so we didn't have a team of pack parents. My dad was always the one at home, always the one taking us to school, or doing the shopping, or dropping us to swimming training. He was always there, but he wasn't always present, if you know what I mean? His mind was always on the next story, the next cast of characters, or on his research. Sometimes, it felt as if we were competing with another world.' He ran a hand through his hair. 'Except it's not a competition – it can't be. The world isn't yours, and the characters aren't real, but it's still more fascinating to him than your homework, or whatever silly argument you had with your friends. Actually,' he went on, lips curving into a rueful smile, 'I'm not being fair. Dad is a really good parent. Kids just want to feel as if they're the centre of everything, don't they? And my sister and I would act out if we thought we weren't.'

'I was never the centre of anything,' Sebastian said bleakly, after a moment's silence. 'I'm the only child of five parents, and not one of them could tear themselves away from their work to care for me. I had a nanny from two weeks old.' He sniffed. 'I fucking loved him, too. I was devastated when my parents decided to let him go. They sent me to boarding school instead. I've never been big,' he continued, and I frowned, because he certainly seemed pretty perfect to me, 'and I was a weird-looking kid. I didn't grow into my face until I was eighteen. And so, I was bullied.' He shot a smile over his shoulder, sad and beautiful; my heart squeezed. 'Constantly and mercilessly. Studying was the only escape that I had, and I took it.' He glanced at Byron. 'I don't know what it's like to *not* have a mother like that. All the kids I met from similar families seemed to have a similar experience – their parents were all distant. But the difference was that *they* didn't seem to care. Not as much as I did, anyway. So, when I grow up –' he threw me another smile, this one devastating '– I'm going to have a thousand babies and spoil every single one of them rotten.'

'A thousand is certainly a number,' Tristan – who would possibly parent said babies – commented dryly. 'This way.' He gestured to a wooden staircase, fastened precariously to the side of the cliff. It cut across the rock and down to the sand, with one wooden handrail standing as a valiant barrier between us and the considerable drop below. 'I hope no one is afraid of heights.'

I was usually fine with heights, but this was particularly exposed; a whine escaped my throat, so softly it was almost silent.

My cheeks heated with embarrassment, but Tristan was already on the staircase, and Sebastian followed close behind him.

For a moment, I thought I'd gotten away with it, but then Byron stepped to my side, putting himself between me and the empty drop.

Alpha, my instincts purred.

Did you do that on purpose? I fumed at them.

They didn't answer; all things considered, their silence was probably a good thing. I made my way down the staircase slowly, fixing my eyes on the wooden planks beneath my feet and refusing to glance to the side as the wind whipped through my hair. Byron's hand occasionally brushed mine, and every tiny touch sent a shiver up my arm.

The sand on the beach below was white, almost blindingly so, and the ocean a mess of breathtaking blues. The beach wasn't one of the kilometres-long stretches common further north; it was small, secluded, and private, bounded by rocky outcrops and bush. It was beautiful, and there was something quintessentially Australian about the untamed bush stubbornly encroaching where the local council had cleared a tiny, sandy car park. This country didn't take kindly to attempts to tame it; it never had.

It was part of what I loved so much about it.

There was another small group of people on the beach – not students, or at least not students we recognised – but they were far enough away that a friendly nod sufficed. Tristan scanned the beach, then seemed to come to a decision, heading for a patch of sand partially shaded by the cliffs and sheltered from the sea breeze. He knelt in the sand, pulling a pop-up dome tent from his backpack, and my mouth hung open as he and Byron made short work of setting it up and filling its sandbags. Byron carefully lay down some towels inside, Tristan unpacked the picnic, and it became something that made my insides go all melty.

It was like a *nest*. A *beach* nest.

'Fuck, *yes*,' Sebastian breathed, then grabbed my hand, dragging me inside.

If we'd really squeezed in, there would have been enough space for all four of us, but the alphas didn't even try to come inside. Sebastian lay down on his stomach on one of the towels, close enough that his elbow brushed my knee when I sat down.

I'd been right about the picnic; there wasn't a sandwich in sight. It was a cheese board instead, done the way I liked best, with dips and a tonne of fruit.

I'd never been spoiled like this before. My omega purred with contentment.

Sebastian and I reached for the same raspberry.

'All yours,' he said as I blushed, grabbing another one. 'Though we may need to fight – maybe even to the death – for the last one.'

He had a serious sweet tooth, even worse than mine, so we faux-sniped at each other until all the raspberries and the expensive-looking chocolate were gone. It was heavenly, eating with the waves and white sand just in front of us.

And then Tristan stepped into our line of sight, dragging his shirt over his head, and I realised exactly what I'd done.

SEBASTIAN

I COULD TELL THE MOMENT ROSE REALISED.

She went still, and I could see the hairs on her arms stand on end. She was wearing a tank top and the sexiest denim shorts I'd ever seen, her arms and legs bare. Her thighs were dimpled and *fuck*, it took every ounce of self-control I had not to bend down and lick every divot on her skin.

I didn't know what was going on with me. I'd felt off-balance all morning, too sensitive, like my chest had peeled open and my heart was on display for all to see. I was alternately close to tears and holding back a laugh, skipping from sadness to delight in a heartbeat. I was right next to Rose, so close we were touching, but it wasn't enough; something inside me wanted to be closer.

I knew it was insane. I knew it couldn't work between us. But apparently nobody had told my body that, and my body wanted to be all over Rosemary Morris like a fucking weighted blanket.

But it wasn't *me* she was thinking about. It was Tristan, my alpha. Tristan, who had just tugged his shirt over his head to reveal the perfection beneath it, every line and curve of muscle, every shadow and dip and swell of light brown skin.

It was a view I knew intimately; I'd seen it every day since I was twenty. I had every pathway memorised, every rise and every valley on the map of Tristan's body a muscle memory beneath my fingertips. I knew how every hard ridge felt pressed against me, how warm his skin was beneath my tongue.

I *knew* how fucking irresistible he was.

I was seeing Rose realise it in real time; seeing the moment it dawned that this innocent trip to the beach would be torture of the mind-blanking, sexy, masculine kind.

I might have felt sorry for her, but the torment was worth it.

Her entire body tensed, as if she wanted to flee, and my instincts clamoured, *hating* that. I nudged her gently. 'Hey. I brought extra blockers. Just in case.'

She glanced at me, and awareness dawned in her expression. 'Fuck, Sebastian, I'm so sorry,' she said in a rush. 'I didn't mean –'

To drool over my alpha? I thought, smiling. I wasn't jealous. I wasn't sure *why* I wasn't jealous, but there was nothing in me but arousal for Rose, concern for Rose, and faint, affectionate amusement at Rose's predicament. *And cheese. There was also cheese.* 'I know you didn't,' I said. 'Trust me. I've been there before. It's totally fine.'

'It's *not* fine. I'm so –'

She broke off, because Byron had apparently decided to send the pair of us to an early grave by doing the same thing.

Fuck. Me.

He wasn't chiselled, not like Tristan. I'd stared often enough at his biceps to have memorised the swell of them, and his black shirts clung in such a way that I'd been able to imagine the planes of his chest. The other parts had been a mystery; now they were unearthed and making my mouth water.

He was all slabs of muscle, roughly-hewn and so fucking sexy I shivered. His stomach was flat, the kind of flat that begged for the scrape of fingernails to find the muscle beneath, and there was a line of dark hair running from his navel to disappear beneath his board shorts, bracketed by two perfect v-lines.

I licked my lips.

He turned, giving us a view of his back – how could it stretch *forever?* – and his ass, my teeth aching with the sudden need to *bite.*

What the fuck, Sebastian.

'Um,' Rose said breathlessly. 'I think I'll take the blockers.'

She glanced at me, and we both broke into peals of panicked laughter. I found my backpack and fished around until my fingers closed on the blister of blockers. Rose poured us both a glass of juice – sensibly avoiding the champagne Tristan had packed – and she swallowed down two of the little pink pills.

And raised her eyebrows in surprise when I did the same.

Betas still needed blockers at Banksia, but not the same dosage as alphas or omegas. Though betas did have scents, they weren't as strong as the other designations, and betas didn't perfume like omegas, or go into ruts like alphas, so a half-dose a day was more than sufficient.

'I haven't taken mine for a few days,' I said, after I'd swallowed a second mouthful of juice.

She made a noise of assent and then offered me a strawberry. I grinned and ate it from her fingers, because who could have resisted?

I tamped down the urge to lick her skin clean, though.

'So what's your sad family story, Rosemary Morris?' I said, mostly to distract myself. 'Please make me feel better about vomiting out mine.'

'I don't have one,' she said faintly. Her cheeks were flushed; she tore her gaze from my lips, looking out at the water. 'I'm an only child, but apart from that, I'm disgustingly well-adjusted. I have two alpha parents who were momentarily astonished to find they had an omega daughter, but rose to the occasion and gave me everything I needed and wanted. My mum and dad have always been a massive support. They call or text me every day and send me dog videos they find online. I've never told them I'm a cat person,' she went on, with a smile that warmed my body from the inside out. 'We've barely ever fought, not even when I was an obnoxious teenager. Which doesn't make for a very interesting backstory, I'm afraid.'

'I'm glad,' I said, and I was. 'It's nice to know that families like that exist. Tristan's family is similar, though he's got two mums and two dads, betas and alphas, and he has two younger brothers. They're all hideously nice, even if they are disgustingly rich.'

'I looked you both up,' Rose said, looking faintly embarrassed. 'I didn't realise ...'

'That he's so rich the numbers don't even seem real?' I supplied. 'Don't worry. It doesn't really sink in until the private jet takes you to the island Tristan's mum bought for him when he got stressed about exams in high school and you realise that the *house* there has a walk-in-wardrobe bigger than your entire apartment. Or when he takes you home to meet his family and it's a five-thousand-acre estate in the north of England with an honest-to-fuck *castle* sitting in the middle of it.' I grinned at her. 'Again, how sad for me, right? Having an alpha who can give me almost anything I desire? But it did take a bit of getting used to. They have an *orangery*, Rose. And *stables*. Like, what the fuck? I thought I was hallucinating.'

Rose laughed. It was a lovely sound, smooth and surprisingly deep, a melody I wanted to hear played on repeat.

'Holy shit!'

The expletive came from the shallows, where Tristan was letting the whitewash ripple over his feet. His beautiful face was carved into a comical expression of shock, and I couldn't help laughing. It really must have been cold, because my alpha had been wild swimming and in ice baths before without complaint.

'Told you,' Byron crowed, then turned and shot us a wide grin.

Fuck.

'I haven't seen him smile before,' Rose said blankly, as if she was in my head and knew exactly what I was thinking. 'Not properly. Not like *that*.'

Because Byron Griffiths happy was *devastating*. All straight white teeth and curving lips and grey eyes full of depths I wanted to swim in. His smile was a secret, a revelation.

What the fuck is wrong with you, Sebastian?

I put a hand to my forehead. I did feel hot. Hopefully I was getting a cold or the flu, and could pass all of today's insane thoughts and feelings off as some kind of fevered delirium.

'The next time I have an *idea*,' Rose said tightly, 'it's your job to shut it down.'

'Absolutely not,' I said immediately, smiling. 'I'm a chronic enabler. The only word you'll ever hear from me, Rosebud, is *yes*.'

She frowned at me, before her lips curled up. 'Is that so?' she said slowly, and it wasn't my imagination – she was leaning closer, her eyes on my mouth.

Fuck the fact this couldn't work. Fuck the weird feelings. Fuck the flu.

Fuck yes.

I want a kiss.

Her berry-sweet breath sugared the air, and my body tensed, ready. I'd kiss her slow and soft, I decided, because that was what she deserved, something romantic and unforgettable, with my hands tangled in her hair and my lips a caress she'd think about for weeks. I'd swallow her sweet sighs, and keep them to myself until I shared them with Tristan later, when his hands were on my skin and I could imagine the two of them –

'Race you to the water,' Rose said, and jumped to her feet.

She tugged her tank top over her head with surprising speed, and my body didn't know what was happening, because I'd been expecting a *kiss*, and instead she was stripping off, revealing an elegant one-piece swimsuit and the generous curves beneath it, but she wasn't technically stripping for *me*, and apparently I was extremely salty about it.

She unbuttoned her shorts and shimmied them down her thighs, and *fuck*, I couldn't stand up now, because my cock was twitching at the sight of her rounded ass and my imagination already had his hands on it, cupping and massaging and spreading so I could kneel behind her and –

'Come on, Seb,' she said with a wild smile, and ran across the sand towards the alphas.

I'd been dealing with getting erections at unfortunate times for years, so I subtly reached to tuck myself into the trunks I wore beneath my board shorts, then scrambled to my feet, tearing off my shirt and sprinting after her.

She shrieked when she ran into the water, then laughed. I followed a few moments later. Apparently, my body was doing its own thing today, because before I knew what I was doing – before I could think it through – I'd swept her up into my arms. I didn't feel the cold as I waded in, not with her warm heat pressed to my stomach and chest.

'I won,' Rose crowed, but as she linked her arms around my neck and I breathed in the sea and the scent of her hair, it felt as if *I* was the one with the prize.

'Don't be so certain,' I warned, and waded out further, until the waves were pushing at my waist and Rose was squirming against the cold, squirming against my *body*, laughing and shrieking as the water surged high over her stomach.

Byron's lips were curved into a smile as he watched us. He was only a few metres away, and when he caught my eye, he shook his head and mouthed *menace* before diving under an oncoming wave. The tide was getting higher – Tristan had checked online, and it would peak before lunch – so I turned back towards the beach.

And caught sight of my alpha.

His expression wasn't jealous, or resentful, or even surprised.

He looked *worried*.

I knew I should have been worried, too, far more so than I was. My body was writing cheques to Rose it couldn't cash; I knew this could never be. I wanted it regardless, wanted this sun-soaked, sea-sprayed moment of happiness, wanted the warmth seeping through me, wanted Rose's smooth skin sliding over mine.

Tristan's lips twisted.

If he'd bitten and bonded me, I'd feel it. His worry would be under my skin, trembling through my veins, carried from his heart to mine. It seemed ridiculous that *this* was what I wanted so badly: his worries, his insecurities, his hurts. I wanted to carry them inside myself so he could feel them halved, *shared*.

His lips moved, shaping my name.

A wave slammed against my back. I stumbled, my feet trying to find purchase in the shifting sand. Rose cried out, but I managed not to drop her, and to hold myself upright as white water surged around us. I pushed forward unsteadily until we were back in the shallows, then lowered Rose to her feet.

Omegas ran cold, so I took her hand and dragged her back across the sand to the tent. She let me pull her inside. I wrapped her in a huge towel, then once I had one tight around my own shoulders, I pulled her into my lap, snuggling close until we both stopped shivering.

Tristan had packed a thermos – he was always three steps ahead – and Rose and I shared sips of decadent hot chocolate until my tongue was coated in cloying sweetness. I knew she could feel the hard bar of my cock beneath her, but I couldn't bring myself to care, and she made no move to shift away. Nothing in my life had felt this *right* since I'd met Tristan, so I fed her strawberries and fixed my eyes to her lips, pink and shining.

After a while, she pulled her phone from her bag. I looked over her shoulder as she edited a photo of the beach and started posting it to her social media.

'Post that one, too,' I said bossily, pointing to one where Tristan and I were in the frame – well, our backs were, anyway. 'You can tag us.'

I didn't really know why I'd suggested it. Maybe so there was proof outside the odd, scentless bubble of Banksia that we were part of her life, even if it had only been for a couple of weeks. I tensed, not knowing how I'd feel if she said no.

She didn't. She fussed over the photo until she got the edits right, then posted it. She tagged us, and Byron too, and to me, it felt like in that tiny action she was staking a claim. The notion calmed me. There we were, on her feed, my alpha's broad back, and mine. We were in her life, and there it was, online, proof where anyone could see it.

Mine.

Rose made a small noise of surprise, and I realised that my nose was trailing up her neck, seeking her scent gland.

I jerked away. 'Fuck, Rose, I'm so sorry –'

'Seb.'

We looked up as one to see Tristan watching us, his hair slicked back from his face, sand dusting his calves. 'We should head back soon,' he said. 'Byron is having lunch with his parents.' He paused. 'If you'd like to, I mean. I figured we'd walk back together.'

Together.

Mine.

Warmth spread through my body. *Pack*, my instincts whispered.

The possibility pulsed beneath my skin like a living thing.

Rose didn't seem put out by my non-consensual sniffing, helping me tidy up the picnic while Tristan hovered outside the tent. I could tell he wanted to do it, wanted to take care of me – of *us* – but I refused to let him clean up a mess I'd made.

I held out the last square of chocolate to Rose, then almost hyperventilated while she ducked to eat it from my fingers.

The alphas packed up the tent – with their shirts back on, unfortunately – and Rose took my hand as we walked back, apparently unbothered by the fact that my skin had heated past the point of comfort and my palm was sweaty and grainy with sand. I put myself between her and the empty drop as we panted our way back up the staircase; she flashed me a thankful smile that made my insides melt. I forced myself not to bring her wrist to my nose, not to brush my lips over her delicate pulse.

She doesn't know this couldn't work, I told myself. *You're going to hurt her.*

But my body didn't want to listen, and I put one foot in front of the other in a kind of daze. White edged my vision and heat rose unceasingly beneath my skin in blossoms of fire.

'Seb,' Tristan said, his voice breaking through my stupor. 'We're back, baby.'

I looked up, confused. We'd stopped, and I was holding Rose's hand, staring at her wrist. I wasn't sure how long I'd been doing it, but Banksia waited before us, its windows staring down intently.

'Let's go inside, yeah?' Tristan murmured.

I nodded, but because I couldn't help myself, I lifted Rose's hand to my lips.

I couldn't scent anything but soap, sand, and salt, but it jolted through my veins regardless.

She stared at me, her eyes slightly glazed.

I inhaled and caught a hint of sweet scent.

My own.

Tristan reacted immediately. 'Come on, baby,' he said, and I was swept inside in a whirlwind of alpha. There were a handful of students in the entranceway beyond the double doors, but they scattered – literally *scattered* – when Tristan glared at them, dominance flowing outwards like a fucking tsunami.

The last thing I glimpsed through the doors was Rose's startled face.

'It shouldn't be for another fortnight,' Tristan said under his breath, half dragging me up the stairs. 'Those motherfucking doctors will be hearing from me.' He got me into our room, locking the door behind us and immediately turning up the air purifier as my scent thickened. '*Fuck*, baby,' he murmured, his pupils blowing out, his thick erection pressing against his board shorts. 'What do you need?'

'You,' I managed, and a handful of moments later I was standing in the shower and my cock was halfway down his throat.

He bundled me up on the couch afterwards, checking the calendar as he dragged a hand through his damp curls. 'It isn't supposed to come for another fortnight,' he repeated, his distress pressing against my skin. A purr rumbled through my chest in response as I tried to soothe him, but it didn't seem to help.

'This has never happened,' he said tightly. 'Those suppressants are supposed to work. Those doctors *assured* us. Maybe we need –'

He fell silent as a loud, insistent knock sounded on the door.

TRISTAN

I KNEW WHO IT WAS, even before I opened the door.

He let me step outside and close the door before his fists found my collar and he pinned me against the wall.

'What the *fuck*?' he hissed. His expression was furious, his knuckles white. There were two perfect spots of outraged red on his pale cheeks, and I'd never seen his grey eyes so stormy.

'Not here,' I answered tersely, pushing him away – with more difficulty than I'd anticipated – before striding to the study room at the end of the hall. Two later-year students were sitting inside, studying. 'Get out,' I said, and after scrambling to collect their laptops and phones, they did.

Byron waited until they'd closed the door, then rounded on me. '*An omega?*' he raged. '*He's an omega?* You brought your omega here, *unbitten and unbonded?* Whose idea was it to pass him off as a beta? *Fuck*,' he went on, raking his hands through his already-dishevelled hair. 'A *male omega*. I didn't even know there was one in the *country*. Is he registered? He can't be registered,' he growled, answering his own question. 'There'd be OPF officers here if he was; they'd never leave him alone. And packs would *kill* to have him. *Fuck*. This is so dangerous I can't even comprehend it.'

'Do you think you're telling me anything I don't already know?' I said coldly.

Byron stopped and looked at me, really *looked*, and I felt suddenly exposed. I was used to being the dominant alpha in most places, but it struck me that right now *I might not be*. This huge alpha with his gentle grey eyes could be the one to put me on my back.

His eyes weren't gentle now, though. They were dark, intent, his pupils blown out with anger.

Or lust.

Possibly both.

'Did Rose catch his perfume?' I said abruptly.

His scent hadn't been strong. He'd taken extra blockers through the day, and it was a heat spike, rather than the prelude to an actual heat – something that Sebastian had never had. The moment he'd emerged as an omega – a few months after I'd met him, and later than people usually revealed – he'd taken so many heat suppressants that the doctors I'd paid to keep quiet were sure he'd done permanent damage to his hormonal cycle.

I can't, he'd said, terrified and determined all at once. *I can't be this. I can't let* this *get in my way*.

Every instinct in me had roared to life, wanting to protect my beta – my new omega – from everyone, from every*thing*. Watching him fight his newly emerged nature and his own instincts had been a new kind of torture, but it was what he wanted, so I'd clamped my inner alpha down tight and done whatever I could to support him. Which included helping him through the monthly heat spikes, which the doctors had assured us were his body's way of reconciling his suppressed heats.

Until now, the heat spikes had been like clockwork. But this one was *two weeks early*, and I was riding a wave of anxious worry as my instincts shouted at me to run back to Sebastian's side, to cool his fever, soothe his hurts, and tend his aching cock.

Byron shook his head. 'The wind was blowing the wrong way. I don't think she caught it. Shit, Grace.' He spiked his hands through his hair once more. '*Cherries*. My mouth is still full of it, and I only caught a hint.'

I went still. 'Was it complementary?'

My voice was level; I had no idea how I'd managed it. My heart was pounding and I was suddenly covered in cold sweat.

Byron gave an odd half-shrug and my spine went tight. 'I …' he started, then trailed off. His blown-out pupils and the strength of his reaction suggested that he *did* like Sebastian's scent – perhaps even liked it *a lot* – but I could see his mind working: how did he admit that to *me* and walk from this room with his limbs still attached? 'You're playing a dangerous game,' he said instead, darkly. 'What if it wasn't *me* who scented him? What if he went into heat here? Heat suppressants and scent blockers can be affected by all kinds of things – the flu, antibiotics, hormonal changes, a scent match. My sister –' he cut himself off abruptly.

I already knew the story. It had taken me a while, but I'd teased out the pieces that made up Byron Griffiths. I was sure there was more to it, but I was confident that I had the bones of him in a folder on my laptop, backed up to the cloud.

I didn't tell him that, though. *Never show your hand*, my dad had always told me. My papa would chuckle and elbow him, and my mother would roll her eyes and joke about the kind of children he was raising, but I'd always remembered that advice.

'For someone who thinks he knows so much about omegas, you seem to be forgetting something fairly basic,' I said, making my voice as cold as I could. I was irritated that he thought so little of Sebastian's choices, and that he thought so little of *me*, though I wasn't sure why I cared. 'Omegas are *people*. I *know* this is dangerous. I *know* we're taking risks. But if you think for a moment that *I* made those choices, that these things were *my* decisions, then you need to think again.'

He glared at me. 'Sebastian *loves* you. It's so obvious it's painful. Are you telling me he refused your bite? That he doesn't want your bond?'

I bristled, because of *course* this alpha would hit the sore spot. I knew what Sebastian wanted, and it was *that*, exactly. 'Do you think that's all he is?' I countered. 'A vessel to be bitten and bonded? Do you think that's all he's good for?'

Real anger flashed in his eyes. 'Of course not. But the world isn't made for omegas. Sebastian could still do everything he wanted with your bite on his skin. Only he'd be *safer* doing it.'

'Except you can't take back a bite,' I snarled. 'You can't break a bond. What if he found his scent match tomorrow? Would *you* take away his freedom?'

Silence was my answer. We stared at one another, neither of us willing to back down.

'Isn't love its own freedom?' he answered at last.

'Sebastian is *already* loved. Already cherished. Already free.'

His expression was troubled, but it wasn't my job to coddle him through the realisation that *protection* and *love* weren't synonymous.

I pinned him with my best stare. 'Will you tell anyone?'

He growled, clearly insulted, but he could hardly blame me for asking; he didn't exactly have the best track record when it came to keeping important things quiet. 'Of course I won't,' he answered, his voice as stiff as his spine.

I nodded and turned to the door, pulling my phone from my pocket. 'Good. But just in case you think about changing your mind …' I let the sentence hang, then held up my phone.

His eyes widened in shock before his face settled into an expression of fury that sent a shiver running down my spine. 'How did you get that?' he hissed.

'Does it matter?' I angled the screen and watched dispassionately as a younger Byron drew back and let his bloody fists loose, pummelling a body on the ground, over and over. 'Just know it's not the only thing I have.' I blacked the phone screen. 'If you so much as *think* of exposing Sebastian, I'll release everything.'

I stepped towards the door, but found myself stopped short as his fingers encircled my wrist, his grip firm but not painful. His touch sent another shiver through me. I ignored it, meeting his furious grey stare.

'You don't need it,' he said, his voice calmer. 'I *like* Sebastian. I'd never want to see him hurt.'

I knew he was sincere. I could hear it, *feel* it. But I didn't trust him.

I *couldn't* trust him.

'Even so,' I answered, and shook him off.

I left him in the study room and hurried back to Sebastian. But as I unlocked our door, it occurred to me that this new problem might just help solve an existing one.

ROSE

'Say that again?' Chloe demanded. 'You, Rosemary Morris, my best friend, went to the beach with *the son of Carwyn Griffiths?*'

I winced. 'Fuck, Clo, I don't think they heard you in Tasmania.'

'Sorry,' she said, unfazed and entirely unapologetic. 'Can you get me a signed bookplate?'

I laughed. 'You're impossible.'

'Well, failing that, can you bond him – the son, I mean … *unless?* – so I can come to the ceremony and *coincidentally* sit next to Carwyn and casually drop that oh, I don't know, *he's my favourite author ever and I want to be him when I grow up?*'

'What happened to *you're there for a degree, not a pack?*' I countered. 'Or *that motherfucker did* what *in the dining hall?*'

On my phone screen, Chloe waved her hand dismissively. She'd let her hair grow; it fell beneath her shoulders like shining black water. 'Exceptions can be made, Rosie. For Carwyn Griffith's son, specifically. And even *I*, the best friend, think he apologised sufficiently for the dining hall incident.'

I fell silent for so long that Chloe squinted worriedly at her phone screen. 'They're nice,' I said at last.

'Ask them for their scent cards, then,' she answered practically. 'I know you're not supposed to have them there, but surely people do it anyway. Only if you want to, obviously, not because I'm a crazed fan.'

'It's just …' I chewed my lip. 'That makes it all *real*. And at the moment it's like this … summer haze. Everything is golden and warm and full of possibility. If I ask them …'

'It ends,' Chloe finished, reading my mind like she always did. 'You'll know for certain what it could be – or not. And the summer will be over.' She paused. 'It's fine to live in the haze, Rosie. You deserve it. But autumn always comes, yeah?'

'Yeah,' I sighed. 'Autumn always comes.'

When Chloe had hung up – after extolling the writerly virtues of Byron's father for a little while longer, then moving on entirely to her pros and cons list for two different Masters programs, one in Singapore and one in Shanghai, both close to different family members and with that, having different complexities – I decided to go to the First Year Library to study. Despite what I'd just said to Chloe, Tristan, Sebastian, and Byron had been absent for the last couple of days. Byron had gone with his parents to visit his sister, though he hadn't mentioned where; Tristan had sent a rather curt group text saying that he and Sebastian had caught a cold. I'd responded, saying that I hoped they were okay and asking if they needed anything, but I hadn't heard anything back. I'd spent some time with both Marina and Alessia, but after giving myself the weekend as a break from studying, I decided to get started on the second assessment.

We didn't have class that day, but I went to the First Year Library anyway. It was nerve-wracking, going there by myself without Byron's comforting bulk, but I spotted James and Pravin at one of the desks and they immediately waved me over with matching smiles.

'Second assessment?' Pravin said, by way of greeting.

'Second assessment,' I agreed, smiling in return.

I set myself up next to them, opening my laptop and getting started. We worked in a companionable silence for half an hour or so, until James stretched and looked across at Pravin. 'Did you hear about the commencement party?'

'I heard it's organised by the Revels,' Pravin returned. 'Apparently they organise most of the social stuff here.'

A later-year student a few desks away stood up, then stepped towards us, his eyes flicking between me and James. Pravin glanced at us, then raised an eyebrow at the other student in challenge. The student turned away, grumbling. 'Sorry,' Pravin muttered. 'Did you want to talk to him?'

'Nope,' I said.

'Absolutely not,' James agreed.

'Well then. Anyway, I heard they're making tubs of sangria.'

James made an appreciative sound. 'Will you go?'

Pravin nodded. 'Alessia wants to,' he said, flushing slightly. I smiled at his obvious crush, though I didn't know whether Alessia returned it. Either way, Pravin didn't seem like the kind of alpha who would pressure a beta; James' relaxed presence next to him rather proved the opposite.

I shifted in my seat. I wanted to go, too. I could ask to go with Pravin, or maybe check whether I could go with Marina.

A familiar anger warmed me. If I wasn't an omega, I wouldn't have to worry as much. And if I was an alpha, I wouldn't worry *at all*. I could simply go to the party and enjoy my life.

But I *was* an omega, and I knew it was a waste of time to complain. It wasn't like anything was going to change, at least not soon. Our current government was progressive – compared to other countries, anyway – and their policies supported universal access to scent blockers and the right to a safe education. But their political opponents were loud, and the opposition's policies pushed the notion of the *traditional pack*, even though designations had barely been around long enough to *have* traditions. They were simply parroting a recycled sexism from earlier times. In their eyes, alphas protected, betas served, and omegas – who were mostly female – bred, and that was all there was to it. You didn't have to look very far back in history to know that notions like that left a lot of room for the loss of opportunity, of autonomy, and for outright abuse. The government struggled with balancing their policies with the opposition's demands, and, worryingly, with the opposition's growing popularity, so things hadn't moved forward quite as far as they could have.

'You're welcome to come with us,' Pravin said, interrupting the depressing direction of my thoughts, his smile directed at both James and me. I thanked him, but I couldn't crash his time with Alessia, and it wasn't his job to protect me.

But it's fine when Byron does it?

I stared at my laptop screen, mulling over why it felt different. I eventually settled on *because Byron volunteered.*

It didn't make any sense, because Pravin had, too.

I pushed aside the notion that it was because Byron felt like pack. I couldn't feel that; I didn't even know what his scent was.

I shifted in my chair again, restless, then looked down at my fingers, remembering the way Sebastian had twined his own through them.

'Rose?'

I blinked, startled, then turned to see Byron studying me with a frown.

'You're back,' I said stupidly.

He nodded. 'An hour or so ago.'

'How was your sister?'

He didn't answer for a long, uncomfortable moment. 'The same as the last time I saw her,' he said at last.

I wasn't sure what to make of that. 'Are you okay?'

His grey eyes darted around the library. 'I ... I just came to make sure you were all right.' His gaze settled back on me; his fingers flexed, as though he wanted to reach out, but stopped himself. 'I think ... I need a walk.'

With that, he turned and strode from the library, leaving me gaping after him.

'Rose.' Pravin nudged me gently with his elbow. I turned blindly towards him, my eyes pricking, my stomach churning at the rollercoaster of emotions evoked by Byron's sudden appearance and even more abrupt departure. I'd *missed* him. 'Oh. Ah,' Pravin said awkwardly, when a tear spilled down my cheek. 'You know none of that was because of you, right?'

I wiped my face angrily. 'No, I don't know that. Sometimes it's hard to know what he's thinking.'

Pravin laughed softly. 'No, it's not. Not usually. Because most of the time, his mind is on one thing – you.'

◇◇◇

Sebastian and Tristan reappeared at breakfast the next day. They both looked tired, and Sebastian's expression was unusually hollow. Despite that, he sat down next to me and slung his arm over the back of my chair as if nothing had happened, saying *Hi, Rosebud*, with a wide grin. My instincts loved it; if we weren't on blockers, his subtle beta scent would be all over me.

'So, are we going?' he said, taking up a lock of my hair.

'Going where?' His closeness muddled my thoughts; it was dangerous being near him.

'To the party.'

I glanced at Byron, whose eyes stayed glued to his coffee cup. 'I –'

'Your alpha will come,' Tristan said, with the hint of an eyeroll.

That got Byron's attention. 'Will he?' he said, one eyebrow raised.

'Have you got something better to do?'

Byron snorted. 'I can think of a hundred things. I'm good, thanks.'

'Rose clearly wants to go,' Tristan said impatiently. 'Stop being obtuse.'

Byron's eyes fell on me. 'Do you?' he said, surprised.

I hesitated. It was another opportunity to see my friends, and I *did* want that. It was so nice, being able to chat to Pravin and James and Alessia, to have coffee with Marina. I felt more like a regular person, and less like an overly hormonal princess locked up in a scentless tower.

But I knew better than to be alone around alphas and alcohol.

'If you three are going, then I want to go,' I decided.

It was sneaky of me, and I knew it; I was essentially forcing Byron's hand. Sebastian shot me a sideways grin, pointedly twirling my hair around his finger.

Byron's expression was thoughtful. 'I'll have to talk to my liaison officer,' he said at last.

Tristan's phone buzzed. He picked it up, frowning, then his eyes widened. 'The marks for the first assessment have been released.'

It took a moment for what he'd said to sink in; by the time my brain caught up, Sebastian had already let my hair go and had opened his laptop to scroll through the online classroom to the grades page. I hurried to do the same, my fingers trembling. I clicked into the grades, then froze when I saw the mark there.

'The class average was eighty-two,' Tristan read. 'And the top mark was ninety-four.'

My chest went light with happiness. I hadn't realised how worried I'd been until the weight lifted.

'Ninety-three,' Sebastian said. His expression was a mix of pleased and disgruntled.

'Ninety-one.' Tristan glanced at his beta. 'Good job, handsome.'

I looked across at Byron, who hadn't bothered to check his mark at all; he was smiling, a soft, knowing smile that tied my insides in knots. 'You got ninety-four, didn't you?'

I flushed.

'Congratulations, Rose,' he said roughly, and my body went hot from his praise. His eyes flickered to Tristan. 'Told you that you'd be a threat to anyone.'

◇◇◇

I spent ages picking an outfit, because I'd never been to an adult party before, and I didn't really have the right clothes. I didn't even know what the right clothes *were*. I eventually settled on a cream-coloured smock dress, paired with some Roman-style sandals that laced to the knee. I left my hair down and added some gold eyeshadow, then dabbed a light stain into my lips, hoping it wasn't too much.

I made sure, too, that my underwear were the new ones I'd bought before coming to Banksia, with the most up-to-date, slick-proof lining, and that my skin was coated in scent canceller. I sprayed myself once I'd dressed for good measure, then dabbed some synthetic perfume on my wrists.

When Byron knocked on my door and his eyes went heavy at the sight of me, I stopped caring about whether my outfit was *too much*.

There was something so powerful about making his heart beat faster; something powerful and *addictive*.

'Rosebud. You're killing me,' Sebastian said from behind him, raising his eyes to the moulded ceiling. He wove around Byron to grab my hand, pulling me into the hallway. Byron closed my door, then checked it was locked. He was wearing his customary black, though he seemed to have donned slightly shinier boots for the occasion. Sebastian, however, was in chinos and a linen button-down, his sleeves rolled up in a way that had no right to be so enticing. Tristan was wearing something similar, only in lighter tones. His hair fell forward over his glasses.

It hit me, then, how beautiful he was. Sebastian was so blindingly lovely that he all but eclipsed everyone around him. Tristan's beauty was quieter, all angles and shining curls, all calm self-assurance and piercing green eyes.

I swallowed.

'We've got you,' Sebastian said comfortingly, and tucked me into his side.

Everyone had spoken about the commencement party in vaguely hushed tones, as though it was a secret, but there was no way the staff didn't know. Two unfamiliar, muscled alphas stood outside the entranceway, clothed all in black, their shirts proclaiming *SECURITY*. The First Year Library was lit by fairy lights and LED candles, and there was a tonne of food – clearly made in the Banksia kitchens – arranged on the study desks. The chairs we used in class had been pushed along one wall, leaving an open space that students were already using as a dance floor. The speakers Professor Heathcote used had been co-opted for a playlist; dance music pumped through the room.

James waved from where he, Pravin, and Alessia stood next to a study table, which held a huge bowl of what looked like the anticipated sangria. There were canned drinks in bowls of ice, too; I grabbed a gin and tonic with a silent sigh of relief. It didn't matter that I was with alphas – I couldn't afford to drink something without controlling the alcohol content, let alone something that might have been spiked.

There were a few more security alphas scattered unobtrusively around the room, and I spotted Marina in a corner, making out with Jasmine, a third-year student. There was a lot of it going on, but I supposed it made sense. Before designations emerged, people would have gotten this out of their systems by our age, and many would have had steady jobs, or even been parents. But in the post-Unveiling age, it took so long for our bodies to adjust to the new hormones and instincts that it was almost like we prolonged our early twenties, as if we were trying to catch up on the things we'd missed while we were at home sweating and crying through the adjustments to our unreliable bodies. It was *the* question of contemporary psychology: whether we, collectively, would ever really recover from the emergence of our designations.

I thought about it often. It was all too easy to remember the *before*, when I was simply a woman with a faint, sweet scent and regular periods. When my mind didn't blank if I caught an alluring scent; when I didn't slick with arousal, but simply got wet.

When I didn't turn into a sex-hungry demon once every three months, begging for a bite. When I could have fucked someone and have it be simply *that* – a fuck. Not the potential for a lifelong, irrevocable bond via an alpha's sharp teeth if they lost control.

When I didn't have to take a cocktail of medications every morning to make sure those things *didn't* happen.

I took a mouthful of my drink, trying to push the thoughts away. There was no going back; I could only make the best of what I had.

Byron smiled at me, his dark eyes almost black in the dim room, the angles of his face lit by flickering fairy lights, and I knew it wasn't all bad.

Tristan pulled Sebastian close, muttering something in his ear before he gently pushed his beta towards the dance floor. 'Dance with me!' Sebastian hollered over the music, and at first I wasn't sure who he was talking to – not until he grabbed my hand.

I let him pull me into the small crush of students, trying to avoid pressing against other people's bodies until Sebastian carved us a space, right in the middle. He danced like he did everything else: perfectly. My limbs went tingly and hot watching him, seeing his hips move, his body swaying to the beat, my eyes tracing the curve of his throat as he threw his head back.

Fuck, the things I wanted to do to that neck.

Contrary to popular belief, omegas could bite, too. We could forge bonds just as strong as an alpha if we bit first, tying a pack together with an omega at the centre, rather than a dominant alpha. But because so much about omegas was still tangled up in historic gender norms, the popular imagination cast us as soft, submissive, small; as people who were made to follow, not lead. It didn't help that our instincts sometimes forced us into obedience over bravery, and our heats made us dependent on others, but those things didn't mean we were *weak*, and they definitely didn't mean that we couldn't lead.

Bite the pretty beta, my omega purred.

My teeth ached, but I pushed the feeling aside, determined to have a good time. I wanted to be no more than a woman dancing with the ridiculously handsome man in front of her. I didn't need a designation for that, or a claiming bite – just some music and to move my body.

Sebastian grinned at me, and I echoed his movements until we were dancing. He stepped closer, his eyes on my face, and it was like the day at the beach all over again. A pull towards him tightened in my chest as he slipped his arm around my back and tugged me forward, bringing our bodies together.

I could feel him *everywhere.*

My breasts pressed against his ribs, and he nudged a thigh between my legs. Heat shot through me and my arms linked behind his neck without me telling them to; he bent until his forehead was pressed to mine.

I was hot – too hot – but I didn't care, because Sebastian was close, his breath smelled like sangria, and one of his hands spanned over my back, pressing me closer.

I licked my lips without thinking; his pupils blew out as he stared at my mouth. 'I can't even scent you, and I still want to eat you alive,' he murmured, his lips brushing over my ear. I shivered, my knees going weak; if I hadn't been leaning on him, I would have staggered.

I knew that this was stupid. I knew that there was only so much my blockers and suppressants could take before they began to fail. I *knew* that I was in a room full of alphas, and that I was putting myself in danger.

I kissed him anyway.

His lips were still for a moment before he moved and they moulded to mine. He tasted sweet, *so* sweet, with a cherry aftertaste to the fruit and red wine. It was a combination that I wanted to drink down, and I sighed into his mouth when his tongue flicked my lip.

My mouth slanted and I opened for him properly, our tongues touching. He moaned and pressed me closer, his free hand sliding to cup my ass. Arousal jolted through me at the touch, and my brow was sticky with sudden sweat, but I didn't care because Sebastian Worthy was kissing me as if he really did want to devour me whole.

His hard chest crushed my breasts as he pressed even closer, one hand moving to tangle in my hair. I couldn't have escaped if I'd wanted to, but I couldn't think of a single thing I wanted less. I wanted my mouth on his for hours – days, weeks – and to have his hands on my skin and his heart against my body, to have the strange pull I felt in my chest eased by his closeness. I shifted my weight, then went still as something pressed against me.

He was hard.

He was hard for *me*.

The realisation was too much; I should have known it would be too much. I gasped into his mouth even as my core flared with new heat and I felt a familiar heaviness as slick began to gather between my thighs.

He jolted back, his nostrils flaring, and *fuck*, I wished I was dreaming, wished I was wrong, but I caught the faintest hint of my natural perfume in the air.

'Rosebud –' he said hoarsely, but I couldn't respond, because someone was wrapping me in a hoodie – one a few times too large for me – and I suddenly found myself cradled in a strong pair of arms, my face pressed into a broad chest covered in a black t-shirt. *Alpha*, my instincts sighed, and I relaxed, because he was striding out of the First Year Library with me held close, growling savagely when a third-year student got in our way.

I whimpered, trying to press my thighs together to ease the ache between them. He tightened his hold as we passed the security alphas, and the omega in me liked that very much.

Alpha, my instincts said again.

I pressed my face into his chest, trusting that he was taking me somewhere safe – somewhere he could give me what I needed.

And what I needed right now was for someone to fuck me until I screamed.

'Alpha,' I begged, my voice muffled; I wasn't really sure what I was begging for. I peeked out sideways, recognising the corridor; he was taking me to my room. That was fine; he could come into my bed-nest. I hoped he'd let me ride him. Some alphas got funny about omegas being on top; the heat alphas had never let me be anything but face-down beneath them.

I didn't think Byron would be like that.

I whined, pressing my thighs together again, shifting restlessly in his arms.

'Fuck, omega,' he growled, as I felt more slick gather. 'Fuck. *Fuck*.'

He stopped, then set me down gently before my own door.

'Open it, Rose,' he said, his voice gravelly, as if he was grinding his teeth.

I fished inside the hoodie for my dress pocket, finding my swipe card and opening the door, my hands trembling. 'Alpha –'

'Lock it behind you with *all* the locks, okay? The deadlock as well as the chain. Then turn the air purifier on high, sweetheart.'

I paused, one foot through the doorway. 'What do you mean?'

He was coming with me – wasn't he?

'I only caught a hint of your scent, Rose, but fuck … You're sweet. Sweet and rich and … I didn't catch enough to place it.' He ran one hand through his hair, frustrated, while the other covered his nose and mouth. 'I only caught a hint, but it's driving me insane. And I might not be the only one, omega. If you don't want your neck covered in bites, lock the door, beautiful. Please.'

He wasn't coming with me.

I whined again, but this time, it was with hurt. 'You're leaving? But I need –'

'Rose. Sweetheart. I fucking *wish* I could stay. I wish I could help you. You have no idea how much. The things I want …' He swallowed. 'But this wasn't the plan, was it? We're both operating on instinct. If I come in there …' He tugged on his hair. 'Rose, I want to bite you so fucking badly. That isn't what you want. That isn't what you *need*. You're here for a degree, not a pack.'

I stared at him, hearing the echo of Chloe's words – and my own – but there were voices coming from the end of the corridor, and sudden unease made my stomach churn. I knew he was right. I was slicking, my blockers were wearing off, and if I didn't lock my door soon, someone might find their way in – and it wouldn't be the person I wanted.

'Fine,' I growled, feeling almost as savage as the sound. I turned and slammed my door behind me. My underwear was damp, and my cunt was throbbing, begging to be filled, but I hooked the chain and flicked the deadbolt like Byron had said, then turned the air purifier up to its highest setting. For good measure, I grabbed a clean towel from the bathroom, rolling it up and stuffing it along the base of my door before opening the windows. I wasn't in heat, so hopefully my scent would dissipate easily in the night air.

I heard a *thump* from the other side of the door; when I checked the camera, I saw that Byron had slumped down against it, his head in his hands. As I watched, he threw his head back, thumping it against the wood.

'Fuck,' he swore, his voice somehow deeper over the camera. '*Fuck.*'

I pulled my phone from my pocket and called him.

He picked up immediately. 'Are you okay?'

'Do you really want to help me with this?'

He was silent for a moment. 'I think you know that I do,' he said at last, his voice low and hoarse.

'Then go to your room.'

On the camera, he turned and stared at my door, startled. 'What?'

'Your room,' I repeated. 'Go there. Then call me.'

'I —' He swallowed audibly. 'Okay. Whatever you want.'

I watched him end the call, then get to his feet and walk away. I made my way to my bedroom and opened the drawer in my bedside table.

He'd been right to walk away, but it didn't mean that nothing could happen.

I could still make both of us feel good.

BYRON

GO TO YOUR ROOM.

No one had said that to me for about fifteen years, but I found myself striding down the corridors regardless. I had no idea what Rose intended, but I'd do whatever she wanted.

My mouth was still full of sweetness; I breathed as lightly as I could, trying to keep what was left of the taste on my tongue. It was sugary, but not sickly; rich, but not overwhelming. An edible scent for sure, which lifted a weight from my heart I hadn't realised I was carrying.

But I hadn't caught enough to identify it, and not knowing would drive me insane. My cock was straining against my jeans, my tongue watering at the notion of diving between her legs and lapping at the source. I'd pressed my nose and mouth into my shoulder as I'd carried her, resisting the temptation to bury my face in her neck and breathe her in.

Torture wasn't fiery pits and pain, I decided. It was carrying an omega close to your chest, her plush thighs hooked over your forearm, and not being able to dip down and sink your teeth into her soft skin.

'You are not a good person,' I muttered to myself. 'She's your *friend*. You're thinking with your knot. You're –'

My phone buzzed in my pocket; I fished it out.

Are you there yet?

I called her. 'I'm here. But what –'

'Do you still want to help me? And to be clear, Byron, I mean *do you want to help me come*?'

My mind blanked.

She waited.

Words. I know words. 'Yes,' I choked out. 'Yes. I want that. Very much.'

'Thank fuck,' she sighed, and a moment later, I heard a new sound start through the phone.

I swallowed. 'Rose?'

She gave a shuddering exhale. The faint buzzing sound in the background changed pace, and *fuck me*, I knew that noise.

I took the advice I'd given her, rushing inside my apartment and locking the door with the deadbolt, then turning my air purifier up to its maximum setting. I didn't think I'd moved that fast before, ever. 'Rose, beautiful?' I said, and you could've grated a fucking rock on how rough my voice sounded. 'Are you …?'

'Mmm,' she gasped, and if I thought my cock was hard before, I'd been wrong. It was steel now, or titanium, or chromium.

I was basically a fucking cyborg.

I held my breath. 'Will you tell me what you're doing?'

She gave a breathy little moan. I had the urge to swallow it down, so the sound was only for me, so that no one else ever heard it. 'I'm on my bed,' she answered unsteadily, her breathing fast and shallow. 'I left my dress on, but took my underwear off. I'm lying on my back with my skirt around my waist.'

The picture my mind made was obscene. I'd tried so hard not to do this – not to objectify her, not to turn her into a fantasy, not to stamp my own desires on the shadow of her – but I couldn't help imagining how she looked now, flushed and trembling, her hair spread across her bed, her knees parted. 'I didn't need lube because I'd started to slick,' she went on, and my brain shorted. 'I'm so wet, Byron.'

It wasn't a groan I gave; it was closer to a sound of pain. 'You didn't need the lube for what, beautiful?' I grated out, though I already knew the answer.

The buzzing sound changed again, and I heard rustling as she shifted on the bed. 'For the vibrator.'

I made it to my bedroom; I didn't so much as *lie* on my bed as my knees gave way and I collapsed there. 'Will you tell me about it?'

'It's big. Thick. Long. With a rabbit for my clit. And it has a part that expands.'

I ran my hand over my face. My cock was throbbing so hard I was sure there'd be an imprint of my zipper across my skin. 'Like a knot?'

'It's not as good as the real thing,' she panted, and for a moment, I was blind with jealousy that someone had knotted her — someone who *wasn't me*. Reason kicked in a second later; Rose was twenty-six. She would have had at least one heat before, possibly many more. She had no pack, so she would have asked a trusted friend, or accessed a public heat clinic, or paid for accredited heat alphas to visit her at home. During a heat, she'd beg for knots, and who the fuck wouldn't give that to her? 'But it does the job,' she went on, oblivious to my useless rage, the slightest hint of a whine in her words. The buzzing intensified as she changed the setting. 'Oh, *fuck*.'

'Rose,' I said desperately. 'I'm not … I don't know what you need from me here. Can I –' I inhaled. 'Can I touch myself?'

There was a moment of silence, long enough that my heart began to sink. 'You're not already?' she said, clearly disgruntled.

I barked out a laugh. 'I'm not going to do it without your consent, omega.'

She gave a wordless whine. 'Fucking *fuck*. Say that again.'

I put her on speaker, then undid my zipper and shoved my jeans and trunks down, palming my cock. It hurt to touch, but it was a pleasure-pain I enjoyed. 'Say what again?' I teased. 'Consent?'

'I mean, yes,' she said tartly, a hint of her usual self shining through her need. 'Obviously. But I meant the other thing.'

I gave my cock a few hard pumps, biting my lip when sensation stirred at the base of my spine and precum welled beneath my palm. 'You mean *omega*?'

I'd put a hint of a purr into the word, and she cried out. There was a soft thump – I assumed her phone had fallen – but I could still hear the buzz of the vibrator. She must have put me on speaker; there was a rhythmic wet noise, and I realised she was pressing the toy into her body before pulling it out again. My hips pushed up as I lost all semblance of control, fucking into my hand.

'Please,' she cried, and fuck, I was so selfish, but I didn't want her to come yet; I wanted to draw this out forever.

'Tell me how it feels,' I growled.

'It feels so good,' she gasped. 'So sweet. I'm so close I can feel it in my toes.'

The notion of her toes curling with pleasure was almost enough to undo me. 'Have you inflated the knot?'

She made a wordless sound of disagreement.

'Will you do it for me?' I purred. 'Will you show me how you can take a knot?'

The buzzing changed again; I imagined her body stretching and settling around the artificial swelling. With enough practice, some alphas and betas could take a knot, too, but omegas were made for it, with extra nerve endings to ensure they could come from the pressure of a knot alone.

'Sweetheart?' I grated out, when she didn't speak again. 'Rose?'

'So good,' she whimpered. 'Alpha, I'm so close, *please* –'

'Come, omega,' I growled, and the bed rustled as she moved, the buzzing erratic as her body clenched around the vibrator, muffling the sound.

Her cries were the sweetest melody.

My body tightened and my knot flared as sensation pooled at the base of my spine. I squeezed my shaft tight, the discomfort forcing the pleasure to fade.

I wasn't coming until she did that again.

'Rose?' I said at last, when her breathing calmed.

'Alpha?' she answered, sounding dazed.

'Did you deflate the knot, sweetheart?'

There was a low whirring as she must have deflated it; she made a strangled sound.

'So good,' I praised. 'So good, coming around a knot like that.' I stroked my cock; it jerked beneath my hand.

'I'm still so slick,' she whispered.

'*Fuck.*' My cock jerked again. 'Fuck, Rose. I bet you taste amazing.'

'You want to taste me?'

I laughed. 'Like I want my next breath. I want to taste you for *me*, and I want to lick you for *you*.'

'What else?' she gasped.

I squeezed my cock again; it wouldn't take much to tip me over the edge, and my imagination was dangerous territory. 'I want my mouth on every inch of your body,' I grated out. 'I want your legs around my fucking neck. I want my hands on your skin, your sweet mouth on mine. I want to feel how slick you are when I slide inside you. I want you to stretch around my knot, and I want to watch your face when you come.'

She gave a sighing moan, and the buzzing started up again. 'Fuck. So sensitive,' she muttered. She laughed breathlessly. 'So good.'

'I want you to come again,' I growled.

'I will.' She paused, taking a shuddering breath. 'Would you want me to present for you, alpha?'

I came without warning, my vision going white as I groaned through the pleasure, picturing her with her cheek pressed to the soft bed and her ass in the air, offering herself to me. Picturing her cunt, swollen and slick, as my cock pressed inside her, picturing her ass beneath my hands as I thrust, picturing the pretty slope of her back and her hair streaming across her shoulders. Imagining her writhing beneath me as my fingers toyed mercilessly with her clit.

I couldn't catch my breath.

She gave a throaty laugh, and I realised she'd outplayed me. 'Too clever by half,' I bit out, as my cock twitched and the last of my load hit the rest of the mess on my stomach. 'I was trying to last. You knew that would set me off.'

'You're an alpha,' she said thickly. 'I know you want me on my knees.'

I blinked; there was a lot to unravel there. 'It's not about your knees,' I answered. 'It's about you trusting me enough to give you what you need.' I paused. 'And for the record, I'd rather have you above me. I'm lazy.'

She huffed another laugh. 'I'll believe that when I see it.'

Something stirred in my stomach, something that took me a moment to recognise. I hadn't felt like this for so long, it was almost unfamiliar.

Happiness.

Happiness, because this was messy and silly and *wonderful*. Happiness, because I'd see her tomorrow, see her brown eyes alight with curiosity, see her auburn hair escaping its bun to frame her lovely face, see her lips purse as she thought something through.

And her words sounded like this wouldn't be a one-time thing.

'You're right,' I said thickly. 'I'd work so fucking hard for you, Rose. I'd work until you were so blissed out you couldn't stand up. I'd work until you couldn't tell where one orgasm ended and the next one began. Until you were begging for my knot. And I'd give you that, too, sweetheart. I'd give you everything.'

'Oh, fuck,' she gasped. 'Alpha –'

'Come for me, omega.'

It was as if I'd pressed a button; she shrieked, and the sound muffled, then cut out.

I turned my head to the side to stare at my phone.

She called again a moment later. 'I rolled on the screen and cut the call,' she said sheepishly.

Could she be any fucking cuter? 'No worries.' I paused. 'Do you need another?'

I winced as soon as the words left my mouth; it sounded as if I was asking if she needed another tissue, or a shopping bag, not an orgasm.

'You'd give me what I needed, wouldn't you?' she said thoughtfully, seeming not to mind.

'Always,' I answered.

'I think I'm okay.' I heard the rustle of material. 'I'm going to kick Sebastian in the shin, though.' She swallowed. 'I should have known better.'

'You like him,' I said gently. 'You like each other. It's obvious, Rose.'

'Yes, but that's no excuse for logic flying out the window every time he blinks at me,' she said crossly. 'I put myself in danger because my impulse control is suddenly non-existent.'

'It's –' I started, then stopped, as a knock came from my door. 'What the fuck?' I muttered.

'What happened?'

'Someone's knocking on my door.' I settled one arm behind my head. 'They can fuck right off, though.'

She huffed a laugh. 'What if it's your mum or dad?'

'They'd call, which would have been an even *worse* interruption.' The knocking continued, louder. 'Fuck, they're really insistent.'

'Then you should answer it.' She sighed. 'I should have a shower, anyway.'

My cock twitched as my imagination ran riot once more. 'Mmpfh,' I managed.

'I'll see you tomorrow?' she said, a smile in her voice.

'I'll see you tomorrow,' I answered, and hung up before I could do something stupid – like profess my undying adoration.

I rolled off my bed as the knocking on my door continued, grabbing a towel from the bathroom to deal with the rapidly-cooling mess on my stomach before spraying myself with canceller and pulling on a fresh shirt and pair of jeans. I padded into my lounge room, unbolted the deadlock, and pulled open the door.

Sebastian stood outside as if we'd summoned him, looking as miserable as he did freshly fucked. His lips were swollen and downturned, his eyes on the floor. 'Can I come in?'

'Are you okay?'

His eyes flickered up. 'I don't …' He trailed off.

I stood aside to let him in.

His nostrils flared as he came inside. This was why the Banksia House guidelines warned against this. We could suppress our scents with blockers and cancellers, and it worked on our bodies – albeit imperfectly – but it was far less easy to remove a scent from a space, especially when you spent a lot of time there.

'Fuck,' Sebastian breathed. He pressed the heel of his hands against his eyes. 'Salted caramel. Fuck me.' His hands moved to his hair; he tugged at the golden strands. 'Of course you'd smell edible.'

He didn't seem to hate it, and at any other time, I'd ask the questions I was dying to know the answer to. *Do we have complementary scents? Do you want to devour me whole, or is it just simply … nice? Does my scent make you as hard as your eyes make me?*

But at that moment, I was too bemused by his presence. 'Sebastian, what happened?'

He turned to face me, his expression a mask of misery. 'I think he did it on purpose,' he said.

I shook my head. 'Who did what on purpose?'

'Tris,' he answered. 'Tristan. I think he wanted Rose to slick.'

SEBASTIAN

I HATED THE WORDS, even as I said them. I hated that I was here, in Byron's room – trying to make sense of what had happened – behind my alpha's back.

Dance with Rose, Tristan had murmured into my ear, pushing me gently towards the dance floor. *It's okay with me if you want to kiss her.*

We'd never really discussed the boundaries of our relationship before Banksia – we'd never needed to – and I'd resisted, frowning back at him. *I know you'd like to*, he'd said, smiling at me indulgently, relaxed.

And I *did* want to. Had wanted to for days, *weeks*, even. Tristan knew how much she'd been occupying my thoughts. And while I'd wanted to talk about expectations and limits first, Rose had also been *right there*, and I'd been immediately caught up in how she felt beneath my hands and how sweet her tongue was when it flicked inside my mouth.

The moment I'd caught a hint of scent in the air – a sweetness I knew, somewhere deep inside, could only be hers – Tristan had dragged me from the First Year Library, all the way to our room, and pulled me into bed before my brain could clear enough to wonder about it. Why had he said that, and without warning? Not just *why* – but *why now*?

My alpha didn't do *anything* by chance. The only impulsiveness he ever showed was with spur-of-the-moment present buying; everything else he did was meticulously planned, calculated, careful.

So *why* had he encouraged me to kiss Rose?

'You think Tristan *wanted* Rose to slick?' Byron repeated carefully. 'What makes you think that?'

'Because he told me to dance with her, and said it was okay if I kissed her. Because he *knows* I can't keep my fucking hands off her.' I looked up, meeting his gaze. 'And because he knows what omegas are like.'

Byron had clearly been doing *something* before I'd pounded on his door. His cheeks were flushed, his grey eyes heavy, and he'd sprayed so much canceller that my nose twitched. He looked delicious, so eminently fuckable, and his apartment smelled so *devourable* that it almost distracted me from my confusion and hurt.

He looked back at me evenly. 'I know you're not a beta, Seb.'

'Then you *know* how bad this is,' I said. 'You know that Tristan wasn't just risking Rose's safety.'

He'd risked mine, too.

Byron frowned. 'He got there at the same time I did. I noticed him pulling you away.'

I worried at my bottom lip. That was true; Tristan's eyes had been on Rose and me the whole time we'd danced, and he'd dragged me from the library just as Byron had carried Rose away. I could put his quick reflexes down to instinct – or consider the possibility that he'd known what would happen and had planned for it.

I clicked my tongue. I'd trusted Tristan implicitly for six years. He had never done a single thing that had made me question his motives, or his dedication to me. I knew that he loved me. I knew that he'd kill for me, die for me.

It was possible he'd never risked my safety at all.

But I also knew that he could be single-minded. And I knew he'd do anything to keep me safe – including hurt other people.

I sank down on Byron's couch without invitation. His room was nice, though different to ours. Tristan's living spaces always looked as if he'd taken part of his family's manor house with him, no matter where he was. My idea of decor was books, plants, and more books, and together, it worked.

Byron's space was less cluttered, though his bookshelves were still stuffed to overflowing. The walls were hung with framed prints, mostly black and white line drawings. One of the bedroom doors was shut; through the other, I could see a green coverlet spread across a low bed, and a huge Aubrey Beardsley print – a scene from *Le Morte d'Arthur* – hanging above it.

I wasn't going to get a closer look, obviously. But I wanted to. Byron's scent made me want to know *everything*, to gather and hoard all the pieces of him that he hid, to examine them all with care, noting every smooth stretch, every rough edge.

I pushed the thought away before it could veer into dangerous territory. Tristan's permission didn't extend to Byron. Rose was different; she wasn't a threat to Tristan's dominance, not like Byron could be. That shit didn't matter to me – alphas could be fucking fools sometimes – but it would matter to Tristan. He needed to be at the top of the food chain, always, and I suspected that Byron's calm facade hid strength for days.

'How can I help?' he said gently.

I shivered. He was good, this alpha; too good, almost. He knew the right way to speak to an omega, careful to always phrase his words in a way that acknowledged we had different needs to the other designations without making us feel weak for it.

I should have been worried to know that he'd realised my greatest secret. Instead, it was a *relief*. I didn't have to pretend with him any longer. I'd still need to be careful, but now I had a second person I could be myself with.

'I just needed a sounding board, I think,' I answered. Byron didn't need to know that, if anything, this visit had confused things further: he didn't need to know that salted fucking caramel would be haunting my dreams.

Growing up with a super-dominant alpha mother, I was used to alphas calling the shots, and their omega following behind. I'd been fantasising about a pack for *years*, always assuming that, if it ever happened, it would be Tristan who found the other members.

Musing about my parents' pack, I wondered if they had it wrong. Maybe it shouldn't have been my alpha mother calling the shots. Maybe my omega mum should have been the one making decisions about the members of her pack.

'Seb,' Byron started, pulling me out of that train of thought. 'Rose.'

I glanced up at him. 'Will you tell her that I'm not a beta?'

'No,' he said, flushing slightly; I assumed it was with remembered shame. 'Not if you don't want me to. I just … I don't want either of you to get hurt.'

I studied him. There was genuine concern in his expression, and sadness in his eyes.

I loved my omega mum. I loved joking with her and listening to her talk about her latest inventions. She was the most permissive of all my parents, and the one who had never made me feel *less* about my choices.

But I couldn't be in the same room as her. Literally. Our relationship was largely conducted over video calls and messages, and when I was at home, I couldn't step foot in her room, because omegas *never* had complementary scents. To others, my mother smelled like just-baked cake – delicious, comforting, and warm.

But to me, she smelled so sweet it made me want to gag, with an edge of too-burned sugar.

Scents weren't real. Byron didn't *really* smell like salted caramel, in the same way Tristan didn't *really* smell like vanilla, and I didn't *really* smell like cherry. Other people's pheromone receptors just interpreted us to smell that way. If two people were compatible, then they smelled like something the other couldn't live without. But if they weren't a good match, they each smelled less pleasant to the other. It was the basis of how packs were formed, or not. The warring scents of omegas ensured that we were evenly distributed across packs, and meant alphas couldn't collect us like living dolls.

I shouldn't have even *liked* Rose. She should have made my hackles rise.

I wanted to rub my cheek all over her instead. I wanted to lick her skin until she was writhing.

I couldn't explain my need to touch her, to bury my face in her neck. I couldn't explain the pull in my chest when I saw her. But I knew that I was living on borrowed time. I knew that it couldn't go further, because our scents wouldn't be complementary. When I dreamed of a pack, it hurt more than it should have to know that Rose could never be part of it.

But *she* didn't know that, and I couldn't bring myself to tell her, because I *needed* to be close to her. It was selfish and cowardly and I hated myself for it, but I was going to draw it out as long as I could, and stay close to her for as long as possible before it all fell apart.

And what about Byron then?

His loyalty would be to Rose. He liked me, and I suspected he would probably bend me over a table if given half a chance, but he was *obsessed* with Rose. He already had an omega, and I already had an alpha. He couldn't be pack any more than Rose could.

'I know,' I said at last, my stomach twisting. 'I just can't … I just can't leave her alone. I know she'll hate me for it in the end, but it's worth it. Any time with her is worth it.'

Byron didn't answer, but his brows drew together.

'It's late.' I stood and made for the door. 'Thanks, Byron.'

'Seb –'

'I'll use scent canceller once I'm outside, don't worry.' I forced a smile. 'No one else will scent you.'

His frown deepened. He opened his mouth as if to respond, but I closed the door.

I took a deep breath in the corridor, the sweetness of his scent coating my tongue. Now that I was outside, I could properly catalogue its effect on me: the warmth spreading through my body, the goosebumps on my skin, the pleasant ache of arousal building deep inside. I didn't want to get rid of his scent; I wanted it to cling to me for days, wanted to drink it, wanted to fucking *roll* in it.

But I couldn't do any of that, so I pulled my spray from my pocket with a sigh, taking one last mouthful of Byron Griffiths before coating myself in cancellers. When all I could scent was their metallic aftertaste, I walked back to our apartment.

Tristan was waiting for me. He wasn't pretending to read, or scroll his phone, or watch TV; he just sat on our couch, his back painfully straight, an expression on his face I'd never seen before.

Guilt.

'You did it on purpose, then,' I said dully.

'I should never have thought you wouldn't notice,' he answered evenly.

'*Why*, Tris?' I tugged angrily on the hem of my shirt. 'Why on earth would you *do* that? Why could you possibly want her to slick in public? And why would you put *both* of us in danger like that?'

'Neither of you were in danger,' he said. 'Byron Griffiths has a white knight streak wider than the Pacific fucking Ocean, and he'd lose a limb before he let Rose stub her toe. If anyone tried to hurt *you*, I wouldn't be held accountable for my actions. Plus, I'd made … contingencies. You were both perfectly safe.'

'Contingencies?' I frowned at him. 'What …' I trailed off. I'd noticed the alphas dressed in black – who wouldn't? – but I hadn't thought anything of it. 'You hired security?'

'Specialists from the APF,' he confirmed. 'Alphas trained to protect omegas and diffuse difficult situations. I also asked Pravin and Marco to keep their eyes on Rose, if, for some reason, myself, Byron, and the security alphas couldn't get to her first. And all of that was on the slim chance that firstly, Rose's scent was complementary to anybody in that room, and secondly, that they were unable to control themselves upon scenting her.'

I rubbed my temples. 'That doesn't answer *why*, Tristan.'

He studied me, his expression intense. 'I can't tell you why.'

'You can't tell me why,' I repeated slowly. '*You*, who tell me *everything*, literally *everything*, including some things I'd be totally fine *not* knowing. *You* can't tell me why.'

'Exactly.'

'And you're *telling* me that you can't tell me.'

He gave me a look, and I realised.

He wanted me to work it out.

It didn't take me long, because there were so few things it could be. I strode to him, splaying my hand over his chest to push him down so I could straddle him. He flicked an app on his phone to turn some music on over the Bluetooth speakers; once the volume increased, I put my mouth to his ear.

'The Revels.'

His hand settled on my hip. 'The fact you're not running this country is criminal.'

'Don't try to turn my head with compliments,' I said tersely. 'I'm so angry with you, Tris.' I lowered my mouth again. 'What did they ask you to do?

In answer, he tapped something out on his phone.

Compromise the omega.

He deleted the words as soon as I'd read them, but I'd already turned cold. It could mean oh-so-many things. *Compromise* was nebulous in itself, but –

'Which omega?' Tristan whispered, his free hand tightening on my hip. 'I couldn't know. But I couldn't *ask*, either, because I could have been volunteering information *they* didn't know. We've been so careful – *you've* been so careful – but I have no idea how closely they're watching, Seb.'

'So you compromised us both, just in case,' I murmured. 'Made us vulnerable together.'

'Not truly vulnerable,' he insisted. 'I would *never* leave you in danger, *never*. I was ninety-nine percent sure about Griffiths, but if he – and the security alphas – didn't rise to the occasion, I could have taken Rose with us, too.'

'And then what?' I grabbed a handful of his hair; he groaned, tipping his head back. His lovely green eyes darkened as they fixed on mine. 'I guarantee you that Rose just spent a good half-hour in the company of her favourite vibrator. If you'd carried *both* of us out of the library, then what?'

He gave a one-shouldered shrug, an action which had always looked unfairly sexy on him. 'You would have either fucked it out or scented each other and lost interest immediately.'

I let go of him in surprise. 'You'd let me fuck her?'

'*Let* you?' He scoffed. 'I'm not that kind of alpha, Seb. You know that. Your body is your own. Until I bite you, at least. I don't know how I'll deal with it then, though I'll try not to be an asshole about it.' His fingers stroked circles on my waist.

I frowned. 'Do *you* want to fuck her?'

He paused, which was telling. 'I'm not sure,' he said at last, which was a very definite *yes*, because in all the years I'd known him, the only answer to that question in relation to someone other than me had been an absolute, immediate, and heartfelt *fuck, no*. 'But it's really up to Rose, isn't it? And it wasn't my throat she stuck her tongue down.'

I inhaled, digesting that. 'I'm *so* angry with you.'

'I know.'

'I told Byron.'

He passed a hand over his eyes. 'Is that where you went?'

I opted for honesty, though I wasn't sure he strictly deserved it. 'I went into his room.'

His lips parted in surprise, then he swallowed. 'And?' he said, barely a whisper.

'Our scents are complementary.'

His hands tightened on my hips, as if he couldn't help himself, as if he needed to hold me tighter. 'And did you like it?'

I fucking loved it. 'Yes.'

'So he and I –'

'Could be complementary, too.' I paused. 'But he's ass over head in love with Rose.'

'Mmm.' Tristan shifted beneath me. 'I wonder if he knows that.'

'If he didn't before, I expect he'll realise after tonight.' I paused. 'What now?'

'You mean *right* now?' he said, gently teasing. I could feel him shift beneath me, and I knew he was trying to lighten the mood.

Unfortunately for him, anger was burning hot in my stomach, and there was zero chance I was going to let him quench it with sex. I took his chin in my hand, forcing him to look at me. 'Tristan, I need you to know that this is our first fight. I love you, but you have to understand that I'm serious. You manipulated us. No matter your *contingencies*, you still put Rose in danger. You put *me* in danger. What if *I'd* slicked and someone noticed? It would have blown *years* of cover. If you pull something like this again, I might not forgive it.'

After six years together, we sometimes took each other for granted. Not in a bad way – I didn't think – but rather we just *assumed* that we'd always be together, that there was nothing we couldn't get through. We'd squabbled over silly things before – what to binge watch next, usually – but this was different. It was a betrayal of my trust, regardless of whether there'd been danger, too.

His hands relaxed their hold on my hips. 'I understand,' he said quietly, his expression serious. 'What do you need from me?'

'I'm going to study.' I slid off his lap. 'I'll be in the nest. I think I'll sleep there tonight.'

His face fell. That made it sink home; we hadn't spent a night apart the entire time we'd been together.

He bit his lip as I headed for the nest, but he didn't try to convince me otherwise.

My nest was little more than a separate bedroom. Tristan had asked me what I'd wanted it to look like, so I'd dutifully picked out some things online, and I usually half-heartedly rearranged them in the days before a heat spike. Sometimes, it made my chest feel hollow that I didn't have more of a connection to it, as if I were somehow being an omega *wrong*.

The low bed took up almost all the floor space, canopied by diaphanous cloth of silver. Tiny fairy lights stretched from the middle of the ceiling to all four bed posts, and more fell in gentle arcs across the walls. The bed was covered in the softest royal blue coverlet Tristan's money could buy, and cushions of blue and silver – all soft, none hard or scratchy or rough – were piled at the bed head.

I'd never spent the night in here before, because I'd never had a heat; I'd barely spent an *hour*. When I'd realised that my designation was changing, I'd taken every heat suppressant I could get my hands on. But I'd revealed late, and I'd been so surprised – and so *scared*. I didn't know *how* to be an omega; I'd always been a beta. And that had been enough to manage, to be honest. I didn't know what to do with heats, or scent marking, or biting and bonding, or the urge to be fucked into the floor. It had all been new, all unfamiliar, all *terrifying*, and I had still been fresh to university and had just found the love of my life.

I didn't want being an omega to ruin all that.

Which was *without* considering all the horror stories I'd read about male omegas, and the lengths that some packs would go to get their hands on one.

The internet really was the worst, sometimes.

So I'd suppressed my designation, both chemically and mentally, refused Tristan's gentle suggestion to register myself, and thrown my energy into pretending that nothing had changed, that I was still a beta who dealt with the occasional complication of a pesky heat spike. A beta with a *really* good nose, a beta who craved my alpha like I did food and water.

But it was hard to keep pretending in my nest.

I smoothed my hands over the coverlet, shivering at the softness against my palms. Without thinking too much about it, I pulled my shirt over my head and threw myself down.

I wondered whether Rose would like my nest.

I wondered whether she had one of her own.

I pulled my phone from my pocket and called her.

'Sebastian?' she answered, her voice unsure. We hadn't spoken since the dance – since the *kiss*.

'Rosebud. What's your favourite colour?'

'I …' She trailed off, evidently thinking about it. 'I'm not sure that I have one.'

'Col*ours*, then.'

'Um. Green? Pink, maybe? And blue. Oh, red.' She huffed a tiny laugh. 'I think I like all of them.'

'That is supremely unhelpful,' I drawled. 'What colours make you feel calm?'

'Blue, I think. And green. Like, dark greens. Golds? Ocean colours.'

'Ocean colours.' I looked around the nest. I could do ocean colours; I was already halfway there.

'Why do you ask?'

I smiled. 'No reason.'

There was a short silence. 'Seb,' she said tentatively. 'Are we going to talk about what happened?'

'I'd rather talk about something else.'

'Oh,' she said, and I could hear the hurt in her voice. 'Okay. Did you have something in mind?'

'Yes, Rosebud, I do,' I purred. 'When are we doing it again?'

◇◇◇

It wasn't until hours later, when I was lying in my nest, the fairy lights casting a soft glow across the bed, that it occurred to me – I'd never asked Tristan why the Revels had asked him to do it.

TRISTAN

IT TOOK ABOUT A WEEK for things to return to normal between Sebastian and me. After the first night spent in his nest, he came back to our bed, but things were strained for the first few days. He didn't talk about it again, and I didn't volunteer to start. Even when the tension between us had eased, I wasn't sure that he forgave me; it was more that he couldn't hold a grudge any longer than that. My golden love was too good-natured.

He clearly hadn't told Rose; her manner towards me didn't change. She treated me as she had before: with nervous warmth.

Something had changed between her and Byron, though. She went bright pink every time he opened his mouth, and his grey eyes went dark with heat every time he looked at her.

And he, clearly, *did* know what I'd done.

He didn't speak to me for days; not until he was standing behind me in the dinner line, Rose and Sebastian safely tucked into seats at the end of a table, deep in a teasing argument about a contestant on a reality TV show.

'I can't believe you did that,' Byron said, his voice low.

Despite myself, I stiffened. No matter how comfortable I was in my own strength, knowing that Byron Griffiths was looming behind me, *angry*, wasn't easy. 'And what, exactly, did I do?' I said flatly.

'Risked the safety of two people you had no right to risk.'

I turned and looked him in the eye, watching them darken like a storm. 'I understand that you're angry about Rose, and I can't take exception to that. But you have *nothing* to do with my relationship with Sebastian. Take your outrage elsewhere, because I don't want it.'

He studied me evenly. 'You really are something, Tristan Grace.'

Unaccountably, my stomach twisted into an uncomfortable knot. I couldn't easily identify the feeling – was it guilt? Shame? – but I knew it wasn't good.

A moment later, I was doubling down. I could tell him, I supposed, explain everything I'd done to make sure there had been no risk – but why would I care what he thought about me? He wasn't Sebastian. In a few years, he'd be nothing but a handsome memory.

I raised a disdainful eyebrow and turned away. It didn't matter what he thought. Sebastian and Rose had always been safe, and the return for these few weeks of discomfort would be membership to the Revels, and Sebastian winning the Banksia Prize.

Byron didn't say another word. When we walked back to the table, each with two plates in hand, he fell into step beside me, but it was for show; he didn't want Rose to know that something was wrong. It wasn't hard for either of us to pretend, because we'd never been overly chatty anyway. All he had to do was hide his repulsion for me, and Rose would never know the difference.

I was more worried about the attraction between Rose and Sebastian. Sebastian knew it couldn't last, but Rose didn't; I could tell he was trying to draw it out for as long as possible. I had a strong suspicion that the length of time would only make it worse when it came to an end, but Sebastian's choices were his own. When we studied together, Rose practically perched on his lap. In class, Sebastian dragged his desk so close to hers that their knees touched. Neither of them paid much attention to Heathcote, too busy messaging and biting back smiles at secret jokes.

I took copious notes and shared them after class without comment.

Heathcote would have been a good teacher, if he weren't a bigot. He was knowledgeable and passionate, and although I'd studied some anthropology as part of my undergraduate degree, he expanded on what I knew and made it far more interesting than my other teachers had.

I wondered if that was how he'd gotten away with his bias for so long. Most of the students at Banksia were alphas because most of the students at *university* were alphas. How many alphas would even *notice* Heathcote's comments? And how many of them would *say* something?

I despised him, but I learned a lot.

Byron's cold shoulder continued as we finalised and submitted our second assessments. Sebastian had been pushing himself in his spare time, making up for his distractedness in class, spending long hours frowning at his laptop in an effort to make sure he got the top mark this time.

After he submitted his essay, he promptly fell asleep on the couch, his brow free from worry for the first time in weeks. I covered him in a blanket, then got a bottle of water and a plate of snacks for when he woke up. After brushing a kiss across his hair, I went for a walk.

A small cluster of students stood on the main staircase, talking. I knew one – a second-year, Jun.

He waved me over. 'They're planning a scent party.'

I stared at him. I'd heard the rumours, of course – Sebastian was unnaturally good at uncovering gossip – but I hadn't really thought they'd risk throwing one; scent parties were *very* illegal in every state and territory except the ACT. There were federal laws against large groups of alphas gathering together, but the ACT local government squirmed around them by hosting the parties at official government venues and terming them *sporting events*. In other states, they were invite-only and held in warehouses or shitty bars, and anyone attending risked eye-watering fines and a jail term. Sebastian had encouraged me to drive to Canberra to attend one, but I'd always decided against it.

He was my pack. I didn't need to find anyone else.

'Will you go?' I said to Jun.

He shrugged. 'Of course. Apparently Banksia hasn't held one for six years – the old Dean was a legal academic, and there wasn't much leniency. Carla Griffiths seems more ... reasonable.'

'Hmm.' I adjusted my shirt. 'Where will it be held?'

'In the maze. A week from now.'

I studied him. Jun was handsome, tall and wiry. 'Do you want to find a pack here?'

He shrugged again. 'Definitely. Don't you?'

When I returned from my walk, Sebastian was waiting.

'You *have* to go,' he said, the moment I walked through the door. I rolled my eyes, fishing the handful of lemon myrtle leaves from my pocket and putting them in a tin for him. 'It's your chance, alpha.'

'I already have everything I need.'

It was his turn to roll his eyes. '*Tris.*' He bounced over and threw his arms around my neck. 'You need another alpha for *me*. If I ever go through a heat, one knot won't be enough.'

'I'd manage,' I said stubbornly. Part of me suspected he was right, and part of me *hated* the notion of Sebastian needing someone else.

'You're amazing, babe, but you're not a god,' he said practically. '*Please* go to the scent party. It would be incredible if you found someone here.' He paused, sucking his bottom lip between his teeth. 'Maybe I could go off my suppressants one day.'

I shook my head at the blatant manipulation, smiling; for all his talk of babies, Sebastian would need time – and probably some therapy – before he willingly went off his heat suppressants. Even so, the thought of him being in heat was more tempting than it should have been. I loved it when he was desperate and begging, and the thought of him slippery with heat-slick and ripe for breeding was my every fantasy come true.

'I'll think about it,' I said, and I did.

✧✧✧

Three days later, I was *still* thinking about it as we ate lunch in the dining hall. Sebastian and Rose were scrolling through her social media feed, their heads close together, murmuring to each other and occasionally breaking into peals of laughter. Byron's eyes were on his eReader; he was eating one-handed so he could tap to the next page with the other. I had my laptop open and was skimming articles about omega scents in medical journals.

A notification popped up on my screen.

I clicked into it, and felt my lips curl up. Heathcote had marked our second assessments in record time, and I was satisfied to see a comment reading *Second in cohort – well done* at the end of my essay.

Sebastian let out a loud *whoop* as he scrolled his phone, making everyone in the dining hall look across at us. When they saw it was him, their frowns smoothed out.

He had that effect on people.

'First?' I said wryly.

He nodded. 'Ninety-eight,' he said, which was impressive, even for Sebastian.

Rose was silent as she scrolled her own phone; Byron fished his from a pocket and did the same, giving a quiet, satisfied rumble a moment later. He didn't seem inclined to share his grade, so I did my own investigating, and a moment later, I was in his profile in the student administration system.

Ninety.

I blinked at my laptop screen. I'd known that he was smart, but I didn't think he'd be quite *that* good, coming from a completely different undergraduate discipline.

Rose was still frowning at her phone, so I clicked to view her grades.

Fifty-two.

I frowned at my screen. *There's no way.*

'You okay?' Byron murmured to her.

I looked up in time to catch Rose forcing a smile. 'All good,' she said with false cheeriness. 'It isn't what I wanted, but it's not too bad.'

Curiosity got the better of me. I clicked into the learning system, then brought up Rose's essay and comments.

Weak argument. Awkward phrasing. Poorly supported. Needs fleshing out. Citation?

I read her essay. I picked up my coffee cup, drained it, then read it again.

It was no different to mine. We'd used the same sources and had similar arguments. I'd used one extra source to support one of my points, but her writing was stronger. She didn't *need* the extra source to demonstrate her hypothesis.

In no world was it an essay that deserved a barely-pass mark.

Anger simmered low in my stomach. I checked James' essay, then Alessia's. Their marks were undeservedly low, too, though not as low as Rose's.

Heathcote was still targeting them. Sebastian had escaped because Heathcote knew I'd speak up if I noticed anything unfair about his grades.

But the others didn't have the benefit of an alpha's public protection.

I was so angry my vision blurred, wisps of white creeping into the edges of my perception as a rut threatened to break through my suppressants. I inhaled and exhaled slowly, forcing myself to be calm. When I could blink away the white, I clicked back into Rose's essay and re-read Heathcote's parting shot.

You should seriously consider whether you deserve your place here.

I should have been celebrating. That mark would knock Rose out of consideration for any award; the threat to Sebastian would be gone.

This was what I'd *wanted*.

Wasn't it?

I *wanted* Sebastian to get what *he* wanted. I wanted him to get the prize he coveted. But I'd imagined him getting it through well-deserved marks and my own influence, not because a bigoted professor committed academic misconduct.

This could lead to the result I'd wanted, but it wasn't *right*.

I caught Byron's eye and stood. 'There's something I need to do.'

He glanced at Sebastian and nodded. He might have hated me, but he knew what I was asking. He'd stay close to Sebastian until I got back.

I kissed the top of my omega's head. 'I just remembered something. Stay with Rose, handsome,' I murmured, too softly for her to hear. 'Get her a hot drink, yeah? Something sweet.'

Sebastian frowned at me, but nodded. I pressed one last kiss to his hair and strode from the dining hall, my hands curled into fists at my side.

Banksia's administration office was on the ground floor in the south wing, next to a cavernous room that held two grand pianos. The office was much smaller, with a window at the front for students.

The woman working closest to the window looked to be in her mid-thirties, blonde-haired and blue-eyed with curls even wilder than my own escaping her bun. She was wearing so much scent canceller that my nose prickled, and she had a quiet command that screamed *alpha*. When she caught my eye, she gave me a warm smile. 'Hi there. What can we do for you?'

'I need some advice.'

'Of course.'

I lowered my voice. 'Anonymous marking is SECU policy, right? And it's not any different at Banksia? I need to know what to do if I suspect a teacher isn't doing it.'

Her smile dropped. She studied my face, her expression serious. 'Do you have evidence to support your suspicion?'

'I believe so.'

She glanced back at her office, then leaned forward. 'You're a first year, yes? The *Origins* course?' I nodded, and her expression turned hard. 'I'll get you the form.'

She turned away to rifle through a drawer, then came back with a handful of paper. 'This is the complaint form. If you search the website, you'll find an online version, too. It's entirely anonymous. Fill it out, give as much support to your suspicions as you can, and either drop it into the box over there –' she gestured to an ancient-looking wooden box bolted to the wall behind me '– or submit via the online portal. It would help,' she said slowly, 'if there was more than one complaint. When we have a submission, we go back through the records to check whether anything similar has occurred in the past. Repeated complaints can see swift … action.'

'Thank you,' I said quietly. 'I can think of a few other people who might have something to say.'

She lowered her voice again. 'There's something else you can do. Something that will guarantee a response.'

Her lips were slightly twisted, and I wondered if betas and omegas were the only ones Heathcote targeted. Universities were famous for their bizarre hierarchies, and support staff were usually at the bottom of the power pile. 'What's that?' I asked.

'If you were happy putting your name to it, you could email the Dean and copy in the Banksia board. There'd be no way they could ignore it, then.'

'Do you think they would? Ignore it? The complaint form, I mean.'

She pursed her lips. 'The old Dean did.'

Byron didn't strike me as the kind of person raised by a woman who would ignore an injustice, but I might have misread him. 'I'll do that. Thanks.'

'Just ... be careful,' the woman said seriously. 'The world of academia is small, and any one of our teaching staff has the power to make things ... difficult ... in the real world. If you put your name to the complaint, there could be ... repercussions.' She paused. 'Did you want to specialise in anthropology or archaeology? The lecturer in question is quite well-known.'

I looked down at the complaint form. I understood what she was telling me: I might have a win here, cocooned by process and bureaucracy, but outside Banksia, Heathcote would have the power to affect my future career – or perhaps even end it before it ever began.

I'd *loved* my undergraduate archaeology degree. Being on digs were some of the happiest moments of my entire life, and Sebastian wasn't the only one who wanted to do further research. If I did this, Heathcote could seriously complicate the plans I'd had for my own higher-degree study and the profession I'd coveted for years.

I thought about Rose's forced smile. *You should seriously consider whether you deserve your place here.*

Fuck. That.

'No,' I said. 'I'll be fine. This is worth the risk.'

The woman nodded. 'Then send the email as soon as you can. You could copy in the administration office email address, too. For our records.'

I nodded, understanding her subtext. An email to the Dean and the board might go missing or be overlooked. An email to the administrative office, where multiple people had access to it, could forward it, and save its content? That would be harder to *overlook*.

This woman was on my side, and it was a nice feeling.

'I'll send it today,' I said. 'Thank you. Truly.'

She nodded. 'Universities are odd places,' she mused. 'They're like their own little worlds, with their own rules. Sometimes, people forget there's a whole universe outside them, and the power goes to their heads.' She smiled at me again. 'It isn't real life here. It's good to remember that.'

I thought about her words as I headed for the First Year Library to draft my email.

Once it had left my outbox, I started my next project – but it wasn't study.

I clicked into an article about Heathcote winning his high school's History medal. Within minutes, I had his academic records, his family details, his early medical records – and I was deep into an archived exchange on social media where one party seemed to be heavily implying that Heathcote had been implicated in contract cheating.

I smiled.

If there was a chance Heathcote could threaten my future, then I'd be ready for it.

ROSE

'How has your week been, darling?'

My mother's voice was comforting. It felt like warm hugs and safe places, like cosy winter mornings and kisses on the forehead.

'It, um –' I faltered.

I was trying not to be dramatic, but I hadn't had a week this bad in quite some time.

Fifty-two.

The thing was, it was a pass mark. It was fine. Thousands of students would respond to a mark of fifty-two with nothing more than a relieved sigh. They'd skim through their comments and put the entire thing from their minds, because who cared? It was a pass.

But before this, my lowest mark – *ever* – had been eighty-three.

I was a high achiever. It was the cornerstone of my personality. If I wasn't that, then I didn't know who I was.

Moreover, the conditions of my scholarship depended on me getting higher marks than that. A *lot* higher.

I cleared my throat and tried again. 'It hasn't been the best week.'

'Are you safe?' Mum said immediately. I could hear the concern in her voice, and a rustle of movement, as if she'd just sat up straight.

'I'm safe.' I cleared my throat again. 'I, um, just got a bad mark on an essay.'

'Oh, little love.' Mum didn't tell me it was silly; she knew how much it meant to me. 'Do you know what happened?'

I'd combed through the comments so thoroughly it felt as if they'd been tattooed on my brain. *You should seriously consider whether you deserve your place here.* 'Ah. I ... um. Needed more sources. My argument wasn't strong enough. And my writing was poor.'

I could almost *hear* my mum frown. 'You've never written poorly in your entire life, Rosie.'

My parents were both primary school teachers. They'd encouraged my interests from an early age and read every essay I wrote during my school years. They only stopped during my undergraduate degree because my dad declared *you've bypassed me, darling. I can't keep up.*

'I, um. I must have messed this one up.'

'Okay.' Mum was quiet for a moment. 'Would you like us to look it over?'

It was kind of her to offer, but I didn't think it would help anything. I was so angry at Heathcote – and angry at *myself* – that I wanted to scream. 'No, that's okay. I'll just … I'll just do better next time.'

Mum and I chatted for a few minutes; my dad hollered *hullo* from the background. I imagined him sitting at their kitchen table, doing a sudoku. The thought made my chest tight.

I missed them, I realised. I'd been so caught up with Banksia House that I hadn't thought much about home, and I hadn't known how much I'd needed to hear their voices.

Mum told me she loved me, and I told her the same; I hung up and slumped on my bed, staring up at the ceiling.

I'll just do better next time, I'd told mum, but I was finding it difficult to concentrate, my confidence shot to pieces by Heathcote's comments.

You should seriously consider whether you deserve your place here.

My phone buzzed. I ignored it at first, but the buzzing continued. I answered it listlessly. 'Why can't you text like everyone else?'

'Rude,' Sebastian said. 'And I've sent you like, ten texts now, Rosebud, and some super cute cat videos and a collection of pretty good history memes, and you haven't even *seen* them. Calling is a last resort.'

'Seb, I saw you three hours ago.'

'Three hours is too long. Come study with me.'

'I …' I closed my eyes. 'I don't think I can.'

'Which is exactly why you *need* to,' Sebastian said ruthlessly. I hadn't told him my mark, just that it was much lower than I'd been expecting. 'If you don't study, sweetness, then that asshole *wins*. And we don't let alphas win, do we?'

I made a non-committal sound. It certainly seemed like alphas won at most things.

'Okay, different approach. Rosebud, if you don't come out of your room in the next two minutes, I'm going to set off the fire alarm and you'll *have* to come out.'

I opened my eyes. 'You wouldn't.'

'My hand is on it. Literally.'

'They'll know it was you!'

He snorted. 'Do you think I care?' His voice dropped. 'Come on, Rose. We don't have to study if you don't want to. We could go for a walk instead.'

'A walk?'

'Outside,' he confirmed. 'Bring your hat; it's sunny. We'll take a page from Tristan's book and go say hello to some trees. It'll be character building, or something.'

I smiled despite myself. 'Okay.'

After we hung up, I took a moment to rake my hands through my hair and brush my teeth, before grabbing my hat and spraying myself with scent canceller. When I finished, Sebastian was waiting outside my room, his sunglasses hooked on the collar of his shirt. They dragged the material down, baring a mouthwatering stretch of skin.

He shot me a megawatt smile. 'Come on,' he said, taking my hand. 'Tris is waiting outside, but he promised he'd give us space. We can walk, just you and me.'

'You and me alone is dangerous,' I said without thinking.

'I think the term is *incendiary*,' Sebastian answered.

I flushed. He was so beautiful that it was hard to believe he really thought that, but he was here, with *me*, and his grip was firm around my fingers. He hooked a lock of hair behind my ear with his free hand, then rubbed his thumb across my cheekbone, as if he couldn't help himself.

'You know what else trees are good for?' he purred.

I shot him a startled glance. 'What?'

'Making out under.'

I swallowed, my mouth suddenly dry. 'Seb —'

'Don't worry, I'm joking. Unless you want to, in which case I'm as serious as a first-year politics student.'

I laughed.

'Honestly, Rose. Literally any time. *Any. Time.* You could knock on my door at three in the morning and I'd make out with you. Whenever, wherever.'

I knew I should have been more sensible, but the pull in my chest was so strong. I lifted his hand to my lips and brushed a kiss over his knuckles. 'It should be somewhere private next time.'

I looked up to find him staring at me, his blue eyes sparkling in the afternoon light. He leaned closer. 'You don't know what I'd do — what I'd *give* — to take you somewhere private, Rose,' he murmured. 'You don't know how badly I want you to myself, just for a little while.'

The pull in my chest turned painfully tight. 'Seb,' I said again, but it came out more like a breathy little whine.

He swallowed, then looked away. 'Come on, Rosebud. I promised trees, so trees are what you'll get.'

It wasn't until after we'd walked across the green beyond the manor's wide back doors that I noticed Tristan, trailing after us from a distance, seemingly engrossed in his phone. I knew better than that, though; whatever he was doing, one eye would always be on us.

If it was anyone else, I'd feel creeped out. But Tristan made me feel safe in the same way Byron did – as if neither of them would hesitate to leap between us and danger.

It was also difficult to forget the way he'd looked that day at the beach. I shivered, remembering the way he'd tugged his shirt over his head, my memory catching on the hard planes of his chest and the lines of muscle crossing his stomach.

Sebastian pulled me past the maze and into the line of trees to the south. They were all towering river red gums, covered in alien-looking white flowers. I breathed in deeply, filling my lungs with the scent of eucalyptus. It was cathartic, being able to smell something natural after being so long inside the manor, where the air was full of the artificial, metallic scent of cancellers. I picked up some fallen leaves and crushed them between my fingers, breathing more of it in.

'It's weird, isn't it?' Sebastian said musingly. 'Being without human scent. Sometimes I feel as if I've lost a limb. Even though our scents outside Banksia are technically muted from the blockers in the water, it's still … comforting … having an echo of them. But here, where there's nothing at all … It's almost eerie.'

'I didn't realise betas had such good noses,' I said absently.

I looked up in time to see a flush of pink spreading across his cheeks. 'I don't know how it is for others, but my sense of smell is pretty good. I've always been able to pick up scents easily.' He bit his lip, as if considering what to say next, then blurted out: 'I wish I could scent you.'

Fuck, I wished the same thing. Would Sebastian be sweet? A floral scent, perhaps? Or would he have a lifestyle scent, like leather? Or some other nature scent, like rain or freshly cut grass?

Whatever it was, I was sure it would be delicious.

But just like with Byron, if I scented Sebastian, this was over. The delicious anticipation would be replaced by biology. And if I didn't like his scent, I'd lose someone who made my stomach flutter. Someone who made me dream.

It would be difficult to be friends with Sebastian Worthy, knowing how he made my stomach tighten. I'd always remember what might have been, and it would colour what *was*.

I wasn't sure how I'd handle that.

'I wish it didn't matter,' I whispered.

He smiled. 'Does it have to?'

'What do you mean?'

His eyes were intent as his fingers found my chin, gently tilting my face up. I could have drowned in his gaze, in that limitless sapphire lapping at the sharp edges of my soul, soothing and caressing. Those eyes darkened as they searched my face, his pupils dilating in a way that made my instincts squirm.

Our pretty beta, they crooned.

Not ours, I reminded them, but it was hard to hold onto that as Sebastian's thumb traced my bottom lip.

'I think,' he said, a moment – a *lifetime* – later, 'that some things must be stronger than scent, stronger than biology. If you scent me, and I smell like a public pool bathroom, then I'll take blockers and use cancellers every fucking day, if it means I'll get to stay close to you.'

The air left my lungs. 'Fuck, Sebastian.' I rose up on my toes, as if I couldn't help myself, and I brushed my lips over his.

His hand cupped my face before moving back to bunch in my hair, knocking my hat to the ground. I wanted to crawl inside him, to feel him wrap around every jagged part of me, tending my hurts until all the rough edges were gone, smoothed beneath the force of his golden light. He nipped playfully at my bottom lip, then soothed the hurt with the tip of his tongue. An arrow of arousal shot through me. I was wearing slick-proof underwear again, for all the good it had done me last time; the memory of the dance made me pause, just for a moment.

'This is a bad idea,' I managed.

'Is it?' he murmured, and kissed me deeper, his free hand splaying across my back.

'No.' I took handfuls of his shirt and pulled him closer as his mouth moved on mine. 'It's not. It's the best idea I've ever had.'

He made a satisfied sound and pushed my back against a river red gum. His hands found my ass and I hooked my knees around his hips, letting him hold me up, pressing myself against the hardness I could feel between his legs.

He made a growling sound. 'You're dangerous, Rosebud.' He ground himself against me; pleasure sparked through my core.

'You don't seem scared,' I gasped.

He laughed. 'I'm terrified, mostly of fucking things up. But I'm not scared of *you*. Or of *this*.' He dragged his nose down my throat, leaving a trail of soft pleasure in his wake. 'I'd like to hear you scream, though.'

I groaned, because it was all too easy to imagine him working me into a state where I'd do just that. He brought one hand up to cup my breast, kneading and caressing me through the fabric of my shirt until my nipple was hard between his fingers. It felt so fucking *good* to be under his hands; I tipped my head back, baring my neck to him, and a moment later his teeth were raking across my scent gland.

I whimpered at the resulting spike of heat, squirming to get closer.

I wanted to feel his teeth. Wanted his canines to push down, to pierce, for my blood to well and spread across his tongue.

No, Rose, I told myself.

He dipped his head, running his nose over the skin just scored by his teeth. Omegas were extra sensitive there; he might as well have been toying with my clit. I squirmed again, pressing against him, trying to get friction where I needed it, and giving zero fucks that anyone inside the manor could look out at the trees and see me rubbing myself against my beta friend.

His fingers walked to my shirt buttons, and he made short work of the first three. His lips found the newly exposed skin; he pulled my blouse to the side so he could kiss the swell of my breasts, first one, then the other.

'I've been wondering a lot of things lately,' he murmured, his breath fanning over my chest. 'What your skin tastes like.' He licked a line across my breast, following the lace of my bra cup. 'What colour your nipples are.' I shuddered in pleasure as his mouth closed over one hard peak, sucking until wet heat spread over the lace. 'How sensitive they'll be.' My core clenched as one hand slid down my side, skirting the curve of my waist and hip before his fingers spread over my thigh. 'Exactly what you'll sound like as you come for me.'

I cried out at that – that, and because his fingertips had trailed over the skin of my inner thigh, then travelled out and around to find the swell of my ass. I was wearing a loose skirt, which posed no barrier to Sebastian; he shifted his stance, and a moment later, I gasped as his fingers began toying with my underwear.

'Can I touch you?'

'*Please*,' I panted.

'And can I touch inside you?'

My body told us both how much it wanted that with a fresh trickle of slick. The magic of slick-proof clothing only stretched so far; Sebastian's pupils blew out as my perfume swirled around us.

'Sweet,' he ground out. 'I knew you'd smell sweet. But the eucalypt … I can't catch …' He shook his head, his expression almost desperate. 'What *is* that?'

I opened my mouth to tell him, but a shrill alarm cut through the air. I stared at him. 'I thought you didn't pull the fire alarm,' I said stupidly.

His blue eyes were dark and wild, his cheeks flushed. 'I didn't.'

I heard a noise and turned to the side to see Tristan jogging through the trees towards us. My face went hot as Sebastian relaxed his hold. Tristan pretended not to see as I straightened my skirt and buttoned my blouse, pretended that his beta hadn't just been about to push his fingers inside me in a public garden. 'It's a lockdown alarm,' he said, his voice low.

'Two quick whoop-whoops,' Sebastian said, his eyes widening. 'Fuck. That means –'

'A feral alpha,' I finished, because I'd memorised the Banksia House handbook, and the third chapter was entitled *On-Campus Safety*.

'I need to get you back inside,' Tristan said, his gaze travelling over Sebastian and me. 'We need a room with a lockable door.'

I looked back at Banksia manor. From here, it didn't look friendly. Its staring windows were full of shadows, its hallways ripe for stalking, leading to corners ready to help pin down prey.

Sebastian shook his head, his expression suggesting he was thinking along the same lines. 'What if the alpha is near the entrance?' He turned, looking over the garden. 'There's a shed that way. The map said it's used by the horticulture staff.'

Tristan's frown was sceptical. 'And if the alpha comes outside?'

'That's why you're here, Tris.' Sebastian grabbed my hand and tugged me through the trees as the alarm changed pitch, becoming more insistent.

The shed wasn't what I'd expected. For starters, it was more like a house, not a corrugated iron square. Second, it was unlocked, which seemed like an oversight, given that it was neatly packed with what looked to be top-of-the-line power tools.

Tristan ushered us inside, then closed the door, locking it with a satisfying *thunk*. 'Pull the blinds,' he murmured, and Sebastian and I hurried to obey as Tristan closed the door on the other side of the room. It looked to lead into a workshop, but I wasn't curious enough to confirm it. There was no lock, so Tristan dragged one of the cupboards in front of it, blocking us in.

Once he'd straightened, he cleared his throat. 'Rose, would you mind …?'

He held something out to me; it took me a moment to realise that it was scent-cancelling spray.

My face went red hot.

I needed the spray because I'd slicked – *while I was rubbing against his beta.*

I looked up at him. 'Please,' he said roughly. His pupils were blown out, and when I dropped my eyes, I could see his shorts were bulging at the crotch.

And it hit me that I'd locked myself in a room with an alpha – while I was damp with slick.

'Chocolate,' Sebastian blurted out, raking in a breath. 'Motherlicking *fuck*. Your scent is *chocolate*.'

'Dark chocolate,' Tristan agreed, his voice a deep rumble. 'Rich and sweet, with a hint of ...' He trailed off, inhaling – *breathing me in.* 'Fuck. Mint?'

'The heat alphas ... They couldn't agree,' I said, the words coming out unaccountably shy. 'Some thought it was mint, others citrus. One thought it was pistachio, another, cranberries.'

'I get raspberries,' Sebastian grated out. 'Sweet and tart and fucking *perfect.*'

I stared at him; I hadn't realised that his sense of smell would be good enough to detect the secondary hint in mine. I wasn't the only one; Tristan was looking at his beta with wide-eyed worry.

The alpha shook his head, as if in disbelief. 'The spray, Rose. Please.'

I took the spray and moved away from them, misting it liberally around my body, wishing I could shower and change my underwear. I turned away and, cheeks burning, sprayed beneath my skirt, coating the skin on my thighs, then made sure the scent glands on my neck and smaller scent points on my wrists were similarly covered. I moved to hand the spray back to Tristan, who, without a word, gave it to Sebastian.

I raked in a breath, but all I could scent was eucalyptus and the metallic tang of canceller. There was no hint of another scent at all, even a less potent beta one.

Or perhaps it was *me* Tristan was scenting – all over Sebastian.

I hadn't known that alphas could have self-control like this, not the kind that Tristan – and Byron – had. I'd thought they were all like the assholes who'd tried to force me to walk with them, ruled by hormones, dominance, and their ruts.

If those other alphas had found me out here, they wouldn't be handing me canceller and keeping a respectful distance.

The alarm increased in speed again, making the hairs on the back of my neck rise. 'They *still* haven't stopped the alpha?'

Tristan glanced at me. 'Have you ever seen a feral alpha?'

I shook my head.

Sebastian shivered. 'It's almost unbelievable. Their eyes go red as the blood vessels in them expand, and they can't see you, can't hear you. All they know is whatever caused their instincts to take over. An enemy, a threat … An omega.'

'Their strength is increased multiple times by a huge adrenalin rush,' Tristan continued, 'which also blocks pain receptors. If they start to fight, they usually just … keep on fighting. Their humanity is stripped away, and the only thing that remains is their alpha. The creature that lives beneath our skin.'

'Is that what Byron would have been like?'

I clapped my hands over my mouth almost before I'd finished the sentence, horrified, but Sebastian only looked thoughtful. 'It must have been,' he said. 'I mean, that's what happens, biologically speaking.' He glanced at Tristan as something occurred to him. 'Fuck, you don't think –'

'No,' Tristan answered calmly. 'Griffiths is in control. This isn't him.'

The thought hadn't even occurred to me; I couldn't imagine Byron like that. 'I didn't ... I didn't think you knew him that well,' I said tentatively.

Tristan peered through the gap between the blinds and the window. 'I don't. Not very well.' He turned and gave me a searching look. 'But I know this isn't him.'

There was respect in his tone, even though they'd seemed distant lately. I supposed that you didn't have to *like* someone to respect them, though it made some small, secret part of me sad they weren't better friends.

I wasn't really sure why.

Sebastian stumbled back from the window. 'Fuck, there's somebody out there.'

Tristan's back went ramrod straight. He pointed to the solid worktable in the middle of the room, its wooden top covered in tools. 'Under that, both of you.'

My feet were moving before my brain registered what he'd said, even though there was no hint of a bark in his tone. Tristan had probably never *needed* to bark; between his wealth-earned confidence and the dominance that poured from him like waves, I suspected people jumped to obey the faintest *hint* of a suggestion from him.

Sebastian and I dove under the table. It was closed in on three sides, and the tight space made me feel safer. I felt even better when Sebastian wrapped his arms around me.

A low, menacing growl came from outside.

Sebastian and I froze. It was one of the things I hated most about being an omega: my fight response was non-existent. It was freeze, flight, or nothing. My instincts weren't encouraging me to look around for a weapon; they were screaming that if I stayed still and quiet, the scary alpha outside might not see me, might not scent me, and might move on to terrorise someone else.

'I know you're in there, little omega,' the alpha growled, and I recognised the voice: Glynn, one of the men who'd tried to make me walk with them during the discipline mixers. 'Come out. Come to me.'

The outer door rattled as he tried the handle. I knew it was locked, but I wasn't sure how locks stood up against six-foot alphas running on black-out levels of adrenalin. Sebastian clutched me tighter, his breathing erratic.

I was struck with the oddest urge to purr.

I forced myself to swallow it down; omegas purred only for their pack. It would be mortifying if I made my little rumble and he pulled away.

I settled for splaying my hand over his rapidly beating heart.

The door shook as Glynn tested his strength against it. 'Come out, omega,' he crooned again, and I broke out in gooseflesh. It felt all kinds of wrong, him speaking that way. It was metal over metal, a knife against a bottle. The shiver skittering down my spine left a bad taste in my mouth. 'I know you're wanting, know you're hurting. I can smell it. I can make everything better. My knot is waiting just for you.'

Bile rose up my throat. There was no way in the world I wanted Glynn's dick anywhere near me, but the fact that he was clearly turned on by *my* scent made me wonder. If I'd scented him, would I want him back? Would my body decide that he was a good alpha, a good *match*, because he was physically strong and my instincts liked the way he smelled?

They couldn't have made a worse choice, and it scared me that it *might happen*. Not just to other omegas, but to *me*. What if I scented someone one day, they made me slick, and I ended up with a bond mark on my neck, never to escape – but they were unsuitable? Sexist, manipulative, controlling? Abusive? Violent?

Sebastian pulled me closer as I shivered again. 'It's all right, Rosebud,' he whispered. 'It will be all right.'

I wondered which of us he was trying to convince.

'*Come out!*' Glynn roared, and I was scrambling out from under the desk before I realised what I was doing – Sebastian's arm still tight around my waist as he moved with me – because that fucking alpha had *barked* at me.

Sebastian didn't let me go, keeping pace as I hurried towards the door, my mind blank of everything but the alpha's command. Somewhere inside, I was fuming, but the anger – and conscious thought – was buried so deep I couldn't touch it. When someone slid in front of me, I didn't understand what they were doing – the alpha had given me an *order*, and they needed to get out of my way – but a gentle hand gripped my shoulder, stopping me.

'You don't have to do that, omega.'

There was no bark in Tristan's voice, just a gentle calm that reset my brain. I stopped resisting – Sebastian paused at the same moment – and we stared at the locked door, at the rattling handle, and then I tipped my chin up to stare at the green-eyed alpha.

Tristan had broken Glynn's command simply by *speaking*.

'*Omega! Come out!*' Glynn roared again, but Tristan simply shook his head.

'You're safe here, omega,' he murmured, and I sighed, because *of course I was*. Who the fuck was going to challenge Tristan Grace?

His hand was a warm, comforting weight on my shoulder. He stroked Sebastian's cheek with the other. Sebastian was pale, and he leaned into Tristan's touch as if it was the only thing keeping him upright.

'I have you,' Tristan said. I didn't know which of us he was speaking to, but it didn't matter. My spine went soft and I lay my head on Sebastian's shoulder. 'You're safe.'

A sharp *crack* split the air, and the door began to splinter.

Tristan brushed a kiss over Sebastian's brow. 'Go back under the table, baby,' he said softly. 'Keep each other warm.'

I hadn't realised how cold I was until he said it. It was shock, the after-effect of a bark from a non-bonded alpha. Sebastian was shaking, so when we crawled back beneath the table to the sound of splintered wood hitting the floor, I wrapped myself around him as best I could, straddling his lap so I could link my arms and legs around his back.

An odd *pop* came from outside: once, then twice.

Sebastian gave a shuddering exhale. 'Finally,' he said hoarsely. 'That's a tranquiliser gun.'

'It's almost over,' Tristan murmured. He paced back and forth before the ruined door; light shone through from outside, bringing the scent of eucalyptus. The wood was heavily splintered, even on the inside, and it was impossible to tell whether Glynn had used his fists or something else against it. 'You've been so brave. Both of you. I'm so proud.'

It wasn't true – I was cowering under a table, for fuck's sake – but his words gave me a warm glow regardless.

Tristan's praise was downright dangerous.

Sebastian buried his face in my neck and breathed in. 'He must have caught your scent in the garden,' he whispered against my skin. 'I'm so fucking sorry, Rose.'

'Seb, it's not your fault,' I whispered back. '*He* lost control, not you. It mustn't have taken much to push him over – my scent would have been diffused when he caught it. If he loses control that easily, then he's not safe *anywhere*.'

He made a noncommittal noise.

There was another thud from outside, and someone gave a wordless shout. A few moments later, a knock sounded on the side of the building. 'Rosemary? Are you in there?'

'Is the alpha contained?' Tristan answered sharply.

'He's locked in the back of a wagon and headed for the nearest Alpha Retreat,' the voice responded, and I recognised it as Harry, the groundskeeper.

I disentangled myself from Sebastian, and we crawled out from under the table. I hadn't cared before, but now the sticky dust on my hands and knees made me feel disgusting. I wanted a hot bath, a blanket, and to drink a chai latte bigger than my head while I watched a trashy TV show.

'You okay?' I turned to see Sebastian studying me. He reached to tuck a lock of hair behind my ear with trembling fingers.

I exhaled. 'I think I need an omega moment.'

Sebastian forced a half-smile. 'Something warm and something sweet? I think I need a moment like that myself.'

'Let's get you both back to the manor,' Tristan said, and unlocked the splintered door.

A number of staff were outside, waiting. A woman strode towards me. I'd met her once before, but even if I'd never seen her, I'd recognise her stormy eyes, high cheekbones, and plush mouth.

'Ms. Morris,' Byron's mother said, her voice deep and calm, like her son's. 'Mr. Worthy. Mr. Grace. Were you hurt?'

I shook my head.

'They're both suffering from shock,' Tristan said. 'Glynn barked at them.'

Professor Griffiths' eyes widened as she took in Sebastian. 'I didn't realise barks affected betas so acutely.'

Sebastian forced another smile. 'I hadn't realised it myself.'

She gestured. 'The campus doctor is here. She can help –'

'I just want to go back to my room and have a shower,' Sebastian interjected. 'Please.'

Griffiths studied him, her brow creased. 'Of course. If that's what you need.'

'It is.' Sebastian turned to me. 'Rosebud. What's going to help you the most?'

I wiped my dirty palms on my skirt. 'A bath.'

Our dean nodded. 'All right. But I will insist you both visit the doctor later. I'd say it's just to satisfy my concern, but we also have a legal obligation to your safety.' Her eyes found mine. 'I'll need a report, too. But, given the situation, I'm happy to speak with Mr. Grace now, and leave yours until later today. Or tomorrow,' she added hastily, as Tristan bristled. 'Tomorrow morning will be fine. The faster we get it done,' she went on, lowering her voice, 'the faster we can expel him.'

It was the right thing to say; Tristan visibly relaxed, his shoulders rolling back. 'We'll come and see you tomorrow morning,' he said. 'I'll take them back now and come to your office once Sebastian is settled.'

It should have sounded condescending. But when he offered me his arm, I took it, leaning on him gladly, because it felt like caring, instead. I was shaky and my skin was clammy; I was still finding it difficult to catch my breath, and my stomach churned.

'You shouldn't be alone,' Tristan said tightly, and after a moment, I realised he was talking to me. 'Omegas can die of shock. You need to stay with someone.'

'She can stay with us,' Sebastian said.

'Baby,' Tristan sighed. 'I have to go back to the dean. If I leave you two alone, someone is going to end up in heat, and the next time you leave the apartment you'll have bonding bites on your necks.'

Blood rushed to my cheeks ... But he wasn't wrong.

Sebastian and I apart were measured, considered, smart. But together? We were reckless, impulsive. We'd proved it, barely ten minutes ago. If I wasn't an omega, and he wasn't a beta who already had an alpha, it wouldn't be a problem, but that wasn't the case. Our recklessness affected more than just ourselves.

I opened my mouth to say I'd ask Byron, but paused. Letting him into my space – or going into his – meant that he'd scent me, or I'd scent him, and everything would just be … over.

I wasn't sure I could deal with *that* on top of everything else that had happened today. And even though I had other friends, my omega wasn't keen on the idea of them in my room.

'I'll be okay,' I said, forcing a smile. 'I'm feeling okay. What if I called someone?'

Tristan frowned down at me. His green eyes were dark with some strong emotion as he considered me, but I couldn't read what it was. 'You'll text Sebastian, too,' he said at last, and it wasn't a question.

The hallways were deserted as they walked me back to my room. I leaned heavily on Tristan; his other arm was wrapped around Sebastian's shoulders. Sebastian seemed almost as affected as I was, and I wondered if he was having some kind of flashback to the first time he'd seen a feral alpha; his face was bloodless, and I could see him trembling. I was as reluctant to leave him as he seemed to leave me, but I knew that Tristan was right.

We couldn't be trusted together.

They waited until I locked my door before they left; we didn't say goodbye. I clicked every single lock into place and pushed a rolled-up towel along the bottom of the door; I even dragged the dining table and leaned it against the door to barricade myself inside for good measure. My air purifier was already set to high, but I turned on my scent diffusers as well, filling my room with a calming lavender blend.

I was still shaking with cold, so I ran myself a bath, using a thermometer to make sure the water wouldn't scald me. Between heat spikes and shock reactions like this one, omegas sometimes needed help to make sure they wouldn't lie in a bath that would either give them actual burns, or hypothermia.

Stripping off was the last thing I wanted to do – a wave of gooseflesh broke out across my skin when I unbuttoned my blouse – but I forced myself to do it anyway, leaving my fuzzy winter dressing gown by the side of the bath for afterwards, along with a pair of heavy-duty winter bed socks.

Sexy.

When the bath filled, I flicked off the tap and clambered in, unable to stop a moan when my shoulders sank beneath the water. I lay there for a moment, willing my body to warm before I reached for my phone.

I had several texts and a number of missed calls from Byron; he picked up immediately. 'Rose?' he said urgently. 'Are you okay?'

I sighed and put him on speaker, setting my phone on the side of the bath. 'I'm okay.'

'My mum told me what happened.' He paused. 'Are you with Sebastian?'

I couldn't stop flushing at that. 'No. I'm in my room. In the bath.'

He exhaled. 'How can I help?'

'Tristan didn't want me to be alone.' I bit my lip. 'I thought about asking you to come. Into my room, I mean. But if that happens … If you scent me …' I trailed off, my teeth worrying at my skin.

'I know,' he said gently. 'If we scent each other, and it's not complementary …' He was silent for a moment. 'But Rose … I caught enough of your scent the night of the party to know that I like it. It doesn't mean you'll like mine, but I can tell you right now that I wanted more.'

'More of my scent?'

'More of *you*,' he purred, and it heated me more thoroughly than the bath had done. 'More of *everything*.'

'Because I'm an omega.'

'Because you're *you*. I've known other omegas. Many of them. None of them ever made my alpha take notice in the way you do.'

I sighed again, melting against the side of the bath. 'Then what do we do?'

'Firstly, I'm going to bring you a chai latte and every dessert I can scrounge from the kitchen,' he said dryly. '*Okay* my ass; Sebastian just messaged to let me know you're in shock, little liar. I'll leave everything outside your door. Then, when you're ready, we can –' He faltered. 'I don't know. What usually happens in this situation?'

'I don't think this situation has a *usually*,' I answered.

'You're the historian. What did people do before the Unveiling?'

'They dated,' I said. 'They went to bars, or out for dinner or coffee, or they saw movies.'

'A movie night!' He sounded so enthusiastic that I couldn't help but smile. 'In my room, so that –'

'My scent won't be too strong, but I'll be able to scent you,' I finished.

'That sounds good. There's only one problem.'

I frowned. 'What is it?'

He laughed. 'What will we watch?'

BYRON

THE MIST WAS EVERYWHERE.

I froze. Fear closed my throat and seeped down my limbs. I couldn't move, couldn't speak, couldn't cry for help. I hated feeling so helpless – as an alpha, it was torture – but there was nothing I could do and no way that I could fight. The mist thickened at the edge of my sight, swirling inwards until all I could see was white.

Red disrupted the vision. 'Byron,' Tina whispered, emerging from the mist, her face covered in blood.

I sat up in bed, gasping for breath, shaking off the nightmare with a groan. It was the dream I hated the most, and the one that came most often. My body was on high alert, my skin tingling as my nerves fired, my alpha riding close to the surface, my instincts roaring.

Most alphas wouldn't think twice about the white mist. It was simply the way our vision clouded when we were in a rut, our sight narrowing to the person we were fucking or fighting. It was a survival response, allowing us to serve or protect, to cherish or damage.

But most alphas didn't know what I knew: that a rut was how an instinct blackout – going *feral* – started. It was indistinguishable from a rut; that was, until you couldn't stop falling into the white, and your conscious thought went with it.

If the general populace ever found out, the outcry would be instant and wide. Scent blockers wouldn't be the only thing in the water supply. Alphas would be permanently on rut suppressants.

The government had to know. They were the ones who funded the Alpha Retreats – where *at-risk* alphas were taken for recovery – and the APF. But the government was good at keeping secrets, and it wasn't as if most feral alphas came back to tell the tale.

Five percent was the number I'd been told. Five percent of alphas who descended into a state of pure instinct were rehabilitated completely back into society. Some larger number – twenty percent or so – had a partial return to their former lives, working or shopping or socialising in the outside world before returning to Retreats where they were monitored and cared for by APF doctors.

But the majority – around seventy-five percent – were termed *unrecoverable*. Seventy-five percent of feral alphas were hospitalised permanently, or until their hearts gave out under the pressure of their raging hormones, and they died.

Ruts are natural and needed, Dr. Ford had told me more than once, his voice gentle. *Ruts help an alpha serve an omega for the duration of their heat, a feat they would otherwise be unable to manage. Ruts help an alpha protect their pack from danger. Ruts, in themselves, are not the problem.*

An alpha had control during a rut. Their vision might narrow, but they knew what they were doing, who they were fucking or fighting, knew whether their hands were caressing or hurting. It was only when a rut turned into something else – when the alpha inside overrode humanity – that it became dangerous.

I didn't remember what I'd done when I'd blacked out. I had flashes occasionally, mostly when they changed my meds.

I rubbed my face with my hands. When Tristan had shoved his phone under my nose in the study room those few weeks ago, the screen showing my face contorted with rage – the grey eyes that came from my mother blank and empty, my fists covered in blood – I'd recoiled.

I'd looked like that. Like a fucking *monster.*

And I'd never stop hating myself for it.

I checked the clock; seven-thirty. It was Sunday, so I forced myself out of bed, trying to shake off the dream.

Tristan and I had a tacit agreement that he took the omegas to the dining hall by himself on Sundays, while I made my way to the staff wing and had breakfast with my parents. Today, I didn't feel like going *anywhere.* Seeing Rose would have grounded me, but I hated the thought of looking at her while I remembered the dream of Tina's face dripping blood.

And seeing my parents always made the past bubble to the surface.

Progress isn't linear, Dr. Ford reminded me.

My phone buzzed. I picked it up, half-hoping it was him. Somehow, he always knew exactly what to say.

The text was from Pravin. *Are you coming tonight?*

'Fuck,' I muttered. I'd been so focused on planning my movie night with Rose that I'd completely forgotten about the scent party.

My eyes flickered to the blister of scent blockers next to my bed. If I decided to go, I'd need to skip this morning's dose.

I dialled Dr. Ford.

He answered immediately, as he always did. 'Good morning, Byron.'

Did he ever sleep in? 'Hi, Dr. Ford.'

'I'm glad you called me. How are Rose and Sebastian recovering?'

'They seem to be fine. Mum made them both have follow-up appointments with the campus doctor, and she didn't have any concerns.'

'I'm glad to hear it.' He paused. 'Was there something you needed to talk about?'

I inhaled. 'There's a scent party tonight.'

He took a moment to answer. 'Ah.'

Scent parties were illegal, so I understood his wish to navigate carefully. 'I've been invited,' I added.

'I assume this conversation is to be kept between you and me?'

Some of the things we discussed – my general progress and Tina, mostly – were shared with a team of

APF doctors, and reports were sent to my parents, for the purpose of them offering more support when I needed it. But other things were entirely private. 'Yes, please. I haven't decided whether I'll tell mum yet.'

'I imagine that's a decision you're thinking seriously about.'

He was right, because I had no idea what mum would think. She'd ignored the commencement party – well, she'd helped set some of it up – but commencement parties weren't illegal. I didn't know how she'd respond to this one. 'Yes. I have been thinking about it.' *Before Rose mentioned a movie night and my priorities changed.* 'I've been thinking about whether … Whether I should attend.'

'What are the reasons to go?'

'I might catch a scent I like. I might have fun.' I dragged a hand through my hair. 'Fuck, I might be able to relax for five minutes.'

'And against?'

'I might catch a scent that I like,' I repeated dryly. 'I might have a fucking awful time. I might … I might …' I inhaled. 'I might lose control.'

'Do you think that's likely?'

I answered honestly. 'No.'

'I agree.' I heard a buzzing sound, and then the slurp of liquid meeting liquid, and I realised Dr. Ford was making himself a cup of coffee. *Fuck, now I wanted one.* 'From what you've told me, you're in full control, Byron.'

I fidgeted on the bed. 'I still worry about keeping it around the omegas.'

'I know you do. I won't tell you that it's not a legitimate concern. It's something a lot of alphas struggle with until they bond, including alphas who have never experienced instinct blackout. But scent parties are usually just for alphas, are they not?'

'Yes, they're just for alphas.'

'The omegas won't be present, then. Given that, what is the worst-case outcome?'

I raked my hand through my hair again. 'That I black out.'

'And what is the worst-case, *most likely* outcome?'

I sighed. 'That I go, I don't find a complementary scent, and am in bed before midnight, slightly more disappointed than I was before.'

'And the best-case scenario?'

'That I have a great time.'

'*And* that you find a complementary scent,' Dr. Ford added. His voice was warm. I had no idea about his personal life, but I found myself hoping that he had a large, loving pack who appreciated his gentleness. 'It's not an everyday occurrence, finding a complementary scent, but neither is it impossible.' He paused. 'I'm not going to give you advice about whether to go or not, Byron, because as we both know, scent parties are illegal, and I would be incredibly irresponsible if I didn't remind you of that. But I *do* think that you're in control, and that you've been in control for years now, and you deserve some time to relax a little bit. Remember not to drink or smoke on your rut suppressants, though,' he cautioned. 'Not because

I think you'd do something stupid, but because you'll probably fall asleep.'

'I promise you that I will not be doing either of those things.'

'Good. I'd hate for you to nod off, mid-party.' He paused. 'Is that what you needed? Did you want to talk it through further?'

I shook my head before remembering he couldn't see me. 'I'm good. Thanks. That's really helpful.' I glanced at the morning light coming through my curtains. 'I'd better go.'

'Breakfast with your parents,' he said. 'I hope your dad hasn't eaten all the bacon this time.'

I hung up, smiling, then texted Pravin.

Yeah, I wrote. *I'm coming.*

◇◇◇

I let myself into my parents' apartment, not bothering to knock.

Dad was sitting cross-legged on the lounge room floor, paper strewn around him. I took in the printed articles, photocopies of books, and – for some unholy reason – printed *web pages* scattered around the room. 'Fuck, dad, you've deforested an entire state for this.'

'As if you can talk, sticky tab king,' my mum said wryly, not lifting her eyes from her tablet. With one hand, she dug around on the couch next to her, then held something up, which I took – a new packet of sticky tabs in a rainbow of pastel colours.

'I tried the tablet, I really did,' my dad said absently, pushing his silvered hair back from his eyes. Even after thirty years in Australia, he still retained a soft Welsh accent. 'I just like paper, I'm afraid.'

The print outs were covered in highlighter and handwritten notes. 'Is this for the new book?'

He and my mother gave matching groans. 'Yes, but not the one you think,' dad said. 'Rita *suggested* that I make *The Light In His Eyes* a series.'

I frowned. 'But you said it was a standalone. You said you didn't want to write historical fiction again.'

'Apparently the publisher – and therefore my agent – would prefer to milk it for all it's worth. Thus, *this*.' Dad waved his hand at the paper-covered lounge room.

He'd spoken lightly, but I knew him well enough to notice the slight slump to his shoulders, which meant he was genuinely upset. I twisted my lips; he'd written three-quarters of a new sci-fi novel over the last few months, and his eyes had lit up every time he talked about it. 'I'm sorry, dad.'

'Not your burden to bear, B. But thank you.'

'How are Rose and Sebastian?' mum said, shifting the subject.

Well, Rose likes to call me every time she's in the bath now, and although we haven't had phone sex again, I think about the way she sounds when she comes every fucking night, and I know enough about her now to have a decent stab at answering her credit card security questions. And yesterday in the dining hall, Sebastian made toast and licked honey off his knife while holding eye contact with me, then asked what kind of sandwiches *I preferred, and did I like the* filling *or the* outside *better or did* I not mind, *and no, he was absolutely not talking about actual sandwiches. Rose and Sebastian are a danger to any human with a heartbeat and I'm currently spending every spare moment planning a movie night in the secret hope that I might actually get to kiss Rose for real. She told me she's kissed Sebastian twice now, and I am simultaneously turned on by it and so jealous I could die.*

I was obviously not going to say any of that to my mother, so instead I answered: 'I think they're fine.'

My mother looked up from her tablet screen. 'Hmm.'

'*Hmm* what?' I collapsed to sprawl in the only armchair not covered in dead trees.

'Just *hmm.*' Mum studied me for a moment, then changed tack. 'I got an interesting email the other day.'

I quirked an eyebrow. 'What kind of email?'

'The kind that my Executive Officer insisted I read immediately.' Mum turned the tablet around so that I could see the subject line and sender.

'Tristan sent you an email?' I said, bewildered, then took the tablet when she offered it.

And almost crushed the thing when my fingers began to curl into fists.

'Heathcote did *what?*' I snarled. '*Fifty-two? Rose?* Are you fucking *kidding* me?'

'Okay, Mr. Hyde, pipe down,' my mother said, completely unperturbed. 'So Tristan's concerns are legitimate, then.'

'Entirely. Rose couldn't get that kind of mark if she tried.' I scanned the email once more before I handed the tablet back, noting its dispassionate tone and the dates and times Tristan had provided for other notable incidents, along with the fact he'd copied in the Banksia House *board*.

Tristan Grace was apparently scared of nothing.

'I can verify everything Tristan says, though Rose didn't tell me she got fifty-two. Fuck, it must have been killing her.'

'You know her so well?'

I looked across to see that dad had stopped reading through an article and was studying me with a hopeful look. 'I, ah,' I started hesitantly. 'I know her well enough to know she's a high achiever. That isn't a mark she'd get under usual circumstances.'

'Then a re-mark it is.' Mum didn't sigh, though I knew how much extra work remarking an entire cohort would be, especially because there would need to be extra checks, and she'd have to manage Heathcote's reaction, along with complaints from students whose new mark might be worse than the first. She simply grabbed her laptop from the side of the couch and opened it. She liked reading on a tablet but refused to write on it; everyone in my family had their little quirks.

'So ... breakfast?' I queried. 'Or has dad already eaten all the bacon?'

'No, but only because we haven't cooked it yet,' my dad answered, going back to his article. 'Do you want some help?'

I tried to groan, but it turned into a laugh instead. *Sneaky fucker.* 'I'll remember this when I'm putting you both in a nursing home.'

Mum snorted. 'That was Tina's favourite threat,' she said, her voice at once fond, and very, very sad.

I fled to the kitchen before I could see her tear up.

I heard her sobs anyway, even over the sizzling of the frying pan. Dad was murmuring to her, and if I went back out there, I knew I'd see his arms around her, and mum crying for the daughter she missed so fucking much.

It was my fault, I knew. Mum could hold it together like a trooper until I was there. Because Tina and I had looked so similar – all dark hair and grey eyes and matching smiles – and we thought the same way, too. We loved the same TV shows, read the same books, played the same sports. There was only a year between us, after all.

We'd both revealed our designations far too early: Tina at fourteen and me at thirteen. I'd revealed a month after Tina, as if something in my body had kicked into overdrive, knowing I'd have to protect my omega sister. And I had, for years. No one fucked with Tina, because her scrap of a brother stood like a shadow behind her, always ready to bloody someone's nose with his fists.

Until.

Until. Until.

It didn't matter that it had been seven years ago. It could be seventy and the grief would still be there, lurking just below the surface, waiting for an opportunity to smash our hearts again, again, again. Tina simply wasn't the kind of person who *faded*. Even now, her voice was so sharp in my memory that she might have been standing beside me. *You don't cook bacon like that, B. Fuck, who raised you?*

I fried some eggs and got the hashbrowns out of the oven. By that time, mum had recovered enough to get the juice from the fridge while dad made me a coffee, going through the everyday motions as if they hadn't just broken open with grief.

'I have to tell you something, mum. But before I do, I want you to know that I think you should let it happen.'

She frowned at me, setting the salt and pepper on the table. 'That sounds ominous, B.'

'It's less ominous and more illegal. But I think … I think it could be a good thing for some of the students here.'

Her frown deepened. 'Okay. I'm listening.'

'There's going to be a scent party tonight,' I said. 'In the gardens. They're illegal —'

'Because of the Alpha Gathering Act,' my mother said, nodding. 'I know. But you want me to let it happen? Why?'

'Apparently, the old Dean was a stickler for the rules. But some people here want packs, and they won't be able to know who might suit them until *after* they leave Banksia House.'

'Why should I support my students forming packs? They're here to study.'

I shrugged. 'It would settle some of the alphas down, for starters. Allow them to make better informed choices, maybe. And it might be good for philanthropy.'

'Because people donate more money when they have fond memories of a place,' my father interjected, serving himself a larger-than-necessary portion of bacon.

Lucky I made extra; checkmate, dad. 'Imagine the endowments you could get if some of the students here packed up.'

'That's right. And it's ... It's so strange, being completely without human scent. I feel like I've got one hand always tied behind my back. One night without blockers would be ...' I trailed off, thinking about the right word. 'Freeing.'

'And what did Dr. Ford think about it?'

I shook my head wryly. My mum was too good. 'You know he wouldn't advise me either way about something like that. But he *did* say that he thought I was in full control.'

'Of course you are,' mum murmured. 'We're so proud of you, B.' She considered her eggs for a moment, pricking the yolks with her fork so that yellow-gold spilled across her plate. 'Fine. I'll let it happen – within reason. I'll ask for an extra security team tonight, and they *will* be in the outskirts of the garden and patrolling the halls. Any hint of discomfort from a beta student or Rosemary, and I pull the plug immediately. And there *will* be a curfew, depending on levels of rowdiness.'

'Thanks, mum,' I said, meaning it, sipping on my coffee.

'Will you go with Tristan?'

'Pravin, actually. Tristan and I aren't ... friends. We just kind of put up with each other.'

'That's a shame,' dad mused. 'Tina always said you'd need an alpha as strong as you are, so you could let down your guard every once in a while.'

This time when my mum cried, I wrapped my arm around her shoulder and let her tears fall on my shirt.

I felt odd twelve hours later, after missing two doses of blockers. My scent clouded around me, a little thicker than it should have been, perhaps because of the nerves churning in my stomach.

I had no fucking idea what I was nervous about, but there was something in the air, as if everyone was full of the same mix of anticipation and excitement. When I passed other alphas in the corridor after lunch, they inhaled, hoping against hope for the rush of adrenaline that came with finding a complementary scent.

I took a shower, catching myself as I reached for the scent-cancelling body wash. *This is what it was like before the Unveiling*, I thought, bypassing my scent-cancelling spray and throwing on clean clothes, then pressing some buttons on my monitors to let my APF team know I was attending a party and my heartbeat might be erratic. I'd still have to check in every hour, but that was easy, no more than sending a code via the monitors, then letting them know when I was about to go to bed.

A knock sounded on my door. 'Ready?' Pravin called.

'One sec.' I shot a text to Rose, who knew what was happening and who had triple-locked and barricaded her door at my request. *Have a good night. Wish me luck.*

She responded a moment later. *Why is there a security team prowling up and down my corridor?*

I chewed on my lip. *That might be because of my mum. Sorry.*

I stared at the three dots until her next message came through. *No worries. It's good, actually. I can hear music, and I think I'd be nervous if they weren't there. Good luck, Byron.*

Pravin inhaled as soon as I came through the door.

'You, too?' I said, smiling.

'Can't hurt, right?' He sniffed. 'Oof. That's sweet. Like, I think I just got a cavity.'

'I take it you prefer savoury?'

'Nah, I'm a lifestyle scent.' Pravin held his wrist out, and I caught the notes of sunshine on freshly washed linen. Nice, but it didn't make my alpha pay attention.

I clapped him on the back. 'Too bad. You would have been a good packmate. I bet my complementaries are all assholes.'

He grinned. 'My parents always say you get the pack you deserve.'

I laughed, and we headed downstairs together.

I didn't know how they thought they'd ever keep the party a secret, because dance music was blaring through the gardens, and there were alphas with drinks in hands standing in front of the maze. It was still early, but it looked as if a few of them had already turned to liquid courage; inhibitions were dropping. A few alphas were making the rounds, blatantly sniffing wrists, some looking more and more crestfallen each time.

Which was why it was dangerous to get your hopes up. Everyone *wanted* a scent match, but you had as much chance of winning the lottery.

'Oh.' Pravin grabbed my arm. 'Can you smell that?'

I glanced at him; he wasn't looking at me. 'I can smell a lot of things, man.'

'Leather.' He inhaled. 'Leather and hay. Oh, *shit.*'

Just like that, he dropped my arm, disappearing into the garden, and I was left alone.

I sighed, but figured I may as well stay out for a bit. The night was warm, and I swiped a can of soft drink from the fountain, which some enterprising soul had filled with ice. The air was thick with scents, battling with the lemon myrtle from the maze. Some of them were nice – freshly baked cookies, strawberry syrup, even a toffee that smelled fairly similar to my own scent – but none did anything much for me, not like Sebastian's mouthful of cherry had.

Fuck, I wished he was out here, so that I could smell him *properly* and see whether we were complementary.

Then we could talk – *at length* – about sandwiches.

Some scents made my nose itch – there was a cloying rose that gave me all kinds of conflicting feelings – but some were downright turn-offs: a too-strong jasmine that almost made me gag; a peaty whiskey that burned my throat; and even – though I could barely believe it – a strong, sharp cheese.

That's unfortunate.

The overwhelming mass of them started to make my stomach churn, so I turned into the maze, where the lemon myrtle blocked most of it out.

It was pitch black, but in a comforting way. The night was clear, and when I looked up, I could see the stars. I could still hear the music, and I figured it was the perfect place to hide for a little while, until I could call it a night and find a barrage of memes to torment Rose. I knew there was a bench not far into the maze, and I let my eyes adjust to the dark as I took the twists and turns to find it.

Once I did, I pulled my eReader from my pocket and got comfortable.

TRISTAN

I DIDN'T KNOW WHY I WAS HERE.

That's not true. You know exactly why; his name is Sebastian Aurelius Worthy.

A pair of alphas were fucking in the bushes to my right, apparently unbothered by the fact they were on full show. They were third years, I was fairly sure, a woman and a man; her mouth was bloody, and so was his neck.

Nothing like booze, bites, and bad decisions.

I continued walking into the fray because I was here now, and I might as well. The scents made my head spin. Some were tolerable. There was a hint of toffee that caught my interest until I realised there was no depth to it; it was all surface sweetness. Others were less pleasant – I swore I caught a hint of *cheese* before a blanket of jasmine descended and I had to cover my nose.

My phone buzzed.

Anything yet?

I could almost hear the hope in Sebastian's voice. *Not yet, but it's early!* I texted back.

It *was* early, but I'd already had enough.

We'd had a long talk before I'd left our room. Well, *Sebastian* had talked, while I listened. And it was less a conversation than a litany of descriptions, all delivered in excruciating detail, of what he was okay with me doing tonight, provided I found a complementary scent.

Not much was off the table, as it turned out. *Sucking is fine*, he'd said, ticking it off his fingers. *Fingering is in — ha — and fucking is all good with me, as long as they're clear or you're using protection.* He'd given a long list of suggested positions and techniques — *do that thing with your tongue, babe, we want to impress them* — before pausing. *Oh, I suppose kissing is okay, too.* He'd studied me for a moment. *But only if you think they're a keeper.*

I grabbed a bottle of water from the fountain. The groundskeepers would be furious; someone had knocked the grotesque cherub off the top and it lay on the ground next to an empty soft drink can. I took a swig of water, trying to clear some of the scents from my mouth, then wove through the packed bodies, intending to skirt the party once more, and then head back to bed. I hated disappointing Sebastian, but I hadn't been hopeful, and nothing about the party was changing my mind.

I'd taken two steps when I caught it, faint through the lemon myrtle.

This scent was sweet, too, like the toffee, but it was the kind of sweet that had layer upon complex layer. The kind of sweet that settled over your tongue until it coated your throat and when it was gone, you craved it, desperate for another hit of delicious burnt sugar with its undertone of butter and offset of salt.

My mouth started to water.

I was sniffing like a dog before I could stop myself, trying to catch more. My heart was beating in my ears and my alpha rose to the surface, howling at me to find its owner. *Mine*, my instincts roared, and my body listened, because I was weaving through the crowd of alphas like a shark through a school of fish – only I didn't want to eat any of *them*.

I inhaled again. The scent was still in the air, but faint, as if its owner had been and gone. *No*, my instincts insisted. *Mine*. The owner of that scent couldn't be *gone*, because it was making my skin tingle and my blood rush around my body at speed.

I'd never felt anything like it.

My canines ached, pushing down through my gums as I caught another hint, closer to the maze. I paused at the entrance, breathing in deeply.

The scent was stronger there. Most of the alphas were in the garden, desperately searching for complementary scents. But the scent I was following – the scent that was *mine* – was stronger in the maze, so I strode inside.

A few steps in, I was rewarded with another mouthful of salted caramel, and with it, the sudden and painful swelling of my cock.

I snarled wordlessly with need and prowled further into the maze.

It was pitch black, and it took my eyes a few moments to adjust. I followed the scent through the walls of lemon myrtle as if there was a rope pulling me forward, attached to my ribs, and someone was holding the other end, tugging. By the time I saw a faint light, my hands were shaking, and I realised the square of brightness was too wide for a phone, it was an eReader instead, and –

Byron fucking Griffiths was getting to his feet, his eyes almost comically wide in the faint light. He inhaled in surprise. 'Grace? What –'

I saw the moment it dawned; he took another half-gulp of air, and his pupils blew out as he staggered.

'*Vanilla?*' he said, his voice half-incredulous and half a groan. 'Your scent is *vanilla?* Are you fucking with me, Grace? I –'

I didn't hear what he was going to say, because I closed the distance between us and seized two handfuls of his shirt, pulling him down so I could devour his mouth with mine, my tongue invading, searching for another hit of caramel. For a moment, his lips were soft with surprise, then he groaned again, wordlessly, and dropped his eReader on the ground so he could bunch his hands in my hair.

The kiss turned *hard*.

I wanted to crawl beneath his skin, to take his heart in my hand and hold it, just to keep him close, so I knew that he was safe – and I wanted him to do the same thing to me. I wanted him simmering in my blood, wanted to breathe his every breath, to know what every inch of his body felt like beneath my hands and against my tongue.

I'd never felt like this before: so uncontrolled, so fucking *desperate*. His tongue swept over mine, hot and sweet, and my knees threatened to buckle. Our kiss was a clash, a furious battle of lips and tongues, so I tried to slow it down, to slant my mouth against his and show some shadow of skill, but it was impossible; I wanted him too badly. My body and my alpha were driving the show, and my mind was lurking somewhere beneath my instincts, lulled into quiescence by his scent.

When did he get so fucking perfect? some far-away part of me mused. *When did he get* irresistible?

I suspected he wasn't either of those things, but biology was at play, and logic had flown far, far away.

He held me just as tightly as I grasped him, his hands tugging at my hair, one moving down to clamp hard on my waist, keeping me flush against his body. My hips were rolling shamelessly against him, chasing whatever friction I could find, my cock rock hard. From what I could feel, he was in a similar state; when I moved back, he made a wordless sound of protest and followed. I had the sudden notion that if I didn't taste him I would die, so I broke the kiss and dropped to my knees.

'Need you,' I rasped, my hands going to his belt.

'Fuck, yes,' he hissed, and let me open him up like a present, shoving his jeans and trunks down until his cock sprang free.

Fuck. Me.

Sebastian was going to lose his mind.

I took him in hand, using my thumb to spread the precum beading at his slit over his head. His cock was beautiful, curving gracefully and carved with veins that begged tracing with my tongue. I did just that, listening to the music of his moans before throwing caution to the wind and swallowing down as much as I could manage.

I was going to need to practise if I wanted to take all of him.

'Fuck, Grace,' he swore, but held himself still, letting me work up and down, taking him further into my throat with every dip. I'd be hoarse and sore tomorrow, but I gave zero fucks as the taste of salted caramel covered my tongue and made my mouth water. I popped off his cock, panting and wiping the saliva off my chin, then looked up to see him staring down at me, his eyes wild.

'What is this?' he whispered, half-desperate, half-anguished. 'Grace. *Tristan*. I don't … I *need* you.'

'Yes,' I said roughly, because I *needed* him, too. 'Strip for me.'

His expression turned wary, and the air pulled tight between us. It was a risk, I knew, giving orders to another alpha, but we needed to sort this out now.

I knew what a complementary scent felt like; Sebastian was one. I knew the heady sense of connection, the pleasant shiver as one body recognised its link to another, the *hunger*.

This was entirely unfamiliar. I didn't just *want* Byron; I wanted to *consume* him. I wanted to be under his skin, and for him to burrow beneath mine. I wanted to break down every barrier between us, to taste his blood as it flowed over my tongue after I sank my teeth into his neck. I wanted to mark him as mine, and be marked in return; I wanted every single person on the planet to know that I belonged to him, and him to me.

He was pack. But we weren't just complementary. We were something Sebastian's talk hadn't covered.

We were a scent match.

And as scent-matched alphas, we needed to work out which one of us was in charge.

'Strip for me,' I said again, gently, my voice a caress. An invisible wall of dominance washed over me in response, so strong I stepped back.

He was stronger than me.

Byron was the dominant alpha of our pack.

I inclined my head, acknowledging the fact as my heart raced like a freight train, holding eye contact all the while.

Even if he was stronger, I still needed to be in charge.

He stared back – then pulled off his shirt.

I let out a shuddering breath, my eyes hot with unshed tears.

He'd ceded to me, and I'd give him the fucking *world* in return. Starting by making him come so hard he saw stars.

'I need to be clear about what I want,' I said, reaching out to trail my nails lightly over his skin, teasing. 'I want to be inside you. Yes or no?'

'Yes,' he said hoarsely, immediately.

'Have you done this before?'

'Not for years,' he answered, and I was suddenly murderous at the notion that someone else had been *inside my alpha.* Because that's what he was – *mine*. Entirely and forever. And I couldn't bear the thought of some stranger touching him.

'I need to be clear, too,' he said, catching my wrist and holding it, his grip almost uncomfortably tight. He gazed at me with a mix of lust and rage. 'I still fucking hate you, Tristan Grace.'

For the second time that night, the universe shifted around me. My stomach dropped and my throat closed over. *Of course he hates you*, I told myself. *He hasn't forgiven you for what you did to Rose.*

I didn't want him to hate me. I wanted him to feel the same desperate need for me that I felt for him. I wanted his universe to realign with Sebastian and I at its centre.

But I didn't think I was going to get that, and I needed him so badly.

I reached out with my free hand and grasped his hip. 'You don't have to like me to fuck me.' My voice was calm, though a thousand emotions were rampaging through me – guilt, shame, and regret not least of them. 'You don't have to like me to be my mate.'

He exhaled, his eyes closing for a moment before he pulled me forward and kissed me again, forcefully, *angrily*, tasting of paradise and resignation. 'As long as we're clear,' he said, and bit my lip.

I pushed him down on the bench, making short work of his boots before wrestling his jeans down his muscled legs. My breath caught when I took him in, naked and fucking *glorious* before me, his cock jerking every time

I touched his skin. I ran my hands up his legs, slowly, *tortuously*, watching him twitch and writhe until I took him in hand again and he swore, one arm falling across his face in the darkness. I worked his cock up and down as my free hand slipped between his legs.

He lifted his knees to make it easier, which earned him a quick suck, as much as I could manage, tears welling in my eyes as caramel spread over my tongue. I traced around his ass – he hissed in response – before I broke away to fish a small bottle of lube from my shorts pocket.

I'd been with Sebastian too long not to carry both lube and scent canceller *everywhere*.

I made my fingers slick before I traced him again, circling and pressing until he was writhing on the bench, then pushing gently inside. His body resisted, so I waited for him to relax before pushing deeper, then withdrew to add another finger, gently stretching.

He was so fucking hot I couldn't think straight. All I knew was that I needed to be inside him, *now*.

I looked up to see his eyes on my face. I couldn't read his expression, but his cock was still rock hard. He didn't hate what was happening in a physical sense, at least. I swallowed. 'I don't know how patient I can be.'

'Does it look like I want you to take your fucking time?' he said, reaching to fist his cock; precum glistened under his fingers. 'I need you inside me so badly it feels like I'm dying. Fuck me already.'

'I might hurt you.'

He snorted. 'You could try, Grace.'

I pushed in deeper. 'Call me alpha.'

'Fuck off,' he panted.

I found the spot inside him that made Sebastian lose his mind. It was smaller in alphas, but no less sensitive. I pressed on it gently.

'Fuck –' Byron bit off, his cock jerking against his stomach. 'Fuck, Tristan. *Please.*'

I bit back an approving purr. I loved him begging, his eyes wild and his hair falling into his eyes. '*Alpha*,' I insisted, because I was a power-hungry asshole and I needed him to say it.

I moved my fingers again, pressing and rubbing and stretching until he keened. 'Alpha!' he snarled, and I gently withdrew my fingers, cleaning them with a wipe – I was always prepared – before rubbing more lube over my throbbing cock.

I notched it where my fingers had been. Byron groaned, arching beneath me, and the universe felt entirely *right* as I pushed slowly inside.

I stopped almost immediately once my head was buried inside him, letting him adjust. He was impatient, reaching towards me to hurry me up, but I resisted; I wanted to own him, not hurt him. He rasped praise as I pushed in once more, and I filed the image of him partially impaled, panting and writhing, away in my mind, because I would be absolutely reliving this moment in the shower tomorrow. He was so tight it was almost painful, and so hot I was losing control; when he moaned *yes, alpha, more* I was gone, and I thrust home with one sharp kick of my hips, a bead of sweat falling from my brow onto his skin.

He inhaled sharply, but his cock stayed hard.

'Touch yourself,' I ordered, because I needed to see him come. I wanted him messy and painted with white and so fucking wrecked he could barely function. 'Touch yourself, *mate*.'

He keened again at the word, and his hand wrapped around his thick cock. 'It won't take long,' he panted, half a plea and half a warning, but I didn't care, because if he didn't climax while I was inside him, I'd lose my fucking mind.

'Good,' I rasped, 'because I want to fill you with my cum.'

'Fuck.' His eyes were grey slits as he watched me roll my hips, so deep inside him that I wasn't sure where I ended and he began. 'Fuck, *yes*. Like that.'

I spanned my hand across his broad chest, feeling his heart beat beneath my palm. It was kicking like a fucking racehorse, but mine was matching its tempo. *Two hearts, one beat*. I was full of so much emotion – and so much *lust* – that I didn't know what to do with it all, so I concentrated on plunging smoothly in and out of his body, reaching down to toy gently where we were joined with my free hand.

He gave a wordless shout, cum painting his stomach and chest in thick white jets, hot and wet on the inside of my wrist. His body squeezed me so tightly I couldn't help but follow, thrusting deep as I emptied myself inside him, my eyes glazing as pleasure exploded at the base of my spine. I panted, raking in air, delicious pain spearing through my mouth as my canines pushed down.

I collapsed on him, nuzzling his neck. He arched, giving a deep, wordless whimper. I grazed my teeth over his scent gland, hard enough to leave a red mark on his pale skin, then sucked until I left a love bite. *Mine*, the action said, and my instincts chanted the same word. *Mine, mine, mine.* My teeth closed on his skin.

'Don't,' he snarled, and pushed me off, so hard that I slipped from his body and staggered a few steps back.

He sat up, dishevelled and ruined and covered in cum, and I'd never seen him look so glorious. The only thing that could make the picture more perfect was a bloody neck after my teeth made new scars, but he reached up and covered both scent glands with his hands.

'I still. Fucking. *Hate*. You,' he grated out. 'You don't get to bite me.'

'But we're a scent match,' I answered, trying – and failing – to keep my voice level as my alpha roared inside me, angry and hurt and bewildered. 'You're *mine*.'

'You think Sebastian might want a say in that? You know, *your omega*?'

'He sent me here tonight.'

Byron slid off the bench and started pulling on his clothes. I found my packet of wet wipes and handed them to him silently. 'He probably thought you *might* find a complementary scent and make out under a tree, Grace. Not find your *scent match* and try to bond him before you deign to do the same for the man who's been by your side for six fucking years.' He wiped the cum from his chest with a look of disgust, the expression hitting me straight in the stomach.

My scent match didn't want me.

But I'd had a lifetime of practise at schooling my expressions, so I pushed down the devastation and began straightening my clothes with focused precision. My instincts were shouting at me to claim my mate, to bind him to me with a bite, to never let him out of my sight.

But that wasn't what Byron wanted.

'Sebastian and I got checked before we came here, by the way,' I said coolly, as if that made a difference now. 'We're clear.'

'So I assumed,' he answered shortly, bending to pick his eReader off the ground. 'I'm clear, too. But if you want to be head alpha, then you should have that conversation *first* the next time you fuck someone new.'

'There won't be a *next time*,' I hissed, my control snapping. 'This is *it*. You're *pack*.'

He studied me in the soft light of the stars, and I gazed back, trying to take in how truly beautiful he was. His expression was closed and his eyes were cold; a moment later, he pushed past me, barging my shoulder.

'Pack is a *choice*, Grace.'

SEBASTIAN

WHEN TRISTAN DIDN'T RETURN after a couple of hours, I tried not to worry.

My mind played out a hundred different scenarios. Best case was that he'd found a complementary scent and was blowing its owner's mind beneath a tree, getting ready to bring them back to our room so we could make sure they were complementary with me, too.

Worst case, someone had spiked his drink and he was lying dead under said tree, with a bunch of drunk alphas fucking all around him, taking no notice.

Which was impossible. *Everybody* noticed Tristan.

At two in the morning, I gave up and texted Rose.

To my surprise, she answered immediately. *What's wrong?*

Tristan isn't back yet.

She called a moment later. 'Byron hasn't checked in, either,' she said, by way of greeting.

I stretched out on the couch, staring at the ceiling. 'Maybe they got wasted together.'

'I don't think Byron can drink. Because of all the medication.'

I sighed. 'Tristan refuses to drink anything that costs less than three hundred dollars a bottle, anyway.' I rolled onto my side. 'All I could see from my window were cans of bourbon and cola.'

Rose made a noise which could have been disgust at the alphas' drink choices, or a scoff at Tristan's pickiness, or perhaps both. 'Maybe … Maybe they're just having a really good time?'

'I don't know if I prefer that thought, or hate it.'

'Because you're not out there, too, being the centre of Tristan's world?'

I snorted. 'I'm the centre of his world whether I'm with him or not.'

Rose was silent for a moment. 'That must be nice,' she said, not bothering to hide the wistfulness in her tone.

I'd never really thought about whether it was nice or not; I'd always taken it for granted. I frowned, shaken by the notion that other people – that *Rose* – didn't have the same kind of unwavering devotion, the same kind of steadfast security.

A moment later, I realised that I wanted to *give* that feeling. To her, specifically.

The realisation shook me further.

I took a shuddering breath. 'Rosebud –'

A scratch outside interrupted me, and after some scraping noises and some thumps – maybe Tristan *had* drunk some of the pre-mixed drinks? – the door opened.

'Alpha –' I started, intending to playfully needle him, but something was terribly wrong.

Tristan staggered into the room, looking all kinds of wrecked. His curls were a mess, his glasses askew. His shirt was crumpled, the buttons undone to just below his pecs, showing a stretch of skin I wasn't sure he *wanted* exposed.

I didn't freeze because of any of that, though. It was his eyes, glazed and unseeing. He stumbled to the couch and collapsed to sit, cradling his head in his hands.

I darted to close and lock the door behind him, seized by the sudden notion that someone was after him. I'd been briefed by his family, after all; I knew it was a possibility, and always would be.

But no one came after Tristan; no one beside the demon he was battling, anyway. I knelt before him, tentatively placing my hands on his thighs. 'Alpha?'

He gave a shuddering exhale. 'Seb. My love.'

He smelled like vanilla-scented sweat and cum – his own – and *salted fucking caramel*, which meant he'd spent the night close to Byron.

Perhaps *very* close, given the cum.

I tried to fight against the rising tide of heat that swept over me at their combined scents. Tristan smelled like a dessert platter, and it was *mouthwatering*. All that was missing was the elusive hint of chocolate –

'Seb?' Rose's voice came from the couch. 'Are you all right?'

I cleared my throat and fished my phone out from between the cushions. 'Something's up with Tristan, Rosebud. I have to go. I'll text you.' I stuffed my phone back where it had fallen. 'Tris, handsome, what happened?'

'Doesn't want me,' he said numbly.

I blinked. 'What?'

'Doesn't want me,' he repeated, a little louder, as if that would help me understand.

I bristled. 'Who doesn't want you?' *I'll fucking end them. Somehow.*

'My scent match doesn't want me.'

I'd never had vertigo, but imagined it would be something like the sensation I experienced hearing his words: my head swam, and it felt as if the world spun on its axis. I swayed; if I'd been standing, I would have fallen.

Tristan had refused to bite me for *years* on the chance that my scent match might miraculously appear in my life. While I'd understood – to a point – I'd never taken the possibility seriously. Why would I? I was statistically more likely to be struck by lightning or be killed by a shark – or a cow.

And never *once* had I worried about *his* scent match appearing instead.

Jealousy exploded in my stomach like a dying star. I coughed, trying to control the feeling, to push it away, push it down, but it was hot and awful and it made my throat close.

Perhaps I shouldn't have been so confident about my place in Tristan's world.

I bit back a hysterical laugh, forcing myself to inhale slowly. Tristan was staring sightlessly at the floor, clearly in pieces; I could have my breakdown later. I slid my hands over his thighs, trying to catch his attention. 'Alpha. You found your scent match?' My voice broke; I swallowed. 'They're *here*?'

He gave a bitter laugh. 'Yes. They're here. It's Byron fucking Griffiths.'

I closed my eyes.

Of course it was. Tristan was covered in his scent; I should have already realised. My stomach twisted. I imagined them side-by-side, imagined breathing in their combined scents, one pair of green eyes and one pair of grey gazing back at me.

Abruptly, the jealousy dissolved, replaced once more by approving heat.

Fucking omega instincts, I fumed, but I was distracted once more by Tristan's scent as I breathed in. *Vanilla* and *salted caramel? Cover me in fucking sugar.*

I couldn't be mad at Tristan. This was what I'd wanted; this was the *pack* I'd wanted. He was doing exactly as I'd asked him to. 'What happened, my love?'

Tristan leaned forward, pressing his forehead to mine. 'We fucked in the maze.'

Okay, wow. I let that sink in before waving a hand. 'Yeah, I got that part, Tris. You're covered in cum and you smell like something I want to *roll* in. But fucking your scent match is supposed to be *amazing*. Don't tell me it was bad, alpha. I'll never recover.'

He cupped my face, forcing a watery smile. 'What the fuck did I do to deserve you?' I made a dismissive noise, but he gripped my chin tightly, his eyes locked on mine. 'You know this changes *nothing* between us, right, omega? My love for you is here.' He rested his free hand over his heart. 'It's so deep and so strong it will never fade, Seb. You *own* my heart. But Byron is … *beside* it, somehow. Even if he doesn't want to be there.'

I frowned. Byron didn't exactly worship Tristan, but they were a *scent match*. 'Why do you think that?'

'Because he said it,' Tristan answered wryly, a hint of his usual self shining through. 'He told me that he hated me, let me fuck him, then told me again after I –' he faltered, inhaling, as if steeling himself '– after I ran my teeth over his scent gland.'

My stomach dropped. 'You bit him?' I hated how my voice wavered, thinning into a pathetic whisper.

'I didn't.' Tristan moved back, still looking me in the eye, and I tensed. 'But Seb … I *wanted* to.'

I whined before I could stop myself, a high, needy sound. Tristan pulled me into his lap, wrapping his arms around me so tightly I almost couldn't breathe. I shoved my face into the curve of his neck, needing comfort, even though it was him who'd caused the pain.

It hurt. It hurt all the way to my bones, a jarring agony of rejection. I'd been so *certain* that Tristan worshipped the ground I walked on, but knowing that he'd almost bitten someone else?

Fuck, it hurt.

'I wasn't thinking,' he whispered, and I was almost as shaken by *that*, because my alpha thought about things even when he was asleep. 'I *couldn't* think. My instincts were so loud, Seb, and my canines had pushed through, and all

I wanted was his blood in my mouth. *Needed* it, even. I would have done it,' he went on, his voice muffled by my shoulder but still heavy with shame. 'If he'd let me, I would have done it, Seb.'

I whimpered, and he responded with a full-body purr, making my omega instincts roll over and show their belly as my limbs went limp and my head lolled on his shoulder. I would have protested that I didn't need it, that I could bear the pain, but I could tell it was comforting him, too, as he fell back into the alpha role he was made for.

'As much as you hate me right now,' he whispered, 'just know that I hate myself far more.'

'Oh, Tris,' I said thickly, forcing my head up to drag my nose over his scent gland. 'I don't hate you. I never could. I won't say that I'm not upset, because I *am*. That shit hurts, alpha. You know how much I want your bite, and you nearly gave that to someone else.' I pressed a kiss to his tender skin. 'But you and I are endgame, scent match or no scent match.' I shook off the effects of his purr with difficulty, pulling back to study his face. He was drawn, haggard, even. 'Do you want to work through this?'

'Of course I do,' he said hoarsely. '*Always*, Sebastian.'

'Then we will.' I smoothed down his unruly curls. 'We'll work it through.'

◇◇◇

The next day we skipped class and went down to the beach, just the two of us. It was overcast and windy, so we had it entirely to ourselves. I waded through the frigid shallows, feeling the push and pull of the waves on my feet and calves, while Tristan sat on the white sand, watching me.

He wasn't okay. It felt odd to term what he was going through *mourning*, but that's what it felt like, as if he were grieving for something – or someone – he'd lost. Though he tried to contain it, devastation and longing poured off him, and it added fuel to the fire of my hurt.

Even in pain, he was careful with me, endlessly considerate. He didn't use me as a crutch, didn't seek to find solace in my arms. I wasn't sure I could have given it, anyway.

'Bluebottle, Seb,' Tristan called, gesturing with his chin.

I looked to my left to see what he'd spotted; the barely perceptible creature buffeted by the whitewash. I backed out of the water, then folded next to Tristan on the sand.

'It's beautiful here,' he said after a moment's silence, his soft accent stronger in his contemplation. 'I wasn't expecting to like it so much.'

I looked out across the waves. 'There's a lot here to like.'

I felt his eyes on me. 'You know I'd take you away,' he said carefully. 'If you wanted to go. There are other schools as good as this elsewhere. We could go to the UK. Or to the United States, or Switzerland, or China. Singapore, Canada, Japan … Anywhere you wanted, I'd take you.'

I studied the waves. The tide was going out. I knew what he was saying; that if I wanted, I could pack up and leave. Go somewhere his scent match wasn't living down the hallway.

That even though he liked it here, even though he had a chance for a biological perfect match, he'd give all that up – for *me*.

'You know I don't agree with my mother much,' I said, brushing the drying sand from my calves, 'but when I was in high school – when she couldn't ignore the bullying any longer – she said something to me. She said resilience was a strength that no insult or fist could match.' I turned to look at him; his expression was blank. 'If you want to go, we'll go. I'll follow you back to England, or anywhere else in the world. But I'd prefer to stick this out, Tris. I'm not a runner, and you're not, either. You just need a few days to adjust, and to remember that.'

Tristan didn't say anything; he just dropped his head to rest on my shoulder, and together we watched the waves roll out.

❖❖❖

When we went back to class, Byron ignored Tristan completely.

If I hadn't realised how strong – or stubborn, perhaps – the big alpha was before, I certainly knew it now. Ignoring a complementary scent was difficult enough. But ignoring his *scent match*?

He must have been in the same circle of hell as Tristan, but he didn't show it. He carried on as if nothing had happened, as if his entire universe hadn't realigned with Tristan at its centre. He was protective of Rose and flirted with her just enough to leave her in no doubt of his interest, but not enough to be pushy. He joked with Pravin, and struck up a friendship with Pravin's new boyfriend, Chul.

When he looked at me, I could still see the hunger in his eyes, but his manner was cooler; he was careful not to touch me, or to sit too close.

It was odd, being near them both, and knowing I wasn't just sitting between two alphas – I was sitting between a *scent match*. Between two people who'd won the biological lottery, and one of them was *my* alpha. The alpha I'd loved for six years, ever since he'd asked me out for coffee after class and I'd fallen straight into his clear green gaze.

I was simultaneously consumed with jealousy and with the need to make it better. The more I thought about it, the more I wanted it – the togetherness; *pack*. If I had it my way, Tristan, Byron, Rose, and I would be together, and nothing more would need to be said. But Byron didn't want Tristan, and two omegas in one pack was impossible – no matter how much I'd liked Rose's scent, she surely *couldn't* like mine – so I knew it wouldn't happen.

But neither could the uncomfortable, silent tension between the alphas continue.

I wondered how long it would last, and who would be the one to break it.

'Those hormone-addled dickheads,' Rose fumed, when I told her what was going on; Byron had apparently kept it quiet. 'They should get the fuck over themselves and be grateful that their perfect match lives down the fucking hallway.'

I snorted. 'Savage. I love it.' I paused. 'I don't know what to do.'

She searched my face. 'Is it your job to do something, Seb?'

'No, of course not. But it's in my best interest. In *our* best interests,' I amended. 'I've never seen Tristan heartbroken, and I don't like it.'

'I'm not sure what you can do about it,' Rose said tentatively. 'It seems like they need to sort it out for themselves. But they're not speaking, so –'

'So we *make* them talk,' I said, struck by sudden inspiration.

If the alphas wouldn't break the silence, then *we* would.

'*We* make them? How?'

Rose hadn't grown up in a pack, but I had. I knew how hard it could be to manage multiple personalities, especially when they had egos like my parents did. It wasn't true that a pack's emotional balance stemmed from their omega – while my omega mum was a lovely person, she wasn't interested in mediating pack squabbles; that role fell to my dad – but I was willing to take up the task if I needed to.

I bit my lip. 'You were talking about a movie night.'

Rose frowned; a lock of hair fell into her face. She tucked it behind her ear. 'Yes, with Byron. We hadn't organised a date yet. But –'

'What if we had one for the four of us?' I blurted. 'Just all of us in one room, with popcorn and something to watch if it gets too intense, and we just let the alphas … sort it out? If they need to snarl at each other, they snarl at each other. If they need to fuck it out, they fuck it out. But we'll be there to make sure they stay human – partially, at least – and hopefully by the end of the night, they'll be past this bullshit.'

'Sebastian,' Rose said, obviously working hard to keep her voice level, 'do you really think that's a good idea? You and me –'

'I know,' I said, reaching out to cup her jaw, stroking my thumb over her cheekbone. Her eyes fluttered. I didn't seem to be able to stop touching her, and the library was almost empty, so I wasn't about to hold back.

'And *them*,' Rose went on, a faint look of horror dawning over her features. 'I can barely contain myself with *you*, but if they're with us, I –'

'Would it be such a bad thing?' I said gently.

She still thought I was a beta. I knew I liked her scent and wanted more of it. I wanted to scent her *properly*, not just a hint on the breeze, not when it was dampened by blockers and cancellers. Maybe – just *maybe* – if she scented me, she'd feel the same.

More likely, my scent would make her nose itch and she'd leave, but I was getting sick of wondering.

'You'd be safe,' I went on, when she didn't answer, 'and with people who'd rather cut their own hands off than hurt you.' I slid my fingers down to cup her nape. 'You'd be safe with *me*. We'd all be on blockers, so it wouldn't be like the scent party. What have you got to lose?'

She gave me a wry look. 'Besides my heart?'

My own beat faster. 'Your heart is safe with me, Rose.'

'I'm not sure I believe that.' She looked away, her brow creased as she thought about it. 'So much for *a degree, not a pack*.' She was quiet for a long moment. 'Okay,' she said at last, just as I was beginning to sweat. 'Okay. I can do it. But how do we get Byron there?'

I grinned. 'That's the easiest part of all. All you need to do is tell him it's happening.'

She directed her frown at me. 'That won't work.'

I rolled my eyes. 'Try it and report back.' My mind was working overtime, planning what we'd eat, what we'd drink, which movie to choose, and what music I could put on when it became clear that we weren't going to watch a movie at all.

I could make a *let's-watch-the-alphas-fuck* playlist.

Or an *eat-Rose-out-until-she-screams* playlist.

Why not both?

My cock jerked as my mind conjured a picture of her spread out in my nest – naked, of course – her lips swollen from my kisses and her arms reaching for me.

I stifled a groan, because I wanted – I needed – *that*. I needed to hear what she sounded like when she unravelled, what her skin felt like beneath my fingertips, what her hair looked like wrapped around my fist.

That.

'Seb?'

I shook myself, realising she'd been speaking. 'Sorry?'

'We got our re-marked essays back.'

'Oh, fuck.' I spun back to face my laptop, clicking into the learning system.

Ninety-eight. 'Mine didn't change.'

'Mine did,' Rose said happily, a flush spreading over her cheeks. 'Oh, thank *fuck*. I can't believe this happened. I've never had a re-mark before. I wonder why they decided to do it?'

I bit my tongue. I could have told her, but it was Tristan's story, and it wasn't his way to blow his own metaphorical trumpet. 'No idea, beautiful, but I'm glad you're happier.'

'Forty marks happier,' she muttered, and my heart wrenched for her.

She made a pleased little *hum* sound, her eyes on her essay's new comments, and I went back to planning an orgy.

With my *pack.*

◇◇◇

Tristan didn't realise I was up to something until the snacks I'd ordered online began spilling from our cupboards. Which, to my mind, proved how much the situation with Byron was affecting my alpha.

'Baby?' he said, bewildered, when I'd received another delivery while he was out on his afternoon walk. 'What's this?'

'We're having a movie night,' I informed him. 'Tonight. And I've invited Rose and Byron.'

He froze; a thousand emotions flickered in his eyes. 'Seb, I … Are you sure that's a good idea? Rose could scent your designation, and Byron …' He trailed off, looking away.

I went to him and tipped his chin towards me, then said something I'd never said before, something that took every ounce of courage I had. 'It's time for no more secrets, don't you think?'

He studied me warily, biting at his lip. His eyes flickered across to the mountain of food. 'Do you think they'll come?'

By that, he meant did I think *Byron* would come. 'Rose was pretty determined,' I answered.

He deflated. 'All right.' His eyes slid back to me; he gave me an unreadable look. 'What do you need me to do?'

I threw my arms around him. 'Thank you.' I buried my face in his neck. 'I know you don't really want to do this.'

He sighed, his arms wrapping tight around me. 'I'd do anything for you.'

I knew they weren't empty words. He was reluctant, but he was going to do this anyway – because he knew it meant something to me. I pressed a kiss to his throat. 'You're the best, Tristan Grace.'

I put him to work cleaning, while I took care of the snacks. Everything was sweet – because omegas craved sweetness like bees needed pollen – but it was *themed*. I'd bought every kind of chocolate I could get my hands on, along with salted caramel popcorn, and cherry clafoutis and vanilla slice from a patisserie further up the coast. While Tristan pushed around a vacuum and I pretended not to ogle him, I made a packet mix of salted caramel brownies and another of cherry blondies, both of which would go perfectly with the homestyle vanilla bean ice cream I'd ordered from a specialty ice cream shop. I'd bought cookies, too: browned butter toffee chocolate chip, chocolate cherry, and vanilla snaps shaped like hearts, covered with thick icing and sprinkles.

Thank fuck for delivery drivers.

When Tristan caught the smell of salted caramel, he stiffened, his neck muscles corded. I left the kitchen to wrap my arms around him, my chest rumbling in a gentle omega purr.

He relaxed, stroking my hair. 'You're amazing,' he said quietly. 'Do you know that?'

'Obviously,' I answered, running my nose over his scent gland. 'It's going to be okay, Tris. I'm going to *make* it okay.'

He was silent for so long that I pulled back, searching his face.

'I trust you,' he said at last. 'If I can't see a way forward, I know that you'll find it for us.'

'Good.' I rose up on my toes and pressed a kiss to his cheek. 'Because if this goes the way I hope it does, then we need to talk about boundaries again.'

❖❖❖

Rose and Byron arrived on time because Rose was a compulsive over-achiever and her understanding of *fashionably late* was strictly academic. It didn't matter, though; I'd been ready for hours, sitting on the couch with my laptop on my knees, trying – without success – to concentrate on the draft of my final essay. Tristan had convinced me not to put the food out no fewer than four times, but he was on edge himself, inexplicably choosing that afternoon to rearrange our bookshelves.

They didn't look that different afterwards, but it was a good distraction for him.

'Hello,' Rose breathed nervously, and *fuck*, she looked more appetising than anything I'd laid out on the coffee table. Her pants were a sage-green plaid and she'd buttoned herself into the sweetest cream cardigan I'd ever seen, which was to say that I wanted to *un*button her, immediately. Her hair was caught up in a claw clip and her cheeks were flushed a deep, delicious pink.

Byron closed the door behind her, his face unreadable as he flicked the locks into place.

I was struck by a barrage of worries. *What if I liked her scent, but she hated mine? What if she didn't like Tristan's scent? What if she liked his, but not mine? What if –*

Her nostrils flared. 'That's …' She spun around to Byron, searching his face, then turned back to me. She inhaled deeply, a flush spreading down her neck. 'Oh, *fuck*,' she said. 'Vanilla. Vanilla and *cherry*.' She gave a tiny groan, the sound hitting me square in the stomach and travelling down. She inhaled again, desperately. 'That cherry ... Wait. *There's an omega here?*' She looked around wildly, as if waiting for someone to spring out and surprise her. When no one emerged, she looked at me in confusion, her eyes wide. 'Seb?'

I guess it's go time. 'I'm sorry we kept it from you, Rose, but –'

She stepped towards me, her chest rising and falling rapidly. 'You?' Her pupils had blown out, the brown of her irises almost invisible. '*You* smell like cherry?'

I swallowed nervously; there was no indication of whether she thought that was good or bad. 'I, ah. Yep. That's me.'

She whimpered, closing her eyes and balling her hands into fists. 'I feel ... I feel ...'

'How do you feel, Rosebud?' I whispered, barely daring to breathe.

And inhaling in surprise when a hint of her raspberry tartness spread over my tongue.

'Rose?' I managed.

She opened her eyes; the desperation in them pinned me in place. 'I feel –'

'Please tell me it isn't ill.' My eyes tracked the lovely curve of her throat, exposed by her upswept hair. I inhaled, chasing another elusive hit of her sweet scent. 'Rose, please –'

'No,' she choked out, pressing a hand to her heart. 'I need to –'

My stomach dropped. I took a step back. I didn't think I'd ever felt sick with disappointment before. I'd known it was a long shot, but I'd held out hope because I knew what her scent did to me, and I'd wished – *prayed*, even – that it would be the same for her.

'Rose –'

Her eyes flickered up. 'Mine,' she hissed, her expression wild. I had the sudden notion that it was her omega looking out from her warm brown eyes. *'Mine.'*

Something inside me shifted.

Mine.

Yes.

That was *exactly* what she was.

My chest bloomed with a sudden ache, pulling me towards her, so strongly it was almost painful. At some point, my cock had woken up, and my trunks felt damp with precum. My hands trembled, shaking with the need to touch her.

I'd been wrong. I didn't just want to fuck her.

I wanted to be *inside* her. All of me. And I wanted her inside me, too. I didn't know how, exactly – although obviously I could think of a few things – but it was as if sex wouldn't be enough. A simple physical joining wouldn't give me what I needed, which was to possess her at the same time she possessed me.

I'd never felt this way before, so base, so desperate, so *instinctual*. It was overwhelming and quite frankly terrifying, but I couldn't stop my feet moving towards her.

She held out a hand, splaying her fingers across my chest, her warmth like a brand. For a moment, I wasn't sure what she was doing – stopping me, perhaps, or warding me off – but in the next breath, her fingers were curling into my shirt to fist a handful of linen.

I inhaled, catching the distinct scents of her hair product, her perfume – and, beneath it, a trace of her scent. My hands slid up her forearms and curled around her elbows.

'Yours,' I grated out, and pulled her up to kiss me.

Her lips were ravenous and mine were no better, as if we were both trying to crawl beneath each other's skin. Her tongue slid into my mouth and I sucked on it lightly before biting down on her bottom lip, licking over the hurt when she gasped. One of her hands dragged a path through my hair and bunched, holding me in place while she took what she wanted from my mouth.

What she *needed*. What *I* needed.

I'd never seen her so forceful, and I liked it so much that my cock was pulsing. I wanted her to push me down, to use me, to *own* me.

Her lips slid over mine once, twice, before she pushed me aside with an adorable growl. I staggered a step back before I regained my balance, reaching up to touch my mouth, which was swollen and smarting.

'What *is* this?' Rose demanded, sounding close to tears. Something inside me bristled at the notion she was upset. *Mine*, it said. *Make it better.* 'I feel like – I feel like –'

'What do you feel?' I managed, when she didn't continue.

She met my eyes. 'I feel like if you're not inside me in the next minute, I'll *die*,' she said angrily, sniffing.

Byron made a wordless sound of surprise, and I wrenched my eyes from Rose just in time to see him glance at Tristan.

I'd been so caught up in Rose that I'd all but forgotten the alphas were there.

'It shouldn't be possible,' Rose continued, pleading. 'It *can't* be possible. You smell like an omega – and you smell like *mine*. But omegas aren't supposed to –'

'Have complementary scents?' I supplied.

'Do you think this is *complementary*?' Rose cried. She gestured to Tristan. '*This* is complementary. I scented Byron when I walked to his room tonight, and *that* is complementary.' Behind her, Byron twitched in surprise, a flush reddening his cheeks. 'But your scent makes me *lose control*, Sebastian.'

'Because you're a scent match,' Tristan said, his voice flat. 'That's how a scent match feels.'

Because he knows that now.

I had that sense of vertigo once more, but this time, it was as if the world was righting itself, not turning upside down.

And I understood *perfectly* how Tristan had almost bitten Byron on that night in the maze.

'But *how*?' Rose's eyes were shining with tears. The omega inside me whined, hating the fact she was upset. 'It's not supposed to be –'

I closed the distance between us and picked her up. She hooked her legs around my waist, and her arms around my neck; my instincts settled immediately. 'It doesn't matter how it's *supposed* to be,' I murmured. 'This is how it is. I'm yours. You're mine. And those two stubborn dickheads are our alphas. We're *pack*.' She sniffed, a tear running down her cheek. I stopped it with my lips. 'And now I'm going to sit your lovely ass on the couch and lick you until you scream. Unless you don't want that, in which case I will respect your boundaries and let you choose a movie.'

'Of *course* I want that,' she snarled, rolling her hips against me. Fuck, Rose was *fierce* when she was desperate, and I loved it. She was usually so controlled – like Tristan, in her own way –and it was compelling to see her starting to unravel.

Make her come apart, my instincts advised, and I thought it was a good idea to listen.

I seized her mouth with mine, groaning at the way she opened and her tongue traced my bottom lip. I carried her to the couch without breaking the kiss.

Which I was pretty proud of, actually.

The pack rooms all had a sunken space in the middle of the lounge room, though Tristan had replaced the Banksia couches immediately with ones we'd chosen. They were wide and soft, a calming navy blue, and perfect for falling asleep or fucking on, both of which we did often. I lay Rose down on one wide cushion, careful to support her neck. She reached to undo her claw clip, her hair spilling over her shoulders and onto the couch like a mermaid.

'So fucking beautiful,' I rasped, cupping her cheek, my thumb tracing the shape of her mouth. She opened it for me, so I trailed the pad of my thumb over the moisture on the inside of her bottom lip. Her mouth moved, sucking me in. 'Fuck, Rose.' I watched her play, sucking and licking my thumb in turn, before she released me with a light bite. *Minx.* 'You need to be naked. Like, now.'

'You sound desperate, omega,' she said thickly.

I leaned back at the sound of my designation – my *true* designation. I flicked a glance at the alphas. They were both watching, their expressions a matching mix of stoic and slightly pained. Tristan's lips pulled up on one side in a tiny, approving smile, before his eyes dipped to the plate of salted caramel brownies for a moment and he stiffened.

Is this okay? I mouthed at them, and received two sharp nods in response. Neither of them made a move to join us, and I didn't invite them to; this moment was for me and Rose.

I looked back down at her. 'I am desperate,' I said, unashamed. 'Are you angry with me? For hiding my designation from you?'

She frowned at me. 'Yes,' she admitted. 'I'm angry that you lied. But I'm mostly angry at myself for not realising sooner. It's so fucking obvious, now that I know.' She studied my face, reaching up to brush my hair from my cheek. 'And I understand why you needed to do it. If I were in your place, I'd lie, too. I just wish you could have trusted me with your secret.'

'No more,' I promised, tracing my fingers down the column of her throat. 'No more secrets. Just this. Just us. I'll tell you anything. Everything.'

She smiled shyly. 'I'd like that.' Her eyes fluttered closed as I stroked her collarbone. 'Oh. And I like *that*.'

She arched beneath me; I took the cue and kept stroking, moving down to her breasts, tracing the shape of them through her cardigan. Without opening her eyes, she unbuttoned it, revealing a white tank top and the shadow of a black bra beneath it. The sight took my breath away; I willed my hands not to tremble as I cupped her, my thumbs working over her peaking nipples.

'Seb,' she sighed, opening her eyes to watch me through her lashes. 'Yes.' I leaned down and sucked a nipple into my mouth, my tongue stroking the fabric of her shirt, making it damp. She shivered beneath me, squirming when I switched to the other breast, doing the same thing. '*Oh.*'

Her breath quickened, and mine did the same. I sucked on her peak with a soft snarl, lowering my body to provide friction when her hips pressed up. We hissed in tandem as the bulge of my cock settled between her thighs. Heat was pouring off her body, but it was pouring off mine, too. I nudged my hips against her, mimicking small thrusts and hoping I was pressing against the bits that mattered.

Tristan had a long-term girlfriend in high school, but I'd never slept with anyone but him. I'd never even kissed a girl properly before Rose. I'd done so much research to prepare for tonight that my browser history looked like it belonged to a straight teenager given access to the internet for the first time. I was confident about some parts – thanks to Tristan, I knew *exactly* what my mouth could do – but I was less sure about others. I'd topped Tristan so few times I could count them on one hand because that was the way we both preferred it, so I was downright nervous about the potential business end of this, even though I was trying not to show it.

Rose shuddered, her eyes fixing on mine. 'I can't believe I have a scent match.'

'And I can't believe I got so fucking lucky that my scent match is *you*,' I told her, nuzzling down her body, peppering kisses over her soft belly. 'This is *everything*, Rose.'

I could scent her better here, catch hints of the delicious sweetness between her legs. Even though her perfume was weak because of the blockers, it still sent my brain offline. I rubbed my cheek over her belly, my instincts demanding I scent mark her. It wouldn't work, of course, but I enjoyed it anyway, especially as I moved lower, nuzzling between her legs as she gasped, rubbing my cheek on her thigh.

'Seb,' she panted.

'There are clothes in my way, Rosebud,' I said, mock-severely. 'I'd very much like to remove them.'

She laughed softly; the sound went straight to my cock. 'I can help with that,' she breathed, shrugging out of her cardigan and unceremoniously yanking her tank top over her head. Her bra was lace, and I reached out to touch it, trailing my fingers along the edge of the cups, delighting in the difference between the feel of the lace and her skin. Her hands went to her pants; she flicked her button open, and I hooked my fingers beneath the waistband to drag them down her thighs. She'd chosen pink lace underwear, and I could see that the material was damp.

'Fuck,' I said hoarsely. 'You're so beautiful.' She made a needy noise in response, one impossible to ignore, so I tugged her pants all the way off and ran my hands from her ankles to her thighs, spreading her wide. I lowered my mouth to her skin, kissing and licking and nibbling from her knee upwards. She squirmed as I teased her, her pretty gasps filling the air; some far-away part of my brain registered that someone had turned on my *Let's Fuck!* playlist.

I turned my head, taking the alphas in again as I swapped thighs. Byron and Tristan were now almost mirror images on opposite sides of the kitchen bench, their bodies in the same state of ready-to-snap tightness, their knuckles white as they grasped the counter. Tristan's shorts were tented and Byron's jeans looked painfully tight, a deliciously proportionate bulge behind the big alpha's straining zipper.

'Is this still okay?' I managed.

Byron cleared his throat as if he were about to speak, then clearly thought better of it, nodding silently, his jaw working as he swallowed.

'Yes,' Tristan said softly. 'This is about you, Seb. Not us.'

I lifted my head long enough to mouth *thank you* to him before turning back to Rose. Her cheeks were pink with a hectic blush and her teeth were embedded in her bottom lip.

I ran my hand up her thigh, stopping just short of the lace of her underwear. 'Can I touch you, beautiful?'

'Please,' she answered, half a breath and half a moan, and I was gone.

I peeled her underwear down – they were *absolutely* going in my nest – and she wriggled, helping get them off. It didn't help me at all, because I got an eyeful of her luscious ass and the curls between her legs and all the blood in my body rushed south. The hint of her perfume wrapped around me and I was snarling without really knowing why.

Rose knew, though.

She let her knees fall apart, her eyes on my face.

'*Fuck*, you're so pretty,' I said, feeling dazed.

She traced her fingers down my arm, leaving trails of heated skin in their wake. 'Will you take your shirt off for me, Seb?'

I was obeying before I even thought about it.

I'd give her anything she wanted.

She made a happy humming sound when I was bare to the waist. 'Fuck,' she breathed. 'I could look at you all day.'

The feeling was mutual and I told her so, dragging my fingertips up her thighs until they met with slick.

Slick was different to alpha or beta arousal. There was more of it, to start, and it was thicker, to help an omega stay lubricated during a heat. It also had self-healing properties, which I hated was a biological necessity.

Tristan would rather die than hurt me, but I knew that some omegas weren't so lucky.

I traced the crease of her thigh, swirling through the wetness. I brought my fingers to my mouth and sucked; I couldn't help myself. My eyes fluttered closed as chocolate spread over my tongue; I swallowed down the tart raspberry kick.

'Seb,' Rose murmured, a note of amusement in her tone.

I peered at her through slitted eyes. 'Give me a moment, Rosebud. I'm having a religious experience.'

'Do that on your own time,' she said. 'I need my scent match inside me.'

Oh, fuck. That was me. Her scent match.

I touched her again with a groan, tracing over where she was slick and shining. She was soft – *so* soft – and I stroked her for a moment, trying to remember everything I'd read. When I thought I'd worked out where everything was – mostly – I circled my fingertip around her clit. She gasped, tipping her head back, so I repeated the action until her hips were pressing up of their own accord.

'Tell me what you like,' I murmured thickly.

'What you're doing is just fine,' she gasped, but I didn't want it to be *just fine*.

I brushed my thumb over her clit, then pressed down lightly. 'Can I touch inside you?'

'Please,' she panted. 'Please, Seb.'

I traced around her entrance, making sure she was slippery. I loved the way she felt beneath my fingers, so hot and so forgiving. I dipped inside her, slow and tentative, then pulled out; when she sighed and squirmed, I did it again, with more confidence.

'*Oh*,' she breathed.

I'd read about a thousand different articles on what to do next. Holding my breath, I slid my fingers inside her, then settled my thumb back on her clit.

'*Yes*,' she moaned.

Female alphas and betas had a spot inside that some said gave them pleasure, but omegas had extra nerve endings to ensure they felt as good taking a knot as their alpha did giving one. I gently moved my fingers, pressing where the internet had suggested she'd be the most sensitive, then dragging over her inner walls. She squirmed again and gasped; I watched her eyes flutter close and her lips part. She made another soft, plaintive noise, and I decided I wanted to hear that sound every day for the rest of my life.

'Like that, Rosebud?'

'Mm-hmm,' she managed.

I bent to press a kiss to her clit, groaning as her sweet taste filled my mouth. I wanted more, so I pressed my tongue against her swollen bud.

She made a needy sound and ground up against me. 'Fuck – Seb!' she cried, her walls tightening around my fingers. I knew I needed to keep going, which was no hardship. I couldn't get enough of the way that she tasted, of the way she felt, of her mouthwatering scent, of the heat of her body. I couldn't wait to explore every inch of her, to feel our bodies moving as one.

'Fuck,' she sobbed, her cunt squeezing me. As an omega, her body was more malleable than the other designations, and her internal muscles were stronger. My knuckles took a beating because of that, but I didn't care, working her through her climax with my tongue until she shuddered and tried to squirm away.

I didn't let her, though I eased up, pressing kisses to her hips. When her breathing slowed and her muscles relaxed, I withdrew my fingers and licked them clean, swallowing down her addictive taste. 'Are you okay, beautiful?'

'Mmm,' she answered dreamily. 'I think I've needed that for years.'

I frowned down at her. 'Your heat alphas didn't do that for you?'

She shook her head. 'They don't … They don't get you *ready*. You just … take care of yourself until they provide a knot.'

'But they get you off then, right?'

She flushed. 'No, not on purpose. They don't touch you at all, other than the, um, penetration.'

I stared at her. 'That sounds fucking awful.'

'It is.' A savage growl came from the kitchen. *Right – the alphas. Who probably don't want to hear about other alphas knotting one of their omegas.* 'It was,' she amended. 'I hated it. But I didn't have a choice.' She licked her lips. 'But I don't want to talk about that right now. Not when you could be inside me. If you want that.'

I groaned, dipping down to press another kiss to her sweet clit. 'I do want that. But I want you completely naked first.'

Satisfaction rolled through me when I saw her hands tremble. Her eyes were glazed and slick coated her rounded thighs. Then she unclipped her bra, and it was *me* who trembled.

'You're fucking perfect,' I blurted.

Rose was all curves, her breasts full and heavy, tipped with dark pink nipples. Her waist dipped like an hourglass, and I wanted to lick every inch of her stomach.

She gave a soft snort, and there was something self-deprecating in it. I'd read that heats were about more than just knots and cum; they were about bonding as a pack. If Rose hadn't had that – if she hadn't had the adoration, support, and care that she deserved, that she *needed* – then it could have affected the way she felt about sex – and herself.

But I could try to make up for it.

'I showed you mine,' she said, in a breathy, teasing voice. 'But you still have pants on, Seb.'

It took me all of two seconds to unbutton my jeans and shove them down. I was so hard and slippery with precum that it should have been embarrassing, but I'd ceased to be humiliated by my omega body years ago, when Tristan proved, over and over again, just how much my desperate arousal turned him on.

It seemed to do something similar to Rose. Her tongue wet her bottom lip as her eyes fastened on my cock, goosebumps rising on her naked skin. I gave her a show, wrapping my hand around my shaft to pump lazily, encouraging more precum to bead in my slit.

'Oh, *fuck*,' Rose whispered. She sat up; her eyes flickered to meet mine. 'Can I?'

I didn't know what she was asking, exactly, but I didn't really care. I nodded, and she reached up to circle her fingers around my cock, leaning forward to lick a swipe over my head with her hot pink tongue.

Fuck.

Her tongue was heaven, and it was bliss when she sucked me down. She was tentative, her eyes on my face to track my reactions. 'That's amazing, Rosebud,' I purred, my hand cupping her cheek. 'You feel incredible.'

She popped off with a quiet gasp and a wet sound that shouldn't have been as hot as it was. 'I like this. I didn't think I would, but I do.'

Oh. My instincts loved the idea of me being one of her firsts. I stroked my thumb across her cheek. 'I'm going to get an inflatable knot for you. I want to make you feel so good.'

'You will,' she murmured. 'I know you will. Lie down, Seb. Let me drive.'

Fuck. Yes.

I dropped and spread myself out on the couch, my hands finding her hips when she crawled over me. She pressed a kiss to my cheek, then gave me a less chaste kiss on the mouth, her tongue flicking against mine as she settled her wet heat against my cock. I held on for dear life, trying not to explode as she slid her cunt over my shaft.

She gave me a smile – so beautiful, so hopeful, so very much *mine* – and her fingers wrapped tight around me as she lined our bodies up.

Yes, yes, yes –

'Stop!' Tristan shouted.

ROSE

I FROZE IN PLACE.

Tristan hadn't barked, but his voice was forceful, and there was no fucking way my omega was going to disobey one of her alphas right now. Not when Sebastian was spread out beneath me, beautiful and golden and so deliciously hard.

All for me.

'Rose,' Tristan said sharply. 'Are you on birth control?'

I bristled at the question, though I knew why he was asking. Omegas were hyper-fertile; biologically speaking, female omegas were made to pop out babies on the regular, like pedigree dogs.

I didn't know whether Sebastian could conceive or not; though male omegas were rare, there was evidence to suggest that some could both carry and birth babies. *Hey, Seb, can you give birth?* didn't really seem like a polite question to ask, though I supposed we'd have to talk about it sometime, given the events of the evening. Whether he had the extra organs a male omega would need for birthing or not, his sperm would be super potent, which – combined with my overactive ovaries – was a potential complication if we wanted to finish our degrees on time.

I wasn't overly maternal, but I had nothing against babies, either. However, studying was hard enough on its own; I couldn't imagine how people did it while they were exhausted from caring duties. I'd prefer to wait until my life felt a little more stable before I faced the realities of morning sickness, teething, and sleepless nights.

'Yes, alpha, I'm on birth control,' I answered. My tone was tart, because Sebastian's pretty cock was *right there* and my patience was waning. 'I had a full STI check after my heat, and I haven't fucked anybody else since then.'

'Heat? As in, singular?'

I glared at Tristan. He frowned back. Fuck, he was gorgeous, and he smelled *so good*, but I had other things – like my *very naked scent match* – to think about. 'Yes, alpha. Heat: singular.'

'And you're on suppressants?'

'You know as well as I do that they're a requirement of my enrolment. I wouldn't risk my place here, Tristan.'

The alpha visibly relaxed. 'Carry on, then.'

It hit me then that the alphas were just *there*, watching. I'd been so absorbed in Sebastian that I hadn't even thought about it. Their presence could have been creepy – or nerve-wracking, at the very least – but a thrill spread through me as I took in their obvious appreciation. The notion that Sebastian and I were their own personal entertainment – of the sexy kind – unlocked something within me that I hadn't known existed.

I like being watched.

Huh.

Or perhaps more accurately: *I like being watched by* them.

The grey of Byron's eyes was swallowed by his blown-out pupils. At some stage, he'd moved into the kitchen, perhaps to put some distance between himself and Tristan, who stood on the other side. They both held onto the barrier as if it was the only thing stopping them from crumpling to the floor, their expressions equally tortured.

They like this just as much as I do.

Having them there – *watching us* – didn't just make me feel safe; it made me feel *desired*. Precious. The heat alphas had fucked me because it was their job; these alphas wanted us for *ourselves*. They wanted us for our brains and our hearts and our idiosyncrasies. And our bodies, of course. But I had the feeling that if all they got to do for the rest of their lives was watch us, they'd count themselves lucky.

They were ours. I knew it as surely as I knew Sebastian was mine. We were a bookended set: two scent-matched alphas, and two scent-matched omegas; a buffet of tooth-achingly sweet scents.

But before we could claim our alphas, Sebastian and I had to claim each other.

I lined him up and sank down on his cock without warning, impaling myself with a hiss. It had been years since my one and only heat, and although I used toys regularly, they didn't prepare me for Sebastian's thickness and length, and they definitely didn't prepare me for the heat. His cock was as lovely as the rest of him, slightly curved and elegantly veined, his head a beautiful blush-pink; it felt as good as it looked. The stretch was delicious as I rose up and worked my way back down, Sebastian's hands tight on my hips.

'Fuck, Rose,' he grated out.

'Let me know if you want me to stop,' I whispered.

He laughed. 'It feels so good I can't see straight. Do your worst, beautiful.'

My worst was that I was determined to blow his mind; it occurred to me that this would certainly be his first time with an omega, and, given what he'd said about his experience with high school bullying, possibly his first with a woman, too. If that was the case, then he needed a whole sheet of gold stars for the way he'd used his fingers and tongue. I hadn't come so hard in months.

I rolled my hips, watching his face. Emotion welled inside me; I wiped my tears away before he could see them. There was something overwhelming about this moment, about seeing the man beneath me, a lock of golden hair falling into his clear blue eyes, and knowing that I'd found my scent match. It was incredible that he existed at all, but having him *here*, so close to me? And the fact we were friends beforehand, as if, even then, we knew we had a connection?

It was pure magic.

Sebastian groaned, more hair falling in disarray across his brow. I picked up my pace, angling to take him deeper. 'Rose,' he panted, his hands moving to my ass.

I splayed my fingers across his chest and ground myself against him. He rose up to claim my mouth, his tongue dancing with mine as I felt pleasure start to build in my core.

'Yes,' he hissed against my lips. 'Use me, omega. Come all over my cock.'

Sebastian had a filthy mouth, and I *loved* it.

His hips began to roll, fucking up into me with smooth, hard strokes, even as I slammed myself down. I cried out as he hit some place deep inside and pleasure sparked like stars in the night sky. It was so different from my heat; I wasn't desperate for a knot, wasn't begging for an alpha's bite. I was doing this because I *wanted* to. My body was singing like a melody, and Sebastian's face had taken on an expression of rapturous wonder as he watched me move.

'Sebastian,' I whispered, realising that the sparks of pleasure were spreading, meeting, and catching alight in a blaze of bliss. It broke in a wave that made my body tight as a bowstring, then boneless, floating.

Sebastian gave a wordless shout as his body tensed and his cock pulsed. I felt the warmth of his release as he moaned my name, and when I shifted forwards to collapse on his chest and listen to his heart beat, his cum seeped from my body, sticky and wet.

It made my heart race. *Mine*, I thought fiercely. *Mine*.

'Mine,' Sebastian croaked, echoing my thought as he nuzzled my hair. 'You're mine, Rosebud.'

My teeth ached, begging to descend and mark him as my own. I ran my tongue along them, trying to ease the pain.

'Fuck, I want to bite you,' he muttered, and I was glad I wasn't the only one.

My eyes flickered to Tristan. It struck me how calm he was, given the situation. His omega – the man he'd loved for six years – had just fucked someone else right in front of him.

And not *just* someone else – his *scent match*.

Not many people would be holding it together like Tristan was.

I turned my gaze back to Sebastian. 'I want to bite you, too,' I whispered. 'But I think we need to talk about it later. All of us.'

His eyes searched mine. 'All right, beautiful. Whatever you want. But *this* –' he gestured between us '– doesn't have to be about anyone but us.'

I tilted my chin to kiss him. 'You're amazing, omega.'

He did something I wasn't expecting, and *blushed*.

Fuck, he was so beautiful when he blushed.

Heat flared through my body once more; he lifted his hand to brush back my hair. 'Do you think we've made them wait long enough?' he murmured, his eyes darting to where the alphas were standing, watching. 'Or do you want me to tell them to fuck off, and I'll show you my nest?'

I had a suspicion that if Sebastian showed me his nest, we wouldn't leave it for days.

'They've been waiting so patiently,' I said, loud enough for the alphas to hear.

Sebastian chuckled, shooting Tristan a taunting grin. 'The head alpha waits until last, don't they?'

Tristan tensed even further, but gave a curt nod.

I blinked in surprise. The alphas weren't bonded – were barely even *speaking* – but they'd had *that* conversation?

'Go get your alpha, Rosebud,' Sebastian whispered, but it wasn't Tristan his eyes lingered on.

Byron's gaze was fixed firmly to my face. He could have been looking *anywhere* – I was entirely naked and dripping cum – but his eyes were on mine as I pushed myself off Sebastian. I didn't go to him, because I was starting to realise that I might get off on power, too, and it felt right to make my alpha come to *me*.

Something deep inside whispered that it was what I *deserved*.

I knelt on the couch, lifting my chin and spreading my knees in a blatant invitation.

'Alpha,' I whispered.

BYRON

AM I EVEN ALIVE RIGHT NOW?

I certainly wasn't breathing as I took in the sight before me.

Sebastian rolled on his side, propping up his chin with one hand as he watched Rose, watched Tristan, watched *me* through heavy blue eyes. Fuck, he was even more beautiful naked, his body patterned with dips and shadows that defined his slender muscles. A line of golden hair trailed from his belly button down like a mouthwatering arrow pointing to his still-hard cock. It was beautiful, too; long and thick and slightly curved, shining with Rose's slick and his own cum.

I wanted my mouth on him so badly that my lips twitched. I lifted a hand to my face to check I wasn't drooling.

Rose smiled in a way that suggested she knew what I was thinking, but if she knew *that*, I doubted she'd still be in the room. She was glorious, her cheeks flushed pink, her hips reddened from where Sebastian's fingers had dug into her flesh as she rode him. Her eyes were lidded and dark as they fixed on mine and my alpha clawed at me, more insistent than I'd ever known before.

She spread her knees in an invitation that almost had me dropping to my own. She was pink between her legs, too, and swollen, glistening where Sebastian's release was leaking from her body. It was obscene and erotic and the most seductive thing I'd ever seen. I wanted to lick and suck until she was clean and writhing, and then I wanted Sebastian to make her messy all over again.

'Alpha,' she whispered.

She was talking to me.

Never in my life had I imagined being this lucky.

'Omega,' I purred, surprised and relieved when my voice didn't break. It had dropped an octave and was gravelly enough to pave a fucking driveway, but Rose shivered at the sound, so I wasn't about to complain. 'Are you inviting me in, beautiful?'

'Yes.' Rose bit her bottom lip – as though I needed *more* reason to go to her, as if her naked body and flushed skin wasn't draw enough. 'I want you, alpha. *Need* you.'

If my ego wasn't already sky-fucking-high from her invitation, it might have rocketed to the *stars* after hearing *that*.

I pulled off my boots and socks – why was taking shoes off always so fucking unsexy? – and ignored the way

Tristan's breath caught when I tugged my shirt over my head. Having my scent match so close but still being so fucking *angry* at him made me feel as if my insides were made of crepe paper and I was being slowly torn to shreds. I simultaneously wanted to offer him my neck – and other places – and punch him in the face, and I was sure he was feeling something similar towards me.

But this wasn't about him. Not yet, anyway.

After the scent party, I expected that somehow, my life would *always* be about Tristan Grace, but I tried to push the thought aside as the alpha inside me fixed on Rose with an unnerving focus.

Mine, he growled, and I didn't disagree. I wanted both the omegas with a fire that – for the first time in years – made me feel whole.

I sank to my knees.

Rose's eyes widened and she inhaled. I caught a hint of her sweet scent in the air as I crawled towards her. My mouth immediately watered; I wanted it stronger, wanted it spread over my tongue, sliding down my throat. I wanted it to fill my lungs and cover my skin.

She whimpered, and I realised that I was less *crawling* and more *prowling*. I'd wanted to show her that I'd do anything for her – that I'd get on my knees for her – but instead I was showing her that even crawling, I was a predator.

I just hoped she knew that I was collared, and that she was holding my leash.

She tilted her head, unconsciously showing me the elegant curve of her throat. It was pretty now, but it would be even lovelier covered in tooth-shaped scars. Sebastian would bite over her scent gland, as was his right, but one day, I was going to make a beautiful chain across her silken skin that would tell any other alpha in no uncertain terms *exactly* who had the honour of belonging to the perfect omega.

If she asked me, I'd leave room for Tristan's bite.

But only if she asked.

I reached the back of the couches when my vision started to go white.

Fists pummelling, knuckles covered in blood, broken moans rising and falling like music to my ears –

I shook my head slightly, swallowing, trying to brush off the memory.

I was close enough to feel the heat pouring off her; I sat back on my feet, looking down at my omega, at my little *queen*. I studied her adorable nose, her perfect jaw, her lovely neck. I took in her pink-tipped breasts, her spread knees, and the curve of her soft belly.

Beautiful.

Dragging him from the doorway of his pack house and throwing him down on the grass outside. Picking him up when he stayed down, when he didn't get to his feet and face me, me, *whose life he'd ripped to shreds with one careless decision –*

The white spread.

I tried to breathe through it. *The rut is normal,* Dr. Ford said in my memory. *Natural. A rut helps alphas service their omega through a heat. It helps them protect what is most precious to them.*

I blinked furiously, trying to will the mist away, but my vision was clouding. The only thing I could see was

Rose, in the same way that the only thing I'd seen on that night seven years ago was *him*, and the blood on my hands.

The rut is normal, Dr. Ford said again.

But what if this wasn't a rut?

I inhaled, desperate for Rose's scent and the peace it might bring me, but all I could taste was copper.

'Alpha?' she said tentatively, and reached out to touch me.

What if I hurt her?

I reared back, out of reach. The white spread. Tristan was saying my name, and there was a hand on my back that must have belonged to him, warm against my bare skin. Sebastian sat up, moving towards Rose, and –

What if I hurt them?

Once the thought had taken root, I couldn't shake it. The mist thickened mockingly; I blinked furiously, willing it to disappear.

The rut is normal –

'Get up!' I roared at him, my voice shockingly deep and shockingly strong, my dominance carried by my bark. I'd never used it before; it scared me and made my throat feel raw. But he deserved it. 'Get up!'

He did, somehow. He got to his knees, and his body made all sorts of sounds with the movements, sounds it shouldn't have made, squishing and cracking and everything wrong. He was hurt, badly hurt, and I'd done that to him – I'd done it with my fists. I'd made him this human-shaped pulp, but it wasn't enough.

It wasn't enough.

It could never be enough, because he'd taken the most precious thing in the world from me.

'Alpha?' Rose said again, her voice breaking through the memories, desperate.

What if I hurt her?

I staggered to my feet, stumbling backwards. I hit Tristan with my shoulder on the way; his expression was half imploring, half understanding. 'I'm sorry,' I choked, tearing my eyes away from him, away from *them*, and stumbling, shirtless and barefoot, to the door. 'I'm sorry. I can't.'

TRISTAN

My scent match closed the door behind him with a thud.

I stared at it, waiting for it to open again, waiting for Byron to walk back in with a smile and another *I'm sorry* – with a different meaning this time – and claim the little omega he'd wanted so desperately for months.

One heartbeat.

Two.

Three.

Byron didn't come back.

A wordless whine cut through the air.

I turned in time to see Rose hug her arms across her chest. Her eyes were glassy, and all the colour had drained from her face. 'Alpha,' she said numbly. She looked across at Sebastian, but I wasn't sure she really saw him. She was trembling. 'Doesn't want me.'

I almost reeled at her words, so similar to what I'd said the night of the scent party.

'No, Rosebud, I'm sure that's not –' Sebastian broke off when he noticed her shivering. 'Oh, *fuck*.'

I moved, grabbing the throw blanket from one of the couches and settling it around Rose's shoulders, careful not to touch her. 'Skin to skin, Seb,' I said, struggling to keep my voice calm. Research on rejected omegas was thin on the ground, because who the fuck would reject one? But I *did* know that the symptoms mirrored those of an omega fighting an alpha's bark, and the shock of it could literally kill them.

I inhaled slowly. I wanted to shout, wanted to *roar*, wanted to leave and find Byron, then drag him back by the scruff of his fucking neck.

I simultaneously wanted to tell Rose that Byron would *never* reject her, that something else must have been going through his mind, because I couldn't believe that he would leave her – especially like *this*, bare and beautiful and wanting – without a *very* good reason.

I suspected I knew what that reason might be.

A sharp pain shot through my chest, as if my heart really was breaking.

Sebastian took Rose into his arms. She sagged against him with a soft whimper. 'It's all right, Rosebud,' he soothed, but I didn't think this could be solved with some supportive words. 'It's all right, beautiful.'

'Left me,' she said blankly.

She trembled violently, and Sebastian pulled her closer, shooting me a desperate look before pressing his lips to her hair. A rumbling sound filled our apartment, and a moment later, I realised what it was.

He was purring for her.

The noise eased the ache in my chest, but it couldn't chase away the worry.

Rose looked up at me. 'Alpha,' she whispered, her lips tinged blue.

Oh, fuck.

Everyday Rose was hard enough to resist, with her quiet intelligence and warm brown eyes. But Rose when she was vulnerable and desperate?

She was alpha catnip, and I was seized by the impulse to *make it better*, no matter what, no matter how.

'I'm here, omega,' I heard myself say, and my own rough purr ripped from my chest. 'We're here. You're safe. You're wanted.'

She pressed herself against Sebastian as if she were trying to sink beneath his skin. It took me a moment to understand that the sound coming from her was keening.

'Take her to the nest, Seb,' I said softly. 'Keep her wrapped up and warm. Make her feel safe.'

Sebastian glanced at me, his face creased in a rare expression of indecision.

'Seb, baby. She thinks Byron rejected her. She's in shock. She needs warmth, comfort, and she needs *you*. You've got this, handsome. Take your omega to your nest and make her feel better.'

He nodded, scooping Rose into his arms. The blanket slipped but didn't fall, baring one of Rose's smooth shoulders. My chest wrenched to see them that way, both vulnerable and hurting.

Usually, I would have waged a one-alpha war against anyone who dared to make Sebastian's life even the slightest bit inconvenient.

But my *scent match* had done this to him. To *them*.

A fissure rent through my chest.

'Will you come with us, alpha?'

I shook myself, realising that Sebastian had paused outside the door to his nest, Rose pressing her face into his neck.

I swallowed. 'Are you inviting me into your nest, omega?'

'I am,' Sebastian answered quietly.

I'd never been in Sebastian's nest.

I'd seen it, of course – from the doorway, handing Sebastian pillows and coverlets and watching as he fastened swathes of gauze to the ceiling and strung fairy lights over the low, wide bed. But it was his space, not mine, so I'd never stepped foot in there, and as he was yet to have a heat, I never had reason to ask for admittance.

Which didn't mean I didn't want it, desperately.

My eyes pricked with tears. 'It would be an honour.'

Sebastian carried Rose inside and laid her gently on the bed. He touched her lightly, carefully, rubbing the blanket on her limbs and chafing her bare feet and hands to warm them.

'That's it,' I murmured. 'She needs your touch, your skin. Your body heat.'

Another blanket lay folded at the end of the bed. It was one I'd bought Sebastian, so soft it felt like touching a cloud, and I draped it over them both. Rose was still worryingly pale, but her eyes were focused on Sebastian, which I hoped was a good thing.

The nest smelled like him, the delicious cherry scent making my mouth water, but my instincts protested that the scent should be stronger. It should have been on every surface, and so heavy that it pulled me under the moment I stepped through the door.

My scent should have been in here, too, but of course there was nothing. It wasn't just the lack of scent; there should have been memories in this place, days of fucking and lovemaking, of comfort and cuddles and kisses in the dark, of falling asleep with limbs entwined.

I hadn't realised how desperate I was for Sebastian to have a heat. Not until I was here, in the place it would happen.

'I'll make you both some hot chocolate,' I said, because a hot drink containing too much sugar could never be a bad thing.

'Don't go,' they said as one. My stupid alpha *preened* at the idea of my omegas needing me.

'Stay, Tris, please,' Sebastian added, and that settled it.

I wasn't going anywhere.

'Alpha,' Rose croaked, and lifted her hand towards me.

I reached and took her fingers in mine, glancing at Sebastian for permission before climbing into the bed. The omegas had snuggled on their sides, so I settled behind

Rose. She rested her head on my bicep and I tentatively lay my other arm across her waist, my hand cupping Sebastian's hip. A purr rumbled in my chest as Rose nestled against me.

There was no way to stop my cock from hardening — it had softened after Byron left, but apparently it loved being pressed against Rose's plush ass — but I held myself still. Even so, I caught a hint of Rose's scent in the air, with the undertone of mint my senses seemed to find in her perfume. The mix of chocolate and cherry was closer to how the nest should have smelled, but it still wasn't perfect. My vanilla should have been here, too, entwined with Byron's salted caramel.

The nest looked slightly different to the last time I'd seen it. It had previously been a mix of navy blues and silvers, simple and elegant. Now, there were some sea-greens, creams, and golds added into the mix, with a splash of white from some new star-shaped lights hanging from the net above the bed. Beach colours.

I wondered why Sebastian had made the changes, and why *now*, when his nest had been the same for the six years I'd known him.

'She's asleep.'

I looked down to see Rose's eyes closed, her lashes shadowing her cheeks. Her lips were slightly parted, her cheeks stained with dried tears.

'She must have been exhausted,' Sebastian added, his voice hoarse. It was understandable; he wasn't used to purring for any length of time, and he'd been shouting with pleasure before that. I made a mental note to brew him some tea with honey.

I shifted, careful not to disturb Rose, and studied him. He was pale and tired-looking, but his eyes were bright with emotion as they fixed on his mate's face.

This must have been what a heat was like, a pack giving their all to keep their omega from the cramping pains, working to keep them satisfied. 'What do you need, Seb?' I said softly.

'What she needs,' he answered. 'Byron back.'

Pain rent my chest once more, but I nodded, slowly pulling away. Rose murmured in her sleep, shivering. Sebastian cuddled her close, and I draped another blanket over them.

It was difficult to leave the nest, too difficult. Everything in me fought against it. I should have been with my omegas, keeping them warm, purring to help them sleep peacefully. But if Rose needed Byron, then it was my job to make that happen.

I called him from the kitchen; he didn't answer. I waited, listening to the ring tone, tapping my fingers on the smooth, cold bench. It went to voicemail. I tried again; this time, the call cut off instead, as if he'd hung up. I dialled a third time; the same thing happened.

I sent him a text. *I'll come to your room if you don't pick up.*

He answered immediately when I called again. 'What is it, Grace?' he said wearily.

My throat went tight. He sounded exhausted – *ruined,* even. 'You need to come back.'

'Yeah, that's not happening.'

My nostrils flared. 'I didn't take you for a coward, Griffiths.'

'Fuck you,' he said, but there was no fire in it; perhaps he didn't have the energy for anger. 'You don't know me.'

'This isn't about you,' I snapped. 'It's about Rose. So alpha up and get your ass back to your omega.'

He was quiet for a moment. 'I can't,' he said at last, and I could hear his heart break in the words. 'I'll hurt her.'

'Byron, the sky would fall down before you'd hurt Rose.'

'You saw the video. I can't risk that.'

The video of Byron turning another alpha into a whimpering mess of bruises and blood. 'This is not even remotely the same,' I said impatiently. 'You're in love with her. You want her. You want her for yourself, and you want her for your alpha. She thinks you rejected her. And if you don't come back, you'll make it true.'

There was another silence, one so long that I began to feel triumphant. I'd convinced him.

'I can't,' he said, and hung up.

I stared at my phone.

'No,' I said to it, softly.

It buzzed, as if in response. I opened my messages immediately, hoping against hope that it was Byron and he'd changed his mind.

Instead, the message was from an unknown number.

9pm beneath the clocktower, it said, followed by a banksia flower emoji.

I inhaled in shock.

I hadn't heard from the Revels since the day they'd abducted me in the maze. I'd assumed I hadn't done enough, that I hadn't *compromised the omega* to their standards.

It seemed I was wrong.

I stared at the words. My hair fell into my eyes, but I didn't bother to push it back.

This was everything I'd wanted. I could make Sebastian's dreams come true.

But this didn't feel like *triumph*.

I'd never been particularly affected by guilt before, but I'd gained this – the privilege of possible membership to the Revels – by manipulating Rose. Suddenly, that notion didn't sit well, not when she was sleeping in my omega's nest, not when she was Sebastian's.

Not when she was *mine*.

I'd used her attraction to Sebastian to bolster my own ambition before I'd really known her. It didn't matter that she'd never been at risk, nor that I'd done it for Sebastian's benefit.

Byron was right to hate me for it.

I pushed my glasses up my nose, swallowing.

Things had changed. Rose wasn't just another student who happened to admire my omega. She was Sebastian's scent match, and she was *pack*.

I had to fix this. I had to make amends.

I exhaled unsteadily. Byron's past was his own business, but he'd let it hurt Rose. And if Rose was mine, then it was my responsibility to make sure she had everything she needed, always.

The omegas were my priority, even at the expense of my feelings. *Especially* at the expense of my feelings.

And even at the expense of my scent match.

They were my sun. They were my *pack*.

'Sorry, Byron,' I murmured to myself. My heart gave a heavy throb. I rubbed my free hand over it absently, trying to soothe the hurt, but it didn't diminish.

I didn't think it ever would.

I deleted the text from the Revels without another thought, then grabbed my laptop, bringing up the videos I'd saved so carefully.

I walked into the nest.

Rose was awake, cradled in Sebastian's arms. Her face was puffy and her eyes were red.

'Omega,' I said, and fell to my knees next to the bed. 'I have something to tell you, and then I have something to show you.'

ROSE

I STARED AT THE LAPTOP SCREEN, watching the videos for what seemed like the fiftieth time.

Do you know why you're here? the APF psychologist asked, her voice made high by the small speakers.

Because I hurt someone, the dark-haired boy answered.

And why did you hurt him?

The boy's shoulders bowed. *Because he killed my sister.*

He wasn't a boy, not really, but at barely twenty, he wasn't quite a man, either. The signs of grief were evident in his heavy eyes and tightly wound body. The skin over his knuckles was broken and red, occasionally weeping; he absently wiped up the blood with the bottom of his black shirt.

The boy in the videos hadn't quite grown into his body, his limbs long and gangly. His hair was shorter, too, shaved at the back and sides. But the sense of power was there, an echo of the alpha Byron would become.

I closed the video and clicked into an article, one I'd already read, and already cried over.

Omega Killed by Drunk Alpha in Horrific Crash in Canberra's South, the title said.

I didn't read it again, just stared at the screen until the text became a grey blur.

'Rose?'

I looked up, my cheeks wet with tears once more.

Sebastian crossed to my side. I was in his bedroom; Tristan had carried me from the nest. The nest wasn't the right place for what he'd told me – or what he'd shown me.

I shivered.

I didn't think I'd gone into proper rejection shock, not really. I wasn't feeling *good*, but I was functioning, and my body was gradually warming. Tristan's confession hadn't helped; Sebastian had put me in the bath afterwards, getting in with me and wrapping his arms around my body until I stopped trembling.

I didn't want to believe that Tristan had used me in such a way, but he'd told me with an even voice and a level expression, with no attempt to hide details or shrink away from what he'd done, and my instincts told me it was the truth. He'd deliberately pit my designation and my body against me to bolster his chances of membership with the Revels, putting me in danger – in *public* – and using Sebastian to do so. The fact he'd hired extra security alphas made no difference to me – it was the intent behind his actions that hurt, and the manipulation.

I could hardly credit it. Sebastian didn't *need* his alpha's help to get the Banksia Prize; he'd get it on his own account. *If I didn't beat him to it*, my snarky, competitive side interjected. But in an odd way, I could also see things from Tristan's point of view: Sebastian had been his entire life for six years, and the Banksia Prize was Sebastian's dearest wish. Were I in Tristan's place, I'd probably do some questionable things to help him get it, too.

But I could barely digest Tristan's confession in the face of what I'd learned about Byron.

I'd been curious about the monitors; who wouldn't be? I'd known it could be bad. I'd been told about what happened to alphas when their instincts took over.

But I'd never really thought about *why* it could happen, about what could have sent Byron into such a state that he'd succumb to the alpha beneath his skin.

I clicked into a different video.

In this one, Byron was wearing a suit, sitting on one side of a long table next to a fair-haired man I knew now to be his liaison officer, Dr. Ford. Beside them were two women, Byron's lawyers.

Trials involving instinct blackout didn't happen in the usual way, I'd learned. There was no prosecution, no judge to arbitrate, no jury; just the alpha in question, their representatives, and senior members from the APF.

The injured alpha refuses to give evidence, one of the APF officers said, sitting unerringly still in her distinctive black uniform.

But he needs to, Byron answered, his voice desperate. *I assaulted him.*

The other APF officer shook his head. *That's not the way this works*, he said gently. *But what we can recommend –*

I stopped the video and clicked into another document.

This one was long; I'd still read it twice. It was wrong to do so, but once I'd started, I couldn't stop. It was Byron's own journal entries, at least one for every day he'd been in the state-mandated Alpha Retreat.

Fuck, I miss her so much today, he'd written. The date indicated that he'd been in the facility for just over one month. *Sometimes, this still feels like a nightmare. Like I'll wake in my own bed and stumble to the kitchen, and there she'll be, blowing on her coffee and stuffing her face with raisin toast.*

Sometimes, I feel guilt for what I've done. Sometimes, I wish Dad had never stopped me, that I'd –

I took a deep breath.

Sebastian wrapped his arms around me. I settled back against him, letting my tears fall freely. 'How did this get so complicated?' I croaked.

He kissed the tears from my neck. 'The truth can be like that.'

'I understand why Byron left the room that night, and why he's kept his distance, but understanding doesn't take away the hurt. And Tristan …' I trailed off. 'I'm so angry, Seb.'

'You have every right to be.'

I twisted in his arms, looking up at him. '*You* hid it from me, too.'

He didn't turn away, looking me in the eye when he answered. 'Yes. I didn't see a reason to hurt you with it. But

I will never hide anything from you again, Rose. I promise you.'

I sniffed. 'I don't know what to do.'

He pulled me close. 'You don't have to do anything right now. Just let yourself feel it.'

I turned back to the laptop, clicking into the last video. It wasn't as clear as the others; it had come from a home security feed.

Come out, you fucking coward, the dark-haired boy shouted, striding across the front lawn of a suburban home. *Come out and look me in the eye.*

Nothing stirred.

Come out, Byron roared, and this time, the sound was carried by his alpha bark. Even second-hand, my spine straightened without me telling it to; behind me, Sebastian tensed.

The front door opened and a sandy-haired alpha stumbled out, clearly against his will. Byron wasted no time, dragging the man down onto the grass. I winced as his fist connected with the other alpha's cheekbone. *You killed her*, Byron said, calmer now. He pulled back, then let his fist fly again, this time straight into the sandy-haired alpha's nose. *You killed my sister.*

I closed my eyes as the sound of fists on flesh continued, keeping them closed until Byron's voice came again. *Get up*, he barked. *Get up. I'm not even close to finished with you.*

Somehow, the other alpha got to his feet. His body looked wrong; all kinds of noises came from his limbs as he straightened them beneath the force of Byron's bark.

The alpha's packmates stood on the verandah, watching, but they made no move to intervene. Numbly, I wondered why; Byron was one boy in the face of four grown men.

Had the sandy-haired alpha made a terrible, tragic mistake? Had he not realised how much he'd drunk when he'd scented Byron's sister – Christina – and convinced her to go home with him before he'd lost control of his car? Or was drink driving something he'd done before?

And either way, did his pack think he *deserved* the justice Byron was offering? Was that why they made no move to help?

I held my breath at the thud of Byron's fists meeting flesh once more, then exhaled when another man sprinted across the lawn, throwing his arms around Byron and putting his own body between the two alphas.

No, no, no, Carwyn Griffiths pleaded, his glasses askew, his black hair in disarray. *Stop, B. You'll kill him, and we can't lose you too. We can't.*

I shut the laptop with a click and burrowed into Sebastian's arms.

◈◈◈

I didn't sleep – how could I? – but I did think. For hours, I thought about what I'd learned: what Tristan had done, what Sebastian had kept from me, what Byron had been through. The hurt I was feeling melded with the hurt I felt on their behalf – for the insecurity that Tristan hid so well, for the pressure he put on himself to give Sebastian the things he wanted, rather than accepting that Sebastian loved him for his own sake. For the torn loyalty Sebastian must have felt in keeping secrets, even in the face of his own guilt. For the way that Byron's actions years ago cast lasting shadows over the potential for his future happiness.

Sebastian stirred awake in the early hours of the morning, and I slid onto him, taking him inside me and rocking slowly until we came together in a gentle explosion of soft gasps and even softer kisses. He nuzzled my neck, scraping his teeth over my skin. I brought his lips back to my mouth. I wanted his bite – *badly* – but not until I'd worked through what I needed to do to fix all this.

Because I'd had enough of crying, that was for sure. But *thinking*?

Thinking was something I could never get enough of, and it was something I was good at.

I'd solve this, one way or another.

❁❁❁

It was, of course, more difficult than I'd expected; Byron didn't come to class for the next week. Nor did he respond to messages or calls, and neither did Tristan see him at the gym, or in the pool, or in the gardens.

Sebastian and I pushed each other to work on our final essays. We'd chosen different topics, so we bounced ideas off one another, testing our arguments, checking our references, helping each other with word choice. It was hard to focus, so we'd work in short bursts and be rewarded at the end with cups of tea, made by Tristan, who spent every waking hour keeping a watchful eye on both of us.

By the weekend, I felt largely like myself again. I'd stopped trembling, my temperature returned to normal, and I could eat properly once more.

I resented my reaction as much as I resented anything about my designation, and I hated the reminder that alphas held so much power.

'It's not right,' I growled.

'No,' Sebastian agreed, absently stroking my calf as he sat on the floor before me, reading through a journal article on his tablet. His fingers paused. 'What's not right?'

'Alphas,' I answered.

He looked across at Tristan, who was in the kitchen, making caramel slice because Sebastian had asked for it, a pained expression on his face. 'Um.'

I put my laptop aside. 'I have to do something.'

'What kind of something?' Sebastian said warily, watching me get to my feet. 'Rosebud? What kind of something?'

I blew him a kiss. 'Don't wait up.'

'Rose, what –' Tristan started, but I dodged past him, smiling, and closed the apartment door behind me.

From their point of view, this would seem impulsive. But I'd thought about this non-stop for a week. I was tired of tiptoeing around my own instincts and the quirks of my designation. I'd been letting things happen *to* me, rather than making them happen for myself, but it didn't have to be that way.

I didn't have to wait for the pack I wanted to form around me.

I could make it for myself.

Byron had left me that night – left *us* – but leaving didn't mean he had to *stay* gone. It just meant he needed time. I could check in, make sure he knew that he was wanted, that we'd be there when he was ready.

He might not come back, I knew, pausing on the main staircase. I might get rejected once more. The pack I'd come to want so badly might never be anything but a dream. The thought wasn't a nice one, but there was zero doubt in my mind that the payoff would be worth the risk.

He was worth the risk.

Steeling myself, I walked to his room.

I knocked on his door. There was no answer, so I knocked again. When nothing came but silence, I called his name.

'Rose?'

I spun to see Alessia poke her head out of a door down the hall. 'Oh, hey,' I said sheepishly.

Her lips twitched. 'He was going out as I was coming back from dinner,' she told me. 'He said he was going for a walk.'

'Thanks, Alessia,' I said, grateful, and made my way back down the stairs.

It hadn't really helped. I now knew the one place he *wasn't*, but there were a thousand places he *could* be.

There was one place he'd talked about, though; one place I knew he went often.

It was a stupid time of day to be outside. The sun was beginning to set, which meant the local snake population would be most active. The eucalypts bordering the Banksia gardens cast long shadows on the ground as I stomped my way down a sandy path, careful to make as much noise as I possibly could. The sky was just starting to darken, lit at the horizon with shades of orange and pink.

With every step, I rehearsed what I would say. When I saw him, however, sitting on the grass near the cliffs and looking out to sea, I forgot every single sentence I'd planned – and possibly every word I'd ever known.

He didn't notice me at first. The breeze was blowing towards us, so I was almost on him before he spun around at the sound of my feet. He'd taken a blanket with him, thick and comfortable-looking, a patchwork of black and blue. His eyes widened at the sight of me, and he went statue-still, the kind of stillness that usually preceded an animal springing to its feet and bolting at speed.

'I watched the videos,' I blurted.

He stared at me. He didn't look well; his skin was paler than usual, and there were shadows beneath his eyes.

'And I read the articles,' I added.

He muttered something under his breath that sounded very much like *Tristan fucking Grace*, then turned his gaze back to the ocean.

The view was breathtaking. I hadn't been out here before; I'd been too wary to come by myself, and I hadn't thought to ask someone else to join me. I'd kept myself shut inside, a habit since my designation had been revealed, and now I knew what I'd been missing.

The ocean stretched before us all the way to the horizon. The water was restless, broken by peaks of white and glints of the late afternoon light. The relentless rumble of the waves filled my ears, so loud I almost didn't hear when Byron spoke.

'Which videos?'

'All of them.'

'And which articles?'

'The same.' I paused, and sank down onto the blanket, an arm's length away from him. I could feel his heat regardless. 'Along with all the legal transcripts, your admission papers for the Alpha Retreat, your journals, your discharge papers, and your psychology reports.'

'That's ... quite an invasion of privacy.' His tone was half-impressed, half-annoyed. 'I can't believe Tristan found all that.'

'There was more,' I said honestly. 'I can safely say that if it exists, Tristan has it. He hadn't planned to share it, I think. Even Sebastian hadn't seen it. Not until –'

'Not until I walked out.'

I didn't answer.

He shifted and plucked at a handful of grass before him. 'Why are you here, Rose?'

'Because I've seen all that, and you're still mine,' I answered softly. 'You're my alpha. But if you don't want to be –' I swallowed, feeling as if I'd suddenly swallowed my own tongue '– you're my friend regardless, and I care about you. I want to be here for whatever you need.'

He glanced at me, his expression unreadable. 'For whatever I need,' he repeated.

I held his gaze, trying to let him see the truth of it. I wanted to let him know that I cared, and I really *would* do whatever he needed – even if what he needed was more space. Even if he needed space *indefinitely*.

He looked away. 'What happened … It's not a nice story.'

'It doesn't matter if it's nice.' I cautiously settled on the blanket, crossing my legs. 'I'm here if you want to share it. That's what *friends* means. And I think –' my tongue felt leaden once more '– I think that might be what *pack* means, too.'

His throat worked as he swallowed. 'Pack.' He said the word reverently, tasting it, then looked down at his monitors. 'I'd never forgive myself if I hurt you,' he said, his voice rough and quiet. 'You or Sebastian. I don't know what I'd do. You're precious beyond belief. And I'd rather deny myself than risk that.' He shook his head. 'I've realised over the last few days that it doesn't matter how much I want it. It doesn't matter how good it would feel, how *right*. Pack isn't for me. It can't be.'

I shifted closer. 'We've never felt anything but safe with you, Byron.'

He closed his eyes.

'It's more than just safety,' I continued softly. 'You feel like … You feel like lazy weekend mornings and talking about our days. You feel like trips away and watching films and buying furniture. You feel like conversations about everything and nothing and cups of tea when it gets cold. You feel like life outside Banksia.' I paused. 'It's terrifying, but you feel like forever.'

He took a shuddering breath. 'You feel like forever, too,' he whispered. 'You feel like everything I've ever wanted.'

My omega preened at that, demanding we be closer to our alpha, but I knew he wasn't done. I shifted again, feeling his warmth on my skin, but still not close enough to touch.

He sighed and opened his eyes to gaze back out at the fiery sky and endless sea. 'My sister, Tina, was an omega.'

My fingers twitched.

'We were always close, always best friends. She was a year older than me, exactly to the day. Our parents used to joke that we were late twins. We even looked that way – both tall, with the same dark hair, the same grey eyes. We did everything together. Tina never minded that I was her shadow; we had the same friends, the same interests. The only way we differed was that Tina loved building things, loved using her hands, while I loved reading and getting lost in other worlds. Our parents would say that I'd dream a world, and Tina would build it.

'She revealed as an omega when she was fourteen.' My breath caught; *so young*, I thought. 'A few months later, I emerged as an alpha. It was way too early – for both of us – but I had to, I think. Can you imagine what a fourteen-year-old omega goes through?' My chest constricted; I *could* imagine it, all too well. 'The staff at our school were on blockers and cancellers – it had just been made law – but the students weren't. They couldn't be, and neither could Tina. They were way too young. But it meant that Tina was never left alone. She was harassed from the moment she stepped onto school grounds by the older students. Even a teacher –' He cut himself off. 'Dr. Ford thinks my alpha emerged in response to that. That my instincts knew my sister needed someone to watch her back. And so I did.'

My heart ached; I rubbed it with the palm of my hand.

'My parents wanted to homeschool her. Tina refused. She said it wasn't her problem that other people wouldn't control themselves. She said they needed to be given the opportunity to try, that things were changing, and they needed to get used to being around omegas. Mum and dad weren't happy, so I went to the principal and demanded to take the assessments from Tina's year. I passed them, and the principal agreed to move me up and place me in Tina's classes. He was relieved, I think. It took the burden of care off his teachers and put it on me.'

For a moment, I was furious beyond belief at an adult I'd never met placing that weight on a child's shoulders. On *Byron's* shoulders.

'Nothing had changed, not really. Tina and I still did everything together, only now I used my height and my weight and, when I needed to, my fists, to make sure she was safe. That became my life – making sure Tina was safe.'

'You were so young,' I whispered.

I didn't think he'd hear me over the breeze, but he did. 'I won't say it was easy,' he answered. 'Tina was headstrong and sometimes she didn't think things through. But the world should have been safe enough for her to make the same mistakes alphas and betas can make, and it wasn't. It isn't. Everything was against her, and it's only human to err.

'When she finished school, she got an apprenticeship with an all-female company of electricians. It was great for her, though I think ...' He inhaled. 'I think she would have moved onto something different, if she hadn't –' He cut himself off again, as though he wasn't ready to say the word. 'She had this amazing creativity. I think she would have ended up in design, or engineering, maybe. She could look at an empty space and see what it could be, you know? She'd take a box of blocks and build a castle, a palace, a dreamscape. She could have ... She could have ...'

He shook himself. 'It was just after her twenty-first birthday, just after my twentieth. Her friends were going out. Usually, I would have gone, too. But we'd had a fight.' He was silent for a long moment. 'It was stupid. So fucking stupid. She'd worn one of my favourite shirts to work and had to plaster and paint a wall. It wouldn't come out of my shirt and the band didn't sell them anymore, and I got cross about it. I stuffed my nose in a book and told her to have a nice night.'

A tear ran down my cheek. The sky was a mess of pink and orange now, with the dark blue blur of night spreading slowly up from where it met the sea.

'He wasn't even her scent match.' There was a tremor in his voice. 'He was a complementary scent.

But Tina's heat was close. She slicked in the bar.' His tone steadied and became detached; I watched his profile fall back into expressionlessness. 'He convinced her to go home with him. She got into his car, and he went into a rut.

'They were two blocks away from the bar when he lost control. He was doing twice the speed limit, the police said, and he'd been drinking. He drove into a shop window.

'Then he left – he left her there.' I swallowed a keen at the way his voice halted and thickened, pressing myself against his side. 'He was injured, but not enough that he couldn't stagger away from the car. He left Tina there. She wasn't dead, not at that point. She was still alive when the ambulances arrived. She died on the way to hospital. She'd bled out from a wound that he could have compressed, if he'd bothered. If he'd stayed.'

I pressed my face into his arm.

'My parents … I can't even describe what they were like, when the police showed up on our doorstep. It broke them, and that's the sum of it. And it wasn't just them.'

For a few moments, we listened to the crash of the waves beneath us.

'Rage isn't a big enough word for what I felt,' he continued at last. 'That alpha had taken my sister, taken my best friend. And he didn't even have the guts to stay with her while she was broken and dying.

'It was easy to find the address of his packhouse. Easy to wait until the police returned him home on bail, pending his trial. Easy to use my bark to make him come outside, easy to let my fists fly.' He swallowed. 'It was what

I was used to. He looked up at me and told me to keep going. That he deserved it.

'The worst thing is that I don't think he was evil. He was stupid, arrogant, and careless. And that was enough. His carelessness took the best thing in our lives. It was enough to break our family. Enough to change everything we'd known, enough to tear our hearts in two.'

He moved, and I could tell he was looking down at me. I lifted my chin, looking back at him.

His jaw worked. 'The government and the APF don't tell the public that a rut and an instinct blackout start the same way,' he went on, his voice lowering as if someone might hear. 'My vision went white. I'd never had a rut before, and I didn't know what was happening. I just saw clouds in my eyes and the alpha who had killed my sister on his knees. So I kept punching, and that's the last thing I remember.' He blew out a breath. 'I've seen the footage. I know what I did, and what I kept doing. I know that it took dad to stop me. But I don't remember it, Rose. It's like I fell asleep. And when I woke up …' He trailed off. 'I woke up in a bed that wasn't mine, in a room I didn't know, with what seemed like a thousand monitors strapped to my body. But my alpha settled, and I *did* wake up. Some alphas don't.'

The weight of his stare was almost unbearable, but I made myself meet it. If he'd been strong enough to get through it, then I could be strong enough to hear about it and not look away. I wondered how many alphas had never come back to themselves, whose bodies became a husk ruled by the creature beneath their skin.

'It took a while to ... adjust,' he went on at last. 'I was watched every moment of the day. They like to study us, because instinct blackouts aren't a common thing. In the past, they didn't even know what caused it. Medical textbooks will say it's *a critical surfeit of hormones, causing permanent or temporary cognitive collapse.* They've found no links to existing illnesses, either physical or mental, and there are no factors they can find that make an alpha more or less susceptible, other than their designation. One of my doctors told me it was simply *a thing that can happen,* which wasn't a comfort then, and still isn't now.

'And then ... I had to relearn my life without Tina in it.' His breath hitched; I felt it beneath my cheek. 'It wasn't easy. I think about Tina every day. I've spent the last seven years making sure that I was never in a situation where I might go into a rut. But when I saw you like that, Rose, flushed and perfect and needing, the rut started to rise and my vision went cloudy –'

'I understand,' I whispered, wrapping my arms around him as another tear ran from my cheek down my neck. 'I understand.'

'Thank you,' he said, a long moment later. 'For understanding.'

The sea was darkening, the points of white silvering as the moon rose. I shivered, even with Byron's warmth pressed against me. 'Do you think it will happen again?'

'I don't know. I hope not. The doctors don't think so, but I can't give any guarantees. And I'll likely be wearing monitors forever.'

'And if we decide you're worth the risk?' I said softly.

He swallowed. 'Rose –'

'Please give us a chance, alpha,' I whispered. 'Please let us in.'

'I need to tell you something else,' he said dully. 'Tristan –'

'Told Sebastian to kiss me at the first-year party so he would make me slick, compromising me in exchange for membership to the Revels?' I interrupted.

He stared at me, frowning, turning his body to face mine. 'Tristan is –'

'Sorry,' I broke in again, looking him in the eye. 'He's sorry for what he did. He told me about it, apologised, and looked after me when –'

'When I left.' Byron looked out at the sea once more.

'Yes,' I said. 'When you left.' I reached up and gently turned his face back towards me. He blinked at me. 'I'm angry about what Tristan did. I won't pretend I'm not. But I've seen his good side, too, and he's genuinely sorry. He's Sebastian's alpha, so he's mine, too, even if he needs to rethink his priorities. He fucked up and so did Sebastian, keeping all the secrets he did; they both know it. But one bad thing doesn't have to define our relationship. One mistake doesn't have to define our future.'

He searched my face, his eyes darkening as the light faded. 'Do you really believe that?'

I knew he wasn't just asking about Tristan and Sebastian. 'How do we learn, if we can't make mistakes?' I answered. 'How do we grow, if we can't change?'

His hand came up; he smoothed my hair back from my face. 'Do you still want the Banksia Prize?'

'Of course I do.' My heart beat faster at the thought of battling against Sebastian. 'Seb might be my scent match, but I'm not giving up on what I want, even if he wants it too.'

'Good.' His thumb stroked over my cheek. 'You deserve that prize.'

I climbed into his lap, pressing my cheek to his chest. He was still for a moment, then his arms came around me, holding me tight. I'd never felt quite so sheltered as I did in that moment, soothed by his solidness and the rhythmic sound of his heartbeat.

After a few minutes of us listening to the waves, he sighed. 'My heart almost stopped that night, you know,' he said softly, 'when I saw you on your knees. You were the most beautiful thing I'd ever seen. But I would have been satisfied with *this*, Rose. Just with the privilege of holding you.'

'It was too fast for you,' I said, realising. 'It was too much, too soon.'

'Maybe.' He nuzzled my hair. 'Although I need you to know that I want you very much. But I hadn't known what to expect, and my alpha … Well, my alpha liked it *too* much, perhaps.'

I leaned back against his arm and looked up at him. 'Your alpha is *perfect*.'

He snorted. 'The preening bastard agrees with you.'

I laughed; the sound died as he dipped down and brushed his lips over mine, once, tentatively.

Oh.

I surged up to make it happen again. *More.*

I hadn't realised I'd spoken aloud until he chuckled against my mouth. 'Whatever you want, whenever you want it, omega. Literally anything. Ever.'

His alpha wasn't the only one preening.

The kiss was sweet, *so* sweet. His hand cupped the back of my head, cradling me like I really was precious, and his lips moved against mine, gently. I lost track of time amidst the nuzzling kisses, the soft caresses, the way his thumb smoothed over my nape. My body warmed from the inside out, as if I'd been drinking something hot and sweet, and a different kind of heat built in my core just as slow and sweet as the kisses.

He made no move to take it further, not until I parted my lips and let my tongue touch his skin, encouraging him to open to me. Our tongues met, and paused, and played, and I sighed with satisfaction as I melted into him.

'I should take you back,' he murmured, pressing kisses to my jaw.

'Should you?'

'Are you cold?' he asked.

I shook my head.

'Getting eaten alive by mosquitoes?'

I laughed. 'No.'

'Hungry? Tired?'

'None of the above.' I kissed him again, biting gently at his bottom lip. 'The view is too beautiful to go back inside.'

'It is,' he agreed, but he wasn't looking at the sea or the sky.

I kissed him harder, lips and tongues sliding, my hands questing upwards until I could bunch my fingers in his hair. It was softer than it looked, slipping like silk over my skin. He made a surprised, approving sound when I tugged on some strands, his arms crossing over my back as I wrapped my knees around his waist.

I hadn't realised how hot my body was, how tightly wound my core. It had been building so gradually and gently, a backdrop to the emotion, to the connection between us. His lips pressed a trail of kisses down my neck; I threw my head back to let him nuzzle at my collarbone, a moan escaping my throat as his tongue flicked out to taste my skin.

'Byron –'

His breath fanned over my chest, warm and tickling, sending a thrill through my limbs. 'Mmm?'

I squirmed on his lap. 'I –'

He pulled back and I squirmed again, this time in disappointment. 'What do you need, beautiful?'

I didn't want to push too hard, not again. I pressed a lingering, closed-lipped kiss to his jaw. 'Whatever you're willing to give, alpha.'

BYRON

Whatever you're willing to give, alpha.

My heart raced. I'd already said what I was willing to give to her.

Literally anything. Ever.

My body was electric, my muscles quivering, my hands trembling.

Because this was *Rose*, and she was in my arms, on my *lap*. This was my omega, and she was staring up at me, her eyes heavy in the now-dark, her tongue darting out to touch her bottom lip.

Fuck.

She shifted her hand, placing it over my heart. I did the same, mirroring her pose, feeling her heart thump against my palm, the soft rise of her breast beneath my fingers.

'Alpha,' she whispered, and that was all I needed.

I took her mouth with mine once more; her tongue licked into me. I groaned, my hand shifting until I was cupping her breast, my thumb brushing back and forth over her nipple, feeling it peak beneath her blouse. She turned her chin, offering the lovely arch of her neck. I bent to nuzzle at her scent gland, loving the way her breath caught. I licked at her sensitive skin, listening to her whimper as her knees tightened on my hips.

I gently nipped her earlobe. 'Tell me what you like.'

She pressed herself closer. 'I, um –' She cleared her throat. 'I'm not sure I've done enough to know. I liked everything I did with Sebastian, but I didn't like – I didn't like –'

'Your heat,' I guessed.

She nodded, swallowing. 'I didn't like the way I felt … used. I wanted to feel *seen* instead.'

It didn't surprise me. She would have wanted to feel grounded, to know that her alphas were there to fulfil her needs. It wasn't the heat alphas' fault; our society treated heats like an inconvenience, something to be suppressed at best, or endured as quickly as possible at worst.

I didn't want anything that happened between me and Rose to be anything like her heat. In fact, I wanted it to erase any memory of those alphas from her mind. I kissed my way across her cheek, finding her lips again. I lingered there as my hand traced the shape of her breast, caressing and moulding until she moaned into my mouth; my cock pressed uncomfortably against my jeans.

'I'm not going to ask to undress you, beautiful, not out here,' I murmured. 'Just in case. But can I touch you?'

'I might die if you don't,' she answered.

I laughed softly. I liked her dramatic streak. There wasn't anything about her I didn't like, I realised, and there were many, many things that I loved.

Like the way her muscles tightened when I lay my hands on her bare knees, and the way her skin felt beneath my palms, warm, smooth, and oh-so-enticing as I slid my fingers up under her heavy woollen skirt. Like the way she gasped when my thumbs brushed over her inner thighs, drawing loose patterns on the sensitive skin, and the way she bit back a cry when I found the lace of her underwear and played there.

I dipped my head, kissing down her neck once more. I brushed my knuckles over her centre gently, once, twice; before the third pass, she was arching and chasing the touch, whimpering.

I wanted to see her so badly; wanted to see her spread out beneath me like a fucking feast, naked and begging. But anyone might walk by, and that wasn't a sight I was willing to share.

'How much do you like your underwear?'

She blinked at me in the dark. 'A medium amount.'

I pulled my hands out from beneath her skirt – she made a flattering sound of disappointment – before spanning her waist and holding her upright. She swayed, shivering, as I delved back below the heavy folds of material and pulled the lace down her legs. She caught on, kicking them off, then sank back down on my lap, arranging her skirt to fan out around her.

I cupped the back of her head with one hand and dipped her gently back, feathering light kisses over her collarbone as my free hand trailed up one soft thigh. Her breath caught and she spread her knees, giving herself over to me as her full weight rested on my hand and arm. My fingers found wetness on her thigh and trailed through it; my alpha purred at the feeling, pleased. *My omega is slicking for me.*

She trembled when I touched her properly, skimming my fingertips over her lower lips, spreading her slick, lingering against her heat. She cried out as I touched her clit, pressing her hips up. I let her set the pressure and speed, keeping my fingers steady as she used me, circling her hips until her breaths were unsteady and I was lightheaded with desire.

'*Please*,' she begged.

I wanted her scent, wanted the taste of her slick on my tongue. I wanted to touch every inch of her, to *kiss* every inch of her, to scent mark her skin and have her do the same in return.

Fuck, I was dizzy with it.

Instead, I gently stroked a finger down, and let it slowly slip inside her as she moved.

'*Yes*,' she hissed, her lips parting. 'More, alpha.'

I wasn't entirely sure I could handle *more* without embarrassing myself; the feel of her wet heat and her inner walls tight around my finger had me concerningly close to the edge. But she was my omega, so I gave her what she wanted, pushing another finger inside her and letting my thumb settle over her clit. 'Take what you want, beautiful,' I grated out. 'Take everything.'

She whined as she rode my hand, the rhythm of her hips becoming faster, their circles tighter. I held her, utterly transfixed by the sudden line between her brows and the movements of her lips as her body grew hotter and tighter and her whine changed to a keen. She clenched around my fingers almost painfully, but I gave exactly zero fucks as she panted through her release and my hand was soaked with her slick.

'Byron,' she whispered, when she'd caught her breath and her body relaxed.

I gently withdrew my fingers and pulled my hand out from under her skirt. Holding her languid gaze, I pushed my fingers between my lips and sucked.

Fuck.

Her taste wasn't as strong as it should have been because of her blockers, but it was enough; chocolate spread over my tongue and down my throat, with its delicious chaser of roasted almond. I groaned and my cock jerked, rubbing painfully against the unforgiving crotch of my jeans.

'Okay, but that is *unfair*,' she said thickly, watching me lick my fingers with evident enjoyment. I caught a hint of her scent on the breeze and dropped my face immediately to her neck, rubbing my nose over her scent gland to try to catch more.

'Please let me do that every day,' I said into her skin.

She gave a soft laugh. 'Are you begging me, alpha?'

'On my fucking *knees*.'

She made a pleased humming sound; her fingers went to my belt. 'Can I?'

I nodded my agreement with a rumbling purr.

She shot me a wry look. 'So you can be naked out here, but I can't?'

'I already have a criminal record,' I joked.

She snorted, and pulled down my zipper. 'Oh,' she said, her eyes widening, a flash of white in the dark. *'Oh.'*

The alpha beneath my skin huffed smugly. 'You don't have to –' I started, then swallowed my words when she shifted back from my hold, ducked down, and licked my swollen head.

My hands bunched in the blanket beneath me. *'Fuck.'*

Her tongue slid over me, then found the sensitive spot on the underside of my shaft. Lapping like a cat, she *hummed* again as I writhed, breathing hard at the sight – and the feel – of her hand wrapping around me as her hot tongue lathed over me. 'I can't tell you how good that feels,' I said hoarsely.

'I want you inside me,' she said, as if in answer.

My eyes began to cloud, and I froze.

A hand cupped my cheek. 'Byron,' Rose whispered. 'We won't do anything you don't want to do. You're so amazing, alpha. We can just talk some more. Or go back inside.'

I inhaled as white misted my vision; it narrowed until all I could see was Rose, kneeling before me, her hand warm on my cheek.

I waited for the memories to come, for the sounds and visions and the pain, but her fingers stroked over my cheek, and –

It didn't happen.

Her fingers traced my brow, my cheekbones, my chin. 'Alpha,' she whispered again.

I pulled her back into my lap and spread her skirt around us.

She made a surprised sound, and a pleased one a moment later when she lowered her hips and my head slid through her wetness. The white didn't leave my vision, but it didn't spread, either, leaving Rose as the only thing I could see, the only thing I could think about. Relief spread through me.

A rut, I thought. *I'm finally in a rut.*

'Byron,' she said softly. 'Do you want this?'

I answered honestly. 'More than I've ever wanted anything.'

She kissed me gently, then I almost passed out as she started sinking down, my cock enveloped by her velvet heat.

Holy fucking hell.

She worked her way down, pausing halfway. Even in the dark, I could see the points of colour high on her cheeks, twin shadows on her moonlit skin. 'Fuck, Byron,' she panted. 'So fucking full.' She rose up on her knees then let herself drop, taking more of me before repeating the motion.

I slid my hands back up her thighs and pressed my thumb to her clit. She arched her back and slammed her hips down, taking me to the root before freezing in place, panting.

I held myself still as she adjusted, working my thumb until her body tightened, her cunt clasping and rippling around me, slick coating us both. She moaned as she came, and I held on by a thread as she rocked, rubbing herself on my swelling knot.

'I don't think I can take that,' she gasped. 'Not outside a heat.'

'I'd never ask you to.'

'But *fuck*, alpha.' She pulled a handful of her skirt out of the way before reaching to caress my knot. Pleasure sparked at the base of my spine; stars danced across my vision. 'Now I can't *wait* to have another heat.'

I snarled, my alpha finally snapping his leash. I thrust up – not enough for my knot to stretch her – shouting wordlessly when she tightened around me once more, determined to make her climax again, wanting to feel her body milk my cock. She planted her hands on my shoulders and met me thrust for thrust, hips rolling, my fingers digging into the flesh of her thighs. She threw her head back, strands of hair escaping her braid as she ground herself against me.

'Alpha,' she panted, a whine escaping her throat as my fingers traced where we were joined, caressing her slick skin. '*Alpha.*'

'Come for me, omega,' I grated out. 'Come. *Now.*'

I didn't bark – I would *never* do that to her – but she came anyway, her body tightening, squeezing around me until the sensation at the base of my spine sparked and spread, flooding through my body. Rose rolled her hips, milking me of every drop of cum until I was shuddering with pleasure. She collapsed forward with me still inside her, her cheek against my heart once more. I nuzzled at her hair as my orgasm ebbed, my canines aching, pushing down through my gums.

I couldn't think of anything I wanted more in the world than for this omega to wear my bite – except maybe making her come again – but I kissed her neck instead, licking at her skin as she sighed.

'You're mine,' she murmured. 'My alpha.'

'And you're mine,' I whispered back. 'My friend, my menace, my love. My Rose.'

She stirred, bringing her lips back up to mine and kissing me fiercely, and there was no more talking after that.

SEBASTIAN

Rose was gone for hours.

I tried not to be a jealous asshole, but who was I kidding? My omega rode me hard, demanding I be with my pretty mate, and I found myself sniffing one of the t-shirts she wore to bed every few minutes like the obsessed loser I was.

'It's because you haven't bonded,' Tristan murmured to me, stroking my hair when I stopped pacing long enough to collapse into his lap. 'Once you have her bite, this feeling will settle. According to the articles I read, anyway.'

'Wait,' I said, looking up at him. 'Do you feel this way about Byron? *All the time?* Like if you don't see him *immediately*, you'll somehow die for want of it?'

He swallowed, but didn't answer.

Fuck. My poor alpha.

What Tristan had done to Rose – and to me – was wrong; I had absolutely no illusions about that. But seeing him so heartbroken – so *tortured* – was, I thought, punishment enough. If what he felt was anything like the feeling churning in my chest and stomach, then he'd been in pain for *weeks* now. Surely he'd paid his penance.

When a soft scraping noise came from the apartment door, I jumped up and literally *ran* towards it. Rose slipped inside, looking beautiful, glowing, happy – and *rumpled.*

She threw her arms around my neck as I wrapped my own about her waist. 'Fuck, I missed you,' she said, the sound muffled as she pressed her face into my shoulder. 'Is that silly?'

I buried my face in her hair. 'No. I've been doing so much pacing, I'm surprised there's not a new path worn through the carpet.' I inhaled, catching a hint of scent – hers, and something else. I pulled back and grinned at her. 'It smells like *the thing you had to do* went well. *Very* well.'

She flushed, and arousal hit as if I'd been punched in the stomach. I kicked the door closed behind her and tossed her over my shoulder, pressing my nose into the fabric of her heavy skirt as she laughed.

Chocolate and caramel. My mouth watered. 'I know this will sound hyperbolic, but I think I need you to ride my face. Like, now.'

She laughed again – slightly shocked, this time – but didn't protest when I lowered us both onto the couch. Tristan put down the book he'd been reading, audibly swallowing. I shot him a questioning look — *are you okay with this?* it said — and he gave a nod in response.

'Can I eat you out?' I asked Rose. 'Please?'

'You can do whatever you want to me,' she said huskily. *Whatever you want* was a silly thing to offer because my imagination was fairly solid, and what *it* couldn't conjure, I was sure the internet could supply.

I unbuttoned her skirt, murmuring wordlessly in approval when it pooled on the ground and I realised my omega was bare beneath it. Byron might have been an alpha and not prone to nesting, but I'd bet my entire inheritance that Rose's missing underwear had a new home beneath his pillow. I settled on the couch and drew her down, arranging her knees beside my head and filling my hands with her plush ass.

'Slick,' I said, surprised; she was coated with it, its distinctive shiny sheen different to the usual arousal.

She flushed, though I wasn't sure why; my cock was so hard it hurt. 'It's been happening for a while now. I think my body wants to have a heat, but my blockers are preventing it.'

'Has it happened before?' I swiped some up with my fingertips, then licked them clean with a purr of enjoyment.

'No, but I looked it up online. Apparently, it's not uncommon.'

My gain.

She was swollen and pink and looked very much as if she'd already come a number of times — possibly the same number of times that Byron had come inside *her*. The faint sweet scent of her slick filled my senses; I groaned, needing to taste more.

I started gently, mouthing at her swollen folds, licking softly at her sensitive clit. She shuddered, rocking slightly as I mapped her with my tongue, indulging in my own need and pushing it inside her. Chocolate and salted caramel flooded my mouth; my cock jerked in my shorts, the material already damp with precum.

Fuck yes.

Rose whined, and I switched my attention to where she wanted it, sucking gently on her clit. She shivered, her knees tightening around my head, and I made sure to keep my mouth gentle and slow so I wouldn't make her sore. She circled her hips slightly, starting to lose herself to the feeling.

A moment later, she went still.

I looked up; Tristan was next to her, stroking her cheek. 'Can I kiss you, omega?' he asked gravely.

Oh.

'Oh,' Rose breathed, as if echoing my thought. 'I … Yes, please.'

'I need you to know,' Tristan said steadily, 'that it isn't about him. That I want to kiss you for *you*.'

I returned my attention to between her legs; Rose bit off a moan. 'U-understood.'

I didn't watch them kiss, but I heard it. Tristan was unhurried and thorough; Rose was increasingly desperate, her whimpers and pants caught by Tristan's mouth as my own worked between her legs. When her body tightened, I thrust my tongue back inside her, desperate to feel – and taste – her climax; while she was still shuddering, I fished beneath my waistband and brought myself off with two quick pumps of my hand.

'I want you to move in here,' I said, when Tristan helped her climb off me and she collapsed on the couch, still catching her breath.

She blinked at me, startled, but it didn't take her long to answer. 'Yes. If that's okay with both of you.' Her eyes flickered to Tristan, who was halfway to the bathroom, grabbing a towel to clean us up. 'But we need to fix this, Seb.'

I knew what she meant by *this*: our pack.

The only issue was that I had no idea *how*.

❖❖❖

Rose went back to her room only to gather her things. It didn't take long with Tristan and I helping; she didn't have a lot to move. The three of us made some unspoken agreement to sleep in the nest instead of my bedroom, and something about it felt *right*, as if that was where we should have been from the start. Tristan had bought the largest nest-bed he could find, and even with the three of us in there we could sleep without touching. Rose and I went through her things and mine together, choosing what would stay in there; we added her sea-green blanket to the end of the bed, and some of her cream cushions atop the pillows. Her fairy lights were pinned to drape with the netting, and her scented candles went on the bedside tables. We moved some of my cushions out, and swapped the abstract painting I'd hung for a set of vintage botanical prints of coastal plants and flowers we found online. I was glad I'd already made some changes; Rose seemed to like it, humming happily every time she stepped into the nest.

Tristan ordered all her favourite snacks and practised making chai tea and lattes just the way she liked them. He emptied out some of our shelves and helped her arrange her favourite books. Within a few days, he knew what she needed when she studied; knew which foods would tempt her to take a break; knew the temperature she liked her baths and which oils to use in her water; and would time exactly how long she needed to be left alone in the mornings until she felt human again.

If I hadn't already been wildly in love with him, those actions would have tipped me over.

Watching him with Rose made me realise just how much I'd taken for granted. I'd thought that he just had an instinct for knowing when I needed something, when in reality he worked hard to know and to anticipate our wants. Rose bloomed under his care and attention, her smiles frequent and beaming.

'You're the best alpha in the fucking world,' I murmured to him one afternoon, after he brought Rose and I hot drinks as we read through a chapter on medical anthropology.

His cheeks went pink, and I was glad I'd said something.

He and Rose hadn't kissed again, though she was happy to snuggle in his arms. Tristan blushed every time he pressed his lips to her hair. I wondered whether that was all it would ever be – packmates didn't have to be sexually intimate, after all – but I suspected there was a spark between them. It was a quiet one, steady and slow-burning, but I had a feeling that when it finally caught alight, it would flare hot enough to scorch.

Byron and Rose saw each other every day, studying after class and occasionally retreating to *hang out* in his apartment. I assumed they spent their *hanging out* time fucking like rabbits, which was what I would do in their situation, but Rose was careful to shower before she came home; she whispered one day that she was worried she'd upset Tristan if she came back smelling like Byron again. I worried even more about Tristan than I did about studying; he was pale, distracted, and anxious. I did everything I could to make him feel wanted, but I remembered how it felt not knowing where Rose was, and I knew it was a problem I couldn't solve. Rose and I talked about it at length – I even called my dads for help – but Tristan and Byron had to sort it out for themselves.

I just hoped they wouldn't take too long.

It was mid-term break when it started.

I had a light stomach ache, just enough to wonder whether I'd pulled a muscle, or had eaten something that didn't agree with me. I didn't spend much time thinking about it – it was easy to ignore – but it persisted through the drafts of my final essay, then through its submission, and into preparation for the end-of-semester exam. It grew worse on the night of the pre-exam party, which saw Rose and I dancing in the First Year Library again, but this time, my heart wasn't in it. I was agitated and anxious, and my clothes rubbed the wrong way on my skin. The smell of scent cancellers made my nose hurt, and every time someone brushed against Rose – accidentally or otherwise – I had to hold myself back from growling.

Tristan watched me, frowning; eventually, he suggested we went back to our apartment, a suggestion I was only too happy to take, for his sake, as well as mine. Byron had been at the party, chatting and laughing easily with Pravin and Chul. The other two alphas had bonded the week before, proudly wearing their bites with content expressions, their hands always touching.

I was happy for them, but fuck was I jealous.

I'd wanted Tristan's bite for years, but he'd always held back. He said he didn't want to take my choices away – what if I found another alpha I liked better? What if I found an entire *pack*?

He couldn't see that I'd already found it, that any pack would need to fit around him, as well as me. Usually, I tried not to let it bother me too much, but tonight I couldn't get it out of my mind.

Rose perched on the side of the bath while I brushed my teeth, her brow furrowed. I couldn't stop touching my neck, dragging my fingertips over my scent glands, bemoaning the lack of bite marks. When I put my toothbrush back on its charger, she caught my hand and pressed her cheek against my stomach, as if she could sense the ache there.

'Something's not right,' she murmured.

I ran my fingers through her hair. 'No. I don't feel well.'

She spanned her hands across my lower back, and it was only with that movement that I realised how much it was hurting. The heat of her palms relaxed my muscles, soothing me. I sighed.

'I'll get you a hot pack,' she said, then led me to the nest, where Tristan was already waiting.

I fell into his arms; he ran his fingertips gently over my skin. Our scents were stronger in the nest now, though I wanted more, and the notion that our scents were weaker than they should be in this special place – this place for *us* – made me irrationally upset. I buried my face in Tristan's neck, raking in breaths, trying to catch a hint of vanilla.

Tears welled when I didn't find it. I wiped my eyes before he noticed, though I couldn't stop myself from sniffing.

'We'll go to the doctor tomorrow,' he said softly.

I didn't feel up to arguing.

When Rose came back, she pulled a soft blanket over my shoulders and nestled the hot pack on my lower back. It felt amazing, but I grumbled wordlessly until her arms were around me and her lips were pressed to my hair.

'The omega is strong today,' she whispered, a hint of laughter in her voice.

'You have no idea,' I returned grumpily, my words muffled by Tristan's chest.

I loved having their hands on me, loved their warmth and their care, loved being sandwiched between them. For a while, I did nothing but lie there, content with knowing my alpha and omega were close, content with listening to their soft breaths and Tristan's heartbeat. But when Rose shifted her hand, her fingers splaying across my stomach, my body reacted as if she'd grabbed my cock, and blood rushed downwards until I was painfully hard.

I gasped at the sensation, so different to the way I usually became aroused. Precum was already dampening my boxers, and the pressure of arousal was sharp and intense. 'I –'

'Seb?' Tristan murmured, worried, lifting up on one elbow.

I shifted restlessly, pressing myself against him. 'I need –'

Tristan inhaled. We hadn't been together, the three of us, since the day Rose had first fucked Byron. I didn't want to pressure them, but my cock was aching in a way that made my mind blank. 'I don't –'

'It's okay, Seb,' Rose whispered. Tristan's eyes flickered towards her, his face glowing faintly under the fairy lights. He gave a tiny nod at whatever he saw in her expression. 'We're okay.' She trailed her hand down and took hold of my cock through my sleep shorts. She stroked me, then pushed my shorts down and took me properly in hand just as Tristan seized my mouth with his.

Having *both* of them touch me was like nothing I'd ever felt. I couldn't think straight; my world split in two, divided between the warmth of Rose's body behind me and her grip on my painfully hard cock, and Tristan's mouth on mine, wet and hard and divine. My body stiffened against an unfamiliar wave of pain rippling through my torso; a wash of pleasure followed it, and I came with a groan all over Rose's fingers.

'Beautiful,' Tristan said roughly, peppering my face with kisses. 'So beautiful, omegas.' With a glance at Rose, he caught her hand and lifted it, licking my cum from her fingers, sucking her thumb into his mouth.

Rose's body tightened behind me; I heard her soft gasp. Tristan didn't go any further, releasing her hand with a kiss to her knuckles before he shifted down the bed to lick my cock and stomach clean.

It should have been enough, but I still felt oddly restless, the pain settling heavy and deep in my stomach. My dreams – when they eventually came – were full of reaching, my hands searching for something that wasn't there.

◇◇◇

I stayed in bed the next morning.

We were scheduled to take a practise exam in class, but I didn't have the energy. Tristan put his hand to my forehead; my temperature was slight, but it was enough that he noticed.

'Seb, baby –'

'I don't want to see the doctor,' I said petulantly. I knew it was silly, but I couldn't seem to help myself. 'I just want a day in bed.'

Neither Rose nor Tristan liked the notion – that much was obvious – but I made them agree to go to class, though my omega was secretly pleased that Rose insisted on skipping her usual study session with Byron in favour of coming back to the apartment early. I knew that if they stayed with me, I'd snap at them, and there wasn't any point in all three of us being miserable. I felt … *needy*, though I didn't know what for. Changeable. I simultaneously wanted to be alone, and needed Rose and Tristan skin-to-skin. I wanted to be covered in blankets, but couldn't bear the feeling of their weight. I wanted a bath, but I was already flushed and sweaty. I wanted water, but only water full of ice, and even then I only wanted a sip at a time. My morning hard-on wouldn't go away, not even after Tristan got back into bed with me and gripped both our cocks in one hand, taking control until I couldn't hold back any longer.

It was testament to just how whiny I was that they both agreed to go to class, though not before making me promise to text if I needed anything.

'I just want to watch trashy TV and feel sorry for myself,' I muttered. There was a severe storm warning for later in the day, so it was the perfect opportunity to stay inside.

Before they left, Tristan made a pile of snacks and some drinks, bringing them to the nest. He'd made hot chocolate in a thermos, so that it stayed the right temperature.

Fuck, I loved him.

I found something terrible on a streaming service and put it on my laptop. I was too irritated to watch it properly, changing position every few minutes, then getting up and pacing around the nest. I ate some of the snacks, but my mouth tasted funny and my stomach churned at the thought of food I'd normally devour. Eventually, I unscrewed the lid of the thermos and sipped the hot chocolate. It was extra sweet, and Tristan had sprinkled some tiny raspberry drupelets and vanilla sugar over the whipped cream.

I couldn't shake the feeling that something was missing, though.

Irritated, I shifted my weight, the coverlet brushing against my skin in a way that made me bristle. Huffing, I got up and ripped it from the bed, tossing it out into the hall. Rose's blanket was balled up at the end of the mattress and I picked it up, rubbing it against my cheek. It was soothingly soft and smelled faintly of her artificial perfume, though I couldn't catch any of her omega scent. My eyes prickled at the thought, my instincts hating that I was missing that all-important piece of my scent match in this special place. I spread the blanket over the bed carefully, then realised the pillows were wrong; I picked each one up, rubbing the cushions against my cheek, tossing some out and keeping some, arranging them around the bed in a rough circle.

But it still wasn't right.

Tapping my fingers absently against my thigh, I made my way to Tristan's room, inhaling. There was a faint hint of vanilla coming from his bed and from his washing basket. I ran my hands over his bed, then carefully bundled up the coverlet, carrying it to my nest and folding it inside my cushion circle towards the end of the mattress. Returning to Tristan's room, I rifled through his dirty washing, finding a shirt he'd worn to the gym and the boxer shorts he'd been wearing that morning before he'd gotten us both off. The material had been wet with precum and remained deliciously sweet and musky.

I clutched the clothing to my chest and sighed, happier.

I took both things back to my nest, stuffing them under my favourite pillow. I left the lid off the thermos, and when I lay back down, I breathed in the scents of vanilla and chocolate. It settled me, though I wished desperately that both scents were stronger.

And something was *still* missing.

Outside, the storm was gathering. The sky gradually darkened and the wind picked up, howling against the nest window. I hoped that Tristan had decided against his usual afternoon walk, but my alpha wasn't foolish; he'd stay safe.

It was early afternoon when pain laced through my stomach, so strong I screamed, but the sound was lost beneath the howl of the wind.

ROSE

My omega stirred. *Something isn't right.*

A sense of wrongness pushed down on me like a weight. I paused in the act of submitting my practise exam, my fingers suddenly trembling.

Sebastian.

Not for the first time, I wished that I'd let him bite me. If he'd bitten me, I'd know more through the bond; as it was, I only knew that something had changed, that something was *wrong*, and that I needed to get back to him.

I clicked the *submit* button and impatiently waited for the confirmation page to load, shoving my drink bottle and reference notes back in my bag. When a message popped up on my laptop saying I'd submitted my exam successfully, I screenshot it, saved the image, then shut my laptop.

'Ms. Morris?'

I looked up to see Professor Heathcote eyeing me with barely disguised distaste. 'I need to go. It's a personal matter.'

His eyes narrowed. 'Class hasn't finished yet.'

'I've submitted my exam.'

He cleared his throat. 'And, as I said, class hasn't finished yet.'

Fuck, this man was an asshole. 'I appreciate that, and I apologise for the disruption, but I need to go.' I glanced to the side to see Tristan watching me, frowning.

Are you okay? he mouthed. I could see his laptop screen was on one of the last questions, though he still had a few to complete.

I spent half a moment bemoaning the fact that *he* hadn't bitten me, either.

I gave a slight shrug, not wanting to lie to him, but not wanting to worry him, either, not when all I had was a feeling of wrongness and he hadn't finished his exam. His frown deepened, but he turned to the front. 'I'll take notes for Rose.'

Heathcote's lips thinned. 'It seems you're making a habit of that, Mr. Grace.'

Tristan's stare didn't waver. 'Isn't that what a good alpha does for their pack?'

Oh.

I felt a rush of emotion – elation, relief, gratitude. Tristan had claimed me, publicly, as part of his pack.

I hadn't known if I'd fully forgiven him, or whether he was ready to take that next step. But my chest went tight and my fingers burned with the urge to touch him;

something in me eased, knowing this alpha – *my alpha* – had my back.

I swallowed. 'Thank you, Tristan,' I whispered, and shouldered my bag, slipping from the library as he and Heathcote continued their staring competition.

I knew which one of them would win.

I rushed to the apartment; *our* apartment, now, I supposed. The promised storm had arrived with a vengeance and it was dark as fuck outside, the wind howling like a pack of wolves. There was supposed to be a movie night after dinner in the First Year Library, and the weather would be perfect for a horror film.

The feeling of wrongness grew stronger as I took the stairs two at once; I all but ran down the hallway, my fingers trembling as I unlocked the door and pushed it open.

'Seb?'

There was no answer. He wasn't in the kitchen, nor the lounge room. I dumped my bag and laptop on the couch, then dashed into the nest.

He wasn't on the nest-bed. 'Seb?' I called again, turning to check the bathroom.

I stopped when I heard a soft groan.

It came from behind the bed, between it and the window. Sebastian was on the floor, curled up in the small space, his arms wrapped around his stomach. His brow was covered in a sheen of sweat and his cheeks were a deep, hectic red.

'Seb, baby, holy shit,' I babbled, sinking to my knees. 'What –'

He groaned again. 'Hurts.'

A wave of perfume washed over me, and the taste of cherries – so potent I might have bitten into a handful – slid down my throat. It was strong, far stronger than it should have been with blockers, and my body responded with a flood of its own perfume and a sudden rush of slick.

I understood, then.

'Seb, fuck.' I hurried to close the blinds. There was no sun coming from outside, but the storm clouds looked as though they were full of lightning, which would be even worse for his over-sensitive eyes. 'Seb, baby, you're in heat.'

'Can't be,' he panted. His body seized as a wave of pain rolled through him. I knew from experience how bad it was, and how he'd be burning up one minute and freezing cold the next, how bright lights would hurt his eyes and how his skin would feel like a livewire.

'I'll run you a bath.' I dashed to the lounge room and fished in my bag for my phone. Tristan didn't answer when I called, so I sent him a text as I ran to the bathroom. I left the light off, running the water until it was hot enough to relax muscles but not enough to burn. I didn't add any oils or bubbles, because I didn't know what scent he'd be craving, but I did light a candle that wafted a delicious, subtle vanilla.

Tristan hadn't responded to my text by the time I got back to the nest. I slowly coaxed Sebastian out of his pyjamas and into the bathroom. Thunder rumbled outside, and I saw the sparking brightness of lightning when it flashed behind the curtains.

Sebastian's cock was red and swollen, precum pooling at the tip as he stumbled to the bathroom. I tried not to touch him, because I knew his skin would be over-sensitive until the heat settled in properly. 'Seb, baby, have you been taking your heat suppressants?'

'Of course,' he said crossly. 'I never forget, and even if I did, Tristan would remind me. I can't be in heat, Rosebud. I just have the flu or something.'

'Sure.' I held out my arm to help him into the tub; he sighed in pleasure as he sank down and the hot water hit his tight muscles. 'A flu that's given you stomach cramps, backache, light and skin sensitivity, and a raging boner. Makes sense.'

He opened his beautiful blue eyes to scowl at me. 'It's not a heat, Rose.'

'Okay. You won't want your alpha, then.'

His pupils blew out immediately; beneath the water, his cock jumped, as if it had a mind of its own. He glared at me. 'That means nothing,' he insisted. 'I *always* want my alpha.'

Which was true, but I suspected that in half an hour or so, Sebastian would be *begging* for him.

I called Tristan again; again, he didn't answer. *Where are you?* I sent, unease churning in my stomach. *Seb is in pre-heat. You need to be here.*

My poor omega sank to lie in the water and closed his eyes. His golden hair flowed out in a waving halo, his cheeks still pink with a heat-flush.

He was the most beautiful thing I'd ever seen.

I slipped from the bathroom and into the kitchen, opening the fridge. We had every snack known to humankind – *thank you, Tristan* – but they were mostly sweet. There was nothing savoury other than artisan cheese and crackers, and dairy wasn't the best idea during a heat. Sandwiches or wraps would be better, or a roasted vegetable salad. There were plenty of energy drinks, at least, and about a hundred bottles of fancy water, because Tristan didn't like the way the Banksia water tasted.

I'd made fun of him, but I was glad for it now. I stuffed some bottles into the freezer and made sure there were plenty of others in the fridge.

I called Tristan again, but he didn't pick up. I brought up the Banksia app on my phone and ordered dinner to our room, selecting *illness* from the dropdown of reasons, and noted that Sebastian and I seemed to have the flu and might need our meals delivered for a few days. I didn't know if there was a limit to it – surely they'd send the on-campus doctor if it went for too long – but we'd cross that bridge when we got there.

I made my way into the nest. I'd already closed the blinds against the lightning, so I turned on one set of fairy lights – the smallest ones that threw the faintest light. I'd seen Sebastian's usual coverlet in the hallway and noticed that Tristan's now covered the bed; my heart ached for Sebastian, building his nest alone, not knowing what was happening. There were untouched snacks on the bedside table already, so I left them where they were. I fetched a couple of drinks to put next to them, then checked that all the food was wrapped up tightly so that Sebastian wouldn't be affected by any errant smells. I had a flashback to my heat, when one of the heat alphas had eaten something garlicky earlier in the day. I'd almost thrown up and I *loved* garlic – in normal times, at least.

I was relieved Sebastian would never experience that. He wouldn't know what it was like to be naked and vulnerable with strangers, even if they were professionals. He wouldn't know what it was like to accept someone he'd never met before into his body, wouldn't beg a stranger for a bite. He'd be touched by familiar hands, loved and cherished by the alpha he'd chosen and his own scent match.

I loved him, I realised. It seemed insane to say so – which was why I hadn't voiced it yet – but I didn't understand how *anyone* could meet my omega and not fall head over heels. He was my scent match, and the way he'd looked at me in the last few weeks … Who could blame me for losing my heart? The warmth of my love for him settled easily next to the pleasant, comforting ache I felt for Byron, the feelings surging together like the tide.

I was keeping space there for Tristan, too. We hadn't talked about it, but he'd shown me that he cared for me, holding me when I cried, stroking my hair when I'd had a nightmare, claiming me as part of his pack. It would be an honour to have him as my alpha.

I called him again, but there was no answer.

I went back into the bathroom. Sebastian's cheeks were flushed bright red, and his hand was wrapped around his cock. He pumped it slowly, but I knew it wasn't because he wanted to draw out the feeling; he was going slow because it was painful to touch.

'Hurts,' he grated out when he saw me. There was no embarrassment that I'd caught him like this; I wasn't sure that Sebastian was acquainted with the feeling at the best of times, and we'd fucked too often over the last few weeks for him to feel shy. I knew what made his cock twitch, what made him moan, what made him shake.

'I know,' I answered, and knelt beside the bath to stroke his wet hair back from his face. 'How are the cramps?'

'Getting worse.' He leaned into my touch. 'Do we have any paracetamol?'

Tristan kept a small pharmacy over the fridge, but I knew it wouldn't have an effect, unless it was placebo. 'I'll get you some.'

He caught my hand when I tried to leave. 'Where's Tris?'

I bit my lip. 'I don't know,' I said. 'But I'm sure he's on his way back.'

It was a white lie – if Tristan had seen my texts, then he was definitely on his way here – but it was a lie, nonetheless. I hated it. Worse, I knew that Sebastian would need his alpha soon, and if he didn't have Tristan, he might go looking for someone else with a knot or a latch.

Thunder crashed with an echoing boom, startling us both. 'I'll get you some paracetamol, then I'll go and find him,' I decided. It was possible, I supposed, that Tristan's phone could have run out of battery, or he could be in one of Banksia's odd dead spots, where Wi-Fi dared not tread. I had a feeling Tristan would rather die than miss a moment of his omega's heat, so really, I'd be doing him a favour, too. Sebastian was still decidedly in the pre-heat phase, so if I had to leave him, now was the time. 'Will you be okay without me for a bit?'

Sebastian nodded. I didn't think he wanted me to go, but he wanted Tristan just as much.

I found him some painkillers and took them and an energy drink to the bathroom. I could tell from Sebastian's temperature that the now-lukewarm bath was what he needed, so I didn't offer to change the water. He pulled me down for a kiss, his hand still wrapped around his cock, and shuddered through a release that I knew would feel like pins and needles. I held him as close as I dared as tears slipped down his face.

'It won't be like this for long,' I promised him.

It would soon be worse, but I wasn't about to tell him that.

I changed my clothes – including my underwear – then sprayed myself with scent canceller. I turned up the air purifier before I left the apartment, locking the door behind me.

I called Tristan again, but I might as well have left my phone behind. 'What's the best way to do this?' I muttered to myself as I ended the call. I made my way to the central staircase and paused there, thinking.

Class had ended twenty minutes ago. Banksia manor was huge, but Tristan was more likely to be in the First Year Library, a study room, or the dining hall than the laundry, the rec room, or the pool. He'd usually be on his afternoon walk, but it was dark as night and the sky was flashing with sheet lightning, so I doubted he was outside, especially as I could hear heavy rain pelting Banksia House's watchful windows.

I decided to start at the top and work my way down.

He wasn't in any of the third-floor study rooms, and nor was he in the First Year Library or the common room. I even checked the PhD common, and got a bunch of dirty looks in return.

I made my way down to the second floor and ducked behind some bookshelves when a third-year alpha gave me a lingering stare. Tristan wasn't in that library, either, and nor was he in any of the study rooms, or the media rooms.

I checked the first floor, then headed to the ground level, checking the dining hall, the pool, and the gym. I even ducked my head into the kitchen, though I backed out again swiftly when one of the chefs eyed me dubiously.

I didn't find Tristan anywhere, but I *did* find Pravin and Chul in the public common room.

'He went outside,' Chul said.

I glanced at the windows. Water streamed down them, so much of it that I couldn't see the driveway beyond. 'Outside?'

Chul shrugged. 'He said he was getting some lemon myrtle for Sebastian.'

'He'd be back inside by now,' Pravin said reassuringly, when he saw my expression.

I made a non-committal sound, because I'd just searched Banksia House from its literal top to bottom. Tristan could have been in one of the areas off-limits to students – the clocktower, which was under repair; the staff wing, which we were banned from entering; or the chemicals rooms, which held the nastier cleaning products and the chlorine mix for the pool – but I doubted it. He had no *reason* to be in any of those places.

I considered my choices. I either risked expulsion by going into the off-limit areas to look for him, or I got a little wet.

It wasn't as if I could tell anyone I was looking for him urgently so he could help his unregistered male omega through a heat that was explicitly against university rules.

Wet it was.

'Rose –' Pravin started, but I just smiled at him and walked away.

The storm wasn't easing; if anything, it was getting worse. Through the rain-slick windows, I could just make out the shadows of trees, thrashing in the gale. It was black but for the ghostly bones of eucalypt trunks; when lightning flashed, the garden lit up in shades of white and silver.

'Fuck this,' I muttered to myself, but I went outside anyway.

It wasn't easy. The wind caught the door and I barely stopped it from slamming against the wall. I had to wrestle it closed behind me, using my full body weight. The gale whipped at my clothes and hair; I wasn't dressed for a storm and I started to shiver. Rain drove sideways, dripping down my back and into my eyes, stinging my skin.

'Tristan!' I shouted, though I suspected it was useless; my voice would be stolen by the storm. 'Tristan!'

Chul must have been wrong. I wiped the rain from my eyes, briefly lamenting what it would do to my mascara. There was no way Tristan would be outside in this.

I shouted for him one more time, because I was already dripping wet and thought I might as well. The sky thundered and I cowered in the doorway, my arms instinctively folding over my head.

I looked towards the maze. Even through the rain and the metallic scent of lightning, I could smell the lemon myrtle. When the sky lit again, I saw it – a shadow moving near the maze entrance.

'Alpha!' I shouted, desperate. I didn't want to leave the relative shelter of the doorway, but I knew whoever it was couldn't hear me.

I took a deep breath and strode out into the storm.

The rain hit me hard enough to bruise. The gale made me stagger to the side; I pushed against it, determined. I fought every step towards the maze, my clothes sticking to my skin.

'Tristan!' I screamed. 'Tristan, please!'

Lightning lit the sky, and I realised the person near the maze was wearing a cloak, their face obscured by its hood.

What the f –

I tripped, fighting to steady myself.

A shadow loomed suddenly beside me, over me. I shrieked in surprise, losing my footing on the sodden ground.

A hand reached out to catch me, but it was too late; I was already falling.

TRISTAN

I woke up in darkness.

'What the f –'

I wrenched my eyes open, but that wasn't the issue; something was covering them.

'No, no, *no*,' I snarled, realising my hands were bound. I swayed from the sudden sense of deja vu. '*No*, you assholes, I need to –'

Something – or some*one* – jabbed me ungently in the shoulder. 'Be quiet,' a voice hissed.

'Absolutely fucking not,' I growled back. 'You need to let me go. *Now.*'

I'd only come outside to get Sebastian more lemon myrtle leaves, planning to be no more than half a minute before heading back upstairs to my omegas and to find out what had made Rose leave class. I cursed myself for not going with her, but Rose wasn't shy about asking for what she needed, and I'd assumed that if she wanted my company she would have said so. I'd barely had the chance to grab a handful of leaves before I'd felt the prick on the side of my neck.

'We were impressed with the way you handled our directive.'

The female voice was the same as last time, imbued with quiet authority.

'You need to let me go,' I repeated. 'I need to get to my omega.'

'To Sebastian?' she said evenly.

I froze. 'To Rose,' I answered, a beat too late.

'We know, Mr. Grace,' she went on, not unkindly. 'You did well to hide it all these years, but we know. And we know why you wanted to join the Revels, why you completed our challenge. We won't help you with *that*, but we *can* help you with something else.'

'I don't need your help,' I snarled. 'I need to get to –'

'We can get Sebastian added to the official OSA database with a backdated reveal.'

I snapped my mouth shut.

It was something I couldn't do, because the official Omega Support Agency database wasn't online. It was a literal office full of honest-to-fuck *paper*, with a security team that made prison look like a farce, and staff so loyal that bribes were impossible. The database information shared with government systems was for medical and legal reference only and couldn't be amended or added to. It was insane, but unfortunately – barring an actual physical heist – it was also entirely secure.

'No more hiding,' she continued softly. 'No more black-market suppressants or buying the silence of doctors. Sebastian wouldn't need to hide his designation. He could be himself, wholly, always.'

I hated the woman – hated the *Revels* – in that moment, because I knew just how valuable that was; a life lived free was worth more than almost anything. 'And what would you want from me in return?' I said coldly, unable to stop myself flexing against my bonds. 'Money?'

She snorted in what seemed like genuine amusement. 'Of course not.'

I went still.

'We know you accessed Banksia's systems before you arrived.'

I frowned, wishing I could see her and read her expression.

'And we know you've accessed APF databases and secure medical records – records that are, I might add, supposed to be hidden behind the best defences money can buy. *That's* what we want from you, Mr. Grace.'

'I'm not a hacker,' I said, shaking my head. 'I have no training, no –'

'No training, no background in computer science or cybersecurity – and yet you've always gotten what you've needed, haven't you?' She paused. 'And it's more than that – you *enjoy* it. You like the puzzle of it. You like knowing things that others don't. We believe in leveraging people's strengths, Mr. Grace, no matter how they come by them.'

I chewed my lip, uncomfortable that she had me pegged so easily. 'What information would you need? And what would you do with it?'

She laughed. 'Nothing nefarious,' she said, assuring, though I wasn't sure I believed her. 'We want you to help rebuild Banksia's systems, that's all.'

Oh.

I'd thought that they needed it, back when we first arrived and I was able to access Rose's personal information so easily, literally over dinner. For a place that housed so many students from well-known families, their system protections were incredibly lax.

'You'll work with an existing team,' she went on, as if sensing my hesitation. 'Your job will be to find the holes. They'll build the walls, and you'll try to tear them down. That's what we want from you.'

'And in exchange, Sebastian's designation would be official?'

'Official and backdated, as if he'd registered the moment he revealed. No furore over the discovery, no OSA officials arriving on your doorstep, no media. What do you say?'

The offer was too good, and she knew it. 'I'm not sure I have a choice.'

'Of course you do. We're not monsters. Walk away and continue living as you always have, or use your skills to help your omega and your school. It's your choice.'

'I'll think about it,' I said, then decided to voice something I'd been wondering for a while. 'Why did you want me to *compromise the omega*? What did it tell you about me?'

She laughed again, surprised. 'Oh, Mr. Grace,' she said. 'What makes you think we wanted to know more about *you*?'

I froze, thoughts whirling as it finally clicked.

The Revels hadn't been testing me *at all.* They'd been testing Sebastian, or Rose – or *both.*

I thought about everything the omegas had been through since they'd started at Banksia. What I'd done, the issues with Heathcote, navigating other students in the close confines of the discipline mixers and class, responding to the feral alpha. They'd managed all of that *and* the demands of Banksia's exceptionally high standards and complex curriculum – while they'd also been balancing the needs of their designation with the drive to succeed.

How often had the Revels been watching?

How many of those *tests* had they *arranged*?

I heard a soft step behind me. 'See you soon, Mr. Grace.'

'Wait,' I said, panicked. 'Could you not knock me out, please? I really have to get back to –'

Something sharp pierced my neck, and I crumpled.

✦✦✦

I woke to freezing water pelting my face, and the sky lit by lightning.

'Fucking *fuck*,' I groaned, rolling onto my side. From the citrus scent around me, they'd put me back in the maze again – *in the middle of an electrical storm.*

'Thank you *very* fucking much, you assholes,' I muttered.

I pushed myself to my feet, trying to ignore the dull pain in my muscles; I realised that my head was covered. Looking down, I could see that someone had thoughtfully wrapped me in a garment – in a *cloak*, of all things. I rubbed the material between my fingers. It was ridiculous and pretentious, but it was also waterproof and warm, so I pulled it more tightly around myself and stumbled towards the maze entrance, wincing at the thunder right above me, its rumbling loud enough to hurt.

At the maze entrance, I heard a faint sound coming from the double back doors.

'*Tristan!* Tristan, please!'

'Fuck.' Lightning flashed to illuminate Rose's pale face, her hair plastered to her cheeks. 'Rose!'

She stumbled, righting herself with difficulty in the gale. I rushed towards her; when she looked up and saw me, she shrieked, stumbling again.

I caught her before she fell – something I planned to keep on doing.

Maybe for the rest of my life.

She seemed dazed, so I bent and scooped her into my arms, holding her tight against my chest. I was already saturated and I could see rain dripping from her nose, so I jogged until we were under cover, protected by the terrace. The door was difficult to open with one hand as the wind slammed against it, but I wrestled with the handle and managed to fight my way inside.

'What the fuck are you wearing?' Rose said breathlessly.

I tugged the cloak off and wrapped it around her. I didn't know how to explain what had just happened, but I did know one thing.

When we'd first come here, Sebastian had wanted the Banksia Prize more than anything. He'd wanted to prove himself to his parents, to set himself apart, to show that his journey – his interests, his strengths – were just as important – and just as *impressive* – as theirs, even if they were different.

Now, Sebastian seemed to want something else. Oh, he still wanted the prize, I was sure of that. But he'd found this omega – found his scent match – and his priorities had shifted. *She* mattered to him now. Prize or not, it didn't matter, because either way, he'd have Rose.

My priorities had changed, too. I'd been obsessed with what I could provide Sebastian, fixated on joining the Revels to ensure he got the prize. But it wasn't just *me* they'd had their eyes on. Despite that, I could now give him something even greater than I'd originally planned: the chance to live life as *himself*, to build a pack, to visit doctors, take a break from his suppressants, and to exist without the constant, lurking fear of being found out. It didn't sound as impressive as the prize, but I was beginning to understand that love didn't have to be flashy. Simply being present was more important than the material things I could provide.

And also, I'd *ask* what he wanted this time.

'Never mind, it doesn't matter,' Rose continued, when I didn't answer. 'I'm guessing you haven't seen your messages. Sebastian's in heat.'

The words washed over me, far warmer than the freezing water on my cheeks; I almost dropped her in shock. 'That's impossible.'

'Of course it isn't,' Rose retorted. 'He found his scent match and his second pack alpha. The only thing I'm surprised about is that it didn't happen sooner.'

'*You* haven't gone into heat, and the exact thing happened to you!'

'No, but I've had one before, and I haven't been on heat suppressants for six straight years.' She poked a finger into my chest. 'He should have had a heat when he first revealed, Tris. Taking blockers for that long without a break *can't* be good for him.'

Which was exactly what the doctors had always said, but I didn't tell her that. 'Okay. Seb's in heat.' I inhaled slowly, trying to calm my instincts, which were suddenly roaring *need to see him, now*. 'What do we do?'

'I've already done the prep work,' Rose told me. 'You've got enough food to feed an army, and you've already got energy drinks. I asked the kitchens to send meals to your room, and I contacted the first-year student advisor and told her we had the flu and would be out for a few days.'

I dipped my head and kissed her. She froze for a moment, then her lips parted and she returned the kiss with a hunger that warmed my chilled body all the way to the bones. 'You're amazing, omega,' I murmured, gently breaking away. 'I'm glad you're his.' I paused. 'And mine.'

Rose flushed, trying not to look pleased. 'Hurry, alpha,' was all she said.

I didn't put her down. We were leaving puddles of water all over the waxed wood floor, but I didn't care.

Sebastian was all that mattered.

'What will he need?' My breath was shaky, but it wasn't from exertion; I was almost trembling with nerves.

'He's in preheat, so he's in pain.' Rose touched my cheek. 'You need to be prepared for that. Preheat usually lasts twenty-four hours, but with the length of time he's been on blockers, I'm not sure if he'll follow the usual pattern. While he's in preheat, his skin will be painful to touch. He'll be aroused, but climaxing feels like pins and needles.'

'That sounds awful.'

'It is. But it's our body's way of gearing up for the heat haze. Our nerve endings get all messed up, and so does our temperature. Our muscles don't know what's going on, so they'll tense and release randomly, which can lead to cramps. If he can stand being touched, a gentle massage will help. Other than that, he'll take comfort from your presence.' She wriggled and I put her down as we reached the apartment door. 'But you need to stop your blockers and wash off your scent cancellers so he can smell you. He'll want that more than anything.' Rose turned to face me, studying my expression. 'Are you ready?'

'No,' I answered honestly. 'I'm so fucking nervous. I've wanted this for so long, but I wanted it to happen in a place of our own, in a beautiful nest full of things Seb had picked out, where I could make sure he was looked after properly. Not in student accommodation.'

Rose smiled at me. 'You're such a snob, Tristan,' she said affectionately. 'Sebastian doesn't need all that. And he *has* a beautiful nest. All he needs is you.'

'And you,' I whispered.

Her smile widened. 'Come on, alpha.'

I scented Sebastian as soon as Rose opened the door. I pushed her gently inside and slammed it shut behind me; *no one* was scenting my omega when he smelled like *that*. Like the most decadent cherry pie I'd ever known, with thick, buttery pastry and sweet, tart filling that made my mouth water at the mere *thought* of it. '*Fuck.*'

Rose inhaled. 'Oh, *shit.*' She turned and locked the door behind us. 'Seb, baby? We're back.'

There was no answer; I strode through the lounge room to the nest, anxious, absently noting the coverlet and cushions tossed on the floor outside the nest. *Was he hurt? In pain so severe he couldn't answer?*

Luckily, it was neither of those things.

Sebastian was curled up on the nest-bed, fast asleep. A hectic red flush spread across his cheeks and down his neck and chest. He was entirely naked – another thing that made my mouth water – but for a pair of thick, woolly bed socks. I'd tease him about it mercilessly after the heat, but, in this moment, I found them so endearing that my heart hurt.

'Oh, Seb,' Rose murmured, rising on her tiptoes to peek over my shoulder, taking in the ring of pillows. 'He's nested properly. Oh, it's beautiful.' She tugged me back from the door. 'This is perfect, actually. Go and have a shower, Tris. Wash off your cancellers.'

I swallowed. I knew she was right, but I glanced back at Sebastian. I didn't want to leave him, not even for a five-minute shower.

'Alpha.' Rose took my chin in hand and tilted it down. Her hair was plastered to her cheeks, her skin still pale from the outside chill. 'You're soaking wet and shivering. You need to get warm and dry. I'll watch your omega while you shower. Go.'

'Our omega,' I corrected. 'And you need to get dry, too.'

She smiled. '*Our* omega. And I will.'

I glanced at Sebastian again. 'He won't wake up?'

Rose shook her head. 'I think he's out for a while, Tris. And even if he did, you're here. He's safe.'

I gave a curt nod, then tore myself away from them both. It hurt to leave, *physically* hurt, my stomach twisting itself in knots.

I showered as quickly as I could, scrubbing off the scent canceller and rinsing my hair. I took several deep breaths, mentally running through everything I'd ever researched about heats.

Academically, I was prepared for this. But in reality?

I was shaking.

My cock was rock hard and had been since I'd walked through the door. But I knew I couldn't just knot Sebastian straight away. He'd want it – at least, I assumed he would – but the more often I knotted him, the more tired I'd get, and I'd be at risk of being unable to satisfy him when the heat haze hit its peak. I'd have to pace myself, and work with Rose.

When I'd imagined a heat before, I'd always been by myself. It had always been me and Sebastian against the world. But now, Rose would be with us, and I felt a rush of gladness at the thought.

I towelled off quickly, pulled on a clean shirt and pair of shorts, then all but ran back to the nest, stopping still in the doorway.

'Hey, alpha.'

Sebastian was awake, lying on his side. Rose stretched out beside him, her body a foot or so away, so she wouldn't accidentally touch his skin.

'Hey, baby. How are you feeling?'

Sebastian frowned at Rose. 'Well, I think Rosebud might be right,' he said grumpily.

'What gave it away?' Rose teased.

'The rampant erection.' Sebastian glowered, this time down at his cock, which was swollen and leaking precum on the blanket beneath him.

'What do you need?'

'Will you lie with us, alpha?' he answered plaintively.

I stepped into the nest, then settled myself on the bed behind him, careful not to touch him. He was glorious like this, all flushed and rumpled. The scent of cherry was thick in the air, coating my tongue, and I caught a hint of Rose's chocolate, too.

I looked around at the circle of cushions he'd arranged, at my neatly folded coverlet, and noticed a shirt of mine stuffed beneath a pillow near his head. 'Your nest is so beautiful, omega. You did such a good job.'

'It's still not right,' he said crossly, shifting his weight. 'There's something missing, but I can't –' He shuddered, his cock twitching. 'I want to go to a proper nesting shop when this is over, Tris. I need to make it right.'

'Of course,' I soothed. 'Of course. We'll go as soon as we can. And we won't stop looking until we find what's missing.'

Sebastian sniffed, then stiffened as his body tensed and his cock leaked precum in a wave of sensation that looked painful, rather than pleasurable. 'Fuck, I *hate* this.'

Rose's brow creased, her expression equal parts stricken and understanding. 'Can I touch, Seb?' she whispered.

He hesitated, then nodded his assent. Rose didn't touch anywhere but his cock, which she grasped with fingers both firm and gentle. Sebastian groaned, the sound half-pleasure and half-pain, as she moved her hand in a fluid motion. I rose up to watch, my own cock leaking at the sight.

'Fuck, Rose, *yes*,' Sebastian hissed, then came without warning all over her hand. 'Urgh, sorry.'

Rose huffed a laugh. 'Why are you sorry?'

'For lasting as long as this sentence.'

She snorted. 'When I had my heat, one of the heat alphas accidentally brushed my *knee* and I came. Your body is all sorts of fucked up right now. Plus,' she went on, grinning, 'you're still hard, aren't you?'

'I know romance novels make a big deal about *steel*,' Sebastian moaned, 'but that's exactly what it feels like.' He shook his head and glared at her. 'And please don't talk about your heat alphas, especially now. You're *mine*.'

Rose's smile went soft. 'Silly omega. Of course I'm yours.'

Sebastian wiped her hand – and his cock – with a handkerchief, which he promptly stuffed under a pillow. In usual times, Sebastian was fastidiously tidy, but I knew he'd want the nest to smell like him – and like *us*.

'I want to talk about something,' he said, rolling onto his back with a wince. He was so fucking *pretty*, flushed and cross, and it took all my willpower not to reach for him. 'And it needs to be now, while I'm still lucid.'

'You'll be lucid during the heat, Seb,' Rose said, frowning. 'You'll know what's happening and you'll be able to make decisions. It will just be a little … fuzzier … than usual.'

'Yes, but I don't want the heat haze held against me.' Sebastian's eyes found mine, searching. 'If I beg for a bite, and one of you is willing to give it, then I *want* it. I'm telling you now, when I'm not thinking about knots. Well, I'm not thinking about knots *every moment*, at least. I want your bite. *Bites*.'

'Seb –'

'No, alpha.' He scowled at me. 'I won't be talked out of this. I fully understand that you might not *want* to bite me. But if I ask for it, and you change your mind – or if Rose wants it – then *I want a bite*.

'You've always been reluctant because it's *permanent*,' he went on, 'and I think I've been understanding of that. But Tris – *you* are permanent. I want to wake up next to both of you every single morning until I don't wake up at all. And before that happens, I want to have my thousand babies with you. Everything I want, I want *with you*. What's a bite, compared to that?'

I reached out and carefully brushed his hair from his forehead without touching his skin. 'Thank you for making that clear. I'll think about it.'

And I would. I wanted to bite him so badly my teeth ached. Rose was beautiful and clever, and I knew she belonged with us; in time, I suspected I'd come to love her as much as I did him.

But there was a ragged hole where Byron should have been, and his absence ate at me.

Sebastian caught my hand and tentatively held it to his cheek. His eyes were on my face and I knew he could tell where my thoughts had gone. But this wasn't about me, so I inhaled and pasted a smile on my face.

'You'll look so beautiful covered with bites, omega,' I purred.

◈◈◈

The preheat ended just before midnight.

I wasn't sure what woke me; a noise, perhaps, or my alpha, knowing better than I did what was to come. I rubbed my face and rolled over to see Sebastian curled into a ball.

Rose was waking, too, sitting back and pushing her hair from her cheek. 'Oh, Seb,' she whispered.

'Hurts,' he grated out. 'Hurts so bad.'

Rose lay her hand on his forehead. 'No wonder. It's time.' Her eyes met mine. 'Your first heat, Seb.'

'It can fuck right off,' he snapped, then gave a wordless moan.

Rose chuckled. 'I know. Would you like me to make you feel better?'

Sebastian held out his arms, and Rose snuggled against him. I inhaled a breath full of cherry and chocolate, watching as the omegas exchanged a sweet kiss.

Rose didn't let the kiss linger, though, making her way down Sebastian's body and rolling him onto his back. Sebastian had made a sound of wordless protest when she broke the kiss; the sound changed as Rose took his straining cock between her lips. He sighed as if every weight had been lifted from his shoulders, then gasped when Rose began to work him up and down.

It was beautiful, but it was more than that. Their connection wasn't just physical; they cared for one another, deeply, and it had started before they scent matched. Their biological connection only deepened what had already existed. They were glorious together, in every way, and a purr tore its way from my throat as Sebastian writhed beneath Rose's ministrations.

'You're both so perfect,' I said huskily. 'So perfect, omegas.'

Rose flushed at the praise; Sebastian received it as his due. He caught my hand and pulled me down, his chin tilted up for a kiss.

I nuzzled at his lips, nipping and flicking my tongue inside his mouth. He was hungry, but not desperate – not yet. I let my hand play over his chest, then found a nipple, pinching and pulling the sensitive peak until he gasped.

'Are you going to come for us, Sebastian?' I crooned. 'Are you going to fill your pretty omega's mouth? Let her see how good you taste?'

'Fuck, alpha,' Sebastian panted, his hips thrusting up. Rose met his movements, relaxing, letting him use her mouth. She rested one hand lightly on his hip, the other moving between his legs to cup his sac.

I trailed kisses over his neck, working my way down to take his nipple in my mouth, flicking the hard tip with my tongue. I kissed and flicked and sucked and nipped until he whimpered, and then I moved to the other side. His body stiffened, and I looked down in time to see Rose swallow – once, then twice. Cum leaked from the side of her mouth; I reached down to swipe it away, then licked my fingers clean.

Her pupils dilated, and her delicious chocolate scent twined through the air. My vanilla joined it, rich and heady, but Sebastian's scent was strongest of all.

'Want to be inside you,' he said, his eyes heavy.

He didn't specify whom, but given our usual dynamic, I assumed it was Rose.

She did, too, smiling as she pulled her tank top over her head, then shimmying out of her sleep shorts. Her underwear was simple – black with a hint of lace – but she looked oh-so-alluring as she peeled the garment down, then swung a leg over Sebastian's hip and sank onto his cock without any further fuss.

Fuck.

'Next time, I'll have a latch toy,' she promised him, her voice hitching as she moved. 'I'll make you feel so good, omega.'

'You already do,' Sebastian gasped, reaching to trace his fingers down her flushed cheek.

She kept a gentle rhythm as she rode him, alternating between working her hips up and down, and rocking back and forth. Sebastian sat up, taking a nipple between his lips. She moaned, arching to encourage him as his hands kneaded her ass.

I wasn't sure which of them came first, but either way, it didn't take long. Omega perfume exploded in the air and I suddenly understood why alphas were so fucking obsessed with heats; it was *heaven*. Their slick made my head spin and my cock ache. I barely held a growl in my throat, my hands burning to touch as they rocked together.

Sebastian kissed Rose's shoulder. His brow was slick with sweat and his eyes were unfocused. 'I need –'

'I know what you need, handsome,' Rose said quietly. 'You need your alpha.'

His eyes flickered to me, wild with longing. 'Alpha,' he whined, and *fuck* – how could I resist?

Rose climbed off him; I noted with satisfaction the cum dripping down her thighs, and the way Sebastian's still-hard cock shone with their combined release. 'Perfect,' I said again, because they were; they were divine in their messiness, and I wanted to be part of it.

I reached out and ran a hand down Sebastian's side. 'Will you present for me, omega?'

He shuddered. I'd never asked him before, and he'd never offered. It was an unspoken thing that we were saving it for a special moment.

For *now*.

He arranged himself with his typical grace, dropping to lean on his elbows and knees, his cheek pressed to the bed, his ass high in the air.

It was the most erotic thing I'd ever seen.

I ran my hands over his back and hips. 'So fucking lovely, omega.' I caressed the hard globes of his ass, then ran my hands down his thighs and back up. He trembled when I cupped his sac, gently moulding.

He was ready for me, his hole shining with slick. I prepared him like usual anyway, massaging and tracing softly around his pucker before sinking a finger slowly inside him. He was hot and tight and he moaned as I gradually breached his body with another finger, then a third, then he shook as I found his most sensitive spot and gently brushed against it.

'Alpha,' he begged. 'Please.'

'How much do you want it, omega?' I withdrew my fingers, then positioned myself. 'How much do you want my cock?'

'I'm going to lose it if you don't fuck me, Tristan,' he growled, with enough bite to let me know that he hadn't been completely taken by the heat haze yet.

I chuckled, then immediately swore as I started to push inside.

I'd been inside Sebastian more times than I could count. But he'd never been this hot, this tight, this slick. His body had never *pulled* at me like this, his internal muscles working as I flexed my hips. It had never felt as if he wasn't simply welcoming me inside, but *demanding* that I be there.

'Fuck, omega –' I inhaled sharply as Sebastian pushed back, impaling himself. 'Fuck. *Fuck*.'

'I don't want gentle,' Sebastian warned. 'I want hard and fast and deep. I want to feel you in my fucking throat.'

While I tried to recover from that statement, I caught Rose's eye. She was pink-cheeked and chewing on her bottom lip. *No knot*, she mouthed.

I nodded, then ran my hand down Sebastian's spine. 'Then that's what you'll get, baby. Brace yourself.'

I took his hips in my hands, pulling almost completely out of his body before slamming back home. Sebastian gasped, fisting the blanket beneath him. 'Fuck, *yes*,' he hissed, so I did it again.

And again.

It was only a handful of moments before I felt his body going tight around me, before his heat cramps bloomed into pleasure. I didn't take him in hand to help him through his climax; I simply kept fucking him, hard and fast and deep, like he'd asked. Cherry filled the air as he came, moaning my name. I gave him a few seconds to catch his breath, then changed my angle, making sure I brushed over some of his sweet spots as I moved, fucking him into a mess of garbled endearments and expletives. I did reach to help him the second time, wrapping my fingers around his cock and letting him rut into it until my hand was covered in cherry-flavoured cum.

My knot began to swell, catching as I plunged in and out of his body. He felt the change, his back arching as he thrust his ass higher. 'Please, alpha,' he begged. 'Your knot. Give me your knot.'

I fucked him shallowly instead, my knot swelling outside his body as pleasure built at the base of my spine. My own body had strong opinions about it – *knot our omega*, my alpha demanded – but I ignored him; I knew this was the first of many times, and knotting would come later. Right now, my omega needed so many orgasms he couldn't see straight, rather than having to lie there, waiting, as my knot deflated.

My fingers dug into his hips. I wanted so badly to plunge inside, but I kept my movements shallow as my knot swelled. His muscles clenched around my cock and I growled, sensation sparking through my body.

'Can I?' Rose said softly.

In the daze of building pleasure, it took me a moment to realise what she was asking. Her hand was outstretched in offering, her eyes were fixed between Sebastian's body and mine, and –

'Yes,' I said hoarsely. 'Fuck, *yes*.'

Rose wrapped her hands around my knot and *squeezed*.

I came with a shout, spilling inside Sebastian as Rose held me tight, the pressure sending the white light of a rut to spark behind my eyes. I shook, collapsing forward, leaning my weight on Sebastian, whose chest rumbled with a contented purr as I slumped.

'Don't think I didn't notice the lack of knot,' he grumbled, as I caught my breath.

'You'll get one soon,' I promised, pulling out gently and rolling onto my back.

'Fuck,' Sebastian said, doing the same and staring at his still-hard cock. 'That barely took the edge off.'

Rose snorted. 'Welcome to your first heat.'

◇◇◇

After a few hours, Sebastian dozed. Rose took a shower while I checked the snacks; Sebastian hadn't eaten anything, but Rose and I had, so I replaced what I could and made sure we had plenty of water. Sebastian hadn't drunk anything, either, which was worrying, but Rose assured me it was normal.

'We're built for this,' she reminded me. 'You can worry if he goes a full twenty-four hours without food or water.'

I took a shower, too, and wondered if I could coax Sebastian in there. With the promise of sex, I probably could; he loved shower sex, though his omega would hate the idea of washing off scents.

When I was done, I went back to the nest. Sebastian had his head in Rose's lap; she stroked his hair with her long fingers. I liked her hands; she had pronounced knuckles and a callous on one finger from long hours of – for some unknown reason – hand-writing notes. They were elegant hands, *interesting* hands, and I loved the way they looked in Sebastian's hair, on his skin, around his cock.

I loved the way they felt on *my* skin, too. Around *my* cock.

And I shivered at the thought of feeling them running through my hair.

'He's slipping in deeper,' Rose whispered to me. 'His temperature is higher and his muscles are more lax.' Sebastian whimpered in his sleep; I tensed in response. 'His pain is worse, too.' She stroked his cheek. 'He'll need a knot soon.'

I'd been so arrogant, thinking I could handle a heat by myself. Rose and I had shared orgasm duty equally – and enthusiastically, it wasn't exactly a chore – over the last few hours, and I was already tired – and that was *without* knotting. 'I thought preheat was longer.'

Rose shrugged. 'This first stage can last twenty-four hours or so. But Sebastian's circumstances aren't usual. He's falling into the second stage faster, but honestly, Tris, I think the heat haze could be *long*.' She studied me. 'We need to be prepared, and we need to pace ourselves. I wish I'd thought about this weeks ago. I could have bought some toys for him.'

'We'll know for next time. Rose, I –' My lips twisted. 'I couldn't do this without you. Thank you.'

Rose smiled and reached to touch my cheek. I leaned into her palm, closing my eyes as she ran her thumb over my cheekbone. 'You're a good alpha, Tristan Grace.'

❖❖❖

Sebastian woke not long after, and it was apparent he was in tremendous pain. Rose took him in hand, but his climax barely seemed to register.

'You're up, alpha,' she whispered.

The words seemed to break through Sebastian's haze; he snarled and pulled her to him. 'Mine,' he growled.

Rose petted him, smiling. 'I'm not going anywhere.'

'Need you.'

Rose kissed him gently, cupping his face with her palms. 'Then ask nicely.'

Sebastian snarled again, but I could hear the amusement in it. 'I need you. *Please*.'

Rose let him position her on hands and knees, then sighed happily as he dipped down to taste her. He didn't stay there long; I took it as a sign he really was in the heat haze. He'd told me a few days ago that he'd live with his face between Rose's thighs if he could, but now he was pushing himself to his knees to take her from behind. For a few minutes, the only sound was the slap of his hips meeting her ass and the wet sound of his cock moving in and out of her, punctuated by their cries of pleasure; a moment later, Sebastian groaned through his release, but the sound was full of pain.

'Alpha, *please*,' he begged.

He made no move to pull out of Rose. 'Now?'

'*Now*,' he growled.

'Demanding,' I said lightly. 'Rose? Is that okay?'

'More than okay,' she panted. 'I've been dreaming about this.'

I positioned myself behind Sebastian. 'Dreaming about it?'

'Mmm,' she agreed. 'Is that disrespectful?'

'Probably,' I answered, 'but it's hot as fuck.'

I pushed slowly inside Sebastian, listening to him pant as his body tightened around me. There was little resistance; he was primed for this, his muscles relaxed. I smoothed my hand down his back, then bent to press a kiss to his spine. 'You're driving this, omega,' I purred. 'Show me how you fuck yourself onto my cock.'

'Holy shit, alpha,' he gasped, but he did as I said, his hips pressing forward – into Rose – and then back, onto me. His body squeezed my cock, almost painfully tight as he impaled himself with a relieved groan.

'That's it,' I crooned. 'This is all about you, baby. Take what you need.'

What he needed was hard and frantic. Sex with Sebastian wasn't usually like this; in normal times, he preferred to take it slow, to tease and be teased in return, to press his face into my shoulder as he came. Now, he was panting, desperate, begging for *harder, faster, deeper*. My instincts lit up in response, my alpha rising to the surface, urging me to fuck my omega until he was marked with my bite and dripping with cum.

'Yes, alpha, *fuck*,' Sebastian whined, and Rose gave a hitched little gasp as he thrust deep. I didn't think the sound was one of pain, though.

'Make your omega come, Sebastian,' I said, mock-stern. 'Don't be rude.'

He reached between her legs, and a few moments later, Rose gave a broken whine, shuddering beneath him as her scent filled the air. My knot swelled as my own climax built, my vision clouding with white as a rut began to rise once more. I let it come, knowing it would help, trusting my alpha to give the omegas what they needed and grateful that my instincts would help me through this first time.

'Please – alpha – *please*,' Sebastian begged, and when my knot swelled larger, I pressed forward.

It took three gentle thrusts for it to lock inside Sebastian. Once I was inside, I rolled my hips, groaning as my knot continued to swell. Sebastian writhed beneath me, babbling broken praises and expletives, shaking and shuddering as my knot pressed against the extra nerve endings clustering inside his omega body and the heat cramps faded from pain into pleasure. I tried not to pass out as he gripped me, his body squeezing around the hard swell of my knot.

'Are you ready, omega?' I grated out. 'Ready for me to fill you up?'

Sebastian gave a wordless whine. 'Now, alpha, *fuck* –'

I came so hard my vision blurred, pleasure rushing through me in an overwhelming wave. Sebastian's body pulsed in time with my own, milking my release. I couldn't stop myself reaching to stroke his flat stomach, my fingers trailing over where it would swell if I bred him. The thought sent another wave of pleasure through me, and I gasped for air as his body squeezed every last drop of cum from mine.

Rose made a happy humming sound and rolled out from under Sebastian, grinning when he growled and clutched at her in response. 'So possessive, Seb. I'm not going anywhere, just moving so I don't get crushed.'

I manoeuvred Sebastian onto his side, sighing when he reached back to touch my hair, his free hand gripping Rose's thigh as my cock shifted slightly inside him. 'Fuck, Tris,' he said dreamily. 'My first knot. *Your* first knot. That was ... good.'

'Good?' I growled, nipping his shoulder.

'Mmm,' he said, sounding almost like his normal shit-stirring self. 'Good.'

'Well then,' I said, as he yawned. 'I'll make sure it's better next time.'

Four days and countless knots later, I realised we were in trouble.

ROSE

'WE NEED HELP,' I WHISPERED, when Sebastian had finally fallen asleep.

He wouldn't stay that way for long. The longest stretch of sleep he'd had over the last few days was two hours – which meant two hours was the longest stretch *we'd* had, too. I'd avoided looking in the mirror when I went into the bathroom, because Tristan looked drained and hollow-eyed, and if *he* looked like that, then I must have looked a hundred times worse.

'We can do it,' Tristan said stubbornly.

'Alpha, *look* at us. What if this goes on for *another* four days?'

'It won't.'

'How do you know?'

He ran a trembling hand through his hair. 'Who would help us, pretty?'

Before this, I wasn't sure I would have said there was such a thing as *too much sex* with Sebastian. But now, I felt weak as a kitten. My hips were bruised and my thighs were red raw with chafing. I was covered in love bites, too; Sebastian seemed to take a primal delight in marking me, though he'd only begged for his own bite once, and he hadn't gone close to breaking my skin with his teeth. Tristan's hips were bruised too, and his cock was red, even after being covered in Sebastian's healing slick. When he walked, he often stumbled, as if his legs couldn't quite hold him up.

My heart bled for him.

'Pravin,' I answered tiredly. 'Pravin and Chul. Marina – a latch from a female alpha would ease his pain as much as a knot does. Jessica from second year. Marco, maybe, from third year.' I licked my dry lips. 'Or we could ring heat services.'

'And tell them we have an unregistered male omega?' Tristan's voice was hoarse. He'd told me about the Revel's offer during one of our quick showers, but he hadn't spoken to Sebastian about it yet, for obvious reasons. 'They'll inform the Omega Support Agency. I don't know what the OSA would do, but it wouldn't be good. They don't answer to the regular police, or the normal courts. And I doubt they'd buy it if we told them Sebastian had a late emergence – he's *twenty-six*.'

I swallowed. 'You know there's another option,' I said gently.

'What –' Tristan shook his head before he finished the thought. 'No.'

'Tristan. Alpha.' I took his hand and brought it to my lips, kissing his knuckles. 'You *know* he'd be good during a heat. And he cares for Sebastian. Genuinely. He'd never do anything to make Seb uncomfortable. You could trust him.'

'How?' he burst out. I'd never seen Tristan look so tortured. 'Even *if* he agreed to help for the heat, he'd leave again, and ...' He trailed off.

'And it would break your heart even more than it's already broken,' I finished. I shifted closer, taking his chin in my hand. Even when he looked drawn and exhausted, Tristan was so beautiful my insides melted when his green eyes met mine. He'd swapped his glasses for contact lenses, so I could see them clearly as they filled with desperation. 'I know, alpha. I know how much you're hurting, and I know how much *he's* hurting, though he hides it. You're both fucking fools, by the way, but that's your own problem to solve. When it comes down to it, *this isn't about you*. It's about Sebastian and what *he* needs. If the heat haze was going to break in an hour, we'd be fine. But it's been *four days*, Tris, and there's no sign of this easing.' I brushed my lips over his, softly. 'I honestly don't know how much more I can take. You know we need help. I suspect he'd be the only person your alpha would let inside the apartment, let alone the nest. He'll give Sebastian what he needs. You know he's the only choice, alpha.'

He ran his hands through my hair, gently untangling a knot. 'That doesn't make it any easier.'

'Of course it doesn't. But you're Tristan fucking Grace.' I pressed a kiss to the tip of his nose. 'You've got this.'

BYRON

IT WAS THREE IN THE MORNING when my phone began to vibrate.

I didn't bother to check it, didn't even roll over to look at the number. It would be a spam call, or someone trying to steal my identity, neither of which I wanted to deal with in the too-early hours.

I rubbed my eyes. I was tired – so fucking tired – but sleep was impossible. I couldn't remember the last time I felt rested. The Banksia clinic had contacted Dr. Ford and my APF team, and they'd prescribed new sleeping tablets, but they were like tranquilisers. They knocked me out for longer than I cared to be unconscious, and I felt like death when I woke up, complete with headaches and nausea. I was getting pretty desperate, though; I suspected that in a few days' time, I'd be reaching for the packet.

My phone stopped vibrating. I sighed with what felt like relief and turned my attention back to the comedy I was watching.

My phone vibrated again. 'For fuck's sake,' I muttered, rolling to pick it up.

I froze.

Tristan Grace calling.

There was no way he was calling me, and equal chance of my answering. I ended the call and threw my phone across the bed.

Where it started vibrating again.

Dread stabbed at my stomach. What if he was calling about Rose? She'd texted a couple of days ago and said that she and Sebastian had caught the flu. She'd sent some intermittent memes since then, but what if something had happened? What if she needed to go to hospital?

I reached for the phone, then balled my hands into fists until it rang out.

Rose and I hadn't defined what was going on between us. I was desperately in love with her, and I didn't doubt her feelings for me, but we didn't have labels yet. I wasn't her boyfriend, her partner, her packmate, or her emergency contact. Tristan wouldn't call *me* about something like that. He'd call Rose's parents.

'Stupid,' I muttered to myself, then my breath hitched as my phone vibrated again. Maybe he'd already called her parents. Maybe she was already *in* hospital. Maybe ... Maybe it was even worse than that.

I swallowed against the remembered grief, against the memory of the officers on our doorstep, their hats in their hands, their faces showing matching sorrow. But if it was that bad, then mum would know, and she'd be calling me, too. There'd been no missed calls from other numbers on the screen.

Why the fuck is Tristan calling?

It clearly wasn't a pocket dial, not when he'd tried so many times. I could hear a number of secondary buzzes that meant someone was texting me, too.

I pressed my hands against my eyes and groaned at the ceiling.

It was curiosity that got me in the end. I reached across and grabbed my phone, reading through the string of text alerts.

Pick up the phone, Griffiths.

Don't be such a dick. Pick up.

I scoffed. As if he could fucking talk.

Please. Pick up.

Byron, I need help.

I stared at the last text, my stomach churning. *Byron, I need help.*

My instincts roared to life. *Your mate needs you.*

'Fuck off,' I muttered at them.

My phone vibrated again. *Tristan Grace calling.*

I answered before I could regret it. 'What the fuck do you want, Grace?'

'You picked up.'

He sounded surprised. I pushed down the sudden wave of longing that came with hearing his voice. 'Yeah, well, calls in the early hours of the morning don't tend to be light conversations, do they?'

'No,' he agreed awkwardly.

Fuck, it was so agonising. I may have been a complete tool, but he'd been just as bad. *What a fucking pair we are. I was right when I told Pravin that my scent match was probably an asshole. I just left out the fact that I was one, too.*

'What do you mean by *need help*, Grace?'

He was silent for a moment. 'Sebastian is in heat.'

I sat up straight. 'In preheat? Fuck. What does he need? I can drive –'

'No,' Tristan interrupted. 'He's in full heat. He has been for four days now.'

'Four *days*?' I repeated, incredulous. 'That isn't … *Full* heat? Are you *sure*?'

'He's not coming out of it.' For the first time, I heard the desperation in Tristan's voice. 'He's still deep in the haze. And I – and we –' He inhaled sharply. 'We need help.'

If I wasn't already sitting down, my knees would have given way. *Still in the heat haze?* Heats generally lasted no more than a couple of days: one for preheat, two for the haze, and a couple of quiet days after for recovery.

We need help.

It wasn't just Tristan – it was Rose, too.

'To be clear,' I said slowly, 'what do you need from me?'

'I can't –' His voice caught. 'I can't keep doing this on my own. Rose is amazing, but he needs knots, and I –'

'Grace,' I interrupted, incredulous. 'Are you asking me to come and *fuck your omega*?'

'I'm asking *my scent match* to come and take away *his omega's* pain,' Tristan retorted sharply. 'I'm asking *my mate* to *do his fucking duty to his pack* and *help his omega through his first heat.'*

Well, shit.

We were both silent after that.

'I don't think I've forgiven you yet,' I said at last.

'This isn't about us, Griffiths,' Tristan answered. He sounded tired, as if he'd used up all his fight in his last retort. 'It's about Sebastian.' He cleared his throat; he almost sounded close to tears. 'Either you're the alpha I think you are, and you'll help, or you're not, and you'll turn your back on an omega in pain. It's up to you. I'll leave our door unlocked for an hour.'

He ended the call.

I sat and stared at my black phone screen. My reflection stared darkly back.

'Fuck you, too, Grace,' I muttered.

Fuck you – because you're right.

If I walked through their door, I wasn't just walking into a heat. I was walking into a heat with an omega I cared about, who happened to be partnered with *my scent match*; an omega who was the scent match of the woman I was in love with. It couldn't get messier if it tried, but at the same time, it was overwhelmingly simple.

If I walked through their door, I was walking into a heat *with a pack*.

The question was whether I could get out of my own way long enough to take my place in it.

I'll leave our door unlocked for an hour.

'Fucking hell,' I muttered, and left my bed.

I showered first, washing off any hint of artificial scent, and all my cancellers. I rinsed my hair, making sure I couldn't smell shampoo or conditioner, then dried off and pulled on clean clothes. When I was done, I messaged my parents, letting them know what was happening, though I didn't expect they'd see it until morning. I trusted them with Sebastian's secret, though I imagined my mother would have a few choice words the next time I saw her.

The kitchen was my next stop; I pulled out all the berries in my fridge. They were already washed and ready to eat, so I divided them into containers, then cut up some apples and pears.

Tina never wanted anything but fruit during her heats, she'd told me.

I grabbed some bottles of water, too, and some elderflower cordial, just in case. If Sebastian didn't want anything, it didn't matter, but it was better to be prepared.

Four days.

I inhaled. I'd never knotted anybody before. What if I fucked it up? What if I *hurt* him?

My phone buzzed. *Are you okay, B?*

My heart constricted at the text from my dad.

I'm okay, I sent back. *I'll update you.*

A moment later, he responded. *Not with too much detail, I hope.*

I snorted. *Absolutely not. Go to bed. Love you.*

Love you, he sent back. *You're an amazing alpha, B.*

I closed my eyes until the pricking feeling stopped.

I sent a message to my APF team via my monitors, then texted Dr. Ford, letting them know what was going on – with no detail, of course; I knew Sebastian wasn't registered – so they wouldn't send someone to check on me if I was radio silent for a few days.

After that, there was no excuse to stay in my apartment, so I grabbed the berries and the drinks and slipped outside, locking my door behind me.

The corridor lights were dim. Clouds had hung around the coast since the big storm a few days ago, so there was no light from the moon or stars when I passed by the windows.

It would have been comforting to see them, but I guessed I was on my own.

I knocked softly when I got to Tristan and Sebastian's apartment. There was no answer; when I turned the handle, the door opened silently.

My groan was not so quiet.

Scent washed over me: cherry, chocolate, vanilla. After so long in the scentless bubble of Banksia, my body went tight as I drew them in. I wanted to drown in those sweet scents, to bury my face in them and never surface. I wanted to taste them from the source, wanted the flavours sliding over my tongue –

'Alpha?'

With difficulty, I pushed my instincts aside and closed the door behind me, making sure to catch every lock. The air purifier on the wall was already set to high. I didn't want anyone else scenting my pack; those perfumes were for *me*.

'Omega,' I said softly.

Sebastian looked terrible. There were huge shadows under his eyes, and his skin was dull and sallow. It seemed as if he'd lost weight since the last time I saw him; his pyjama shorts hung low beneath his hip bones. His lips were swollen and chapped.

He was still more beautiful than he had any right to be.

'I gave permission for you to come, but I wasn't sure whether you would.' It was clear he was still deep in the haze: his pants tented over his crotch and his usually clear blue eyes were cloudy. He didn't look wholly real; he was an alpha's dream come to life; a fantasy made flesh. 'If you run again, there won't be another invitation. I won't let you hurt him – hurt *us* – a second time.'

'I understand.'

His eyes fixed on the bag in my hand. 'What did you bring?'

I pulled out the containers of berries. 'Some fruit and some drinks. Would you like some?'

His eyes narrowed. 'Are they a gift?'

I blinked. 'Not a courting gift. I want to get you something better than berries for that. But they *are* an offering.'

'So you *are* courting me?'

My lips curved up. 'I think we've messed up the proper order of things, but yes. I'd like to. If you want that.'

He appeared to consider it. 'Are there raspberries?' he said at last.

There were, so I offered them to him. His long fingers carefully took a couple and popped them between his heat-ravaged lips. He closed his eyes as the flavour hit his tongue.

'Shall I make you a drink?'

He nodded, so I found a glass and some ice. When he sipped on it, his eyebrows rose. 'Elderflower?'

'It was my sister's favourite. She always wanted it, especially during her heats.'

'Was her scent as sweet as yours?'

I swallowed against the pain that came with that question. 'Marshmallow,' I said gruffly. 'It used to make my nose itch.'

And fuck, I missed it.

Sebastian hummed and drained the glass dry. I took it from him, shivering as my fingertips brushed his skin, and made a second glass.

My alpha derived such a primal satisfaction from watching him eat and drink the things I'd offered that, for a few minutes, I felt calm. I couldn't help my scent from rising, though, still weak from the blockers in my system. I saw the moment Sebastian caught it; his body went tight as his lips parted, and he inhaled raggedly, his chest expanding. His eyes flickered to meet mine as his pupils blew out.

'*Alpha.*'

Cherry filled my senses. 'Can you eat a bit more, Sebastian?'

He shook his head. 'Not hungry for food.'

I licked my lips. 'What about a shower?'

He thought about it for a moment. 'Only if you'll join me.'

I guess I walked into that one.

Sebastian took my hand. My skin tingled at the touch; heat spread through my limbs as he tugged me towards the bathroom. His skin was fever-hot, almost scalding. I followed him, but took over once we walked through the bathroom door, running the shower and making sure the temperature was right before I turned back to him. 'Do you need –'

I faltered as he stripped off his shorts and I was left with a very naked, very aroused omega.

My nerves screamed back into existence.

Sebastian's eyes travelled from my face down my body; he doubled over without warning, clutching his stomach. 'Alpha,' he whined, and my instincts stood to attention. 'Hurts.'

'Step under the water, sweetheart.' I guided him under the shower, arranging him so the water was running on his back. 'That's it.' I paused. 'Can I touch you?'

'Please,' he said hoarsely, so I let my palm rest on the small of his back before starting to rub in small circles. Although the pain would radiate through his limbs, it would be concentrated in his abdomen and lower back, and massage could help relieve it.

'Not what I meant, alpha,' he grumbled, but I could feel him relaxing under my palm. 'Aren't you coming in?'

'If you want me to.'

His fingers caught the hem of my shirt. 'Yes, I want you to.'

He stepped out of the water to pull it up, and a moment later it lay in a black pool on the floor. I stood statue-still as he ran his wet hands over my chest and stomach, trying not to hyperventilate. My cock pressed painfully against my zipper; my breath caught as he reached for the button on my jeans.

He stopped. 'Is this okay?' he said, as if remembering that he should check first.

'Whatever you want is okay,' I answered hoarsely.

'You say that now,' he murmured, his fingers making short work of my button and zip. 'Fuck, alpha.'

I'd never been vain, but the look on Sebastian's face when I kicked off my jeans could have changed that. His tongue flicked out to wet his lips and his eyes hooded as he focused on my cock. I flushed as it jerked under his gaze, as if begging for attention.

'I was worried,' he said, 'that when Tristan asked for your help, you'd do it out of some sense of obligation.' He reached out and trailed a finger up the underside of my shaft. 'This doesn't look like obligation.'

'It's desire,' I grated out.

'For me?'

'For you,' I confirmed.

He shuddered, stepping back under the shower, his hand splaying across his stomach as he was wracked by another heat cramp. 'Alpha –'

I fell to my knees, water spraying in a gentle cascade over my shoulders. 'Let me help you, omega.'

His eyes closed and his head fell back against the shower wall as I took him in my mouth. His cock was over-warm against my lips and tongue, but tasted so sweet. I tried not to think about the hints of chocolate and vanilla I could taste beneath the cherry, or about what they'd been doing over the past four days to mix their scents up in such a way.

Sebastian whimpered as I cupped his sac, swallowing his thickness down as far as I could. It wasn't to the root –

my gag reflex was sensitive – but pushing my limits sent shivers of pleasure up my spine. I popped off his cock with a filthy squelching sound and a groan. 'You taste so good.'

'Your mouth is fucking sinful, alpha,' he muttered.

I swallowed him down again, moving my mouth up and down his shaft before swirling my tongue around his head. Cherry coated my mouth and I was desperate for more. I listened to his moans and expletives; when he started gasping *oh fuck, oh fuck* I knew I was doing the right thing. His fingers speared through my hair, gripping tightly. I hollowed my cheeks and sucked as his hips jerked.

Cherry slid down my throat as he stiffened, groaning my name. I reached to squeeze the base of my cock, hard, trying to stave off my climax. I swallowed one mouthful, then another, my alpha shouting for more.

I gave Sebastian one last cheeky suck, feeling smug as he cried out and shuddered. 'You're incredible, omega,' I said thickly.

He tugged on my hair until I rose up off my knees. He pulled me in for a kiss, which I happily gave him, my breath hitching as his tongue dipped into my mouth. 'Want you, alpha.'

I tried not to lose my mind. He pushed me out of the shower; I hastily grabbed a towel and threw it around his shoulders, though he seemed oblivious to the water dripping from his hair and down his body. He looked like a siren as I followed him from the bathroom, the song of his perfect body and alluring scent seducing me from the safety of my ship and into the wildness of his waters.

I'd happily drown.

I stopped in the doorway of the nest.

The mix of scents was heady here, so strong that I felt dizzy. My mouth watered as vanilla hit the back of my throat. *Mate*, my alpha roared. He knew Tristan's scent, knew that he was close.

Knew that he was *mine*.

But Sebastian's needs were more important. Despite that, I couldn't help but glance to one side of the nest.

The bed was swathed in diaphanous material, and through it I could see Tristan stretched out on his side, asleep, a blanket draped over his hips. He looked exhausted, but one arm was still cradled protectively around Rose, who had curled up against him. She looked pale, too, and the way she'd pressed her face into Tristan's chest in her sleep suggested her omega was comfortable enough with him for complete trust.

Ours, my instincts roared.

Settle the fuck down, I told them, but I knew it was useless.

They wouldn't shut up until I claimed my pack.

I cleared my throat softly. 'May I enter your nest, omega?'

Sebastian dropped the towel to the floor and climbed up onto the bed. The soft light played over the dips and swell of his chest and stomach, catching on the hard lines of his jaw, darkening his eyes. 'You may, alpha.'

For the first time, I stepped into an omega's nest.

My breath caught at the thought.

Sebastian's nest was lovely, all calming ocean colours and soft fabrics. Fairy lights played over the bed canopy like tiny stars. It was soothing and romantic all at once, and my anxiety eased. I took the towel he'd dropped and tossed it back outside; his nest was beautiful, and it deserved to stay pristine.

'Alpha,' Sebastian whispered, and my mind blanked of everything but helping ease his pain.

It wasn't entirely selfless; I'd never been so hard and my blood felt as if it had caught fire.

Three scents invaded my senses, but Sebastian's was the strongest. It caught at me, inviting me forward, drawing my alpha to the surface. My own scent swirled, mingling with the others until the air was almost unbearably sweet.

Sebastian perched on the edge of the bed; I moved forward until I caged him with my arms, rubbing my cheek on his. 'Tell me what you want, omega.'

He fell back, his knees spreading, his cock weeping precum that pooled on his belly. 'I want your knot, alpha.'

I closed my eyes for a moment. *Had a sweeter sentence ever been spoken?*

I shifted my weight to one hand and swept the other over his thigh, feeling the muscle beneath the silky skin tremble. My fingers were equally shaky when they traced between his rounded cheeks, finding him slick and ready. I circled where he was burning hot and quivering. 'Is this okay?'

'Please,' Sebastian whispered, his eyes wide and wild. 'Please don't tease me, alpha.'

I pushed inside and had to hold myself back from shouting.

He was tight and slick and scalding, and I couldn't think of anything but pushing further inside, joining my body to his, and of sliding in and out of that divine place. He groaned, shifting his hips, trying to take my finger deeper. I added a second and gave him what he wanted, my teeth embedded in my bottom lip as he clenched around me. Another time, I'd spend hours preparing him, stretching and slicking and seeing just how much I could make him squirm, but he was already primed, already tilting his pelvis, already begging for more.

'*Please*, alpha.'

I went still as white began to cloud my eyes, creeping in from the edges of my vision. I inhaled sharply, my shoulders tensing. I tried to breathe through it, to acknowledge it and move forward – as I'd learned to do with Rose – but I couldn't push away the sudden panic. I pulled my hand away from Sebastian, my pulse racing.

'Hey. Alpha.'

I looked down at the angel beneath me, an angel who was reaching up to touch my face, his expression a mix of hunger and understanding.

'You're okay, alpha. It's a rut, that's all.' His hands skimmed my stomach; one wrapped around my cock. 'You're doing so well, alpha, and I want you so badly. *Need* you.' I groaned as his thumb swiped over my head, spreading the precum pooling there. 'You feel so good, and I need you inside me.' He guided me down, and suddenly I was pressing against his slick heat. 'There. That's where I need you. And you need me, too. You're so hard, alpha. So swollen for me. We can give each other what we need. I know it.'

The white spread, until my vision narrowed to the omega beneath me. I wasn't too proud to admit that I was still scared, still nervous about knotting him. But Sebastian shot me a hungry grin and shifted, and my instincts took over as my hips thrust gently forward, my cock sinking into the fire of his body.

'Fuck, yes,' he hissed. 'Just like that.'

The white stopped spreading.

My arms shook with the effort of pushing into him slowly, carefully, thrusting forward gently only to pull back, letting his body adjust to my cock.

'You're in control, alpha,' he murmured, and my instincts responded. *Yes, we are.*

It was easy after that.

I sank inside until I was buried to the hilt and his body shook around me, squeezing and tightening and greedily pulling. I'd never felt anything like it before, and I knew I wouldn't last, but the omega beneath me didn't want me to.

He wanted my knot.

Sebastian arched, one hand wrapped around his cock, the other spread over his stomach in an effort to ease the heat cramp. 'Please,' he begged, and I couldn't refuse him.

I pulled out, then pushed back in, hissing every expletive I knew. It was *heaven*, and I wanted him to know it, and feel it, too. I dipped down to take his mouth with mine, my tongue tracing his bottom lip before I bit down. I didn't break the skin, but he whimpered and squirmed beneath me, throwing his head back to bare his neck.

'Alpha,' he whined, and my control snapped.

I pulled back, then my hips kicked as I thrust – *hard*.

'Yes,' Sebastian snarled, arching, his eyes wild. '*Yes*.'

My lips pressed against his scent gland as I gave him everything I could. It wasn't gentle, and it wasn't reverent; it was instinctual and frantic, the alpha inside me wanting to *possess* the omega beneath him. My teeth scraped over his skin, and he chanted *yes, please, alpha, more* as the scent of cherry thickened in the air. I lowered my body, letting him rut against me as I moved. His legs shifted higher and I sank deeper inside him, snarling wordlessly as my knot began to swell.

'Fuck, yes,' he cried. 'Alpha, *bite*.'

I scraped my teeth over his scent gland again, but somehow, I managed to hold back. There were no other bite marks on his skin, and I knew I shouldn't be the first one to leave them there, even if my teeth ached as they pushed down, ready. His scent match's teeth should be the first to sink beneath his skin, and, after that, the alpha who'd loved him for years. I was last on the list, and happily; I knew I just needed to be patient and wait my turn.

He shuddered, his body tightening as his cock jerked against my belly. 'Fuck, *yes*,' I snarled. 'Come, omega.' My knot caught on his entrance as I swelled. I plunged inside him one last time, then rocked as my knot inflated.

Sebastian gave a wordless whine, and his body squeezed as he came, panting frantically, his arms closing around me. '*Alpha*.'

Pleasure flooded through me; I muffled my shout against Sebastian's neck. My vision went white, but I wasn't afraid. I rocked against my omega, my knot lodged in his body, and as the pleasure ebbed and my vision cleared, I heard another sound.

A deep, unbroken rumble, coming from my chest.

I pulled back, surprised.

Sebastian blinked up at me, his lips curving. 'You're purring, alpha,' he said. 'You're purring for *me*.' His hands stroked up my back as his body relaxed. '*Oh*. That's so good.'

I moved carefully, rolling us so that Sebastian sprawled across me. He gave a bitten-off whimper as my knot shifted inside him, but settled quickly, laying his head on my chest and sighing happily as he listened to my purr.

My heart just about burst as his own began to rumble, slightly less deep and slightly less loud, as if we were two different notes in the same melody.

'The nest is right,' he said sleepily.

I kissed his head. 'Omega?'

'The nest wasn't right before. It is, now. It was you. You were the thing that was missing.'

Oh.

'I'm glad, Sebastian.' I stroked his hair, loving the feeling of his weight on me. 'I'm so glad I could give you what you needed.' My head dropped to the side, and I stilled my strokes.

Rose and Tristan were both awake, and both had their eyes on us.

On *me*.

Rose smiled, full and approving. *Hey*, she mouthed, then her eyes fluttered and closed once more. Her smile remained, her expression one of deep contentment.

Tristan's expression was inscrutable. I couldn't tell what he was thinking; it could have been anything. I couldn't imagine that it was *good*; the alpha that had walked away from him was currently knot-deep in his long-term love and omega. I'd be feeling a *lot*, if I were him.

Sebastian murmured, his weight increasing as he slipped into sleep. Tristan focused on my fingers, still caught in the golden strands of Sebastian's hair. His brow furrowed, but it looked thoughtful, rather than angry. He caught my eye once more – my heart skipped a beat and my purr faltered – and there was a long, tense moment where we stared at each other.

I realised I'd forgiven him.

He closed his eyes and buried his face in Rose's hair.

◇◇◇

I started awake. I'd fallen asleep with Sebastian's head tucked beneath my chin, but I woke with my face pressed to his shoulder, his back against my chest, my arms tight around him. I wasn't sure what had disturbed my sleep – not until I heard a voice.

It was loud and clear, but it didn't come from anyone in the bed.

You're a pack alpha, B. Just like you were always meant to be.

I closed my eyes again, smiling.

◇◇◇

Sebastian woke twice more during the night. Each time I kissed him, teased him, fucked him, knotted him, and purred as I held him and he drifted off to sleep once again.

After I knotted him the third time, his skin cooled, and I knew it was over.

SEBASTIAN

COMING OUT OF THE HEAT was like waking from a dream.

I could remember everything that had happened, but it was fuzzy around the edges, like a long-ago memory. I stretched in the nest-bed, feeling unfamiliar aches in my muscles, and a raw feeling elsewhere that I'd not experienced since I'd started fucking Tristan six years ago and neither of us had known what we were doing.

But I also felt *peace*. I inhaled, the scents of chocolate, vanilla, and salted caramel wrapping around me, smoothing the edges inside me that I hadn't even noticed were rough. I felt like a puzzle that had finally been put together.

I touched my neck, but there was no pain, no broken skin.

A mix of disappointment and relief washed over me. Disappointment because I wanted bites and bonds, badly. Relief because in hindsight, I didn't want those memories to be fuzzy. I wanted my bites to be stories I told my grandchildren, something I thought about on my deathbed. In fact, maybe filming it would be better, so I could watch the moment over and over, and force people I'd just met to relive my happiness the way that some people made you watch videos of their kids or pets.

'Seb?'

I looked over to see Rose prop herself on one elbow. My heart expanded as I studied her, my poor, exhausted omega who'd worked so hard and made me feel so amazing. Her hair was a tangled mess, her skin pale, her eyes darkened with bruise-like shadows.

She was incredible.

'Rosebud,' I said. Or tried to, anyway; it came out as a croak. 'I love you.'

'Oh, Seb.' She moved across the bed to give me a nuzzling kiss. 'I suspect that's the hormones talking. But I love you, too.'

I took her in my arms, the omega beneath my skin poking his head up to preen. 'I didn't do anything embarrassing, did I?'

'No.' She scent marked my cheek. 'You were incredible. You were so beautiful, taking your alphas' knots. A perfect omega.'

My cock jerked at that, but didn't harden; I imagined it had done quite enough for the time being. 'You didn't bite me.'

She was silent for a moment. 'You only asked each of us once,' she said eventually. 'And I know what you said, Seb, and I'm sorry, but it didn't feel right. For any of us. I –'

'I'm glad you didn't,' I interrupted. 'I want a bonding ceremony instead.'

Her eyes widened. 'With priests?'

'Fuck the priests – not literally, obviously, and sorry for blaspheming and all that – but yeah. One where we have witnesses, and we bite each other, and ride off into the sunset or whatever. Maybe not on an actual horse, though,' I went on, thinking about it. 'I think Tris is allergic. A car would be better. But something special. Something we'll remember forever.'

Her eyes went misty and she sniffed. *Huh. My Rosebud is a romantic.* 'That sounds lovely. But …' Her eyes flickered to the side of the nest.

Where our alphas lay.

They were both asleep – *sound* asleep – but they'd curled around each other, as if their bodies *knew* they were supposed to be together. Byron's arm was slung over Tristan's waist, and my alpha's expression was peaceful in a way I hadn't seen for months.

'Byron has had insomnia for weeks now,' Rose murmured. 'He fell asleep after the last knot, but lightly. He was restless until Tristan rolled next to him. They haven't moved since.'

'They're such fools,' I said fondly.

'But they're *our* fools.'

I smiled. 'Yes. They're ours.' I rolled onto my back, taking Rose with me. She settled her cheek on my chest, listening to my heart beat, just as I'd done with Byron. 'I think I finally feel like a real omega.'

'Seb,' Rose said. 'You were *always* a real omega.'

'You know what I mean.' I waved a hand flippantly. 'I'd never had a heat, so it didn't feel that way to me. It always felt like I was stuck half-way – not beta enough, not omega enough. It always felt as if I was still waiting for something.' I kissed the top of her head. 'Now I know what it was. A five-day sex-fest and more knots than I can count.'

'I do remember feeling as if my heat had reset my body. Like I'd turned myself off and on again. Everything just felt ... better.'

I frowned. 'I wonder if this could happen to you?'

'That my heat suppressants might fail, do you mean?' She nuzzled into me. 'Maybe we should plan for it, instead. Perhaps I could go off my suppressants at the end of the year, during the break.'

'A Christmas heat,' I murmured, thinking about it. 'Mmm. Yes, please. We could go to Tristan's island. Or anywhere else you wanted. We could fly overseas, have a heat in the snow somewhere.' I rolled us over, licking at her scent gland, pressing my hips into hers. 'We can work it out later. There's something I want right now.'

She blinked up at me, her lips parting. 'You're joking.'

'I never joke about pancakes, Rosebud.' I grinned and rolled off the bed, pulling her with me. 'Let's give the alphas some space and make some breakfast.' My grin widened. 'And if we happened to *accidentally* lock the door on the way and not open it until they've kissed and made up ...'

'It locks from the wrong side for that,' Rose said, ever-practical. 'But maybe the time alone will be good for them.'

TRISTAN

I STIRRED.

At first, I thought the sound behind me was snoring. But then my tired brain realised it was an unbroken, deep, continuing rumble that didn't hitch or fall with breath.

It was a purr.

It didn't belong to Sebastian, though, and nor was it Rose's adorable, melodic crackle. It was too deep and too rumbly and it made me feel *safe*, soothing over every fractured part of me.

My own started without warning, adding an extra layer to the sound.

What the fuck? I thought sleepily, forcing my tired body to roll over.

A wordless noise of complaint was my reward, though the purr continued, accompanied by a deep sigh.

There was a heavy weight on my waist and it shifted as I moved, settling along my back, pulling me closer to a hard wall of warmth.

I wrenched my eyes open, then froze.

Byron's face was inches from mine, his eyes still closed, his purr unabated. I stared at him, taking in the thick black lashes shadowing his cheeks, his high cheekbones, his square jaw, and something I'd never noticed before: an almost-invisible dusting of freckles across the bridge of his nose.

I swallowed.

'Can feel you looking a' me,' he grumbled thickly, a hint of his father's lyrical accent slipping into his voice for a moment. 'Go ba' t' sleep.'

'I don't think so,' I answered softly. I reached out and tentatively stroked his hair back from his face.

'Mmm.' He leaned unselfconsciously into the touch. 'You can stay awake if you keep doing that.'

I did as he asked, shifting my body closer. 'Whatever you want.'

'Want you not to be an asshole again,' he murmured. 'Can you do that?'

'No,' I answered, honestly.

He cracked his grey eyes open to glare at me.

'If someone tried to hurt you, or either of our omegas, being an asshole would be the *least* of what I would do.'

'Oh.' He closed his eyes again. 'That's okay. You can be an asshole *for* the pack, but don't be an asshole *to* the pack. Deal?'

'Deal.' I cupped his cheek, stroking my thumb across his skin. My nerves were buzzing. 'Does that mean you forgive me?'

'Yes,' he said grumpily. 'But please don't do it again, Grace.'

'You think I'd risk this?' I traced his cheekbone. 'You think I'd do *anything* to jeopardise my pack?'

'No.' He stretched, lifting his arm from my waist for a moment, only to pull me closer a heartbeat later. I nudged a leg between his, locking us together. 'You're a lot of things, Tristan, but you're not stupid.'

'You're a lot of things, too,' I told him, 'but the most important one is *mine*.'

His arm tightened around me; he pressed his forehead to mine. 'Yes,' he said simply. 'Yes.'

We lay still for a moment. I breathed him in, the salted caramel scent of him settling over my tongue, making my mouth water. My cock twitched hopefully, then gave up.

Byron snorted. 'The spirit is willing, but the flesh is weak.' He grinned. 'How am I as tired as *you*? You did this for *days*. I barely managed a few hours.'

I smiled. 'Better work on your stamina before next time then, Griffiths.'

He made a humming sound, then pressed his lips to mine, softly, tenderly, before sighing against my mouth.

Happily.

'Mine,' he murmured. 'My mate. My alpha. My pack.'

'Yours,' I agreed, and tipped his chin back for another kiss.

I lost myself for a long moment, caught in the slide of his lips over mine, the way his hair felt as it slipped between my fingers. I traced my hands over his shoulders and back, learning the shape of him, following the planes and dips of muscle. I was going to map every inch of him, learn the places he loved to be touched and just how to do it. I was going to make up for everything – for that first, too-quick fuck in the maze, for the hurt I'd caused Rose and Sebastian, for being an asshole even before then. I'd spend my lifetime making sure that this alpha knew what he meant to me.

He sighed again, and turned his cheek, scent marking me. My purr rumbled contentedly in response; I arched my neck, letting him nuzzle at my scent gland, my limbs heavy with happiness.

A loud crash came from the kitchen.

Byron was on his feet in an instant. 'What the fuck was that?'

It was my turn to sigh. '*That* is Sebastian making pancakes.'

Byron stared at me, then ran a hand through his messy hair. 'Oh. That can't be too –'

Another *crash* sounded, followed by a shriek of surprise that could have come from either omega. I forced myself upright. 'I'd better go help.'

Byron frowned. 'It's pancakes. Sebastian is a literal genius. Surely he can manage.'

'Uh-huh.' I paused. 'Have you ever cleaned egg off a ceiling?'

My mate blinked at me.

'Sebastian is an accomplished baker, provided it comes from a packet. But if he tries to make something from scratch, it all just –' I made a motion with my hands '– falls apart. Spectacularly. I've witnessed it for years and still can't explain it. But I *do* know that it's best to intervene early. Especially if you're hungry.'

Byron's lips twitched. 'It seems I have a lot to learn.'

I stood and closed the distance between us, brushing another soft kiss across his mouth. 'Don't we all.'

ROSE

SIX MONTHS LATER

THE GREAT HALL WAS FULL OF PEOPLE.

I turned around in my seat, trying to spot my parents in the crowd. Tristan's mother waved to me, smiling widely. I waved back and blew her a kiss, then gave a less unhinged smile to Tristan's fathers. Sebastian's omega mum caught my eye and gave me a cheerful salute; his mother acknowledged me with a graceful nod. I knew that was her at her friendliest, so I waved at them both.

My own parents were a few rows back, sitting with Byron's father; my eyes misted as my mum and dad blew me a kiss. I hadn't seen them for months and was looking forward to introducing them properly to my pack.

'Oh, your mum is so cute!' Sebastian exclaimed, waving enthusiastically. 'You look just like her!'

I'd met Sebastian and Tristan's parents on a visit to Sydney during the mid-semester break; Tristan's parents had flown from the UK specifically. Meeting eight parents in one go had been a lot, but I was glad we'd done it; it had made this – the Banksia House annual awards night – and what was to come tomorrow, easier.

Our final grades weren't released until after the award night ceremony, leaving the academic achievement awards – along with the later-year awards and the all-important Banksia Prize – a mystery. Next to me, Sebastian was thrumming with anticipation; we'd spent the last semester in loving competition, challenging each other to work harder, aim higher, to get the best marks possible.

And tonight we'd know whether it had paid off.

Oh, Sebastian pretended very well that he didn't mind which of us took first place in the year, but *I* knew just as well that it was bullshit. He wanted the academic award almost as much as he wanted the Banksia Prize. And after meeting his parents, I couldn't really blame him.

'No matter what happens, you're both amazing,' Byron murmured, leaning down to kiss me, then reaching to cup Sebastian's cheek. 'Plus, there's always next year.'

'Don't encourage them,' Tristan muttered. Our alphas looked so handsome, Byron in a black button-down and jeans, and Tristan wearing a pair of plaid pants and a linen shirt. He leaned down to nuzzle Sebastian's scent gland. 'The real prize comes tomorrow.'

'Yes, yes, the bonding ceremony will be great, but Rose and I need the metaphorical gold stars, Tris.' Sebastian's knee bounced. 'Inherent worth is good and all, but we need validation.' Byron's mother stepped onto the stage. 'Fuck me, it's starting.'

'Good evening and welcome to Banksia House,' the Dean said into the microphone, smiling out at the crowd. Sebastian said I looked like my mother, but Tina Griffiths had been a mirror image of hers; the proof was in the photos Byron had put up all over our apartment, alongside shots of our pack and all our families. I'd taken several of them, developing them in Banksia's new dark room, which hadn't existed until Tristan had politely asked for it on my behalf. 'I'll get my welcome done quickly, never fear.'

There was a smatter of laughter from the audience, and Carla Griffiths continued.

'This year has been one of change for Banksia House. A new dean, new members of faculty, and some updates in pastoral care practices and support procedures, especially in relation to our beta and omega students.'

I cleared my throat softly at the mention of new members of faculty; Professor Brandon Heathcote had left Banksia manor after the first semester's final exam and had not returned. His later-year students all had new tutors, and although I'd searched online, I couldn't find any notice of Heathcote finding another job – at a university, at least.

'Academia is, and always has been, a meeting point of progress and tradition,' our Dean said, her tone serious. 'And it is our responsibility – as people with the incredible privilege of belonging to and participating in this environment – to know that traditions affect and are enacted upon individuals differently, and often, this is not to their benefit. It is our duty, as scholars, to know when to let traditions go, and when to begin new ones.' She paused. 'It is with this in mind that I have the immense pleasure of announcing a change to Banksia's admission procedures. From next year, the two scholarship positions in every Banksia first-year intake will be no more.'

There were some gasps from the audience; a few voices rose angrily. Beside me, Byron tensed.

'Instead, there will be ten.'

There were some more gasps from behind us, and some relieved laughter.

'Four positions will be retained for students of any designation who show above-exceptional academic ability. The remaining six positions will be reserved for students of beta and omega designation who meet or exceed our entrance tests. Banksia's cohorts will remain small, so the hope is that these new positions will significantly increase our percentage of beta and omega students. Our environment and support services will evolve to meet this challenge, with more pack rooms and nests available, and student leave procedures updated to include heats. In this way, we hope that Banksia, over time, will become an institution where *any* designation can succeed – and not just succeed, but excel.'

Sebastian began to clap loudly and, a heartbeat later, the rest of the audience joined in.

Carla gave a pleased smile. 'A full breakdown of our new policies and procedures will be available from tomorrow on the Banksia website. But for now: the fun part.' She shuffled some papers on the lectern and, for a moment, I could see her as a younger lecturer –

charismatic, capable, and slightly harried. 'Without further ado, the academic awards.'

Sebastian took my hand, his body tense.

'The first year academic award goes to Alessia Lupo.'

Sebastian's fingers tightened, then released; we both clapped and cheered as a stunned-looking Alessia stood up and made her way on stage.

'Alessia beat *both of you*? But your marks were *insane*,' Tristan said. 'How –'

'She clearly did better.' Sebastian turned to grin at me. 'Serves us right for thinking one of us had it in the bag.'

'It's not the ego check we wanted, but the ego check we needed,' I agreed, grinning back at him. 'But we'll do better next year.'

'Now we know who to beat.' Sebastian turned back to the front and whooped loudly. 'Way to go, Alessia!'

Byron's hand settled on my thigh and squeezed gently. 'You're not upset?'

I shrugged. 'A little disappointed, I guess. But if Alessia beat *us*, then she clearly deserved it.' I glanced at him from beneath my lashes. 'Maybe I'll ask her to be my study partner.'

'You'll do no such thing,' Byron growled, as Sebastian said simultaneously: 'Absolutely fucking not.'

I laughed and settled back into my chair as the applause died down, snuggling into Byron as his mother read out the other academic prizes. Marco won the third year prize, while Marina snagged the award for best three-minute thesis.

'And now we come to, perhaps, the most controversial and best-known of all our awards: the Banksia Prize,' Carla said, once the audience had settled. 'Awarded by the historic Banksia Revels, the Banksia Prize is given to one first-year student annually. The student may or may not be top-performing in their cohort. They may or may not be active in Banksia's clubs. They may or may not spend their time volunteering. They may or may not be highly valued by their peer group.' She paused. 'I did ask what the criteria of the award was, as no doubt many deans before me have done, and I suspect I received the same answer they did. The panel takes into account many different considerations when awarding the prize, and it simply goes to the student the panel believes deserves it – no more, and no less.' She paused. 'This year, the Banksia Prize will be even more controversial than usual. For the first time in Banksia's history, the prize will be awarded to two of our first-year students.'

I felt Byron's eyes on me and turned to see his face split into a beautiful, proud smile.

My stomach dropped.

'Both students are formidable scholars, placing equal second in the first-year cohort. Both embody the values we strive to cultivate at Banksia House: excellence, dedication, curiosity, and ambition. In addition, both these students have, over the past year, demonstrated traits we hope to see in all our students moving forward – bravery and resilience.' Carla smiled, looking almost as proud as her son. 'I need to add here that I am not a member of the Revels and had no part in the selection; anyone with questions about the process may contact Ada in the administration office.'

Tristan turned to Sebastian and me, his green eyes wide.

'I am pleased to give you the joint winners of this year's Banksia Prize: Sebastian Worthy and Rosemary Morris.'

The audience began to clap; behind us, I could hear Tristan's mother cheering wildly. I sat still, stunned, until Sebastian caught my hand and dragged me upright, towing me towards the stage.

Carla enveloped us both in a warm hug. 'Well done, both of you. I'm so proud,' she whispered. She handed us both a rolled-up parchment. 'There used to be a trophy, but now your name just gets engraved on the wall. I hope that's okay.'

Sebastian turned towards the audience, glowing beneath the stage lights, shooting a smile that could only be described as *gleeful* towards his parents. 'I know it's bad to do things out of spite, but sometimes, it just feels so *good*.' He took my hand in his, and turned his smile on me; it softened, became adoring. 'Fuck yes, Rosebud. You're amazing.'

'So are you.' I lifted his hand to my mouth and kissed his knuckles. 'My omega.'

'My omega,' he murmured back. 'I guess we have to stick around Banksia for longer now.'

My eyes found Byron and Tristan in the audience, both on their feet, applauding, with matching wide smiles. 'I can't wait.'

Sebastian laughed, the sound at once joyful and smug. 'I wonder what the second-year prize is?'

❂❂❂

The audience was smaller the following day.

We'd only invited our families – our parents and Tristan's younger siblings. We'd talked about location for hours on end over the last six months, with suggestions ranging from the ridiculous – Tristan suggested the Natural History Museum in London – to the practical – the tiny local courthouse – but once I'd suggested the beach, we'd all gone quiet.

'Yes,' Sebastian had said, and that was that.

None of us were devout, so we'd engaged a celebrant rather than the traditional two priests for the ceremony. She was a cheerful beta with ash-brown curls and an ever-present friendly smile. She hadn't known who either Tristan or Sebastian were, so we hadn't had to worry about her leaking details to the media, even after two photographers were arrested outside the gates of Banksia trying to get a story about our pack.

The four of us stood together on the cliffs, facing the sea, our parents seated behind us. I wore a flowing dress of soft gold with white sandals, while Tristan and Sebastian had coaxed Byron into tan chinos and a white linen shirt so the three of them matched. He had a pair of aviators perched on his nose, and Sebastian had pinned tiny sprigs of wattle to their breasts; I had a similar sprig tucked into my hair.

My eyes darted to the place – a few metres away – where Byron and I had first kissed. As if he knew what I was thinking, he grinned and brought my hand to his mouth, pressing his lips to my knuckles.

'I never imagined this,' Tristan mused softly, watching the sun sink over the horizon, the sky lit with shades of pink and orange as the tide surged below us, 'but somehow, it's what I've always wanted.'

The celebrant looked us over and began.

'We are here this evening for the best of reasons,' she said, smiling, 'to witness the bonding of the Morris-Worthy pack. All packs are special and all bonds sacred, but this pack's journey wasn't simple, nor easy. They have worked – both together, and as individuals – to overcome the barriers that separated them, and are stronger for it. And as a pack with not one, but *two* scent-matched pairs, I think we can all agree that they have found something rare, something precious, and something worth fighting for.

'They told me they didn't want to write vows which, I must admit, I found surprising, given they are all intelligent, articulate people. But Byron said to me: *how could I ever put this into words?*' She paused. 'I understood, then. Some things are bigger than words, more powerful than language. Some things can never be captured by mere sounds or symbols. So, instead of words, instead of vows, let your bonds speak for you; let your hearts say what your lips cannot.'

I sniffed as a tear ran down my cheek. Sebastian wiped it away, his own eyes bright.

'Usually, the head alpha would bite their pack first,' she continued, smiling at Tristan. 'But that isn't the case today. I was informed by both alphas that the omegas were the core of this pack, and they would be the ones forging the bonds. Rosemary and Sebastian, I invite you to begin.'

I took a shuddering breath and turned to Sebastian. He took my hands in his, gently squeezing my fingers. 'Ready, beautiful?' he whispered.

I was nervous, but I wasn't scared. This was my omega, and I loved him. My canines pushed down, sending a dull ache through my jaw. 'Ready.'

He tilted his head, baring his neck to me; I leaned forward, pressing a kiss to his scent gland, then bit down. His blood spread over my tongue, cherry-sweet with a slight metallic aftertaste. I moaned softly as warmth spread through my body, an awareness chasing after it – not of the environment around me, but of *Sebastian*. Of my other half, my perfect match, my omega. Of his golden sunshine, of his flirty cheerfulness, of the steel backbone he obscured with smiles and his big blue eyes. I splayed my hand over his heart, closing my eyes as his love surged through me. 'Oh, Seb,' I whispered.

'Rosebud,' he said, panting slightly. 'Rose, I –'

I tilted my head. '*Bite.*'

It hurt, but only for a moment; my limbs shook as he gripped me, moaning my name. I felt lightheaded, as if I was floating away; the next heartbeat, I was anchored by the echoes of Sebastian's emotions, by his gratitude and admiration and adoration.

I pushed my love for him down the bond, trying to show him just how strongly those feelings were returned. He staggered slightly; I held him up.

He pressed his forehead to mine, inhaling shakily. 'Rose. This is … This is …'

'No words?'

'No fucking words.' He kissed me; I tasted my own blood on his lips. 'No words other than *I love you, always*.'

I stroked his hair, feeling the strength of his emotion even as he said it. 'There's more to go yet.'

He grinned. 'I can't –' he faltered as he looked towards our alphas, who had fallen to their knees on the grass.

For *us*.

'I love seeing them like that,' Sebastian murmured, echoing my sentiments exactly.

We stepped before them; me before Byron, Sebastian before Tristan. We hadn't talked about it; we'd just known this was how it would be. I ran my fingertip over Byron's cheek.

He closed his eyes, leaning into the touch. 'That was so beautiful,' he murmured. 'You're both so beautiful.'

'Are you ready to be mine, alpha?' I whispered to him.

He smiled. 'I've been yours since the day you arrived.'

I bent, nuzzling at his scent gland. He tensed; I stroked his skin, soothing. 'Are you sure?'

He swallowed. 'I'm sure.'

I pressed one more kiss to his scent gland, then moved my mouth down. His scent gland was Tristan's to mark; I'd bite him on the collarbone instead, where everyone could see it and know that he was mine.

My teeth sank easily through his skin, and my legs went weak as salted caramel filled my mouth. I clutched at his shoulders; his hands gripped my hips, steadying me.

His light was different to Sebastian's, shot through with grief and loss and healing. He was so strong, so much stronger than he ever gave himself credit for. His steadiness, his care, and his devotion flooded through me, along with a hefty dose of desire, enough to make me flush with heat.

'*Byron*,' I said under my breath. 'Our parents are here.'

He chuckled. 'I'm going to have a lot of fun flustering you in public, beautiful.'

'That will work both ways, alpha,' I said tartly.

He gave a rumbling, approving purr. 'Don't get distracted, omega. You've still got a bite to go.'

Tristan reached out and wrapped an arm around my waist, breaking off a kiss with Sebastian, who looked as flushed and as overwhelmed as I felt. It had seemed like a long wait for all of us, but for them it had been almost seven years coming; Sebastian cupped Tristan's cheek lovingly, his gaze full of a calm contentment I hadn't seen on him before. I took Sebastian's hand and he turned his smile on me, before his eyes fell to Byron.

Tristan looked up at me, blood bright on his neck. It didn't seem to bother him, in the same way my bite wasn't even hurting; there were too many feelings swirling around my body to worry about pain, and I was so high on the euphoria I was surprised I didn't float away.

'Ready, omega?' he said quietly.

I twirled one of his curls around my finger. 'I can't wait, alpha.'

He held me steady as I bit his collarbone. I shook as his protective love washed over me, through me, chased by admiration, respect, and – *oh my word* – the *heat*. We'd been taking things slow in the physical sense, and sometimes I'd wondered if he wanted me the way I wanted him, but the craving coming through the bond left me with no illusions. I knew, in that moment, that I would always be safe, always be *wanted*, and that having Tristan watch my back was no small thing. He would always be modest about what he did for the pack – what he sacrificed for us – but now I'd always know just how much he gave, and just how much he cared. I licked his vanilla blood from his skin, feeling satisfied, feeling complete.

Almost.

Sebastian took my hand and gently pulled me away as Tristan turned to Byron, touching his cheek and turning his gaze.

'I am the head alpha of this pack,' Tristan said quietly, 'but I've come to realise over the past few months that a head alpha's job is not to lead, but to serve. I know we said no vows, but I have one. I vow never to take from you, but always to give. And my first action in keeping that vow is to ask you to forge the prime bond, so you can always ensure I keep that promise.' He tipped his head to the side and closed his eyes. 'Bite, Griffiths.'

Byron swallowed, his stormy eyes bright. 'Grace –'

'*Now*, Byron.'

Byron huffed a laugh and bent to nuzzle Tristan's cheek before his mouth dropped to his scent gland. 'Since you asked so nicely, love,' he said, and bit down.

Tristan swayed, groaning. 'Oh, *fuck.*'

I felt his shock and pleasure through our bond like a lightning bolt – and not just his, but Byron's, too, and the echo of Sebastian's approval as he watched. Byron pulled back, his eyes dark, and Tristan struck; Byron's cry of pleasure-pain was lost to the waves as his scent match bit down.

Sebastian's fingers wound through mine. 'I don't mean to hurry you, but –'

I inhaled, scenting cherry perfume through the salty evening air. We'd washed off our scent cancellers earlier in the day, and I didn't have faith that our blockers would continue to work through *this*. My body tightened in response to Sebastian's scent, slick beginning to pool between my legs.

Both alphas got unsteadily to their feet, and a moment later, we were wrapped in their arms. Byron nuzzled at my neck as Tristan barely held himself upright, his body tense. My knees buckled as Byron bit down, the bond completing in a rush of love and heat; Byron held me steady, then turned to Sebastian, his teeth sinking into my omega's neck.

'Fuck, you *do* look pretty with all those bites,' I said breathlessly, then moaned as Sebastian's pleasure rolled through me. 'Tristan –'

Tristan bit Sebastian first, sealing their bond. They gave matching groans; Sebastian caught Tristan's mouth in a passionate kiss as Tristan cradled his omega's head tenderly. When I whimpered, barely holding back a whine, Byron swung me into his arms and presented my neck to Tristan like an offering. The alpha wasted no time, and the circle of pack bonds snapped into place – wholly, finally, and forever – as his teeth pierced my skin.

'Oh, thank *fuck*,' Sebastian moaned. 'I don't mean to alarm anyone, but I need to have sex, like, *now*. Preferably with each of you, multiple times.'

Tristan chuckled. 'That can certainly be arranged.'

I looked across the grass to see the celebrant and our families ... *gone*.

Tristan followed my gaze. 'It's tradition for the witnesses to leave before the last bond is given,' he said, his voice soft and doing all kinds of things to my body. 'I think they all left earlier, though.'

'Because of the orgy?' Sebastian said hopefully. 'Please tell me it's because of the orgy. But I really hope they didn't take your car, Tris, because otherwise the rideshare driver is getting a *show*.'

Tristan pulled him into his arms. 'You didn't think I'd plan for this?' He kissed Sebastian, hard and hungry. 'Come on.'

Tristan led us down to the beach and past the rocky cliff face; Byron kept me cradled in his arms, occasionally dipping down to kiss my forehead or cheek, or nip playfully at my ear. Every caress sent a bolt of pleasure through me, and an answering echo of affection through the bond; I wondered how I'd ever get used to the feeling. The sun had almost set and the night was clear; a thousand stars looked down on us from the navy-black sky, silvering the waves.

Beyond the cliffs, sheltered by their height, a pavilion sat on the white sand, lit from within.

'Oh, Tris,' Sebastian said thickly. 'You did this for us?'

'This is the least of what I'd do for my pack,' Tristan answered.

'It looks so pretty,' I said breathlessly. 'But what if someone walks past?'

'I hired the beach for the night,' Tristan said, unfazed. 'And some security, too.'

'You hired … a beach,' I said slowly. 'An entire *beach*. A *public* beach. You hired … the *ocean*.'

'It's amazing what people will do if you give them enough money.'

'That really shouldn't make me want you more, but here we are,' Sebastian moaned. '*Please*, alphas. I'm wasting away. Dying for the want of a knot.'

'Well, we can't have that.' Tristan picked Sebastian up and slung him over his shoulder. 'Your orgy awaits.'

Byron followed our alpha inside the pavilion. The floor space was filled by a wide, low bed covered in white and gold covers and cushions. It must have been murder to get across the sand, but the romance of it stole my breath away. Lanterns with flickering LED candles were hung around the walls, casting a soft, warm glow over the bed. A narrow table sat to one side, covered in plates of fruit and cheese, two bottles of champagne resting on ice.

Tristan tossed Sebastian on the bed without ceremony then dragged his shorts over his hips, freeing his cock and immediately swallowing it down. My omega moaned, squirming on the bed as Tristan hollowed his cheeks and sucked. I squeaked and pressed my thighs together as Sebastian's pleasure rolled through me, building at the base of my spine and between my legs.

'Fuck,' I whispered. 'Will it always be like this?'

Byron settled me on the bed next to Sebastian. 'Apparently, it eases after a few months, but the feeling – the sense of connection – never goes away.' He waited for my nod of approval before rolling up my dress, though he could feel how ready – how *desperate* – I was through the bond. He dragged my underwear down, pushing my knees apart. 'Best get used to it, beautiful.'

He buried his face between my legs as Sebastian seized my mouth in a kiss. Heat flooded my body, making it difficult to think; all I could do was *feel* as my omega nipped at my bottom lip and my alpha sucked gently on my clit. After murmuring *may I, pretty?* and receiving a gasping *yes!* in response, Tristan's fingers swept through my slick folds and pushed inside, curling gently.

My climax crashed over me; I whimpered into Sebastian's mouth, shuddering as my cunt clamped around Tristan's fingers. Byron gave a satisfied growl. When Tristan withdrew, Byron sucked his alpha's fingers into his mouth, his eyes heavy with want as he licked my slick from Tristan's skin. Tristan groaned, the muffled sound deepening as Sebastian stiffened, his hips pushing up. I felt the shadow of his pleasure as he came.

'Fuck,' Sebastian gasped, dragging me in for another kiss. '*Fuck*, alphas.'

Tristan's chest rumbled with a pleased purr as his throat worked, swallowing down Sebastian's release. '*Mmm*,' he said, licking his lips. 'I'll never get enough of your taste, baby.'

'Share,' Byron demanded, and Tristan bunched his hand in the big alpha's hair, pulling him in for a fierce kiss as Byron's fingers made short work of Tristan's shirt buttons.

'That's more like it,' Sebastian said thickly, watching Tristan yank Byron's shirt from his shoulders. Sebastian slipped off his own, then tugged at my dress until I lifted it over my head. Once my dress was gone, I reached back to unclasp my bra, but he pushed my hands away. 'That's my job.' He stripped it off me, then cupped my breasts from behind, kissing a line along my shoulder while he stroked, pinching my nipples gently. I moaned, arching into his hands as he tweaked and pulled at the sensitive peaks.

Hands skimmed my thighs. 'So pretty,' Byron purred. 'Aren't our omegas lovely, alpha?'

'Beautiful,' Tristan agreed roughly. He knelt on the bed, giving Sebastian a hungry kiss before turning his attention to me. I whimpered as his lips found mine, his tongue stroking until I opened to him. My hand found his curls; I tried to pull him closer, wanting more, wanting my alpha, wanting *everything*. 'Easy, omega. I'll give you what you need.' He pulled back, his green eyes dark. 'You're mine tonight, pretty.'

My breath caught. 'Tonight?'

Desire shot through our bond. I couldn't tell whether it was his or mine; either way, it was strong enough to make my head spin.

He trailed kisses from my mouth to my ear. 'I wanted our first time to be special,' he murmured, so softly only I could hear. 'And I know you've been planning something of your own, omega.' He guided my eager, reaching hand to his cock as Sebastian's fingers trailed over my stomach and found their way between my legs. 'I'm hard as stone just thinking about it.'

My breath stuttered as my fingers closed around his cock, which was, indeed, impressively hard. 'How –'

He kissed my nose. 'It's my job to know,' he said.

I stared at him. 'I want you,' I burst out, need throbbing in my core, settling into my very *soul*. 'I want you *now*.'

My alpha smiled at me, a full, rare smile. My heart expanded in the cage of my chest. 'Then take what you want,' he said. 'It's yours. Always.'

He lifted me from Sebastian's arms; my omega slipped to kneel on the floor. Tristan turned me around as if I weighed nothing at all, positioning me on his lap, my back against his chest.

'You're in control, omega,' he whispered to me.

I turned to kiss him, my teeth sinking into his bottom lip. 'You're mine.'

'Yes.' His arms tightened around me. 'We all are.'

I took his cock in hand, trailing his head through my slick before I lined him up and sank down. '*Alpha*,' I panted, closing my eyes against the stretch. My body lit up with pleasure as I slid down until I was breathlessly full.

Tristan's hands found my hips; one caressed my stomach before rising to cup a breast. 'Talk to me, Rose.'

'So good,' I breathed. 'Fuck, Tris. So good.'

'Good.' He nuzzled at Sebastian's bite; the action sent a jolt of pleasure through my limbs, my muscles tightening. His tongue swept out, tending the wound in a slow rhythm that made me shake. I cried out in surprise as a sudden climax rolled over me, my body clamping around his cock.

'*Yes*,' he hissed against my skin, rocking back and forth gently as the waves calmed. 'Again, pretty.'

'It's my turn,' Sebastian said, smoothing his palms up my thighs until his thumbs met at my apex. He pressed down lightly and I moaned, chasing the pressure when he moved. He shifted to kneel between our legs, his eyes on the place Tristan was spreading me, where I was slick and swollen. 'Show me how you ride our alpha, Rose.'

My core tightened at his words; I splayed my hands on Tristan's thighs for balance, then lifted up, and dropped down.

'Mmm,' Sebastian said approvingly. 'Again.'

I did as he instructed, fucking myself onto Tristan as Sebastian watched, his eyes not moving from the place we were joined, his pleasure evident through our bond. Byron made a strangled sound and moved to kiss me, his tongue thrusting into my mouth in time with the motion of my hips.

Something soft and wet swiped over my clit.

I shrieked, overcome by sensation, by the feeling of Tristan inside my body and Byron inside my mouth and something – Sebastian's tongue, I realised, when he did it again – teasing my most sensitive place. Byron broke the kiss, falling to his knees behind Sebastian and running his hands down our omega's back; Sebastian's breath caught as he lapped at where Tristan and I were joined, making the alpha beneath me quiver.

'So tight,' Byron growled, his fingers working between Sebastian's legs, his love and worship clear down the bond. My mate moaned, shifting his knees further apart, sucking gently on my clit. I rocked back and forth, feeling the pressure build inside me, rolling my hips so that Tristan rubbed against a spot that made me see stars, letting the sensation inside me build slowly as Sebastian's tongue caressed me –

Tristan bit my shoulder, his canines just shy of breaking the skin.

I screamed as the pleasure broke, shuddering over me like a wave. Sebastian gave a matching shout as Byron pushed inside him, smoothing his palm down Sebastian's back, making him moan against me. The soft vibration forced a series of pulses from my over-sensitive clit; my head lolled back to rest on Tristan's shoulder.

'You're not even close to finished, Rose,' Tristan whispered to me, his breath fanning my ear. 'After this, you're going to get on your hands and knees and show your pack how you'll present for us during your heat.' The filthy words sent a fresh wave of arousal through me; I stiffened as he rolled my nipples between his fingers and thumbs. 'Do you want to tell the others, pretty? Tell your pack exactly when you stopped taking your heat suppressants.'

Byron's pupils blew out, his eyes turning black. He bit his lip as he pulled back from Sebastian's body, then slowly – tortuously – pushed back in. Sebastian's limbs shook, but he tilted his hips, trying to take more. 'You stopped taking your suppressants, beautiful?'

'I wanted it to be a surprise.' My voice was hoarse. 'The Banksia rules state that omegas must be on heat suppressants during the teaching terms and mid-semester breaks. They don't say anything about the end of the year.' Sebastian lifted his head, blinking up at me, his chin shining with slick. His eyes fluttered closed as Byron took on a steady rhythm, his hands tight on my omega's hips. 'I stopped taking them after our last class.'

'The suppressants take a fortnight to stop working,' Tristan murmured, rocking beneath me. 'Or so the doctors I called said. Which would make the start of your heat –'

'Next week, when we're on the island,' Sebastian supplied, dipping his head back between my thighs and licking around the base of Tristan's cock. 'Fuck, Rosebud. Want to see you stretched around a knot so bad.'

Byron groaned; his pace quickened. 'Make her come again,' he ordered, a thrum of dominance in his words, though I wasn't sure whether he was talking to Sebastian or Tristan. '*Now.*'

It didn't matter who he meant, it turned out; Sebastian's lips closed over my clit and Tristan took my hips in hand, holding me steady as he began to fuck up into my body ruthlessly, hitting one of the sweet spots on my internal walls with unerring precision. I gave myself over to my pack, swept away in the waves of emotions flowing through my bonds, the circle complete when Byron wrapped his hand around my knee, grounding me. His warmth tethered me as I let go entirely, let my alphas and my omega push me into bliss. The love in our bonds pulsed inside me, pulsed *together* like a shared heartbeat, until I shattered into ecstasy, my cries echoed by my pack as we fell to pieces.

For a moment – or an hour, I couldn't say for sure – I floated dreamily, my body light and my mind blank of anything but our shared warmth, our shared pleasure, our shared love. I came back to earth with lips on my neck, another mouth trailing over my belly, and a pair of gentle hands pushing my hair back from my face.

'Rose,' Byron whispered.

Someone wrapped me in their arms and rolled me sideways; the hard length inside me shifted, but stayed where it was. I made a satisfied noise at the feeling of my alpha's release staying deep inside my body, then sighed as our scents mingled in the night air. I nuzzled forward until I found a stretch of cherry-scented skin, then whined until lips that tasted like caramel parted my own.

'Do you think it could be starting early?' I heard, the voice sounding far-away.

'... could have brought it on.' Something touched my brow. 'She definitely has a temperature.'

A chuckle sounded close to my ear. 'That's my Rosebud,' my omega murmured proudly. 'Over-achieving, even when it comes to heats.'

'... have to get her back to Banksia. I'll call ...'

'... ring Chloe. She was flying in ...'

'... let her parents know, too. They were supposed to have lunch ...'

My alpha slipped from my body, the soft mattress beneath me shifting. I grumbled wordlessly, balling my hands into fists as my fingers began to tingle.

'Shh, omega. I've got you.' A pair of strong arms caught me up. I nuzzled forward, finding the bite mark I'd given, letting my tongue soothe over the wound. My alpha groaned. 'Fuck, beautiful. I'm not going to make it to the nest if you keep doing that.'

The smell of the ocean and the crash of waves brought me out of my daze. It was nighttime, and Byron was carrying me, making his way back up to the cliffs – a process I was not making easier with my tongue on his bite.

'I misjudged the timing, didn't I?' I said crossly.

He huffed a laugh. 'Even you make mistakes sometimes.'

'I'm sorry.'

'For what?' he said, kissing my hair. 'For making our bonding ceremony even more special?'

'For ending our night early.'

'Oh, Rose,' he said softly, the moonlight brightening his face as he smiled. 'This is just the beginning.'

THE END.

ACKNOWLEDGEMENTS

When I first read an omegaverse novel, I hated it.

I didn't finish the first one I tried; I'd stumbled unknowingly into something pretty dark, and it simply wasn't for me. I steered clear of anything mentioning alphas, betas, and omegas for quite some time after that. It took falling down the Kathryn Moon rabbit hole and cautiously opening *Baby + The Late Night Howlers* for me to dip my toes back into the genre, and since then, I haven't been able to stop reading.

As always, this book wouldn't have been written without other people. This one was particularly difficult. You know that meme from *The Great British Bake Off* where James Acaster says 'Started making it. Had a breakdown. Bon appetite'? That is *Want It All* for me. And without my little village and the wonderful alpha and beta readers I worked with on this book, I would never have typed *The End*.

Thanks, as always, to my incredible alpha readers, Kelly, Hannah, and John. I honestly could not function without you. To my beta readers Charlie, Elle, Tiffany, Lauren, Claire, and Erika – I am so grateful for your time and considered feedback; thank you so much, and a special shout out to Elle and Erika, who have been so supportive and incredibly lovely as I worked to get this book into the world. Thank you, too, to Heidi and Raychael, who offered feedback during the ARC process. I'd like also to acknowledge Australian omegaverse authors Eliana Lee and Roxy Collins, whose novels gave me the prompt to think *no, actually, this could work!* when I was daydreaming about a pack finding each other in an Aussie setting that means a lot to me.

It's a widespread joke that during holidays, there's no one left in the city of Canberra, because we've all gone to the NSW South Coast. For me, it definitely has a ring of truth; I was lucky enough to spend many a school holiday at Bateman's Bay, and then, when my grandmother moved south from Sydney, at Callala Bay, Callala Beach, and Jervis Bay. The NSW South Coast is one of my favourite places in the entire world, and I hope you can feel that love as you read this novel.

Hollie xx

ABOUT THE AUTHOR

Hollie Hartwright lives on Ngunnawal land in Australia's capital city with her infinitely supportive husband, their two children, and two feline furbabies. She has degrees in both Literature and Education.

In her spare time, Hollie reads almost anything she can get her hands on. Her favourite genres include monster romance, alien romance, historical romance, epic fantasy, historical fantasy, and dystopia. Despite the last one, she believes in happy endings – preferably happy endings with a lot of fun along the way. Because of that, she writes otherworldly love stories with plenty of spice and happily-ever-afters.

If you'd like to find out more about Hollie and her books, you can follow her on Instagram, Bluesky, or sign up to her mailing list at holliehartwright.com.

ALSO BY HOLLIE HARTWRIGHT

THE ADVENA ABDUCTIONS SERIES

High-heat, why-choose alien romances with heart

Book One: Count Down
Book Two: Into Orbit
Book Three: Dark Space
Book Four: Safe Landing

www.ingramcontent.com/pod-product-compliance
Lightning Source LLC
Chambersburg PA
CBHW050105120726
47904CB00004B/1226